PRECIOUS
CATASTROPHE

BOOKS BY DEIRDRE SULLIVAN

Perfectly Preventable Deaths
Precious Catastrophe

Prim Improper
Improper Order
Primperfect
Needlework
Tangleweed and Brine
Perfectly Preventable Deaths
Savage Her Reply

I Want To Know That I Will Be Okay (for adults)

PRECIOUS CATASTROPHE

DEIRDRE SULLIVAN

HOT
KEY
BOOKS

First published in Great Britain in 2021 by
HOT KEY BOOKS
4th Floor, Victoria House
Bloomsbury Square
London WC1B 4DA
Owned by Bonnier Books
Sveavägen 56, Stockholm, Sweden
www.hotkeybooks.com

A CIP catalogue record for this book is available from the British Library.

ISBN: 978-1-4714-1068-0
Also available as an ebook and in audio

1

This book is typeset using Atomik ePublisher
Printed and bound in Great Britain by Clays Ltd, Elcograf S.p.A.

Hot Key Books is an imprint of Bonnier Books UK
www.bonnierbooks.co.uk

To Adam James and Johnathan McGuinness.
For the most precious heart.

Even though I walk through the Valley of the Shadow of Death, I will fear no evil, for you are with me.

Psalm 23

1

Costmary

(maintaining wakefulness, purging phlegm, worms)

'Catlin Hayes, for the fifth and final time you are not a Dracula.'

I can see the white of Mam's knuckles clutching the steering wheel as the car whirrs over the stony mountain road. I'm in the back, which is annoying as I don't have full control over the music that gets played. When we moved to Ballyfrann for the first time, Brian was driving and my hair was still dark red. I didn't need to nap then, and my throat and my bones didn't ache or twinge unpredictably throughout the day. My voice didn't rasp if I forgot to stay hydrated. I hadn't died. I'd never been in love.

'I rose from the dead,' I point out, not for the first time. Mam sighs that old familiar sigh of hers. The Catlin-you-are-reminding-me-of-bad-things sigh.

'That doesn't make you Dracula.' She has a point, but so do I, and I will beat my point into her as though it were a stake through the heart of a lesser Dracula.

'I'm sensitive to light.' I gesture to the small round tortoiseshell sunglasses perched on my nose. They are exactly the sort of sunglasses a stylish but photo-sensitive Dracula would wear, going about the place, wearing capes and causing havoc. I should absolutely get a cape.

'You're hungover.' Mam is now resigned to the back and forth of this. Which is exactly where I want her. I like winning. I'm good at it. I've been doing it since the day I was born, with several notable exceptions.

'*You're* hungover,' I tell Mam. We're both right. I polished off a bottle of coconut rum with Layla Shannon and Eddie Collins last night, trying to get information out of them. Maddy pussyfoots around the strangeness of Ballyfrann, but I prefer a more direct approach. Plus, people feel sorry for me now, because I got my face eaten off, and when it doesn't clam them up it can make them weirdly gabby. I feel a bit sorry for me too, to be honest, but what they actually should feel is scared. I have a lot of rage inside me now.

A year ago, my sister and I moved to Ballyfrann with our mother and her new husband Brian. And it ruined everything about my life. This town ate my face and stole my sister, and I'm going to figure everything out and make it pay.

Mam's drinking last night was less purposeful. Brian did some big business deal and a client sent him a bottle of something expensive. They normally never open wine on a weeknight, and I wondered if it was an attempt on his part to delay this

2

trip until he could come too, and keep an eye on us. It almost worked, in fairness. Mam is hanging.

I adjust my sunglasses and smile a toothy, Dracula-style smile at Mam and Maddy's sleeping form. I'd been looking forward to catching up properly with my sister, but she conked out as soon as she'd clicked her seat belt on. Which might be for the best. Mam's driving isn't wonderful at the best of times, and Maddy's always one pothole away from a cheeky vomit out the window. I don't know why Mamó let Maddy come with us, she's usually much stricter with her. We get the odd dinner, once a week, on her night off, but otherwise, it's hard to know where she'll be or how to get to see her. When we do talk, she's always asking questions about me. Not that I mind that, I've no problem talking about myself, but when she leaves I often realise I barely know my sister now at all. Mind you, maybe I didn't know her then either. There were a lot of things she kept from me.

'Should you pull over, and take a drink of water, or go somewhere and get a coffee or something?' I ask Mam. I'd love a coffee.

'I'm grand, love. It's mainly anxiety, I think. The last time we visited your father's grave, we were all still together and life was much more normal. The two of ye were getting on okay.'

'Hey! I'm getting on okay,' I say. And it's true. I am. Considering.

'I keep thinking of your name on that wall,' she says. When my ex did what he did to me, it became clear that he had also done the same before, to other girls. He carved their names onto a cavern wall; our names, I mean. Mine was there too. I don't like thinking about it, and when she brings it up, I feel more like a Dracula than ever. Like an undead thing that shouldn't be. Tethered to memory. Mam doesn't mean to hurt me, I know that much, but when she mentions that place, or that night, it's like my bones begin to sweat or something. I've gotten better at hiding it so she thinks I'm healing. She tells me how resilient I am at least once a week. She doesn't hear me when I pray at night, sob to the Virgin Mary to protect me, knowing that when it really counted, she didn't. It was my sister who sacrificed herself so I could live.

Maddy snorts in her sleep, the way she does, and turns.

'It's good she's sleeping,' Mam says, changing the subject, probably more for her benefit than mine.

'I might go to sleep as well,' I say. 'Seeing as the sun has risen. Because of what a Dracula I am.'

'A Dracula wouldn't care about her mam,' Mam says.

'Dracula had impeccable manners,' I say. 'People can be a lot of things at once.'

And then I'm thinking about Lon and it doesn't seem so funny any more. Lon was the love of my life. We met shortly after I moved to Ballyfrann, and we were obsessed with each other. I dreamed about him every night and he was the first thing that I thought about each morning. Both those things are still true, but for slightly different reasons. He keeps coming back, in my dreams. And I relive what happened over and over again. Not the end, but the beginning and the middle. But, with the knowledge of where his love is leading, it's not a bit romantic any more, and I'm trapped in my body, repeating

4

history again and again, and seeing the cave move closer and closer. Lon was a lot of things: charming and brutal, young and old. Maddy could see through him right away, but she's a witch, and I'm . . . I don't know what.

When I don't dream of Lon, I dream of Dad. Dad burned to death when we were two years old. And I keep dreaming about it. Wild warm fever dreams that feel all too real. I wake up gasping, running for the nearest sink to drown my face in, to remind myself that it's out now. I'm home. I'm safe. Only I'm not at home. I am not safe.

I wonder if visiting Dad's grave will be different this time, with all that's happened. It was always a bit sad, but we got used to it. I never knew him really. I just have memories. A murmured bedtime story. A hand dangling rosary beads over my face and me reaching my two hands up to grab them in frustration. Watering the plants in the garden with a little pink watering can we'd gotten as a present from one of Mam's work friends who visited.

When I open my eyes again, we're passing through a village that's much bigger than Ballyfrann, with art galleries and a cute-looking coffee shop.

'Can we stop for a coffee?' I ask.

'We want to make good time,' Mam says. And then she makes a *hmmm* sound and thinks. 'I'll have to stop for petrol anyway. Let's see if there's a station here.'

'I got bitten by a Dracula!' I say triumphantly. 'The least I deserve is a well-made cappuccino.'

Mam shuts up. I've probably gone too far. And Lon wasn't really a Dracula. A true Dracula would have had more finesse, or at least stuck to the neck area. That would have made the marks he left much easier to hide. If only.

Mam pulls the car in, parks and gets her purse out. 'I'll be back in a minute.'

Success.

Maddy stirs and opens one eye. 'Where are we now?'

'Mam stopped to get me an artisanal coffee,' I say. 'She'll probably get you one too. She didn't want to wake you.'

'It was nice to sleep . . .' says Maddy. 'Wait. Did you get her to do what you want again by reminding her that Lon ate your face?'

'I did.'

'You're some bitch, Catlin Hayes.' She's smiling though. I don't know if she knows how she feels about my talent for getting Mam to do whatever I want most of the time. Little bit judgemental, little bit admiring. I grin back, unashamed. I mean, if I can get people to do stuff for me, why shouldn't I? I know that there's probably some rule about not using the bad things that happen to you to manipulate other people, but I can't make them not have happened to me. Lon won't un-eat my face, un-break my heart. So the least I can do is guilt people into doing stuff for me and telling me secrets. Secrets that I hope will be the key to getting my sister free of the old wagon who yanked me unceremoniously back from the dead in exchange for her soul and freedom.

'I do what I can. Plus she's hungover. It's way easier to get her to do stuff when she's hungover. It's like she's a tired puppet.'

Maddy blinks and peels back stray strands of hair from

6

her eyes. 'The way you talk about other people scares me sometimes, Catlin.'

She opens up her bag to check her phone. I know that face.

'Who are you expecting a message from?' I ask her.

'No one. I barely have time to breathe, let alone be messaging people. Mamó has me so busy.'

'You're lying.'

'I might be.' She smiles. 'But I'm not going to tell you either way.'

'UGH. You're so frustrating. I'm sitting here, COVERED in scars. TRAUMATISED.'

'Ah here, you're hardly covered in scars. They're more like birthmarks.' She's not wrong. They're not pocked like scars would be, but they are a mark of violence that was done to me, and *scar* seems the proper word for them. I am scarred now. What he did is written on my skin.

'Don't tell me how I look or what I've been through. Just tell me who's the girl? It's not Oona again, is it?'

Oona Noone is this French one who thinks she's amazing. And in fairness to her, she is a bit amazing. Very pretty, well-liked by everyone, and my sister is thoroughly in love with her. A dose. And much and all as I'd like my sister to have someone to remind her how wonderful she is and make her feel like there's more to life than witchcraft and servitude, I'm pretty sceptical about magical people as romantic partners, for obvious reasons.

Mam comes back with gorgeous fluffy coffees all around. I tell her she's a hero, and she smiles and tells me that there's an expiry date on this 'fancy treatment'.

7

'On what? On being murdered? Do you have any idea how callous that sounds?' I say.

'Shut up, Catlin,' they both say with the exact same intonation, and it's so in-tune that it makes me laugh with surprise. Time passes, and the things we pass on the road bring back old memories. The good kind, from before, when we were normal.

'It's lovely, isn't it, to all be together again?' says Mam. 'We should just stay here and not go home at all.'

'Yeah,' I say, and I hear the sadness in my voice.

There are some things you just can't journey back from.

2

Ragwort

(menstruation, cleansing, aches and pains)

We wheel into the small gravel carpark of the cemetery where Dad is buried. It's a bit of a drive from where we used to live, but it's close to a forest – not the forest where it happened, but another one, and Mam thought he'd like it there. Even though, as Catlin has pointed out on more than one occasion, a forest's where he died and it's a bit like burying someone who got hit by a car beside a multistorey carpark. Only prettier. The way Mam thought about it made sense to me, and now that I know Dad was a bit like I am, with the witchcraft, it makes even more sense. I clutch my satchel in my bag and remember what Mamó told me before I left.

'Make it quick, make it quiet, tell me everything you see.' She never lets me leave the house without at least one order. That's

when I'm allowed to leave at all. Being a full-time unpaid intern for Ireland's grumpiest woman is a JOY.

Catlin's face is half hidden underneath a muffler, and from the back, with her white hair, she would look to a visitor like a tiny nana. Her eyes flash as though she's heard my thoughts. She might not be magical, but she is very good at reading my moods, even now when we're so far apart. Often in the garden, I'll find little crystals or small notes wrapped in tinfoil, mixed in with the plants. I pretend to be stoic about it, but it means the world. My sister is a lot of things: selfish, vain, irresponsible, kind, caring and, now and then, incredibly resolute. We reach the side of the grave, and I brush some lichen off the stone and scrape it into a small jar which I place in the pocket of my big satchel.

Mam takes a swig from a hip flask, which is so out of character we both do a double take. *Where did she even get a hip flask?* I wonder. Did Catlin give it to her? And my eyes must have communicated more than I intended them to, because she responds as though I'd voiced my suspicions.

'I did in my hoop give it to her, Madeline Hayes,' she exclaims angrily, 'I'm traumatised, not crazy.'

Maybe she is a bit psychic now that she's come back from the dead, I think, trying hard to keep my face extremely neutral, in case it happens again.

'Sorry, girls,' says Mam. 'It looks worse than it is. It's just a sort of cold drink. Here, smell.'

I breathe it in. It's earthy and sweet. Nettle and lemon balm, meadowsweet and rosehip. And something else as well. It smells like mint, but not peppermint or spearmint.

'It's only a tea,' I say.

'Aww,' says Catlin. 'I thought I was going to have something to tell that therapist you're trying to force me to go to.'

Mam keeps trying to get Catlin to do therapy, which would be a great idea if she could source someone with experience of the kind of thing that goes on in Ballyfrann, as opposed to a nice, normal woman Catlin would have to dance around the truth with for a hundred euro an hour. Catlin is resistant to going. Mamó was trying to do check-ins with her, at the start of this, to see where her head was at and what she needed, and she has done a few, but Mam keeps stalling and making it difficult, which is understandable because she still feels complicated about what happened the night Catlin was murdered and I gave up my soul and seven years of my life to get her back. I mean, it is kind of a lot to cope with. I should know.

'Where did you get the tea,' Catlin asks, 'seeing as you kind of hate Mamó?'

'I don't kind of hate her,' Mam says. 'I fully hate her. And with just cause. Brian gave me this, for the headache I had this morning. I hate him a good bit less.'

Brian and Mam have been working on their marriage, and here they are, I guess. Brian is trying, turning over new leaves all around. Being honest with her about everything that goes on in the town, his past. Going for daily runs. Drinking endless smoothies pointedly, like he's healthier than the next man. I don't know. It's still hard to get my head around the shift we saw in him the night he brought Lon back, all trussed up like an animal. And the suspicions I have around a sort of spell we found last year, a slaughtered fox, not like the usual animals that litter the corners and paths of Ballyfrann but something that had been tortured with a purpose.

I know all too well the kind of desperation that would drive someone to something like that, but I wasn't able to follow through that night when I felt like there was no other path left to me. The calm on the surface of Brian is deceptive, and I feel like now I watch him with very different eyes. I'm not sure how I feel about how close Mam is coming to forgiving and forgetting. To carrying on. Some of us can't go back to how things were.

'Okay,' I say, with a curt nod of my head, and set to work.

A stone in each corner of the grave. A trail of herbs linking the stones. Some words Mamó taught me to say, that basically translate to narrating what I'm doing. She's not big on flourishes, or incantations, Mamó. No purple velvet capes or expensive wands for the likes of her. It's all very definite and sensible. As sensible as magic can be, really.

'It's safe,' I say to Mam and Catlin. 'Who wants to go first?'

They look at each other.

I sigh.

It always falls to the witch. When things get difficult.

I get the shovel, and start digging. Catlin and Mam stay by the grave, heads bowed, murmuring to each other. When my arms get tired I pass the shovel to Catlin, who manages about half as much digging as me before she passes it to Mam, a film of sweat clinging to the white and red of her skin. Mam really puts her back into it, fair play to her, but she isn't able for a

12

lot. I try to focus on making sure everything is going smoothly, but my mind turns over the contents of that tea. Since when did Brian start blending his own teas?

I take the shovel from Mam and keep going till it hits a *thunk*. There aren't very many people in the graveyard, but none of them have noticed what we're doing, and a part of me feels that Mam and Catlin should be more impressed by that. By my skill. It's hard-won after all.

I meet my sister's gaze and put my hand on the edge of the coffin lid. Thinking of something I overheard Mam say once, about there not being all that much to bury. He's probably a pile of ash and bone. I swallow deeply, then Mam reaches out.

'It should be me, love,' she whispers.

So I let her clamber in her husband's grave and strain at the coffin until the lid gives . . . and parts . . .

And opens.

3

Fingernails

(defence, breaking grip)

When Maddy was getting suspicious about Ballyfrann, at the start I dismissed it as nerves or anxiety. I didn't realise that both of those things could be teachers. Sometimes, beside Lon, my flesh would pucker into goosepimples, and I would feel so cold. I would ask him to hold me then, to warm me up, but he couldn't really do that. Not entirely. Now when I dream of him, I wake up shivering or sweating. Feeling wrong in very different ways. The smell of his cologne still in my nostrils, filling up my lungs. I cannot breathe. I tell myself he's dead now, I am safe.

I don't feel safe.

There was nothing in our father's coffin. Not a speck of dust, a flake of ash. We each took a handful of the earth he was supposed to have been buried in and put it into those

14

small jars Maddy uses. In the absence of ashes, it's nice to have something that's linked to him, I suppose. Maddy'll probably grow a plant or something witchy in hers. And I'll just plonk mine somewhere on a shelf. Maybe it might be good on my altar. Like a Mass card, but more so. I do enjoy a Mass card. I love a bit of religious paraphernalia.

We've booked into a hotel for the night, because Mam couldn't face going 'back there'. Neither me nor Maddy wants to be in the hotel. The reaction people have when they see my face is more about them than me. I know that much. But I still don't like seeing it. In Ballyfrann, people are used to me by now.

Maddy is just stressed that Mamó will be angry with her, and possibly exact a terrible revenge. The second bit is guesswork; Maddy swears that Mamó is pretty fair actually, but it doesn't seem fair, to force someone to give up their soul and work for you for years whether they want to or not. I don't know what souls do, not exactly, but I do know that I don't want to lose mine. If Maddy died, which she won't – I will not let her – I would worry about whether or not she'd be able to get into heaven with no soul. I kind of see them as tickets, or those stamps you get on your hand when you're at a gig. I wonder if without them you'd be a ghost, or maybe just nothing at all. I'd hate for her to fade away. I worry.

I haven't always been fair to Maddy myself. I've said things that were cruel and, when I was at my most Lon-obsessed, homophobic. And I think about that sometimes, particularly when I'm trying to get to sleep, about how hard it must have been to not be out yet, and be waiting for the right time to

15

speak her truth, and for me to just come out with horrible generalisations about lesbians. I've tried to apologise, and she says it doesn't matter. But sorry won't make her or me forget.

I was furious that we couldn't go swimming in the hotel pool. At one point I would have said, 'Fuck them,' and strode out in the tiniest swimsuit I could find, with my scars on show, but when I had that sort of strength my body was unscarred, and now I can't sleep and I can't focus and there are all these little things that remind me of Lon everywhere, everywhere. His hungry eyes, the colour of dull coins and sometimes bright ones. They flickered and they changed when they were fixed on something that he wanted. The feeling of eyes on me used to feed me, and now it makes me feel like I am food. So I stayed up in the room and flicked through the channels. There was one with a slideshow of the pool, which was something. Maddy got sick of me complaining after a while and fecked off out, which, fair. Mam was on the phone to Brian for ages. I scrolled around on my phone, and I kept thinking about the empty coffin, and all the answers that we want and still can't seem to have.

'What do you think it means?' I said when Maddy arrived back later, with a big bag of chips for me, and three kinds of chocolate bar for dessert.

'I have no idea,' she said, and then chewed her lip a bit. 'No, that's not true. I have a sort of theory, but it's not fully formed.'

'Give it to me,' I say, meaning both theory and chips. I suddenly feel hungry.

'Okay. So basically, I think someone took Dad's . . . um . . . remains, to use for magical purposes.'

'What kind of uses would they have for his ashes?'

'So if Dad was a witch, like me, his magic would still exist in him, in one form or another, even after he died. Everything has uses, from a desiccated leaf to a pebble with a hole in it. But the more significance something has, the more useful it could be. I can't be sure exactly what Dad's ashes would be used for, but given our family history it's probably sinister, because look at all the sinister stuff that has happened. I would be so curious to know when exactly they went missing though.'

'It looked like they were never there at all.'

'Mam was upset,' Maddy says, which is an understatement. She full on vomited beside the grave. I held her hair and told her it would be okay, and to get it all up. The sort of things she used to say to me when I was small, but I was trying to take it in myself and it felt a bit like I was reading from a script. I get like that sometimes now, like I've clicked into a weird autopilot. I think it might be my body trying to spare me fear or something, but I don't like it. It reminds me a bit of getting blackout drunk, you know when you have those nights and after a certain point they only come in flashes, little scenes, and the rest is gone, but you were still there all the time, doing things you couldn't make memories out of.

'Why are you smiling?' Maddy asks, and I tell her there's no reason, and that we should do something nice for Mam.

'Like what?'

'Murder Brian?' I suggest.

'She wouldn't be gone on that. At all.'

'You're probably right,' I say. 'But it would be nice if he left her all that money and she could, like, buy your freedom back with diamonds, and we could move back to Cork, or somewhere new.'

'I don't hate the way things are, Catlin,' Maddy tells me. 'They're different, and yeah, it's hard sometimes, but it's not all bad or anything.'

'Oh,' I say. 'That's good. I kind of do though.'

'I know,' my sister tells me, and she reaches out her hand to hold my hand.

4

Rosemary

(opening obstructions, clearing sight)

I wake Catlin around 2 a.m. and she is less grumpy than she should be. Her eyes take a while to focus, and I smile. We haven't really gotten the chance to talk properly, for all that we keep saying how we need to. What we have to say is hard to say, and some of it there aren't really words for, I suppose.

'I've found the code to the alarm for the swimming pool, and a way around the security cameras' is a good substitute for actual constructive healing.

Her face lights up. 'A low-stakes adventure!'

'The lowest. Almost *no* chance of one of us dying.'

She punches the air. I've packed a bag with towels and swimming caps and goggles to take with us, not because I am the organised one but because I am the one who organised this. It's an important distinction. We have these roles thrust on us, you see, and I keep thinking about how I always felt I was quieter and worse and she was louder and better, but we're just two different people and it's fine.

When you spend half your life labelling jars of stuff, it gives you a lot of time for self-reflection.

We go down in the lift to the gym. Ideally we'd find a back stairs, but the keypad is really near the entrance.

'Where did you even get the code?' asks Catlin, like I am a mysterious woman of intrigue in a green velvet smoking jacket, instead of a teenager in pyjamas with bears on them and no chill.

'It was the screensaver on the computer. Genuinely. Which is several kinds of stupid. I can't decide if that's a sign from the universe that they deserve it, or that we do.' My hands shake a little as I key it in, which is weird, as this is a really mundane transgression compared to some of the stuff we've gotten up to since coming to Ballyfrann.

'Are you nervous?' Catlin asks, grinning.

'Yeah. We could get caught,' I say.

'We won't.' She tosses her hair with a bit of her old swagger. 'And if we do, what are they going to do? Call the guards?'

I swallow.

'They won't call the guards, Maddy,' she assures me. 'They'll give out to us, and probably to Mam as well, and she'll be annoyed but also get that it was a nice thing you did for me and that is the actual worst that can happen, which is a walk in the park compared to having my face eaten or you losing your soul.'

'Fair,' I say. Because it is. The door beeps open and we head

20

in. It's dark, but there's a big window that looks out on the terrace and the garden at the back of the hotel. The moon is bright and we can see it reflected on the water.

'Are they not supposed to cover it up or something?' Catlin asks.

I shrug.

She pulls her pyjamas off, plunges in in her underwear and swims a few lengths, I sit on the edge and dangle my legs in. The last time I swam at night, it was with Oona Noone, and she looked so beautiful I could hardly breathe. I still see her sometimes, in passing, in the forest. We exchange a few words, but I'm always with Mamó, or doing something for Mamó, and there isn't space for us to walk and talk together like we used to. She messages to ask me how I am, and it means the world, but it's still not the same. The promise of something is missing. And I don't know where it went, that thread between us. I'm still obsessed with her, but I know it's all one-sided. We had our moment, and it's kind of up to me to be mature about it. To love her like a friend, and not objectify her or make her the star of all my happy-ending daydreams about what life will be like when I don't have to work for Mamó any more.

Catlin pulls my leg and drags me under, bearjamas and all, which is a very Catlin move, and I try to duck her but I don't get very far. Even without a soul, I'm not vicious enough, I guess.

In witch-trial times, that was one of the ways they did it. Threw a woman in water, to see if she would float or sink. We're both floating now, on our backs, looking at the darkly dappled patterns the water makes on the smudge grey of the ceiling. I wonder if it means that we will burn.

'Snap out of it,' Catlin says, snapping her fingers in front of my eye in a move that is both incredibly annoying and also sort of impressive, seeing as she's doing it in water.

'Of what?'

'Whatever mental torture you were inflicting on yourself. You're like Batman.'

'I'm not like Batman.'

'You live in a big house, and make sacrifices to set things right in the world, and you love kissing girls.'

I squinch my mouth. You know, it's oddly accurate.

'Kissing girls is not solely a Batman thing,' I tell her. 'He doesn't like, own, the shift.'

'Not with *you* around,' she cackles.

'Do you talk to your best friend the priest like this?' I ask. Catlin is *best friends* with a priest now. It's weird.

'Father Byrne isn't my best friend,' she says. 'I just like the church. It's safe. I feel like nothing bad could happen in there.'

'Catlin, have you ever looked at Irish history for, like, a second?'

'I know about all the child abuse and the Magdalene laundries and the selling babies to rich Americans and lying about it and covering up rapes and murders and all that. But that's like, *the Church*. This is just a church. And Father Byrne wouldn't want part of any of that.'

'How can you be sure?' I ask. 'People don't go around advertising how shit they are.'

'They should,' she sighs.

'They fully should,' I say, and we both lapse into silence for a while. She swims to a little jacuzzi part of the pool – it's

22

not switched on or anything, but you can still sit in it like a bath – and curls towards me.

'I'm fairly sure he was sent here as a punishment,' she tells me. 'He doesn't say much but I don't think he lies, and that's refreshing. And Mamó likes him.'

'Mamó doesn't like anyone,' I point out. It has to be said.

'I know, but she hates him less than some of the other people in Ballyfrann. I once saw her nod at him.' Catlin doesn't miss much these days. There is a grudging respect in Mamó's voice when she talks about Father Byrne. But I still don't like the idea of Catlin hanging out with a priest.

'There's something off about it,' I say. 'I mean, priests shouldn't have teenage friends. Jesus should be friend enough for them. And you're not short of people to hang out with who aren't in their eighties.'

'You're one to talk.'

'I can't control my situation with Mamó. And she's probably not in her eighties.'

'She could be – we don't know how witches age. I will say she carries it better than he does though. Look, Maddy, I can't go to counselling, because no one will believe me, so I need to go to confession because I have to get it out somehow or I'll lose the plot.' Catlin's voice is a little high and breathy, as if she's getting it out quickly before she can't say anything at all.

'Okay,' I tell her. 'Okay.'

'I know it is. I don't need your permission.'

'I'm getting cold,' I tell her. And it's true. Gooseflesh up my legs. The lights in the hotel garden flicker through the big dark window like artificial stars.

23

'Me too,' my sister tells me, 'but we don't know when we'll get this chance again. Can we please stay a little longer, Maddy?'

I nod and she puts her head on my shoulder. Nothing in the coffin. Just pale grey lining. It looked soft. I never understood that. Surely when they're dead the time to make them comfortable has passed. I don't know what I was expecting really. I should have given up on answers long ago. Ballyfrann doesn't offer anything up easily. There's always an unpleasant sort of price.

5

Coffee Grounds

(motivation, speed)

I didn't dream about Lon last night. It was like he couldn't find me there. It was a relief. I'm not sure that I even dreamed at all. I did only get like three hours' sleep, mind you. Madeline woke us up at the crack of dawn, wanting to get on the road, and not 'cheat' Mamó out of more time.

'She'll make me pay it back,' she told us, looking stressed and crumpled in the clothes she'd slept in, and I'd believe that. It would be less egregious than some other stuff she's done. And we don't know the half of it. But I am going to learn the half of it. Father Byrne has a series of big leather-bound books under lock and key in the back of the chapel that I'm fairly sure are the parish records – births and deaths and marriages and other things as well, because it's Ballyfrann and there's always some dark secret lurking somewhere. I'd

25

love to get a look at them. I know it's unlikely that they say things like 'shape-shifter', 'wise woman', 'local serial killer' but maybe? It would be good to get a sense of how long this place has been dangerous. With that in mind, I've been watching tutorials on how to pick a variety of locks. I've ordered some tools – skeleton keys, bolt cutters and little sets of pliers – off the Internet, using Brian's credit card. I told him it was for make-up, and he didn't ask me anything else really. It's nice in some ways, having a Brian to exploit, even if I'm worried about himself and Mam.

About his motives.

He should have been honest with us, about what this place is, what coming here would mean, and all the healthy morning runs and vegan smoothies won't convince me that there isn't something off about him now. People have more than one face, and it's important to remember every one they show you. To keep counting. I'm also a bit suspicious about this tea he gave Mam. That's witch behaviour, giving people tea with bits of branch in it. And she vomited after. Granted that could have been the shock, or the hangover, but it's something for me to keep an eye on, at the very least. Maddy used to be the one who'd notice things like that, but she's not in the castle any more now, so it's kind of up to me to try my best.

Mam guns it back to Galway, Maddy egging her on and stress-tapping her fingers on her knees. Her nails are very short and a little stained, and we are mostly silent. I try to bring up Dad, and Mam shuts me down with an 'I'm not ready to talk about it, pet.' Which makes me stiffen, but I don't correct her, or point out that we might not be able to talk about it again for ages, not all three of us at least, once we get back, and Maddy has to go down to the basement.

'You know the way the Collinses are shape-shifters?' I ask.

'Yes, Catlin,' Mam sighs, as though I've started describing in detail the consistency of my period blood. Which would maybe be a thing, if I got any. I haven't since I died and came back. The expensive doctor Brian brought me to in a village forty minutes away from Ballyfrann said that it could be stress related, and not to worry about it. It would even out as I grew up. Apparently they could have stopped even if I hadn't been assaulted by someone who was supposed to be in love with me. I'm only young, and I have lots of time to wait for my body to sort itself out. But none of us can know what time we have.

His hot breath on my skin.

His hands.

His teeth.

It doesn't take that much to stop a life.

'Do you ever think about what they shift into?'

'Can't say that I have,' Mam says.

'Ah, COME ON,' I say. 'You *must* have. Like . . . they're shape-shifters. Maddy, do you know?'

Maddy smiles a mysterious smile, and I poke her in the ribcage until she stops looking superior and starts giving out. A poke in the ribcage is a great equaliser.

'I can't reveal stuff I learn while working with Mamó. It's like doctor–patient confidentiality or something.'

'Yeah, but doctors can break that if they need to for the public good. Like if there's a threat.'

'Meaning?'

I lower my voice to its most serious intensity. 'If one of them is a dinosaur, you have to tell us.'

'None of our neighbours are dinosaurs, Catlin. You'd have noticed by now.'

'I don't know, Madeline. Not all dinosaurs were massive. Some were smaller.'

Mam interjects with her curious voice on. I've got her, I think. She's going to be like a dog with a bone until we get some answers.

'So, you've interacted with some of these shape-shifters in your . . . work?'

'Mam, you interact with them every day. Carol Collins works in the deli.'

I picture Carol in my head. A curvy woman with shiny brown hair and a little undercut.

'I'm calling it. Brown Lab.'

'You don't get to decide that sort of thing, Catlin.'

'Hear me out. She's fat, she's pretty, and has an expression that's a mix of hope and loyalty when she prepares a ham-and-cheese roll.'

'Catlin.'

'She always asks how people are. A Labrador would care about that sort of thing. They're really good dogs.'

Mam lets out a big thoughtful *hmmm*. 'I think that Eddie Collins fella is a Brussels Griffon.'

'That's very specific.'

'Google it,' she says, eyes confidently on the road.

'That's uncanny, apart from the eye colour. Look, Maddy!'

28

'Eddie is our friend. I want no part of this.'

'There is nothing wrong with being a good dog, Maddy. Look how loyal this guy looks. He'd give you a lift in his car if you were stuck. If only he had a little doggy car.'

Mam is warming up. She's got a talent for this.

'I'd say Layla Shannon is a white Afghan hound.' She nods. 'She looks the type.'

'Are they shape-shifters too?' I ask.

'They're definitely *something*,' says Mam, nodding sagely.

'I love how you've both decided everyone is dogs now,' Maddy says. 'What happened to the poor dinosaurs?'

'Dogs are better. My God, wouldn't it be so nice if that was it, if everyone was dogs and we didn't have to worry about any more dark secrets?'

Maddy grins. 'It really would. I feel like we've been gathering a few of our own recently though . . .'

'Like today,' I say. 'Are we just going to say to people why we went back to Cork, and what we found?'

Mam swallows. 'I think maybe it would be best to keep it low key, love.'

'Are you going to tell Brian?' I ask, pressing her.

Her eyes are cloudy in the rear-view mirror. 'I don't know.'

'What do you think happened?' Maddy asks her. 'I mean, Dad was in there at some point, wasn't he?'

'He was,' Mam says. She swallows again. 'We didn't have an open casket because of how he died, but I saw him in there . . .' There is a pause. Her eyes are fixed on the road.

'I have this horrible feeling that someone stole your father, girls.'

Maddy looks at me. 'Me too,' she says. 'Something isn't right. There has to be some sort of explanation.'

'Could it have been his family, to like "protect" him?' I ask. 'I mean, that wouldn't be the worst . . .'

We're not in contact with Dad's family. They were never that fond of Mam, and after he died they drifted away. It hurts a bit, if you take the time to think about it, so it's probably best not to.

'That's one scenario. I'll have to keep trying to get in contact with them. They seem to have disappeared. The numbers that I have don't work any more.'

'Charley is a pug,' says Madeline, her voice so determined to lighten the tone that it's actually a little stressful. 'I mean, not that she is a dog. But if she were a dog, I would definitely put her as a pug. She has mournful resting face and big brown eyes.'

I take note of this. It's nice to know Maddy can notice big brown eyes that aren't attached to Oona Noone.

'What would I be,' I ask, 'if I were a dog?'

'You're already a pup,' says Mam, laughing.

'A Chinese Crested,' says Madeline, who has been googling.

'You'd have to be the same dog too,' I tell her, searching to see what they look like. My heart stops in my throat. A Chinese Crested has dappled skin and is largely bald with white hair.

'Not necessarily,' she says. 'There's not, like, a rule.'

'I don't want to be a Chinese Crested,' I tell her. 'I want to be a Yorkshire terrier, like I was before all this.'

'We all want things we can't have, Catlin,' Maddy says.

'Yeah,' I snap. 'Like a bit of fucking sympathy.'

I worry at the rosary bracelet I got in a church we visited on holidays once. It has red beads inlaid with flowers and a little silver crucifix with pointed ends. The beads are spaced out so they make a decade of the rosary. You say a Hail Mary for every bead. Or I do anyway. I taught myself.

A Yorkshire terrier is a nice dog. Everyone likes seeing a Yorkshire terrier. And they can be a bit snappy, but they're so cute that you forgive them instantly. And they kind of move around like they happily own the place.

I'd like to feel that way inside again.

'I think I'd be an Irish setter,' says Mam. 'Or maybe a Kerry blue.'

The road stretches before us, and it isn't long before the mountains start to loom again, and the sick feeling in my stomach intensifies.

'Those are both great dogs, Mam,' I tell her, and the talking fades away into a heavy sort of silence that probably does no one any good.

I look at Madeline, looking out the window at the road, avoiding me. I know that what I've been through is written on my body. I know that I have changed. But it feels cruel in someone else's mouth. I trace my fingers over the delicate beads around my wrist, feeling the inlaid patterns under the whorls of my fingertips. Maddy is a lot of things – stressed, annoying, shy, but cruel isn't one of them. Not usually. I'm the one who hurts other people. The one who speaks without thinking. The one who doesn't care.

I wonder if it's something to do with not having a soul, if somehow her empathy is less. People aren't sure what souls

31

are exactly. The part of you that can go to heaven. The part of you that's spiritual, that loves, I would have said before now. But Maddy can still love, and she needs to be a bit spiritual to practise witchcraft, doesn't she? She broke into a swimming pool for me, to make me happy, I think. She gave her life for mine, almost. She is still here. She is still here. Probably just tired.

Nothing to get all worked up about.

6

Fennel

(strength and courage, cleansing)

I feel the nerves hum through me as we pass though the village, past the school, the shop, the petrol station. I feel like I have a big exam tomorrow. With Mamó, every day is a little like a day with a big exam, to be fair. She's always barking questions. Or orders. And when she tries to explain things, she's really bad at it, because she has no patience. I think in an ideal world, she'd just upload all the years and years of knowledge she's amassed to my head and leave me at it silently. If she didn't distrust computers, and all technology. She barely has a phone. It's essentially an old-timey calculator that rings. I don't know why I said that about the Chinese Crested to Catlin. I suppose I just thought it fit. I like those dogs – I think they're elegant-looking. And she's not as changed as she thinks she is. I mean, it's the same face, the same body. It's just parts of it grew back a little . . . livid. Mamó has ointments, teas and salves that help with that. We make them every fortnight or so and send them up.

'I don't want to drop you back there,' Mam says. 'Maybe we should just have stayed in Cork.'

'Too late for that,' says Catlin, the queen of things that don't need saying.

I tell her that it's fine. And it will be. There are parts of my old life I miss, but it's not forever and it's not that bad. We've got a routine going, and I'm learning things, learning to be stronger and more knowledgeable about what witchcraft can and cannot do. And I suppose as well that there's a part of me that thinks that I deserve this. I left it so long to speak up about Catlin, to intervene. If I had stepped up sooner, we mightn't be in this situation now. Maybe Catlin wouldn't have been murdered, and we wouldn't have done the things we did to Lon, and I wouldn't know what I was capable of.

We turn down the driveway and pull up to the back of the castle. I should be used to it by now, but it still takes my breath away. The size of it, the ramparts and the turrets. I can't believe that Brian's dad built it. It looks like it is hundreds of years old. Of course bits of it are. Lots of other castles in our castle. I look at Catlin, to see if she is feeling some of what I'm feeling, but her expression is hard to read. Mam is staring grimly, straight ahead. Her knuckles on the steering wheel are white. She doesn't look like someone coming home, not in the slightest.

Brian is waiting at the door, like a Victorian butler. His face is thin and pale and drawn, his expression doleful. Brian always looks worried now, the size and shape of the worries flickering across his face at different speeds throughout the day, but there's always something there, to fear, to dwell on.

I just want to have an evening of reading dusty notebooks written by Mamó's predecessors and maybe cataloguing dried plants in jars. The granny flat (though it's more of a spinster cavern to be honest, which I prefer) we live in is full of plants and dried plants and drying plants and bits of plants and other things in jars with labels on them. People in Ballyfrann drop their glass to Mamó instead of the recycling, which I only realised when the fifth client arrived with a big wooden crate stacked high with empty pasta-sauce jars.

I've gotten used to silence, and my own company.

But it was nice, last night, to have that time with Catlin. I feel so complicated about my sister now, in a way I usen't do before. It's like our relationship has shifted and it's now infused with sacrifice and death, with my failings and hers. I didn't tell her everything before, but now I don't more purposefully. She's always trying to make sense of things, make sense of me, to figure all of this out, and there isn't anything to figure out, not really. It is the way it is.

We are the daughters of a burning man.

An empty space.

7

Earth

(creation, or destruction)

Deep in the ground something calls to her. Her eyes flick open. She rises, and feels a sharp, wide pain inside her gut. She clutches her hands to it, as though she could embrace herself, and heal. She finds she cannot even feel herself.

A kiss.

The smell of dust.

The writing on the wall.

Her house, up on the hill.

Her dog.

Her mother.

Her name, before, was Bridget.

Something happened, oh, who is she now?

She opens her mouth, but something is wrong with her ears and she can't hear whatever sounds she makes. Her feet begin to twitch and shudder, like a rabbit sensing danger.

Thump.
Thump.
Thump.
And she is moving. Or part of her is moving. Pulled apart.
She needs to stay together. What happened here. What happened here. What happened here. What happened here.

what

happened.

8

Coins

(transitioning, promises and luck)

There are two confession boxes in the church of Our Lady of the Mountains, and only one priest. Which doesn't make a lot of sense, but this is Ballyfrann so I suppose I shouldn't be surprised. Father Byrne keeps me waiting, but I don't mind. Sitting on the worn velvet upholstery with little bits of horsehair poking through it is kind of . . . meditative.

'Bless me, Father, for I have sinned, it has been two weeks since my last confession,' I murmur as he enters the booth opposite me. I can hear him sighing as he settles his creaky old bones down and gets ready to listen to me. Maddy is right that he's *old* old. Like you could well imagine him sitting in a wheelchair in a nursing home with a blanket on his lap, if he wasn't so sprightly.

'Has it really, Catlin Hayes? My word,' he says. 'It feels

like only yesterday I was listening to you telling me about throwing . . . what was it . . . a hair straightener? At your stepfather.'

'It was a hot brush, Father.' I got seven Hail Marys for that one. He knows Mary is my favourite, so always ladles her on pretty thick, which I appreciate.

'And what does that do?' he asks.

'It's like a hairbrush that is also a hairdryer,' I explain.

'It sounds convenient,' he says. 'Maybe I should invest in one.'

'The one I have is only okay,' I say. 'I expected more.'

'Well, it seems to double as a missile, which is useful.'

'I did my penance for that, Father,' I say. 'Can we talk about my current sins?'

'Which are . . . ?' I can't really see him through the grille, but I know he's steepling his fingers.

'I did some underage drinking,' I say.

'Alone?' he asks.

'You want me to, like, name names?'

'No,' he says. 'I just think it's better not to drink alone. Particularly when you're weathering a storm.'

I feel my eyes well up. I *am* weathering a storm. People act like it's over, but it isn't. It hums through the meat of me. I carry what happened with me everywhere.

'No, Father,' I say. 'It was a social thing.'

'That's good,' he says. 'Not the drinking, but the socialising with children your own age.'

'As opposed to creepy murderous predators?'

'As opposed to very old priests.' I can sense his smile.

'I broke into a swimming pool!' I say as well. I'm kind of

39

not sorry about either of those things, and I'm fairly sure he knows I'm not. I'm rarely sorry, which probably means that absolution doesn't really take. But there's a value to owning the things you've done, I suppose. Even if you'd do them again tomorrow.

'This was in Cork?' he says, as though it were an exotic location where the rules don't apply. Father Byrne has been placed in Ballyfrann for the past fifty years or so, and fully needs to get out more.

'Yeah. I didn't want to go to the pool because of the scars, so Maddy found the code and we broke in after hours.'

'Did you steal anything?'

'We swam a bit and talked a bit. It was nice,' I say. 'But obviously also sinful. I'm very contrite.'

'Of course.'

'Oh!!' I say. 'I have a really good one, and this is a sin but it's also a bit of detective work. We dug up my father's grave.'

There is a long pause.

'Could you repeat that, please, Catlin?' he asks. 'I think I must have misheard.'

'Stop, your hearing is great since you got that new hearing aid,' I tell him. 'You heard right. It wasn't the nicest thing to have to do, but we wanted to see if it would answer any of the questions we have around what happened to him, and how Maddy's a witch and everything. Mam came too. She pulled open the coffin.'

'Indeed,' he says. And there is a pause again. 'And did you find any answers to your questions?'

'No,' I sigh. 'Just more questions.'

'It's often the way,' he says. 'Is that everything?'

'Well, those are the big ones,' I say. 'You're kind of caught up with my life now. How are you keeping?'

'Well. Carol Collins did a lovely job with the new flower arrangements, and I ordered in some votives from a new supplier. They look nicer but I'm not sure they burn as well.'

'I'm sure they'll be grand,' I tell him.

'And how about yourself, Catlin? Are you having any more of those . . . dreams?' His voice is low. I've told him a little about Lon appearing night after night inside my head.

'Oh, now and then.' I brush him off. 'But I'm finding them easier to cope with.'

'You shouldn't have to cope with them alone,' he says. 'Is there a trusted friend you could confide in?'

'You're kind of it, Father,' I say. 'I mean, there's Maddy, but she's hard to get a hold of.'

'Kept busy.'

'Yeah,' I say grimly. 'Can we . . . not talk about this any more? I just . . .'

'Of course,' he says. For a priest, Father Byrne is weirdly good at respecting boundaries. It's one of the things I like best about him. He gives me my penance and tells me I'm absolved of all my sins. I get a few decades of the rosary. Father Byrne is a big fan of an aul' pray. I don't know why. He doesn't look like very many of his have been answered. By the time I leave the confessional, he's already striding up to the sacristy, to sort out one thing or another. I didn't realise how busy priests were before. I thought it was mainly saying Mass and drinking cups of tea, but he's all action.

41

I like to stay still in church.

I like to breathe in the smell of incense and candle wax, put my fifty-cent coin inside the box beside Our Lady of Ballyfrann and light a candle to her. There are always fresh flowers at her feet that aren't really feet. She looks like a lady the way a black-and-white photograph of an ultrasound looks like a baby. It's more a dream, a blob, but everyone pretends. Madeline thinks she's creepy, but I know she's beautiful. She's just survived a lot. They found her in the bog years and years ago, and dug her up and cleaned her and prayed to her. An abandoned thing reclaimed, and given power.

And she is powerful.

The man who found her, he had an injury and she healed him. She has healed others too. Her feet are smooth from being rubbed and hoped on.

I feel a sort of hope licking at me like a flame sometimes when I am deep in prayer in front of her.

The promise of a place beyond my hurt.

Of beauty reimagined.

Power taken back.

Our Lady of Ballyfrann is small as statues go, and she's made of old, smooth wood, dappled different pales, the white of bone, the beige of milky tea, the brown of driftwood. There are no features on her face – she could be anyone. She could be me, or another girl. Like Helen Groarke, who was Lon's ex before me. Or Bridget Hora, who went missing back when Mam was small.

And if I get the words right, maybe she could heal me, like she healed those other people back in the day, after they found

42

her. That's why she's in the church. Because of miracles. And I'm in need of something like a miracle, something to restore my face, my heart. And make me whole and not a broken thing inexpertly remade and always hurting.

I close my eyes and picture Our Lady of Ballyfrann as a girl. What would she have looked like? Bridget Hora maybe, or one of the more old-timey mountain girls. What happened to me was not the first time something like it happened. It had been happening for years and years. But people didn't like to look at it directly, and so they didn't. It was hard to talk about and so people didn't talk about it. And it kept happening.

Is it rape if they try to kill you during? Lon had my consent, up to a point, and then it changed. And now when I think of someone touching me, or when I touch myself, it feels broken. Like there's a link missing in the chain. Because my hands or my imagination will do something to me, always, in the end, that smacks of him, and then I'm frozen. And I don't know what to do with that. Part of me thinks I should just pick someone and kiss them and work through it, like a textbook. Section by section until I feel competent. That doesn't sound very sexy, does it? I used to think that it had to be spontaneous, and wild. I'd love when a guy grabbed me like I was something that he had to have. It made me feel so desired, so powerful. But now, I'd love everything written down beforehand. All predictable, and safe. Because I don't want anyone to grab me, or to put their hands on me in ways I don't ask them to.

I wonder how long this will last. If it's a forever thing, or a couple of years thing. And there's no way to know. It varies from person to person. Victim to victim.

Some people who've been through things like this call themselves survivors, but I don't feel I really have survived. I mean, I died. And I am different now. I breathe. I pray. I visualise the Virgin Mary with Bridget Hora's black-and-white-newsprint face. Barefoot on the mountains where her bones were found. Most of them, anyway.

What do you want? the Virgin-Bridget asks me.

It's my imagination, but I hear it, a sweet and husky voice, sounding as though it hasn't been used in years. I keep my eyes closed and my brain focused on her.

So many things.

I want so many things.

9

Mint

(belly, gnawing heart)

I've spent the day weeding and tending to the physic garden, and checking the dates on all the jars of dried herbs. I've made a list of all of the ones that need replacing or replenishing, and Mamó has stared stonily at it and barked more orders at me. It's exhausting, but I think it's also my punishment for being away for the two days. I don't mind being exhausted, but I do want to unpack what happened in Cork, and see what Mamó thinks it might mean. I'm fairly sure that Mam is kind of right. That someone stole him. Or what was left of him. I have this sense that it was for some sort of witchcraft. I mean, if you can use a leaf, a branch, a drop of blood, there must be some sort of value to a body.

When I get back to the basement flat, Mamó is sitting on the sofa drinking a small glass of red wine. Her raven, Badb, is drinking a saucer of what also looks like red wine.

'Did you give Badb wine?' I ask her.

'No,' she answers. 'What do you take me for? It's obviously blood.' As if that's perfectly normal, which for her it is. Probably.

'Grand, so,' I say, moving closer. I can smell the heavy scent of it, and see the texture, slightly different to wine. It's not that viscous, must be fresh. From the vein of a calf or a lamb, I reckon. Badb laps it up with their little raven tongue. On battlefields, they'd feast on what remained after the slaughter. A death buffet. I hear a hiss behind the sofa, and turn. Button is there. Of course he is. With his bushy tail and long memory.

Button is a fluffy tortoiseshell cat, who is also a glowering, one-eyed reminder of the worst thing that I have ever done. Mamó saved his life, after I almost killed him, that night when everything turned upside down. He's not grown much bigger than when he was a kitten, but his body is differently shaped now, less tubby and more rangy. His opulent fur is kept glisteningly clean by his pink little tongue, and he likes salmon, Mamó, Catlin and hating me, in that order. His ears are pressed back against his head and his pupils are the thinnest slits of black.

'Come on, Button,' I say. 'Be sound.'

Mamó harrumphs. She has an amazing collection of contemptuous sounds. It would be impressive, if it wasn't so irritating.

'Can I put him out, please?' I ask.

'You've done enough to that creature. Let him stay here near the fire if he wants to.'

Initially with Button, I tried to overcompensate, giving him

46

salmon and fine cheeses. But the levels of hatred have remained the same, though his greed has grown bigger, and now my guilt is mixed with annoyance. I don't like it, but it's the way things are.

There are at least three different kinds of magic that you can practise. And the kind Mamó and I do is the most practical kind. We use herbs, and stones, and objects and pieces of things, sometimes even pieces of ourselves. It takes a toll on the body every time, but you know what you're getting into. You pay the price upfront. But there is another sort of magic. Prayer magic. And that was what I tried to mess with the night I hurt poor Button who, while maintaining eye contact and an arched back, traipses to the fridge and hisses at me until I open it and give him a piece of fish. He hisses again, and I move back to the sofa as I hear him start to nom. Button will rule us all one day, I swear it.

Prayer magic is where you ask something older and more powerful than you are to help you. Sometimes these things have names, and sometimes they do not. And you can't be sure, no matter how strong you are, that who you think you've called is who's responding.

They can do favours for you, big impossible things, and more quickly and less painfully than if you try it our way, but you don't know who you owe, and what they want. Praying to something leaves a little door open between their world and ours and they can push a finger through and work at it and widen it until there's no sort of boundary at all between you and them. That's the kind of magic I tried to invoke, without really knowing what I was doing, more than a story I'd been told about devils and favours at the crossroads.

And I almost did invoke it.

'The coffin was empty,' I tell Mamó. 'Nothing there at all.'

'Did you manage to dig it up without being seen?' she asks.

'Yes,' I answer, and she inclines her head very slightly which I could interpret as: Gold star, Madeline, ten out of ten, what an amazing witch you are. Never have I seen such talent in one so young. I am very proud of you and can teach you no more, you're free to go now.

I snort at the thought of Mamó ever being that effusive. Her praise is sparing, and sometimes oddly scathing. But I am proud that I managed to make that particular one work. It took a lot of planning, and a good bit of energy.

'What do you think they're using him for?' I venture. I want to see what she thinks of my hunch.

'It might be nothing,' she says. 'Perhaps his relatives took his remains to bury in their own places, or to protect them.'

Apparently Dad's witchcraft was a family thing. Hayes is an old name and a magic one, according to Mamó. We don't know Dad's family. They kind of froze us out after he died, and we reckon now it might have been to protect us from all this. Something was done as well to Mam's memory. It impacts her, and every now and then she gets flashes of panic or clarity, but then it dissipates. She only really remembers the parts of Dad that weren't witchy. But how do you love someone without loving who they are? If you have the instinct – like I do, like we think Dad did – it's part of you, you can't be something different. Though I have tried.

'What did your mother do?' Mamó's voice cuts through my worries, grating.

48

'She vomited.'

'Ah,' she says, and it is the most cutting *ah* I have ever heard. Poor Mam, I think. I hope she never hears that level of contempt to her face. I remember the little hip flask, and wonder if maybe it was that that caused her to feel sick . . .

'Did you give her a tea?' I ask. 'She said Brian made it, but it's more your area, so I thought you might have passed it on to him to give to her.'

'I did no such thing,' she says. 'No one has to accept my help if they don't want to.'

That isn't strictly true, but I don't get into it. Her eyes flick over me.

'What was in it?' she asks, her voice casual but interested.

'Nettle, lemon balm, meadowsweet, rosehip. And something else as well I couldn't place. Something that was masked,' I tell her. 'Like mint, but not.'

'Hmmm.'

'What do you think?' I ask.

'I think,' she says, 'I'd like to know what that final ingredient was. I might have to have a little word with Brian.'

I don't think Brian would be too gone on that little word.

'And did you bring some of the vomit back?' she asks, as though this was a perfectly normal thing to expect me to do.

'No,' I say, disappointed in myself. 'I did bring some soil though.'

'Well.' She sighs. 'It could have been instructive. I suppose you'll know for again.'

It's one of her less scathing retorts but it's still fairly scathing.

'I'm worried about Catlin,' I tell her. 'She's still not right.'

'She might never be right,' Mamó says. 'Has she done anything to worry you?'

'She's going to the church a lot, and I don't think she's sleeping well at all. Her eyes look tired. And when we were in the hotel she wouldn't go anywhere. It was like she didn't want people to see her.'

'Hmm,' Mamó says, staring into the fire. 'Keep an eye on her. And if anything out of the way happens, report back.'

I nod.

'What am I going to do tomorrow?'

'That's for tomorrow.' She turns to look at the fire, making it clear that we are now done talking.

I roll my eyes, and Badb raises their head from the saucer and does a little caw at me. Button shuffles from wherever he's been lurking to the door, and I rise to let him out. The moon is new, a little slice beginning, and the air is colder than it needs to be. It bites through me, and when I turn, Mamó is rinsing her glass and going to bed. When the door closes behind her, I take the glass from the drying rack and sniff it. I cannot tell if it was wine or blood.

10

Smoke

(connection, divination)

The sleepwalking happened again last night. I dreamed of Lon, and when I woke I wasn't in my room. I was halfway down the stairs. I woke mid-step and almost fell on my face. I don't know what it means that this is a thing I sort of do now. Or, not really a thing I do – it feels more like something that is done to me. And that's what creeps me out. The fact that, even without being here, he's still on some level able to control me.

Ordinarily, the dreams are like visiting old memories, or dreams I used to have when I was with him. But this was different. It wasn't like the others, a repeat of something I've already seen. We were in a shed, which is surprising because Lon wasn't really a shed kind of boy. I needed to get some tools off the wall and they were really heavy and Lon kept telling me I needed to pull, to really pull, and I could feel him getting frustrated and it frightened me, I wanted to tell him to leave me alone but I couldn't speak and my hands reached out for the shovel on the wall, between a saw and pliers, and the wood of it, the shining blade, his voice, made me remember everything that had happened and then I was down in the cave again, the night Brian came to get us, when we stabbed Lon in whatever it is he had instead of a heart. A flash of his eyes wide, and then my feet began to feel the worn red carpet, and then the air, my hands grasping for the banister.

I killed him.

He doesn't have a resting place we know of. Brian took the body and I've never asked him where he put it. For a man who claims to be sensitive, he's very good at telling us only some of what we need to know. When I look at him now, I see the gaps, the little buttonholes where distrust has seeped in. I used to think he was a harmless sort of person, and now I know he's not at all that way. He lied to Mam, to us. I do not trust him, and maybe that's why I feel the urge to dig Lon up, and look and just make sure he's in there.

I could have really hurt myself on the stairs – they're big and curved and made of hard old wood. There are so many things here that are not great from a safety point of view. Sharp antlers poking out from walls, heavy statues, vases. Unopened chests of who-even-knows-what. Secrets. I used to think living in a castle was great, and in some ways it is. It's big and beautiful and full of interesting old stuff. My bed is a four-poster and could probably fit up to nine more people if I was an opulent countess who hosted orgies. The castle is properly vast, and there's always another room, another corner, to discover. I found a room last week that was just full of mounted animal heads on the walls. With some of them I could see where the bullets had gone in. It was fascinating, but I think I would have liked it more before I felt like prey. Scary things could happen here and no one would notice. The statues' eyes were blank, the walls were thick enough that my voice would not have carried very well.

I didn't call for Mam or Brian after the sleepwalking. Mam's been so tired since we got back from Cork, her face pale and the rings under her eyes getting more pronounced with each day passing. Plus, if I had woken her, he would have woken too. And besides, I don't like to worry her. There's nothing she can do to fix my brain. There's no point in telling Maddy about it either. She'd make a bigger deal of it than it is. It doesn't take much to stress her out, and besides, it's only a bad dream, with added extras. I hardly ever see her as it is. And this isn't really the sort of thing that I'd put in a message. She'd probably have to run it by Mamó. And I don't like the thought of being investigated.

When I came back to my room, I scrolled through my phone until I found a picture I'd taken of Our Lady of Ballyfrann. It's hard to take a good picture of her, because she's just a round bit of wood really. Her power isn't in how she looks. It's in the story of her, this chunk of the divine pulled from the bog so many years ago.

I placed her at the centre of my altar, which is mainly Marys and other saints and medals and candles and things. I love the look of them, their faces and expressions. There's this . . . serenity about them. And wouldn't it be nice to be serene?

Their painted eyes, especially the older ones, are made of plaster, flaking flecks of blue on the floor, like birds shedding feathers. Maddy had so many feathers in her pockets the first day we moved here, she just kept finding them in every room. I think of her whenever I see a feather in the castle, a thick white seagull quill, a dark crow's plume, even the small ones that flutter out of duvets when you change the cover. Maddy might have thrown them out, though maybe not; she always liked keeping things. Collecting. She'd squirrel things inside my room in places where she didn't think I'd notice. Mam used to be at her, about her mental health, about not collecting things, or giving in to impulses. It wasn't the best way to deal with it, but I think that it must have been born of fear. Mam has some sort of sense memory about what happened with Dad, and something in her body gets so afraid when Madeline gets witchy. I've seen the muscles tensing in her neck, and it scares me a little. That fear, if it wasn't hand in hand with love, is the kind of thing that leads to burning girls. To 'rooting out' the parts you don't want to tolerate.

Mam doesn't like my altar either, but it's not the same, because my altar is aesthetic. It's pretty. I keep it that way. And prayer is something Mam understands. Like, half of Ireland's Catholic, even if they don't practise. Mass is a normal thing. And Mam likes normal. She was the one who brought us to the church when we were little, who bought our Communion dresses and organised our confirmation party. A lot of the prayers I say are ones I first heard from her, murmuring quietly on the long polished wooden benches while stained-glass windows filled the room with oddly coloured light. A darker light.

Mam doesn't like us having candles in our rooms. After what happened to Dad. But I don't care. I need the calm of this. I take my lighter out and move its flame to each wick, until the altar is glowing around the photograph. I pick dried rose petals, dandelion heads from around them. I must get fresh ones. It's been a while since I properly tended to the altar, made it look as good as it can. I place them in the bin and get a pillow. I find a soft grey feather, very small, under the bed, the vane of it as downy and delicate as a spiderweb.

Huh, I think, and place it where her feet would be if my phone were a statue and not just a screen. The image flickers in the candlelight. It's as though something gentles in her face, although it can't, not really. I clasp my hands and I begin to pray.

Till I feel safe.

11

Flower-de-Luce (Iris)

(eases head pain, ulcers, cankers, wounds)

Because it's the kind of summer day where it rained all night and the earth wants to suck your feet into it for a snack, I've been sent up to the mountains with a list of things to gather, written in Mamó's almost indecipherable handwriting. That's challenge one. Challenge two is that there are things that aren't on the list as well. There always are. It's one of the ways she tests me, though I don't know why she needs to really. I'm here for seven years, it's not like I'm not going to pick stuff up. When I get back, I'll have to clean the bathroom. Mamó orders me to do things as she sees fit, which is horribly unfair as a situation, but in the context of our bargain, fair enough. Like, as well as witchcraft things there are . . . flatmate things, I guess.

I'd love to be around when she has that word with Brian. I'm a bit suspicious of our stepdad. He seemed like a gentle sound man who loved my mam and would never endanger our lives or facilitate the execution of Catlin's ex-boyfriend. He isn't all he seems. Mam thinks he is open with her now, or at least she claims she does. But there are secret passageways in the castle walls, and try as we might, we can't work out exactly how many. There are some things that are really hard to map. Like people's motives.

I'm gathering up a good bundle of costmary when I hear footsteps behind me. It's Layla Shannon, on one of her runs. She's wearing a white T-shirt with dark red sleeves and little white shorts with a red stripe on them. She looks like a ballerina or an intimidating model. She towers over me, her white-blonde hair gathered up into a high ponytail that swoops down her back before curling up a little, right at the end.

'Hi, Maddy!' she pants. 'I thought you might be up here.'

'Yeah, Mamó gave me a list,' I say, wrapping the flowers in cloth, and placing them in my enormous leather satchel. My enormous leather satchel is one of the best things about working for Mamó. It can fit SO MUCH STUFF. Like, think of all the stuff that would fit into an enormous leather satchel you'd imagine. And then DOUBLE IT. It's the little things.

'It's not a bad day for it,' she says, smiling. And it's true. The sun is high in the sky and the clouds are just little wisps of candyfloss against the brightest blue. It doesn't look like Ballyfrann today, it looks like the landscape in a children's cartoon or something.

Layla has been happening to bump into me a lot, when I'm up here. I think she worries that I might be lonely. Which is good, because I am, but bad because I don't want everybody knowing that I'm lonely, and being all 'Oh, there goes lonely old Maddy, off filling her bags of stuff again'. I mean, I do have some pride.

I do like Layla though. She's fun, and doesn't ask much of people. Also, she tried to warn us about Lon. Not in a very constructive way, but it was more than a lot of people did. She sits down on a big rock (we're not short of big rocks in Ballyfrann).

'What are we looking for next?' she asks.

If I were more like Mamó, I'd glare pointedly at her and tell her nothing. But Mamó seems to be able to get by without friends, and even though I don't have a soul, there's still a need in me for human connection.

'Ragwort,' I say.

'What's it for?'

'It depends. Menstruation, diabetes, bruises, rage. You can do lots of different things with it. No plant is just for one thing. It depends on who is using it and what they combine it with, if that makes sense.' I look up awkwardly at her. Whenever I start talking about this stuff out loud, I always get a little overwhelmed by how much I have yet to learn. And how hard it is to get a hold of anything exact.

'It does a bit. I mean, it's probably like everyone's thing. If you don't live it, you'll never fully get it.' Layla trails her hand over a mossy rock and wipes it on the side of her shorts. 'I didn't think it would be this moist . . . it's such a sunny day.'

'Nature can be surprising.'

'For sure.'

'How are Fiachra and Cathal getting on?' I ask. They're her brothers – Layla is a triplet.

'Grand. Same as ever. Loving bikes. Being hormonal. Giving out to Dad loads at the moment. Like it's his fault we are the way we are.' She grins. She has a really good smile. It's a bit goofy, like her mouth is almost closed and you can just see a little flash of teeth, and when she laughs her mouth opens so wide that she could swallow mountains.

'And what way is that?' I ask. Her face falls into something else entirely, so I backtrack. 'You don't have to tell me if you don't want to,' I carry on. 'I mean, I don't want to be rude. Or pry. It's your business.' I spot some ragwort, and take out my blade. Lust is something ragwort can be used for as well.

Her eyes are almost black, maybe they are black. They gaze away from me, as she begins to talk.

'Ugh,' she says. 'It's fine. I mean, most people know. I did grow up here. But it's just . . . embarrassing.'

I nod and keep on going about my work. Silence can be powerful, and also she probably really needs to talk because it all starts coming out at once. She crouches in on herself as she begins to speak, almost folding in half, and hugging her hands around her torso. They splay out wide. Her fingers are so long. Her voice squinter than normal, tentative.

'So, when you think shape-shifter, people generally think wolf. Or hare, or something badass,' she says, quirking her mouth a little.

I smile back. 'I don't think most people think about shape-shifting at all. Outside of Ballyfrann . . .'

'Ah. EVERYONE does. Have you never had the conversation about what type of animal you'd be if you were an animal?'

I nod. 'Yeah, actually.'

'And nobody ever chooses what we – like me and my family – are. I'm –' she rubs her fingers on her temples – 'a were-swan, I suppose is the closest term. It is MORTIFYING.'

I didn't think I could be surprised any more, but there you go. I try to maintain a neutral expression. Keep my mouth closed.

'A completely,' Layla says, taking a little packet of jelly beans from the pocket of her shorts and offering me one before starting in on them herself, 'ridiculous thing to be. And it GETS WORSE.'

'How?' I ask. I mean, it does not sound great.

'That is a fair question, Madeline Hayes. Allow me to explain. There are two kinds of people who turn into swans. There's the kind with magical powers, and the kind who just turn into really big swans for an unspecified period of time and have no control over when they'll turn back. Guess which one the Shannons get to be?'

'The second one?'

'Bingo. And to make matters worse, we live, like, a really long time, which I know doesn't sound like something to complain about, but it means that if I were to turn into a swan any time over the next fifty or so years, I would be a fluffy little cygnet. Just a tiny vulnerable little cygnet, unable to switch back, but weirdly with the power of speech, for all the good it would do me.'

'So you'll live for properly ages then,' I say.

'Yup. Well, I mean, we live for ages provided we don't get eaten by predators while we're out there being vulnerable little snacks for decades at a time.'

'You said your dad was like you. How about your mam?' I ask.

'Fully the same. There's a bit of a thing with marrying your own kind that I don't necessarily get. I mean, if you had a chance of not passing down the weird swan-curse to your kids, why would you not take it?'

'I don't know.' I sigh. 'Why wouldn't you tell your new wife that if she moved to your hometown there was a good chance one of her kids would be murdered? People in Ballyfrann make terrible choices constantly.'

'It's true,' she says. 'Fecking Brian. What was he playing at?'

'I do not know,' I say, shaking my head. 'I mean, at least you're not bound to serve a witch for seven years?'

'That is a bright side. Though I'd be no use to her, unless she needed to . . . I actually can't think of anything. No one ever needs a cygnet. No one. Why would you?' She spreads her arms out wide, a graceful movement, and for a second I get a flash of wide, white wings.

'How are Fiachra and Cathal about it all?' I ask.

'As you can see,' she says, 'I'm not exactly delighted about it. And they are taking it far less well than me. Swans, Madeline, cannot use bikes.'

'That must actually be really tough on them . . .' I say. 'But surely you've known for a while? Your parents wouldn't, like, just not tell you who you were?'

She shakes her head. 'Like parents ever know who their children are, really. But yeah, they did prepare us. But we kind of didn't have to worry about it too much when we were younger. The onset comes in adolescence, so at the moment, every day when we wake up, we're not sure whether or not we're going to make it to sunset as humans, or be stuck as fluffy nonsense clouds for like a year or two. Or more. Makes planning for the future pretty hard. It's not as bad as it could be, but that feeling that there's a stopwatch running on the way my life is now, and that at any second it could beep is . . . something.'

'Um, I don't know what to say,' I tell her. 'That sounds really hard. I mean, even I feel for you, and I have no soul.'

'Yeah, you do,' she says. 'It's just waiting to come back. You're a good person, Maddy. Thanks for listening to me going on about alllllll my troublesssss.'

'Any time,' I say. 'You've listened to me often enough.' I say it to be nice, but then realise it's true. She has been kind to me, Layla. When all this started and I was really lonely and afraid. She'd chat away whenever she saw me and keep things light and kind. It was a gift.

'Are you sure you don't want a jelly bean?' she asks. 'They're almost finished.'

'Go on,' I say, and she passes me a red one. We sit together eating in silence, and then I go off looking for mullein, and she goes off running.

The light is beginning to slowly change by the time I start making my way back down, and the air is cooler than it was before. I trudge step by step in my sensible boots, past the little shed that Oona and I kissed in. More than kissed. It's strange how that night, the night everything happened, had that little harbour in it, something good. I walk inside. It's two little rooms, with thick stone walls, a roof that probably used to be thatch but is corrugated iron now, turned orange with time. The floor is dusty and the old fireplace is full of ashes and little twists of paper. The beanbags leaking on the floor like snow. It's hard to know how long it's been like this. I haven't been back there since that night, and it's strange, like walking back inside a memory, only it isn't how I remember it at all, it's dingier, and older. In the darkness, the details evaded me, unless they were about Oona, and then I wanted to take everything in. Every inch of her. Every facet. I trail my fingers along rough stone. They come away dirty. I venture out the small half-door at the back of the shed, and notice that there's a little garden. Overgrown for sure, but someone grew vegetables here once. Someone tended it. I place my hands on the soft green leaves and wonder who.

Something in me twitches. There's a niggle, an unsettling feeling I get sometimes, a sort of compulsion. It generally happens when I sense a kind of threat, which makes me sound like a startled deer. I don't like run off into the forest or anything, I just have to follow my body and do what it tells me to do. Sometimes that's gathering specific things, and apparently sometimes it's going up a little worn path at the back of the old garden, between some hawthorn trees and browning blasts of heather with fading purple and white blooms.

I walk the path step by step, and turn off it when I'm halfway back to where I met Layla. I come to a big gap in the side of the mountain, a sort of cave, but smaller, and it goes far back. A tunnel might be a better word for it. A passageway. I go inside it, turning on the torch on my phone when it gets too dark to see, and taking small steps to make sure my footing is okay. My hands fly to a pile of rocks at the side of the tunnel, and pull at them and scrape. I feel a nail break but I keep on going, like I am not the pilot of myself. It will hurt the minute I stop needing to do this, or it will hurt more. I suck the finger with the broken nail and instantly regret it as I taste foul dirt and dust and something else. I spit on the floor. Something horrible. My hands worry at the earth beneath the stone until they reach something small and rough and pale. A piece of bone, around an inch long, and slightly smaller than the width of my finger. It could have been discarded by an animal, I think, a passing fox. I clutch it in my fist and inhale deeply, trying to allay the sense of panic that rises in me.

I know that it is human.

Something left a piece of someone here. Discarded it, like it didn't matter.

I have a very good idea who.

I grit my teeth.

12

Feathers

(changes, wishes, messengers)

I'm trying to work out ways to keep track of what's happening, night by night, making notes in case there is a pattern. Ratted paper underneath my fingernails. A leaf caught in my hair. Crumbs on my pillow. A smear of something blue on my nightgown. Dirt on the soles of my feet. And feathers. Always one or several feathers. Even when I don't find them on me, they've snuck into the corners of my room, between the drying flowers on my altar. So many now that I could trim the kind of hat Mam thinks looks good on her at weddings.

Sometimes they smell of blood.

I haven't woken up anywhere except my bed since that night on the stairs, which means that I do something creepy in my sleep that I don't remember and then come back to where I was and tuck myself in tight. I wake cocooned.

I might need help but I am so, so sick of needing help. I want to try to fix this on my own. I want to save myself this time. That's if I even need saving.

Tonight I sprinkled talcum powder all over the floor around my bed. It felt like a mixture of one of Maddy's circles of salt and something you'd read in a child-detective book. I prayed to Our Lady of Ballyfrann, and fell asleep with her image in my head, name on my lips. I hoped she might be able to intercede for me. I would like to be healed. To feel like myself again.

It kind of . . . worked.

I dreamed the way I always do, of Lon.

But she was there too, only with Bridget Hora's face carved into the wood, the skin marked with the grain of it, like scars. She stared at me with wide, human eyes, the kind of blue the sky is in my dreams, sometimes bright and others almost colourless. They looked so strange, so animal.

We were in the cave and he was holding me and touching me and murmuring the things I used to like to hear him say, before he showed me who he truly was. My heart was in my throat, and she couldn't help me. It felt like she was watching what was happening with me and Lon through a veil and I couldn't quite focus on her. Details darted in and darted out.

I wonder if I had managed to call out, to push through, would she have helped me? I have no voice in there. Not of my own. I just repeat the lines that I've been given. He tells me that he loves me. I look at him. I say I love him too. We kiss and I can smell his cologne and the wet, dusty scent of the cavern, and all I'm doing is waiting, waiting to taste the tang of my own blood. My heart beats as quickly and as desperately as a bird against a windowpane, hurting itself so it can get out get out get out . . .

I wake just before he strikes, with a gasp, the sheets wrapped tight around me like a shroud. There are footprints weaving through the talc. And something else. I struggle out of bed and turn the light on. Feathers. Handfuls of feathers – black-and-white-streaked ones, like from a magpie, dark and shimmering ones, and the long thick brutal kind. They may have come from Badb, I muse, looking at my skin for peck marks, wounds. The feathers are new. And they don't feel like they come from Lon, which gives me hope. The praying might be working, at least a little.

I gather them, and place them on my altar, thinking of the girl far away, watching us with her impassive face. Bridget Hora. Will she help or hurt me? I don't know. It's hard to tell. I can't pick up a vibe. I search her name on my phone, and scroll through articles. She was small. Small like us, and older than the others – nineteen, which isn't old at all if you're a corpse. They never found her skull, only some bones, and scraps of clothes and hair. She died the year Mam was born. She could still be alive. Except for him.

She had curly hair, Bridget Hora. Permed. It looked dire, but it was the eighties and that kind of thing was tolerated back then, even celebrated. In the black-and-white photograph that accompanies the newspaper articles she looks like she is from an older time. It's a headshot from a play she had been in, in college. *Sive*. I've never seen it. It's about another girl who dies.

67

People hinted that Bridget Hora might have been pregnant, which was apparently one of the worst things you could be in Ireland back then if you weren't married. The Magdalene laundries were still open back then. I wouldn't like to be pregnant now, but at least if I were, I wouldn't be kicked out on the street or given to some nuns who'd sell my baby or anything like that. Which is a plus. In my dreams, she's wearing a plain blue dress, which is kind of disappointing given that she's from the eighties. I mean, there's nothing wrong with a decent shoulder pad. Or a shell suit.

The names of the girls Lon killed go back for over a century. And it feels disgusting that he pretended he was a teenager to me. That someone that age would want to get with me at all. I thought he was nineteen, and Maddy said it was weird that someone out of school would be going after people still in school, but I didn't think Lon was after 'people'. I thought it was me he loved, that we were special.

I need to move. The floor is a little warm from the underfloor heating. Sometimes the soft old wood feels almost like skin that doesn't give. I wrap myself in a large smoking jacket I found in the attic and lash on a pair of velvet slippers and a big shawl. I run my fingers through my wild white hair and stomp down the stairs purposefully, towards the door near the kitchen. When I get to the back door, the moonlight filters through the glass panel above it, and though it isn't full, it's very bright. I blink.

And suddenly, I sense something or hear something. A presence. My heart pounds in my chest. A cough behind.

'Catlin?' Brian says, emerging from the hallway, looking

like a shadow taking form, so tall and thin and awkward in his body.

'Brian?'

'I'm sorry, love. I didn't mean to startle you. It's just I heard you up, and wanted to check in case you were . . .'

'Sleepwalking?'

'Yes,' he says. 'I think we need to talk.'

I uncurl the shawl from around my neck and follow him into the kitchen. He clicks the kettle on. It starts to boil.

'I've noticed you going about the place at night-time,' he says, as if this isn't super creepy, 'and when I speak to you, it's like I am not there.'

'Yeah,' I say. 'I've been sleepwalking a bit. I think my body wants to get away from my head at night or something.'

'I thought it might be that,' Brian says, pouring hot water into two mugs. 'Which is why I didn't want to interfere. And they say it can be dangerous, you know, to wake a sleepwalker.'

'I think I've heard something about that all right.'

He takes the teabags out and pours the milk. He doesn't ask me how much I take and puts loads in, the way that Maddy likes it. I thank him anyway. His eyes are on mine and I have the strangest feeling in the pit of my stomach, somewhere between sleepiness and nausea. My head feels light and warm. Not warm, but *hot*.

'You need to keep an eye on the sleepwalking,' Brian says. 'And I will too. Have you told your sister about it at all?' His expression is neutral, but it's a sort of mask, I think.

I take a gulp of tea. 'No,' I say. 'Not yet.'

69

'That's good,' he says. 'That's good. Though you might think about waiting a bit. She has a lot on her plate, Madeline, without worrying about how we're all getting on without her.'

'I was worried she would tell Mamó.' I touch my hand to my forehead. It doesn't feel so warm on the outside, but inside I feel I'm burning up. I can't think straight. 'And that it would make, like, a thing of it.'

'If you're worried, Catlin,' Brian says, 'by all means, reach out to anyone you think will help you. But if you're handling this . . .'

'I am.' I square my shoulders. 'I am handling it.'

'Good girl,' he says.

And I tell him, 'Thanks, Brian.' And polish off the dregs of milky tea, and head back to bed. On the stairs my legs feel strange, like they are already asleep. Or somehow not connected to my body. I grip the banister like it's a crutch, my fingers making patterns through the dust that coats it, It wasn't there when I was going down, at least I don't think it was. I bring my fingers to my face, they smell of ash, and suddenly I'm in front of the sink in the bathroom vomiting up the tea he made for me, and everything else that's in my stomach until there's nothing there but yellow bile. It is the kind of vomiting that feels like sobbing, and my eyes and nose are streaming with clear fluid by the time I'm done. I wash my face and brush my teeth, and then, and I have no idea why I do this, I scoop a little of the bile back up, and smear it at the feet of one of my Marys, the one in the red dress who carries a long thin sword, and I light some candles and

I murmur prayers until my body feels calm again. Brian is up to something. I'm sure of it. Just because he comes across all sensitive and plausible in his V-neck jumpers doesn't mean he's not scheming.

I wish that I was better at knowing who to trust.

My hands still shaking, and the candles melted halfway down, by the time I feel safe enough to venture to my bed.

13

Salt

(protection, keeping things in or out)

Mamó was trying to get a hold of Brian all day today apparently. She called him 'tricksy'. This finger bone I found is both old and new. Apparently she knows the place I found it. Of course she does. Sure she knows everything. Her voice was low as she held it in her hand and stared at it.

'That wasn't there before.'

'How do you know?' I asked, which probably annoyed her, but so does everything.

'I have been doing this since long before you were born, girl,' was her response, which isn't very satisfying really. I mean, the bone is small, it could easily be missed.

She's done some stuff to it already, to see who it could have belonged to. Mainly observing, but she also burned some pungent herbs (the combination of them smelled like toast and earwax) and put her hands on it and was quiet for a really, really long time, until I coughed a bit and then she snapped at me to, 'Keep it down, would ya?'

'Should we hand it to the guards?' I have asked her several times in different situations, and her answer is always 'Not yet' or 'Not now' or 'What power have they here?'

I carried on, 'There could be DNA in it. Or something. They could search the place. Some of the girls have family alive. And it could help them to know –'

'Or dredge old sorrows up again. We can't know,' she said, running her fingers over the bone as though it was a precious object. No gloves or anything. Just a woman rubbing what is possibly an important piece of evidence in a missing-person case repeatedly, until she's gotten what she wants from it. Nothing dodgy about that at all. Her face flickers as though she was listening to it tell a story to her. After a while, her mouth settles into a steady line. She stands.

'Get your coat,' she tells me. 'We need to go up there.'

'But it's after midnight,' I complain. I am in my fleecy pyjamas. My muscles are tired from a long day of doing things. I won't be able to see and she's going to boss me around and I also feel like if she goes into the shed she'll be able to tell all of the things that happened there with Oona, and that's private. I'm fine with people knowing I'm a lesbian, but Mamó and sexuality don't really seem to belong in the same place, and the thought of her knowing private, beautiful things about me makes me itchy, vulnerable. I resolve to try to keep her from rubbing anything in the shed if we go in there. Especially the beanbag. This is very stressful.

73

She looks at me. It's not a glare. It doesn't have to be. At this stage in our relationship, the glare is implied. Her eyes are the grey of clouds before they burst, a threat. A force of nature. My eyes are just eyes. They help me see.

I get my coat and put some empty jars into my satchel, along with some torches and spare batteries. Also some hand sanitiser because if we're going around touching human remains I don't want to feel them clinging to me until I reach a sink. Mamó picks up a leather case of tools. It's a roll-up one, like people have for knitting needles, only she keeps knives in there, and assorted other things that look like they could be used to force a confession out of someone in a dungeon. Maybe she got them off Brian. I snort, and she twists her head abruptly.

'We might as well take a shovel.' That means that I will have to carry a shovel up a mountain in my fleecy pyjamas and I sigh without meaning to. Sighing does no good here. In fact, it probably tripled the size of the shovel we're bringing. Which is almost as tall as me, and not that practical.

She hands it to me with an eyebrow raised, and off we go.

We stride back up to the shed, and it takes ages and it's cold. I wish I'd taken the time to put a bra on, I muse sadly. I'd be so much more comfortable with a nice thick bra. And a waistcoat made out of hot water bottles and maybe just not being here, but being in bed instead.

'We could have done this in the daytime,' I mutter.

'Whist,' she says.

Whist means *be quiet*. A lot of things Mamó says mean *be quiet*. When in doubt, silence is a good option around her. I rub my eyes with the heel of my free hand and try to keep pace with a tall woman with no shovel. She has a car. We could have driven halfway there at least. That would have been practical.

We reach the shed, and she strides inside as if she owns the place and looks around with a *hmm*. For all I know, I realise, she does own the place. I don't know where she lived before the basement, but she only moved there after Brian's father passed away. I'm relieved to see she doesn't stop to investigate the inside of the shed, just heads straight out through the garden and up the little path, as though she knows exactly where she's going. We reach the tunnel, and she presses her two hands to the ground and begins doing some very snorty breathing.

I watch her, mouth a little open. She turns to me.

'Take the rocks from the corner and place them in a circle at the entrance,' she says in a low, urgent voice.

I do what she tells me, propping the enormous, and possibly useless, shovel at the edge of the cave. She continues breathing for a bit, then rises and inspects the circle, moving a few stones around here and there, until she's satisfied. She opens up her pack of knives and uses one to draw some swirling shapes and some vertical and horizontal lines into the dusty centre of the circle. When the circle is full she pulls some rosemary and juniper from her pocket, crushes them in her fist and throws the pieces down. Satisfied, she wipes the knife on her coat and replaces it in the pouch.

'What do they mean —' I begin, but she cuts me off.

'I don't have time to be explaining all of this to you. Use your eyes and instincts and follow me. Something isn't right here. Come, now.'

75

And with that she begins striding into the dark mouth of the tunnel. I see her straight back get swallowed up entirely before I begin to follow.

A voice calls from the abyss. 'Don't forget the shovel.'

What is my life? I roll my eyes, and start to follow her. When I look back at the mouth of the tunnel I see moonlight flickering on the symbols she carved, as though they have drawn it to them. And I think of a night when I woke up feeling like everyone in the family was in danger, and went to put salt under their beds. And Mam and Brian were in the room together. For a second I saw something, tattoos or marks upon his skin. Just like these ones, flickering with moonlight, and then all of a sudden they were gone.

I swallow, and quicken my pace to try to catch up with her. She clearly meant for me to go back and notice that. She's always doing sneaky things like that. Forcing my own brain to make me learn instead of just telling me what it is I need to know.

I run, shovel in hand, sometimes awkwardly clanking off the wall of the cave, until I reach Mamó. She's standing at the edge of a padlocked door, cutting off further movement. And both her hands are full of human hair.

She looks extremely annoyed, even for her.

'Hold this,' she says, passing me the hair, and what feels like another bone, but jointed differently, like the case of a woodlouse, or a child's toy. It's about three inches long, and it takes me a while to work out what it is.

And when I do, I really wish I hadn't.

'Is this . . . a bit of someone's spine?' I ask Mamó, who is working at the padlock with something from her rolled-up bag.

'Hmm?' she says. 'Yes. Yes, it was.' Her voice is both very respectful, and very irritated that I felt the need to ask while she was concentrating.

'Ah!' she says at last.

The padlock gives. She throws it down in the dirt in front of the door and turns towards me, standing blankly behind with my shovel and my spine.

'Let's head back.'

'Are we not going in?' I say, aghast. It feels like a let-down.

'No. I just needed to leave a little padlock of my own.' She nods. 'It mightn't take.'

'Do you know where it goes to?'

'Madeline, use your brain. We just found pieces of a girl, and then there was a secret passageway. Where do you think it might be likely to lead?'

I don't have to say it. But it flashes through my brain. The stone. The carved names. My sister's blood. The cave where it all happened.

'You've been through there before though,' I say.

'Aye. I have.'

'And you don't care to go back.'

'Not with you, girl. Not right now.'

I nod, and let out a non-committal grunt. Maybe I am learning something from her after all. Silently, we start to head for home.

Having shovelled nothing.

14

Hair

(binding, keeping, cursing)

So, I'm fully doing something Madeline would call 'reckless'. But I call it good sense. I mean, who wouldn't break into a sacristy and access the secret books that might be full of information about Ballyfrann's history? My skeleton keys have been burning a hole in my pocket since I got them, but weirdly, it turned out I didn't need them.

I waited until I knew Father Byrne was out doing priest stuff. Visiting the sick and elderly. And I did feel a bit bad about it, until I realised that God was literally on my side with this. Which sounds like a bit of an exaggeration. But it's not. So, I snuck up to the door of the sacristy, hoping none of the flower-arranging women would pop in to adjust a freesia, and did my worst. The first step to lock-picking is to check that the door is actually locked. I tried the door. It was. But rather than reach for my skeleton keys right away, instinct took over and I closed my eyes and murmured a prayer to Our Lady of Ballyfrann. I thought of her as she was in my dream, watching me with Bridget Hora's eyes, and I heard the lock click open, which was very strange but also great. I felt the way I used to, back when I believed my prayers were answered. Back when I felt strong instead of weak. I don't know how or why it worked exactly, maybe it's all the rosaries I've been saying, or it might be because I was trying to break into a room in a church, so the holiness of the location helped me do my crime. Or maybe she just took a shine to me.

Once I was in the sacristy, I took it in, the coppery shine of the wood, the chests of altar cloths for different times of year. Spare candles, spare incense. Spare everything. It took an age to find the big old books. Wrapped in silk, they looked like bolts of cloth. I unfolded one massive volume wrapped in red. It smelled of dust and incense, and covered something like seventy years, births, deaths and marriages. Lots of Collins-on-Collins and Shannon-on-Shannon action going on, surprising no one. Shape-shifters are weird, even if Eddie Collins has a sort of talent for making me feel a bit more seen, a bit more safe. I photographed a few pages on the phone, but didn't find too much of interest until I stumbled across one Margaret Cleary, because she had the word *Mamó* written in blue ballpoint beside her name. If it's actually Mamó, she is two hundred and seventeen years old.

She should be long dead.

So . . . why isn't she?

There wasn't a huge amount of other interesting stuff in

the records. Brian's dad was born in 1902, but I couldn't find a record of Brian's birth. Maybe it was somewhere else or something. And who was working as a 'farm labourer' in 1917 is not much good to me while I try to work out which members of my family I can trust, and how to cope with being in the world after what happened to me. But better than nothing, I suppose.

Which brings us up to now.

A sudden noise, and I nearly jump out of my skin, but it is just the heating clicking on. Still, that is enough for one day. I wrap the book up, carefully, so no one can tell that someone has been snooping, and close the door behind me. I picture her again. The lock clicks back.

In my mind I say a fervent, *Thank you*. And kneel in front of her for a bit of a pray before I go. I mean, it isn't penance or whatever, but even when I do that I'm rarely ever sorry.

Father Byrne, when he stomps in about five minutes later, is not in a chatty mood. He offers me a cup of tea, but I can tell he doesn't really mean it. Besides, I could do without tea after whatever that thing was with Brian and the sleepwalking.

He has deep dark circles under his eyes, as though he hasn't slept in days.

'Are you okay, Father?' I ask, and he says that he's grand. I don't believe him, particularly as he goes off and comes back with the cup of tea I didn't want. As if he hadn't registered at all what I'd been saying. I sip it gingerly, waiting for the taste of bile again.

'What's on your mind?' he asks me, the way priests can. They have the power to ask basically anything because they have magic collars. I have that power too, because I have no shame.

'Not much,' I tell him. 'Not sleeping very well, but prayers are helping.' I smile at him, and he smiles back. Priests love prayers. 'What were you doing today?' I ask, curious.

He sighs. 'Parishioner in trouble. Domestic difficulties. I had to go in and mediate a bit.' He swallows and I see his Adam's apple bob up and down. It's really big and his neck is covered in fine white hair. Some old people just start growing hair everywhere. It's already begun for Mam. She plucks her chin. I've seen it. I trace my hand along my own smooth jawline. I wanted to get her a voucher for IPL the Christmas before last, but Maddy said she'd find it insulting because she likes to pretend she isn't growing a beard and so we got her a general beauty voucher instead.

'Anyone I know?' I ask Father Byrne, not that he will tell me, because he doesn't do that sort of thing.

'I can't tell you that,' he says, surprising me not even a small bit.

'Ah why not, Father?' I nag, just to be a dick about it. 'It's not like you were in the confession box when this "domestic" stuff went down. And I'm really good at keeping secrets.' I smiled the broad, trustworthy smile of a prefect. I'm not one, but I can do the smile if I need to. Many skills.

Father Byrne lets out a small sharp laugh. 'You are in your eye, Catlin Hayes. I've probably already said too much. I'm tired.' He puts his hands on his knees like he's about to help himself get up but then sits down again. I try to look sympathetic. I'm not a really sympathetic person, but sure why not give it a go?

'My sister gets like that sometimes,' I tell him. 'When she's had to interact with people too much. Kind of exhausted.'

'I don't know if it's the people. Or the weight of what they're carrying. It's a privilege to hold it for a while, but I always have to leave them with it sooner or later, and that's hard too.' His face is stoic but his eyes are sad. He probably doesn't have to think too hard about how to be sympathetic. Maybe that's what made him want to be a priest.

'What made you want to be a priest?' I ask.

'Why, Catlin, have you a vocation?' He smirks at that. Which is fair. I'd be a terrible nun. Maybe a better priest. Like a fancy one, a bishop or something. I could have a palace, and sexy housekeepers, and fancy robes that got shipped in from Rome and cost a fortune. I mean, if I had to be clergy, I'd want to be the kind with a cushy life.

'I'm just curious,' I tell him, sipping the tea, which has the exact right amount of milk in it, because he listens and remembers. 'I mean, most people I know aren't priests.'

'I'd be worried if they were.' He laughs. 'You don't get a lot of teenage priests. Even Our Lord was in his thirties when he really began to gather his flock in earnest. It's not what you'd call a normal job. And people in my line of work generally don't hang out with teenage girls unless there's something a bit funny going on. I'm older than I look . . .' he begins, and I really want to say, 'Like Margaret,' but I hold off, because I don't want him to know I've broken into his room full of secrets.

'How old?'

'I'll be eighty-five next birthday,' he says proudly.

'Wow,' I say, though I do find adult ages hard to gauge. Like, I kind of sort them into 'twenties, forties, golf? and OLD'. What do I say to someone being eighty-five, like? 'You don't look it'? Except he kind of does.

'When I grew up, Ireland was a very different place. I was the youngest of a large family, and there was no farm for me to inherit or anything, so the priesthood was a good career option.'

'Didn't it have anything to do with God?'

'A bit, yeah. I mean, I do have faith. But faith was more usual back then. The Church directed people's lives in a way that it doesn't any more. A priest was powerful, respected. And I'd be lying if I said that didn't appeal to me every bit as much as the closer relationship to God and prayer. Prayer can be a great gift, if you use it correctly. But there are ways to use it for other ends, and that's where the difficulty lies. People who are drawn to powerful organisations tend to like power. And it's hard to make them see the value of something humbler. It took time for me to see it myself . . .' He trails off, lost in memory.

'Does it take long to become a priest?' I ask. 'Do you, like, do a course?'

'It takes years and years,' he says. 'I went to the seminary, and studied. And I enjoyed it. I really took to the word of God, and when I was ready to go into the world, I was so excited to do some good.' He sighs. 'But you can't always do the things you want, and the bright spots can be few and far between. The fire that was in me then is largely gone. But every now and then, someone needs me, and so I have to go and do my best for them. It's people, and being good to people, Catlin, that matters in the end, not who you worship, or who you love, or how much money is in the bank. It's being good to people, even when it's hard, or when it kills you.'

I drink the last bit of the tea, and think of Maddy and how much she gave up for me. I think of the mountain girls: Helen Groarke, Nora Ginn, Bridget Hora and all the other names carved into the wall of the cave around my own. I don't feel safe in the castle any more, there is the sense of eyes on my back. Watching me.

'It does kill some people,' I say.

'It does. It killed Our Lord.'

'I mean real people,' I snap, and then realise what I've just said. Whoops. 'Excuse me, Father Byrne, I don't mean that Jesus wasn't real, I just mean, it's not just something that happened then. It's happening now too.'

'It is,' he says. 'Someday I'll tell you the story of how I ended up in Ballyfrann.'

'Not by choice?'

He laughs a low, dry laugh. 'No, child, I amn't here by choice. I don't know many people who are.'

I nod and I almost get the urge to ask him about prayer. The power of prayer. Because what I did, with the lock before, I mean . . . it wasn't normal. It was something more. And he is right. About the lure of power. My hands over the lock, asking it to do what I wanted, and hearing the little click.

It felt so good.

I want to know what else I'm capable of.

15

Yellow Rattle Grass

(for coughing, sight)

I'm outdoors again, this time looking for violet bramble rust, for Mamó. It's bright pink spots on the leaves of brambles. She has also asked me to 'Take some photographs of the brambles on the mobile phone', which is the most technological she's ever been, at least in my presence. She can be surprising though, so maybe she has, like, a secret Internet presence where she posts about the best new deals in Lidl. And her grievances.

Violet bramble rust is a fungus, but also basically a plant disease. It's like I'm picking off bits of chicken-poxy plant skin. I wonder what she'll use the leaves I'm gathering for. I have a sense that it'll be to effect some sort of change, maybe a negative one. Though I feel kind of negative at the moment, so maybe that's just me putting my own internal stuff on this innocent and prettily named fungus. My body feels like the air before a thunderstorm. There's a sense that something is going to happen and everything will change. My phone vibrates in my pocket, and I check it.

It's Oona.

She wants to know if we can talk.

I swallow, and carefully snip another leaf from the bramble. If I leave here, Mamó will know. But also, if I go to Oona, I'll have seen Oona. It's been too long. And we were, are, friends. And I don't want to be the kind of person who stops being friends with someone when it stops being physical.

I ask her where she needs me to be.

The lake we swam in once. It's an hour's walk, but I could probably find more things on the way. My heart is pounding. When we were kids, we used to go to this beach in summer, and there was a big high platform that you could dive off, right into the water, and Catlin would, and all our friends would, and I would stand there, looking down, and then I'd sigh and climb back down the safe way. Once Catlin pushed me off, to show me that it was safe, and I broke my ankle.

It isn't always safe to take a leap.

But sometimes there's no choice.

I barely notice my surroundings until I'm there, beside the lake. The water smells cool and fresh and I can see her head bobbing up and down. I sit on a rock, and wait for her to notice me. Which would probably make a good epitaph. I think of the empty coffin our father left behind. Waiting for someone. I shudder in spite of the sunlight on my skin. Oona begins to swim towards me, and I realise that I've been holding my breath for a while. It's like my brain knows we're just friends but my body and my heart aren't exactly there. Maybe they never will be.

She rises from the water and comes and sits on a rock beside me. She's wearing a dark green one-piece swimsuit, and it looks beautiful against the brown of her skin.

'Hello, Madeline.'

Oh God. I love the way she says my name.

'Are you okay?' I ask, and she sighs.

'Yes and no. It's been a heavy time.'

'Your parents?' I ask. Oona's dad has a temper, and it can get messy at home sometimes. I'm not sure what his thing is, if he has one. The Noones are related to the Collinses, but it's distant as far as I know. Oona's like her mam, Elodie. They have an affinity for water. A sort of need. My stomach tightens. I hate to think of her being made to feel scared.

'Yes. We had to get the priest in,' she says, as though this was a perfectly normal thing to do.

'What? To pray for him? I didn't think you were religious,' I say.

'We're atheist, and even if we weren't, we wouldn't be Christian.' She says the word like it's a bad thing, which I suppose for lots of people it has been, and still is. 'But we're desperate, and Carol Collins told my mother that he would be good to help them talk it through. That Dad would listen to him. It kind of worked. I also think he threatened him a bit. Though my mother is more than capable of threatening him herself. She told him that we would move back to France.'

'How did he take that?'

'Not well. He said that he would kill himself.' Her face crumples. 'He didn't mean it, but . . .'

87

'Oh, Oona.'

'It's horrible. I thought, when we moved here, that things would be better, because we could be ourselves. But no one here is fully who they are, it's all so full of secrets and lies and pain and it's like it infects everyone, and I can't . . .'

I put my hand on her forearm, and lean towards her. 'I get it. I mean, not entirely, I can't, but I understand it's hard and that you must be struggling right now, and worried about your mother . . . and your dad.'

'I do still love him. And so does she. He's not . . . he just has a hard time being who he is, and it spills out onto everything and everyone he loves. But I don't want him to die.'

'I know you don't. He's your father.'

'Do you remember your father?' she asks. 'I know he passed when you were very young.'

'I do, a bit. In flashes. Little kid memories, that are more like pictures, or scenes . . . I don't know if they're mine even, or bits of the stories Mam tells us about him. I wish I'd known him more.'

'I feel the same, and I have known him all my life. I don't know who he is, deep down, at all. He can be really kind and sweet, and then it turns, and it's like he's waiting for someone to do something so he can have an excuse to explode.'

'That doesn't sound healthy,' I tell her, wondering how much I should say. It sounds abusive to me. But that's a very big word to say out loud. 'Do you . . . do you feel safe?'

'Father Byrne helped, I think,' she says. 'But he's not . . . I mean, how much good can one conversation on one day do?'

'Have you talked to Mamó?' I ask. 'She's pretty scary, but

I know that she's helped some other people out with stuff like this. And if you ever needed to get away, even for a night, we do have the space. Or Brian does, at least.'

'Thank you . . . It's up to my mother really.' She smiles. 'I don't mean to be . . . I just. I really wanted to talk to you, you know? You have a way of being there for me . . . and I'm sorry we haven't seen each other as much.'

'If it's urgent, you know that I'll be there,' I say. I don't add, 'unless the people around me are actually getting murdered, because here's hoping that will never happen again.'

'I know you will,' she says, and puts her head on my shoulder. We stay like that for a long time, looking at the ripples on the water making the light dance this way and that. And I think of how every wave is doing its own thing, but together they form part of this whole big thing, and I think about all the life under the surface, and how complicated and intricate it is, and how I don't even know the half of it. And I feel Oona's warm skin against mine, and hear her breath slowing and steadying, and I feel both powerless to help and such a deep desire to be able to take it all away and make it right for her.

My phone starts going again, and it's a message from Mamó. *MADELINE. STOP. THIS IS MAMÓ. STOP. WHAT ARE YOU AT? STOP. COME BACK NOW. STOP.*

I imagine her typing it into her big bricky phone. It probably took her longer than a spell. I smile. I quite like having something I am good at that she isn't good at.

'I get the feeling she doesn't send a lot of texts,' I say, showing Oona. 'But I should go.'

'Will you be in trouble?' she asks. 'I know for you it is complicated to find time.'

'It'll be fine,' I say, with more confidence than I feel. 'I have most of the stuff she asked me to get today, and I can probably gather more of it on the way back.'

'Okay,' she says. I turn to go, but she pulls me in for a hug. She's almost dry, but I still feel the damp soaking through my clothes, against my skin. 'Thank you, Madeline.'

'It's not a thank-you thing. We're friends. I'm here,' I tell her, and I feel her soften against me, before she pulls away and walks towards the lake. I begin making my way to the castle, and when I turn she's floating on her back on the surface of the lake, face to the sky and arms out like a star.

I wish that I could have helped her more. I mean, listening isn't *doing*. I wonder if it might be worth saying it to Mamó, what's going on. I spent so much of last year keeping secrets I should not have kept, maybe it's time to just be open. Even though it's not my story to tell. It's hard to know what being a friend looks like sometimes. Is it loyal to say nothing? Or would real loyalty be in getting her help, even if it means she's cross with me?

I'm closer to the castle now. I notice some more blotchy bramble leaves, and clip them and place them in my bag. I was supposed to take photographs as well, of the brambles, I remember, and I whip out my phone and start to do that, when I notice something clinging to the thorns. A scrap of fabric. I peel it off and place it in a bag inside my bag. Looking near where it was, I notice that some of the thorns are stained a little, the brambles parted. I reach my hand through them, and feel around on the ground for anything unusual. I close my eyes and breathe in and out. There is a patch of earth that's been disturbed, and as I brush my hand over it my skin encounters something warm and soft.

It moves, and I startle my hand back and peer down, shining the light of my phone through the brambles to try to get a closer look. I reach my hand out, nervously. I feel a beak, some feathers, and the warm wet of blood. A part-way buried crow. I think of Button, and the sacrificed fox myself and Catlin found back at the crossroads, shortly after moving here. We've worked out since that it was a sort of offering. A prayer. That was the beginning of all this, the first clear sign that things were somehow . . . wrong.

A wild thing murdered, and a tame thing tortured.

Mamó said she needed to fix them, both those times.

And there's a bang of wrongness off of this.

I snip away at the brambles, to make a path for it, and dig with my hands until I've gotten it loose from the earth packed around it. It isn't dead, but lots of its feathers are gone. My fingernails are caked with dirt. The crow is barely moving, barely warm. It opens one beady eye and closes it again. It's close to death. I don't know what to do. I wrap it in my cardigan, clutch it to my heart and stumble home.

16

Air

(whispers, movement, knives)

You wake.
Or you're awoken.
Get to work.
Room by room and piece by piece.
Putting order on it all.
Your bones are scattered in so many places.
And you can feel them all.
Pulling you apart.
Keeping you weak.
Tethered here.
Obedient.
You weren't good at that when she were quick.
Your mother warned you. About him. You warned yourself as
*   well. You should have known.*

You will never see her face again.

Your name was Bridget.

Now you are a nothing sort of thing.

A ghost of a girl not a slip of a girl.

*But there are places you can fold and fit, odd hidden corners where
the dust collects and everything is easier to hide.*

He keeps you hidden there at first.

At first.

*But now you are forgotten unless something stops or something
breaks.*

And then and then.

Your pieces held to light.

*Hands upon the thing that was your face and thumbs and words
that pull at you, and pull.*

The memory of who you were before.

*Faces. Clothes. The feeling of other people's skin. Your skin. Of
being in a body in one place. Of feet upon the ground.*

Of kisses.

Dew on grass. Cider on the hillside.

Cigarettes.

*Earrings too heavy for your earlobes, and pulling at them all night
long but they looked good they found them in the grass when
he dragged you*

out

and up

and round

and over bumps

you thought when you were dead

you

would
just
stop
but back you came because you are a thing for them to use.
like an appliance
serving purposes and all these years you
click
into it
and do not think too much but
something's happened and you can stretch out and touch
the girl
and make her see you
you aren't sure exactly what you want,
but oh it's nice to be the puppeteer and not the puppet.

17

Circles

(Sacred Spaces, Boundaries, Protection)

I am on the mountainside, watching Lon with another girl. He is smiling at her and they are drinking cans. I can feel the tall grass against my bare legs and hear the click of insects in the undergrowth. The sky is a saturated blue, with clouds all perfect white, no grey at all.

And it is Ballyfrann but it isn't Ballyfrann.

And it's my dream but it is not my dream.

I cannot hear what they are saying, and I try to move closer but it's like my legs are made of something else that isn't flesh, they don't obey me and I can't control them. When you make a thing from clay, it will not move unless you use your hand to make it move, and there is no hand rearranging me, bringing me closer.

They are kissing and I don't need her to turn to see her face.

I know it's Bridget Hora, or Our Lady of Ballyfrann. The mix of them, and I see him begin to try to pull away and her arms clutch him so tightly I can see them digging into his leather jacket, long nails leaving moon-marks on the black. His hands scrabble and push and he looks small so small like nobody like nothing. Her face to mine, and blood around her mouth.

She didn't have to take back her power.

It never left.

It was there all along.

I look for Lon, but he is gone, besides he doesn't matter.

And I look at her, her deep blue eyes and wild brown hair her feet are bare and she is wearing a floral dress, white and blue the Mary colours really and the hillside is covered in flowers and they all fade to purple and to blue just like her dress and everything is blue and he is gone and she is holding me, but gently, gently, I am safe. I'm safe now.

Together we can make him go away.

She tells me, and she whispers in my ears.

Three secrets.

I wake.

I can't remember what they are.

18

Hellebore

(melancholy, jaundice)

Mamó is having a chat with Brian, and I am here with her. My job is just to sit in and observe.

'You'll have to learn, sooner or later, how to deal with him,' she told me, as though I were the parent and he the child. I've been instructed to be quiet and listen in.

Mamó has dressed up slightly for this, I think. It's hard to tell, as she mainly wears variations of the same stuff, but her boots are laced very tightly and her hair is in a long, thick braid down her back. My phone buzzes and I check it. It's from Oona, but it's not important. I mean, it's a link to a video of a puppy having a dream, so it is highly important, but I don't have to risk Mamó's wrath by replying right away. I've been sending cute links and memes to Oona to try to distract her from the hellscape of her home life. I mean, I'm powerless to actually do anything, but a fifty-six-second montage of a husky and an owl who are BEST FRIENDS is soothing.

I'm wearing a black jumper and black jeans and my boots, and a white shirt underneath so I don't look FULL WITCH. Darker colours are kind of easier now, as they show stains less, and there is never a day I don't end up covered in stains. Before I used to choose clothes based on what looked nice or suited me. Now it's what can withstand lots of brambles, and possible animal blood. We couldn't save the crow. Mamó has him gathered in her bag like evidence.

When I got home that night she was not happy. Particularly when I told her that I was with Oona. Apparently I'm not allowed to have friends any more. She used words like 'dallying' and 'lolly-gagging' and 'ungrateful'. And I felt this rage rising in me. I mean, Oona *needed* me. Isn't that supposed to be what we do? Help people going through things in the village. Like, am I supposed to just ignore her when she needs a friend, or is there a form I should have got her to fill in? I didn't ask for this. I just didn't want my sister to die, and if she's here to help people and so powerful and capable, why couldn't she have just been kind and helped without asking me to wreck my life? She had the gall to tell me that the trip to Cork had 'gone to my head', and that no more of them would be forthcoming.

'Oh yes, please, Mamó,' I snapped. 'I really wanted to go and dig up my father's grave and find his body missing, and see what that did to my mother.'

'You stayed in a hotel,' she said, as though I had flown business class to Mauritius.

'Mam booked it. I had NOTHING to do with it.'

'Sheila knew the rules. I was very clear on them before I gave permission for you to go – that you had one day to get it done. And were to return as soon as possible. You agreed to that, Madeline. And when you found out about this "hotel" you could have reminded her more strongly. That your actions have consequences now. But sure, why would you, when you have such trouble reminding yourself where your responsibilities lie?'

I raised my hand to make some sort of gesture, I don't know what. It kind of just flapped there a bit like an irate bird, until I moved it down. 'I have a responsibility to my family, and to my friends as well. That doesn't go away just because . . .'

'Of the commitment you made?' She smiled tightly. 'It should, Madeline. You are at the beginning of a very dangerous and complicated path, and the more people you care about, the more potential there is that one of them will be drawn into it.'

'Oona's dad is being . . .'

'I am WELL aware of the carry-on of Johnny Noone, a header. It is being handled.'

'Oona doesn't feel like it is being handled,' I said, though that's not strictly true. I think she just feels deeply sad and worried.

'Handling something isn't going around explaining what you're doing for people and looking for notice. I'm adding the time for today to the end of your sentence.'

I audibly gasped, like a cartoon character, and hated that I was letting her know how much she's getting to me. 'That's so unfair.'

Her expression didn't change at all. 'If it were unfair I wouldn't be doing it. You missed a day in Cork and several hours today. It's escalating, and if I continue to let it slide, you'll be off gallivanting every day, when there's so much learning to be done.'

'But what am I learning? I'm by myself most of the time with lists.'

'Independence. Thinking for yourself. The different sorts of plants and how to identify them and how you connect to them. To use your eyes.' She paused. 'A few months ago I don't think you would have found that crow. I think you would have run home. And you were right not to. What you found this evening needed finding.'

It was almost a compliment.

She took it out and spread its wings and felt its chest and looked into its eyes.

'It hasn't long. Will you get me mugwort, marigolds and a few of those leaves that you picked up today? And there's a jar in the fridge that looks like pickled onions only purple, I'd like that as well.'

'What is it?' I asked.

'If you need to know, you'll find it out.'

I hate not being told things I don't have the skills to find out for myself yet. I brushed imaginary dirt off my jumper, and we headed out the door, towards the castle. We are here now, meeting in Brian's office. All very formal. I am here as her apprentice and not his stepdaughter. It's weird being at home but also at work. We walked past my old bedroom to get here. I was kind of hoping to run into Catlin and Mam, but they were nowhere to be seen. He probably picked a time he knew they wouldn't be around, to keep this intervention, or whatever it is, as secret as possible. Typical Brian nonsense. As if I don't have a mouth or a phone, like. I should message them. But what to say . . .

Mamó turned as she crossed the threshold and ordered me to take the cursed shovel with me. Clearly she hadn't forgiven me for the Oona thing.

'What am I going to do? Bury him?' I asked, outraged.

'Let's hope it doesn't come to that,' she told me.

I swallowed.

Off we went.

Brian's office is a large room with ornate wallpaper and many knick-knacks strewn around. Brian senior, Brian's father, was a monster, apparently. He and Lon worked together, and some of the murdered girls' blood is on his hands. Brian feels a deep sense of resentment towards his father, which might sound a bit therapisty to say, but that's the way he talks about him. Like someone who has done a lot of therapy. I know this because he has told us how much therapy he's done. Brian did some bad things when his father was alive, things he is ashamed of even now. And when Brian senior died, I think (though the timeline is a little patchy), Brian invited Mamó to live beneath the castle, to keep an eye on him in case he ever went off the rails. And he hasn't. He's made mistakes. Like not telling us about the way the village was before he moved us here. Like marrying Mam without being honest with her. I don't think that he thinks that marrying Mam was a mistake. He loves her, and he looks at her so sadly sometimes. But she wouldn't have married him if she'd known what was going to happen. And that has to hurt.

After we found that fox, I suspected Brian. More and more, I wonder if it was some sort of trap. A prayer to keep us here, even after it all came to light. To make my mother stay with him forever. And that's manipulative and creepy, and desperate, but that's the way you feel when you're losing love, or don't think you deserve it.

The shovel is ungainly and large, and it took manoeuvring to get it through the door of Brian's office. I left it plonked against the elegant wallpaper with the pattern of curls and thorns and creatures with cruel beaks. Last year, I found a secret passage hidden in the walls, and I got lost there, feeling through the dark for ages. I came out near the village. The passage also leads into the caves.

I think of the tunnel near the shed, that clearly leads to the castle, and Mamó glares at me as though she can see the cogs turning in my brain and is simultaneously proud and ashamed of me. Brian sits behind his desk, and offers us coffee. Mamó declines, but I say yes, and he puts a pod in his little office coffee machine. There are these vanilla ones I really like, and whatever there is to be said about refusing hospitality from someone you're here to intimidate, there is more to be said for finding space for joy in awkward places. It smells amazing. I bet she's jealous now.

'Thanks, Brian,' I say as he hands it to me.

'You're welcome, pet,' he says, starting his own more pungent coffee going. 'Eh . . . why is there a shovel?'

'Never you mind why there is a shovel, Brian,' Mamó tells him. 'We need to have a chat about some things.'

I sip my coffee and I scan the room. Brian stands perfectly still. He isn't nervous, or fidgety. He meets Mamó's eye. There's something missing from the shelves, I think. Something I can't quite put my finger on yet.

'Of course,' he says, opening his arms like a man with nothing to hide. But everyone in Ballyfrann has something to hide. 'What do you need to know in particular?'

Something in his tone rubs me the wrong way. As if he's trying to placate an older relative. Has he forgotten who Mamó is? What she is capable of?

She takes the crow out of her pocket and slams it down on the middle of his desk. It makes a thud.

'The girl found this,' she says. I bite back that I have a name and they both know it. Well. I will be quiet. I will take everything in and not just be resentful. My arm muscles hurt from carrying the shovel.

'Well, it certainly isn't mine. Where was it found?' Brian asks, looking at it with a disconcerted face, as if he's never seen a dead animal before, when he grew up here, in the depths of the mountains, when dead birds litter the roads after storms and the school bus always passes at least one fox or cat that's been run over.

'Up near the old place,' she tells him, and he nods as though this makes perfect sense, though everywhere in Ballyfrann is old, and there aren't that many landmarks near the brambles. Except the shed. She probably means the shed.

'We found the lock as well,' she said. Definitely the shed then. Ugh, why does everything have to have, like, a dark history? Can't there just be a welcoming kissing shed for girls who

103

love girls? Why is the world always worse than it needs to be?

'I thought you might have,' he sighs. 'Look, after last year, I wanted to make it a bit more safe, you know? I'm aware it wouldn't keep you out, but I thought it might deter someone from going in and getting lost. A stranger or a child who might not be able to find their way out. Who'd end up traumatised. Or worse. You know the history with the tunnels, the cave. It's not a good place.'

'Hmm,' she says. It's barely audible, and basically just acknowledges that he has said something and she has heard it and deemed it unworthy of a longer response.

'Is there anything else?' he asks.

'There is,' Mamó says. And she takes the hair from her bag and puts it on his desk. 'This belonged to Bridget Hora. We've been finding parts of her, around the old place.'

'Oh dear,' says Brian, taking a sip of his coffee. 'That is unfortunate. Such a tragedy. Of course, the killer has been brought to justice now. I mean, we did take care of Lon. Myself and the Collinses, and then Madeline and Catlin.'

Lumping us in with him. He made sure, too, that we wielded the sword. Again Mamó says nothing. This time Brian also tries to say nothing. He drinks his coffee.

'Last year I spoke to you about the fox the girls found,' Mamó says. 'And I am wondering if there's anything you want to tell me now.'

'There isn't,' Brian says. 'I know my father made mistakes. But I am not my father, and I've been trying my best.'

'Your best is honesty,' Mamó says slowly. 'And that is not what I am getting here.'

104

'It is though.'

'Brian. I am too old for this.' She sighs. 'What have you been up to? Why is this room warm?'

'It's summer.'

'Not that kind of warm. There's power here.'

I remember what the missing thing is. Brian's father had a shrunken head, he'd bought it on his travels. I get up. They are staring at each other, and they don't notice me right away. I have some mint leaves in my pocket and I poke my nails into my skin until I feel it part a little. Blood on mint. I crush it in my hand and I smell it and I picture the head.

'Madeline,' Brian says, also rising, 'what are you doing?'

I look at him. As steady as a stone.

'My job.'

Mamó looks at me and nods. She does not rise from her chair. After a moment Brian sits back down. I walk around the room, cupping my hands around my nose. It must look strange. If Mam could see I know she'd be upset, but it's the way of these things. They don't look normal, though they feel natural. It's almost involuntary sometimes. Like when you know that you are going to vomit. That light-headedness, that pull. Your body takes the wheel.

Brian asks me again what I'm doing, but his voice is very far away. It's like everyone else is underwater and I'm still here, on land. There are places that are warmer and colder than others, a little like that game that children play – too hot, too cold – the entrance to the passageway is roasting. I draw my hand back and mark the place in my head for later on. It's not what I need, and maybe it's residual, from what went on before.

The fox splayed out and Catlin on the bed, as pale as wax and bleeding out in front of me, the crow on Brian's desk small eyes dull and wings so dark and delicate, my hand reaching out against the wall, and I feel a nudge, and crouch towards the floor. My hands flat on the warmth of the floorboards, the splinters and the grain of them, the little notches from feet and tear and time. I poke around until I find the space that I am after. There's a floorboard that feels a little different to the others, a little off. A little looser maybe. I try to prise it up, and meet Mamó's eyes. I realise with a pang of anger that I'm going to have to use the bloody shovel. Ugh. I grab it and push it down between the floorboards, prising the one I'm interested in from the others, splintering the wood a little in the process. I need to get to it, to force it out. Whatever little secret he is hiding. On a bed of faded red velvet, nestled in a little hollow space, is the shrunken head. A horrid mimic of a human face, the eyes gouged in with thumbs, the flesh discoloured. The hair, I realise, is the same colour as the hair on Brian's desk.

'Mamó,' I say, 'I think it's her. Bridget Hora.'

There are bundles of herbs around the fist-sized knob of flesh, and some teeth too. A candle and a piece of old, stained paper with nothing written on it.

Brian stands, and Mamó tells him, 'Sit,' and Brian sits. I probably would have sat too, in fairness to him, if I weren't crouched down on the floor, noticing and staring.

Mamó goes over to the head and lifts it up between finger and thumb, eyeing it suspiciously, and a little sadly too, I think. Flesh scraped from bone, reshaped and used – for what?

'This troubles me, Brian,' says Mamó, and she looks at him evenly. No trace of a glare. I feel goosebumps develop on my skin.

'It was Brian senior's,' he says lamely. 'I had it here, and didn't think much of it, but then, when everything happened with Catlin, I found myself unable to look at it, so I placed it somewhere warm and safe.'

'And what about the girl attached to it?'

'She's long dead. It's just an oddment now. A souvenir.' His voice is low and deliberate. He is trying very hard, I think, to be plausible, but it's barely working. What is this?

I turn my gaze to the head again. It's humming with something. It feels like when you walk past a wasps' nest, and you can hear them teeming and sense the power of them and the threat. Keep the head down, don't disturb, leave well enough alone. How is it that I didn't notice this last year when it was just laid out for all to look at? Has something changed? Have I changed?

'Don't insult me, Brian,' Mamó says, holding the head up like she is his mam and has just found drugs in his room. 'You made a commitment when your father died. To this town.'

He nods. 'I know. But . . . I didn't know the half of it then, and some things, as you know, were more urgent than others.' He massages his temples with his hands. 'My father kept her here – to clean the house.'

'What?' I open my mouth, aghast, then shut it. It's not the time to talk. I need to listen. Get a grasp on this.

'She doesn't mind doing it. She was lingering anyway at first, and it gave her the chance to be around. She wanted to keep an eye on things. Because of how she died. What do they call it? Unfinished business.' He's on a roll now, and Mamó's face is still impassive, calm. Like a cat watching a mouse exhaust itself, and biding its time, I think. Oh, Brian, what have you done? He keeps on going.

'And when everything happened with the girls last year, it was kind of resolved for her, but for some reason she got unsettled, and I suppose I tried a few things to . . . calm her down.'

Mamó, still holding the head in her hand, lets out a sigh. 'Brian. I didn't come down in the last shower.'

'I know I'm not . . .' He pauses, and his sentence trails off ineffectually. Maybe he has run out of excuses, I think, or he needs to fill his brain up with more of them, like petrol in the tank of a car. That's about to get driven into the sun.

'Madeline,' Mamó asks, 'can you tell me back, to the best of your knowledge, what your stepfather has been doing?'

'As far as I can tell,' I say, 'he has been exploiting and controlling the ghost of a murdered girl in order to get the housework done.'

'Not all the housework,' Brian says. 'Not hoovering, or laundry. Or cooking. I mean, I do what I can. I'm not bone idle.'

'Interesting choice of words, Brian,' I say. 'From what he said, I also think that the arrangement was initially started by his father, continued running smoothly after he died, and then when everything happened with Lon, and the murder of my sister, Bridget might have felt unsettled, perhaps seeing an opportunity to get away from endlessly cleaning a massive castle day in, day out for all eternity.' I glare at Brian.

'It wasn't only that,' he said. 'She began . . . acting out.'

'How so?'

'Catlin has been sleepwalking, and there have been other things as well. Piles of dust left in the centre of my office table. Finger marks on glasses, shadows on the walls and in mirrors. I think it's mainly me who sees it.'

'Maybe because you're the one exploiting her,' I snap.

'That could be it. But Sheila's not been feeling well, she's exhausted and taking to the bed more and more, which isn't like her at all. And there's a weight to the air here now, it's oppressive.'

I start to say another snarky thing, but Mamó waves her hand at me to quiet me. I close my mouth, and glare at him, thinking of poor Mam. The vomiting at the graveside. That strange tea. No wonder she's been keeping to herself. I must go in and check on her, and soon. Make sure she's safe. When I lived here, I would sometimes wake up in the night with a specific thing I had to do to protect my family – rowan berries hidden in their pockets, salt under their beds. I hadn't thought of how the lack of that could impact them. I bite my lip and try to focus on the task at hand. I don't want Brian to see that I'm unsettled. Or Mamó to think that I'm daydreaming, skiving off.

'And you didn't think it might be worth having a word with me about all this?' asks Mamó.

Brian sighs. 'Look, my priority at the moment is my marriage. And Sheila, rightly or wrongly, blames you for taking Madeline away. I was trying to avoid conflict. But it was wrong of me. I should have let you know much sooner. I owe you an apology. I will be more forthcoming next time, I promise.'

Mamó sighs. 'I'm going to take care of this,' she says, rising. 'I will come back tomorrow and we are going to have a little talk about Catlin's sleepwalking and everything else that has been going on. And I expect your full cooperation.' She puts the shrunken head in her pocket and picks up the body of the crow from Brian's desk.

'Of course,' says Brian, rising from his seat and showing us out as if we didn't know exactly where we were going. We walk down the stairs, through the hall and out the door in silence. Mamó with her glare, and me still with the shovel. It isn't until I hear the click of the latch behind us that I turn to her and ask her if he was lying.

She walks over to the kettle and flicks it on, before turning to me. 'Partly.'

'What does that mean?'

'It means there's more going on than meets the eye.' She removes Bridget's head from her pocket and looks at it.

'What are we going to do with her?' I ask, gesturing to the head.

'We're going to send her on her way,' Mamó says. 'We won't be sleeping much tonight.'

Again.

19

Hagstone

(fertility, seeing through doors)

Lon has been getting smaller in my dreams, while the figure of Our Lady of Ballyfrann gets bigger and bigger. As though she were feeding off of him. They are together in the forest now. I follow them, and this time I'm the one behind the veil, I stare but cannot touch. He looks like a child compared to her. He has to reach up to hold her hand. She leads him over the mountains and I follow. They venture up the hills and through a little cottage and a vegetable garden. Smoke comes from the chimney, and they sneak around the back and up a little dirt track worn by feet and to a tunnel. She stops at the mouth of it. She can't get in, there's something preventing her. She pushes again and again, and it won't move. She tries to push Lon through and he lets out a whimper. I hear the crack of bone as something gives.

She opens up her mouth, but instead of teeth, thorns, as sharp as blades, poke from her gums. She roars and it's so loud I fall back and the world whips from around me. When I wake up, I'm in Brian's office and my hands are full of strips of torn wallpaper. I try to put some of it back, but he'll have to get somebody in, it's a mess. It's all such a mess. I can't explain why this is happening.

I think of Bridget's face.

And of Our Lady of Ballyfrann as well.

What should I do? I ask. Every bit of me wants to go back to bed, but for the first time since the night we killed Lon, I touch the panel on the wall and let it slide open. I stare into the darkness, thinking of everything that happened, everything that is happening. I pray for strength. I gently close it back. She wants me there. I feel it in my stomach, like a cramp. I amn't strong enough. I can't go in yet. Maybe another time. When it is daylight and I'm not alone. I sigh, and touch my hands to my face.

They come away bloody, and I rush up the stairs to the mirror on the wall of the hall leading to our rooms. I switch a dim lamp on and look at my face. It's like I have been crying tears of blood and wiping them messily all over my skin. I turn the light off and traipse back to my room to wash my face. It's weird. It's very weird. But I amn't scared. I think it is a sign. Something is happening. Isn't that a Virgin Mary thing, to cry tears of blood? She has my back. I trust her. She won't fail me. I pad into the bathroom, right up to the sink, and rub cleanser all over my face, and start wiping wiping wiping. One, two, three, four, twenty come back all different shades of red, from scarlet to vermillion to the almost brown of an old bloodstain. I methodically keep on going, until one comes back clear.

When I look in the mirror, I let out a gasp that's almost a scream.

The scars I bore. The stains upon my face.

They've disappeared.

20

Rowan Berries

(resilience, protection)

We've released Bridget's ghost from her cleaning duties, and bound her to the fingerbone, hair, spine and shrunken head. Successfully, I think. It's not tying her down so much as ensuring we have a way to contact her if we need to. It's not something that I thought I'd ever have to say, but there you go. It took all night. Juniper, flower-de-luce, ragwort and rattle grass. Rainwater from the year that she was born, the year she died and this year. And lots of chanting, which sounds kind of peaceful, but not the way Mamó does it, which is basically just barking simple commands, over and over again until they take. I wonder if that's how Brian's dad bent poor Bridget to his will in the first place. We bound her in a field, through the forest, halfway up the mountain between the castle and the shed. The place they found what remains they could find. What would it be like to be scattered in so many places? Would who you were be kind of scattered too, all strewn about?

By the end of it I felt as if my legs were moving in spite of me, my body heavy and my eyes about to fall right out of my head with the weariness.

'Is this how Catlin feels when she's sleepwalking?' I asked Mamó, and she shook her head at me as though it were a ridiculous thing to wonder. I waited for her to say something, and when it became clear she wasn't going to, I asked her why my sister would be doing it at all.

'It could be any number of reasons. It might not have anything to do with what we found today. But, given that she came back from the dead, it's something that I should have been informed of. Brian knows right from wrong.'

'Catlin knows right from wrong,' I said, and she didn't respond. 'She does. She's a good person.'

'There's no such thing, girl,' she said, 'as a good person. Life isn't that simple.'

'I'm a good person,' I said lamely.

'You're a person who wants to do good,' Mamó said. 'It's not the same at all.'

'Isn't it?'

She didn't answer me. We traipsed back through the forest, through the fields. I felt as though something was on my shoulders, a sort of weight, making every movement heavier. The stars were bright, and when we got back to the flat, Mamó told me that I could 'sleep it in' tomorrow. Sleeping it in Mamó-style means getting up at ten o'clock. It is a luxury I have only been afforded twice, and both those times I have

115

felt her judgement keenly. But I'll take my sleep where I can find it.

I dreamed of Mam and Catlin. Well, not them exactly. Me looking for them. I was in the castle calling out, and I could hear their voices on the air, as though they were close enough to touch, but couldn't see them.

I wake desperate to check on them. I mean, I often want to see them, I miss them a lot, but this was something else – a deep ache inside me, a feeling that I had to see them, that if I didn't it meant that something terrible might have happened. I asked Mamó if it was okay, and she gave me a nod. I think, after what happened with Brian yesterday, it's basically witch-work. I mean, it sounds like neither of them's doing well, according to Brian, but I haven't really picked up on it, and normally my instincts are quite good for stuff like that. I suppose it's easier to gauge how someone is when you can be beside them, looking at them, rather than just messaging.

I open the back door to the castle, and take my boots off so as not to dirty the floor. I notice footprints and smudges that weren't there yesterday. Small ones but it's strange. I hadn't realised how clean the castle was before, which I suppose was a sort of privilege.

Everything is a little greyer around the edges. I wonder if it's already the impact of Bridget being gone.

Catlin isn't in her room. Her bed is perfectly made, as though it were a bed in a hotel, which isn't like her. I look at the statues on her altar, covered in candle wax and pebbles, and . . . I reach out my hand . . . feathers. Dark, soft feathers.

Hmmm.

As Mamó would say.

If she'd bother her hole actually saying anything instead of just glaring all the time.

I tuck one in my pocket to take back to her, and snap a quick picture of the altar on my phone, just in case. It takes a few attempts to get it right. The light is fuzzy and the objects seem . . . distorted somehow . . . as though they're moving slightly with each image, masking themselves. It doesn't feel like Catlin's room at all, and the smell is a bit different too, more like a church or something. She has clearly been spending too much time with the priest.

I send her a message to ask if she's around today, to tell her I might have some time off, and tuck my phone back into the pocket of my big baggy Aran cardigan. It makes me anxious when I don't know where she is. As I turn to leave, I have the strangest feeling. Like someone has taken a feather and brushed it across my skin, from the nape of my neck right down to the bottom of my spine, slowly and deliberately. Just to let me know they can. I turn but I don't see anything, though the smell of roses in the room is stronger now, and I feel warm, uneasy. I call for Mam, and move towards her room.

I've brought a little jar of salt with me, with rosemary and clary sage and orange peel. I've made the jar quite pretty so it could masquerade as something for a bath rather than a spell for her protection. I always left salt, whenever I felt worried, and Mam would always take it out and bin it.

I knock on the door, and she says come in and I do. She's curled up in the bed, even though she'd normally be up by

117

now, her hair is loose around her shoulders and her eyes look sunken in her face, exhausted.

'Maddy!' she says. 'I'll get up now.'

'No, Mam,' I say. 'We can chat here, if you're not feeling well or something.'

'Ah, I'm grand,' she says. 'Just a bit tired. I haven't been sleeping well. Or I don't think I have. And my stomach is a bit . . . off or something these days. I find it hard to have an appetite, which probably doesn't help.'

'I could bring you up some toast?' I offer. Mam loves toast. She always gives it to us when we're sick.

'I'll come down for a cup of tea with you,' she says. 'I'm really happy to see you. How did you get away?'

'I just asked if I could visit and she said yes,' I explain.

'Oh, she said yes, did she?' Mam says, as though that is further evidence of Mamó's evil. She kicks on her slippers with venom.

'It's quiet here today. Where's Brian?' I ask.

'He had to work. I think he's in his office. Or at a meeting. I was half asleep when he left.'

'Did he say anything about the meeting yesterday?' I ask her.

'No,' she tells me. 'He doesn't really talk much about his work. Says he likes to leave it in the office where it belongs.' She turns away and, quick as I can, I bend to tie my lace and sneak the jar underneath her bed, behind a shoebox.

'I mean his meeting with me and Mamó,' I say, a sinking feeling developing in the pit of my stomach.

'Oh,' she says. 'No. He did not tell me anything about that. What was this meeting in service of?'

I head downstairs. 'Quite a bit. I'll put the kettle on.'

No wonder she needs salt. I'm both unsurprised and annoyed that Brian hasn't told her. He's supposed to be open and honest with her now. It's frustrating, having to be the one who spells it out. I close my eyes and steel myself to tell her that her husband has lied to her again.

I hear her feet padding down the stairs after me, slowly, as if she knows she won't like what I say next. I go ahead and put the kettle on, source regular, normal-person teabags and none of that nonsense Brian was giving her. She smiles, and sits.

'Mam,' I say, 'you don't look well at all. Is something wrong?'

'No,' she tells me. 'I'm just having an off day.'

'Brian said that you were having a lot of them.'

'Did he now?' Her voice is ice. I almost feel sorry for Brian. 'I get the feeling that's not all he said. Why did that wagon let you come and visit?'

'I suppose . . . to check on you,' I say, lamely, plonking a mug of tea in front of her. She cups it with both hands, smells it and puts it down on the table again with a little *yeuch*.

'Not up for tea?' I ask.

'It just tastes off . . . what do you need to tell me?' she says, even though I've made it just the way she likes it, 'I can't focus on anything else. What's wrong?'

'It's not that bad,' I say, although it is, in fairness, terrible. 'I mean, it's bad, but not Catlin being kidnapped bad.'

'I survived that, I suppose,' she says. 'One way or another.'

I take a sip of my own tea, and look at the grain of the wooden table. I think I'll say it quickly and directly. Like pulling off a band-aid. That would probably be the best way, right? Deep breath.

'This isn't going to be easy for you to hear or me to say, Mam, but here goes. Brian has been using the ghost of one of the murdered girls as a sort of cleaner.'

'This is not where I thought that was going,' says Mam. 'AT ALL.' Her face is pale. Maybe I could have been more gentle with it, but there's no good way to break this kind of news.

'Yeah, we were pretty surprised ourselves,' I say. 'It's –'

'Cruel is what it is. Exploitative. Which poor girl was he . . . using?'

'Bridget Hora,' I say apologetically. 'He said his father set it up, and he just, kind of, let it carry on.'

'Typical fucking Brian,' Mam says. 'Just see how things play out, keep it quiet and keep the head down. Sometimes –'

'I know,' I say. 'We've taken back her head, anyway, and are working on releasing her.'

'HE HAD HER HEAD?' Mam's mouth is open and her eyes are wide.

'It sounds worse than it is,' I say. 'As he would say himself.'

'In fairness, Madeline, it doesn't sound good.'

'Do you remember the shrunken head in his office?' I say.

'Dreadful thing. I asked him to put it away.'

'Well, it was made from her,' I say.

'I feel sick,' Mam gasps. 'What have I married?' Her face is pale and I can see her hands shaking as she moves them to cup the mug of tea. 'My husband. Who I share a bed with. Has been using pieces of a murdered girl's body to . . . what . . . do the hoovering? I mean, he can afford a cleaner. He's loaded.'

120

'He says she doesn't hoover. Or do laundry. Or cook,' I say.

'Well, let me tell you it's been a long fucking time since I've seen Brian with a hoover in his hand,' Mam says. 'I wouldn't believe a word he says. Not any more.'

'Oh, Mam,' I say. 'Why can't people just be simple?'

'I do not know,' she says. 'I'd settle for them not having blood on their hands at this stage, Madeline. My standards have lowered considerably since moving here. If I had . . . I never thought I'd put up with someone who had . . . placed the two of you in danger . . . and . . .' Her eyes are filling up.

I swallow. I hate it when Mam cries. I move over and wrap my arms around her.

'It'll be okay,' I tell her. 'We're working on it, Mam. We'll fix it.'

'Your father was kind,' she said. 'He was so kind. And I thought . . . Brian . . . he seemed kind, didn't he, Madeline?'

'I think part of him is,' I say.

'The part of him that isn't weak and lazy and cruel, you mean?' she asks, and her voice is acid. Brian is not going to enjoy the next conversation that they have, I muse. He might not survive it.

She holds her hands in her face and gathers herself.

'I need to find a way to get you, your sister and myself out of here. Cleanly and calmly,' she tells me. 'It'll take time. I'll clear the joint account out for a start, put it into my own savings. Then, we can choose a place to live. Somewhere as far away from here as possible.'

'Mam,' I tell her, 'we can't leave.'

'The hell we can't!' she snaps. 'None of us signed up for this.'

'Mam,' I say again.

'We'll find a way, Maddy,' she says, gripping my hand so tightly I can feel her fingerbones, the mark they'll leave. 'We can do it.'

'There's more,' I say lamely, not wanting to make her more upset, but aware I have to tell her what Brian said about Catlin too.

'Of course there is,' she says, taking a big slug of her tea. 'Sure, it'd be too simple otherwise.'

'Brian said that you not feeling well and Catlin sleepwalking are both symptoms of the ghost acting out,' I murmur, trying to make my voice as gentle as possible. 'Mamó thinks we need to keep an eye on it.'

'So, once again, a force has been damaging our lives and hurting my daughter, and their solution is, *Let's just wait and see.*'

'It's not that,' I say, even though it kind of is.

'Oh, I think it's EXACTLY that,' she snaps. 'And I, for one, am sick to death of it.'

'But there are more important things at play,' I say, as if I had any idea what they were. I just kind of weirdly have faith in Mamó's methods. I do not like her, but I do respect her. Grudgingly.

'There is nothing more important to me than the two of you,' Mam tells me, her voice low and sure. 'Other people might have their own priorities, but you are mine. And I'm going to work on it. I need you to trust me. And to have a little bag packed, just in case. Of essentials. Passport, phone charger, change of underwear, that sort of thing.'

'A go-bag,' I say, feeling like I'm in a crime drama all of a sudden.

'Yes,' she says. 'I'll pack one for myself, and throw a few bits together for you and your sister as well to get you started, though you might need things that I don't know –' she swallows, and a small flicker of distaste passes over her face – 'witch things.'

Her face is bright with something between hope and rage. 'It's settled then,' she says. She pulls me to her fiercely and I can feel her chin digging into the top of my head.

'Okay,' I say helplessly. I want her to have hope. It gets you through things. Even stupid hope sometimes can help.

I take a sip of what's left of my tea. It's cold.

'I should probably get back to Mamó,' I say.

Mam sighs. 'Of course.' She smiles. She is gearing up for tears, I can tell by her voice.

I look up at her and try to say the things that I can't say with my eyes. But they're just eyes, you know? It's hard to tell how much of it she'll get.

'Madeline?' she says, as I turn to shuffle off.

'Yeah?'

'Any chance you have another hug for your poor old Mam? She needs it.' If she's talking about herself in the third person, she probably needs more than a hug, but I turn to her, and she wraps her arms around me, and I feel safer than I have in a long time, and the tears are pouring out of me all of a sudden, and she strokes my hair and tells me that it will be okay, as though I were a little child again.

As though she could fix everything.

As though anyone could.

21

Mirrors

(to see yourself and not yourself)

Life can happen pretty fast sometimes. My scars are gone, and I am also hooking up with Eddie Collins in the sacristy. Eddie Collins is not a bad kisser, but it is strange to be getting with someone who isn't Lon. A good kind of strange. It reminds me of the old me. The girl I used to be before this place. We've been dancing around this for a while, I think. Eddie's always looking out for me. Not in a creepy way, but if we're in a group and I say something, he listens. And that's very different to how it was with Lon.

Why am I thinking about Lon right now? My brain is so frustrating. I mean, kissing is supposed to be distracting, not an opportunity to examine each and every choice that led me here. Who am I? Maddy? I trail my fingers across the nape of his neck and he pulls me closer. I close my eyes. The sacristy is great. I wish we had one at home. We should probably just have sex right now, to honour all the fallen women the Church abused and shamed, I muse. And feel my shoulders tense a little. No. Not yet. Too soon.

Eddie pulls back.

'Are you okay?' he asks. 'Is this okay?'

'Yeah,' I tell him. 'Fine. Kiss me again.'

He's so polite. It's good. Eddie is really warm, he smells of sweat and body spray and his hair is weirdly soft, like the fur of a cat. I wonder if that's what he turns into. I bet he'd tell me, now that I know what his neck tastes like (like a neck, but nicer).

I didn't go into this church expecting to hook up with anyone. Which, I suppose is what they all say, and then life just happens. But it is a nice place. I feel safe here. There's a good smell of incense. And I locked the door behind us, using my newfound making-the-world-do-the-stuff-I-want powers, so we shan't be disturbed. Father Byrne is off doing visits to parishioners anyway, so it'd only be Carol the Labrador with the flowers and things.

Ohhh . . . that's just delightful. I close my eyes and kind of melt towards Eddie. I only mildly fancy him, but there are not a lot of boys in Ballyfrann, so he's going up in my estimation quite a bit.

He puts his hands on my ribcage and pulls me closer to him. I freeze.

'Could you not do that?' I say, stepping away.

'Which part?' he asks, moving his hands away and stepping back a bit.

125

'The touching-my-ribcage part,' I say. 'It's not something that works for me.' Any more. There are things, I realise, that Lon did to me that I won't get to enjoy again or for a long time anyway.

'Okay,' he says. 'You look upset. Is there anything I can do to help?' He shuffles over to the other side of the room, and I unlock the door and open it a bit so there's an exit, which suddenly seems crucial.

'No. You helped by listening and stopping. Thank you.'

'Catlin,' he says, and it sounds so sensible in his mouth, like Credit Union Account or Homework Notebook. 'That's . . . that's a really low bar.'

'Well, I mean, you didn't try to murder me, and then succeed and actually murder me, so you're doing really well compared to the last person I was with,' I say. I laugh a bit. He doesn't.

'Maybe don't compare me to the worst person you've ever been with,' he says. 'You could hold me to the standard of someone really sound and non-murdery. Like Santa.'

'Santa?' I ask, feeling a bit sceptical.

'I was trying to think of the safest man there is,' he says.

'I don't know if he's the safest man there is,' I say. 'But he's CERTAINLY the hottest. What a ride.'

'A sleigh-ride.'

'Big ice-palace. Team of Elves. Bags of stuff. Cool pets. Iconic dress sense.'

'Opulent beard.'

'Don't get me started.'

'I mean, he is pretty old.'

'But he looks his age, which is refreshing at this point,'

I say. 'There's an honesty and simplicity to Santa. He'd go down your chimney, but only with enthusiastic consent.'

Eddie looks perplexed. I may have gone too far with the deeply erotic chimney metaphor.

'How are you coping with all that stuff?' he asks. 'I mean. It has to be hard.'

'I'm used to it at this stage,' I tell him. 'I do miss the way things were before, but I don't get to go back, so . . .'

'No,' he says, shuffling a bit. I can tell he's finding it awkward. And it is awkward.

'You don't have to be nice to me just because we kissed,' I tell him. 'There's no need to, like, check in on me and stuff.'

'It's not . . .' he says, and blushes furiously, trying to find the words. 'I mean, I know I haven't asked you before about what happened with Lon, and we kissed and then I did, but it's not like I don't feel a sense of . . . I don't know . . .'

'Responsibility?'

'Yeah. I mean, we knew what he was, Catlin, and we let it happen. Of course I've wondered how you were. I'm surprised you're still talking to us, to be honest.'

'Why did you let it happen?' I ask. 'Not that I think you could have stopped it, once he had his . . . claws in me.' I shudder.

'We thought that Brian would handle it,' Eddie tells me. 'And I know my parents would have said to leave it alone, not to be drawing trouble on ourselves. It just . . . It seemed like someone else's business.'

I'm sitting up on top of the presses with the glass cases on top of them, where the parish records live now. I realise I've pushed myself as far away from him as I can possibly go, which

127

is so the opposite of earlier on. It's funny. But not in a nice way. I might cry, I realise. I can feel it starting to happen, and I don't want him to see it. I murmur a quick prayer inside my head for me to keep it together. To have a bit of dignity, composure.

'It was my business,' I say. 'My body. My life. And I didn't have all of the information.'

'It shouldn't have happened.'

'See, people say things like that a lot – Mam, Brian, Maddy – but there are things that people could have done to make it not happen.' I'm looking at the floor, and my voice is low and full of anger.

'Yes,' he says. 'Erm . . . do you want me to go or something?'

And I tell him that I do, but I don't really. I watch him turn and leave, and it's like the loveliness of the kissing is all twisted up by what happened to me and every time this town has let me down. It's better not to rely on another person really. I don't need a Galway boyfriend, or anyone. I just need a way out of this. I slide off the press, rearrange my clothes, and go kneel in front of Our Lady of Ballyfrann. There are seven candles lit to her today. I hold my hand above one until I feel it begin to burn the skin of my palm.

That must have been the way our dad felt, only more and all over.

And even when he was dead, they didn't leave him to us to mourn.

I hold my hand there until I see a mark begin to form.

I hold my breath.

I'm here.

I'm here.

I'm here.

I hold my hand to my face and smell the flame on my skin. I look at Our Lady of Ballyfrann. The pale wood of her. The curves. She looks so stable, so eternal.

Help me, I ask.

The candles flicker and suddenly the smell of roses hits me, as thick and strong as someone else's perfume on the bus. I breathe it in, it's beautiful. She's beautiful.

She's got me.

I hear a rustle behind me, and Father Byrne is there, organising the pamphlets at the door. He's tall and thin and casts a shadow along the carpet like a sinister priest from a documentary.

'Hello, Catlin,' he says. 'How are you getting on?'

'Fine, Father,' I say, trying my best to look more pious than tousled.

'Having a bit of a pray, I see. You do know there are other statues there?'

'She's the best one though,' I say.

'It's not a competition,' he says.

'But if it were, who do you think would win? Jesus probably,' I say. 'Priests love Jesus.'

'It's true,' he says. 'We do.'

'As a teenage girl, I think it's okay to like Mary more,' I say.

'It's understandable. But religion isn't a popularity contest,' he says. 'It's a deeply personal thing.'

'If it's not a popularity contest, why do people try to convert other people?' I ask.

'Because God is good and having Him in your life makes it better, is the reasoning there, I think,' he says slowly and thoughtfully. 'But I've never been big on . . . canvassing . . . myself. People find what they need in their own time.'

I realise there's a small cut on the side of his forehead, like he's been hit with something.

'What happened, Father?' I ask. 'Are you okay?'

'Oh, fine. I got a bit of a wallop is all. It's not the first and it won't be the last. People resent the help they ask for sometimes.'

'Who walloped you?' I ask, feeling outraged on his behalf. I mean, he's eighty-five. I know he's sprightly for it, but that doesn't mean it's punching season like.

'Someone who needed to lash out,' he says. 'And I'll say no more about it.'

'So I could just, like, punch you, and you'd be okay with it if I needed to lash out?' I ask. 'This is new and interesting priest information, pertinent to my interests.'

He smirks. 'Give it a go, Catlin, and we'll see how you get on.'

I look at him.

'You absolutely punched back.'

He says nothing.

'Ah you did,' I say. 'You flattened him. Toxic masculinity for Jesus at its finest. Proud of you.'

'I wouldn't know much now about this toxic masculinity now,' Father Byrne says, walking towards the sacristy. 'Wait, this door is open.' His voice shifts to something far more serious.

'Oh, wow,' I say. 'I didn't notice anyone in there or anything.'

'I definitely locked it behind me,' he says. 'I always do. And the only key –' he pats his pocket – 'is here.'

I make a note of that useful information.

'I don't know what to tell you. I can't even say if it was open

130

when I got here,' I tell him, widening my eyes. 'I went straight over to Our Lady of Ballyfrann and kind of zoned out.'

'Zoned out how?' he asks and his eyes are dark green searchlights, trying to pin down lies, solve crimes and, apparently, seek out the next punchable parishioner. Not going to be me, I can tell you that much.

'You know, like, deep in prayer,' I tell him.

'And what does that feel like for you exactly?' he asks.

'Like everything else just drips away and I'm just kind of taking in the sensations around me, or sometimes like a daydream with prayers that go along with it,' I say, trying to put words on something I've not really expressed before. 'Calming, peaceful. Like a break from all of this.'

'Yes,' he says, nodding. 'That's right sometimes. It can be. And you're sure you heard nothing or saw nothing?'

'Yes,' I say.

'And you're sure it wasn't you?'

'Why would you think it was me? What would I even be doing in a sacristy?' I ask him, outraged.

'I keep a lot of confidential items locked in there, and you could be curious. Looking for answers. Who would blame you, after all you've been through.'

'I can't believe you think it was me,' I tell him, trying to hide the truth without outright lying.

'I don't think it was you, Catlin,' he says with a sigh. 'But you are the only person in the church, and so my list of suspects is kind of short.'

'I didn't realise that priests got to be detectives and have punch-ups,' I say. 'This day has been a revelation.'

131

'I'm glad it was edifying for you, Catlin Hayes,' He turns towards the sacristy. 'Now if you'll excuse me, I have to go and check if anything is missing.'

And with that he's off into the little room, locking it behind him with a click. Much good the click will do him, now that I have magic unlocking hands. I look down at them. I can still faintly smell the roses from earlier. Just a suggestion of them really. I don't think anyone else could smell them, curling around the candle smoke and flowers like a riddle or a promise.

Our Lady of Ballyfrann looms above me, and even though she's small and made of wood, she is imposing. She can change the world. We all can, if we only have the tools.

The skin on my palm is completely smooth, unblemished.

No features on her face, but I feel as though she's smiling upon me.

I whisper, 'Thank you,' bless myself, stand up.

22

Clove

(money, friendship, minding – also teeth)

When I asked Catlin where she was, I got a prayer-hands emoji, three lipsticks and five exclamation points. I assume this means she's gotten up to something in the church. I got the all-clear from Mamó and headed in there. By the time I catch up with her, she is leaving and I am WRECKED: it takes AGES to cycle into the village from the castle. It's not even a short bus ride. My legs are strong from all the walking, but I normally don't cycle much, and I can feel the sweat under my armpits. I'd love a quick spray of deodorant, but she won't judge me. Only she absolutely will, because she's Catlin. Other sisters, not that I have any, would be sound and nice if you sacrificed your freedom for their life. They certainly wouldn't run up to you shouting, 'Hello, smelly, guess who I just hooked up with?'

'Father Byrne,' I say.

'No. UGH. He's eighty-five.'

'Didn't stop you with Lon,' I point out. There's something off about her, but I can't put my finger on it.

'Don't bring him up. He ruins everything. Stupid old creep.'

'Yeah,' I say, narrowing my eyes and staring at her. It isn't a new parting, but there's definitely . . . 'Sorry. Come here. I came to find you because there's a lot going on with Brian and Mam and things . . . Have you been sleepwalking?'

'I've been kissing Eddie Collins in the sacristy is what I've been doing.'

'You rascal. Shifting a shape-shifter.' I'm a little worried about her hooking up with another supernatural boy, to be honest.

She holds up her hand. 'UGH. No. Don't call it that. It was kind of . . . nice?' She has a smile on her that's almost shy, which is not very Catlin at all. I nudge her. I mean, it was bound to happen at some point. The town is small. And Eddie doesn't creep me out like Lon did . . . which is a good sign, I suppose.

'Tell me everything. But first tell me about the sleepwalking.'

'Are we, like, walking home so you can interrogate me? Because Brian said he'd give me a lift, and I would much prefer that.'

'Brian isn't . . . how to put this . . . ?' I say, trailing off. I mean, I'll tell her. Of course I will. But I want to find out about the kissing first because it's way more fun to talk about than human trafficking with ghosts.

'You sound like Oona,' she snorts, as if that was a bad thing, and not a massive compliment. I love the way she phrases things, there's this little jolt of anticipation I always get while she searches for the perfect word.

'I'd like to see you go to school in your second language,' I tell her.

'I'd like to see that too. Because I'd be in another country and not here in stupid Ballyfrann, where everyone is terrible.'

'Not EVERYONE here is terrible,' I tell her. 'Some people are nice. Layla's sound. And you just got with Eddie.'

'We're not *together* together or anything,' she says. 'I mean, he's lovely. He is. And there was a bit of build-up over the summer, like I had a feeling he was into me, and I didn't hate it. But today was just a spur-of-the-moment thing, and to be honest it ended kind of awkwardly. I don't want to run into him for a little while.'

'What did you do?'

'I could draw you a picture,' she says, making obscene shapes in the air with her hands. In another life she would have been a very good, very disturbing mime artist. 'But I do not think that it would be the sort of picture you could hang on the wall. Unless it was a SEX ROOM.'

'Why would I put your picture on the wall of my sex room?' I ask. 'Or his for that matter? It would utterly defeat the purpose of the room . . . You haven't been full on riding him in the church, have you?' My voice comes out a little more judgy than I meant it to, and I try to keep a neutral supportive expression. I mean, Catlin's body is Catlin's business, explicit hand gestures aside.

'I didn't. But it was hot.' She pauses for a moment. 'I'm not sure if it was hot because it happened in a church or because I fancy him. Time will tell, I suppose. It was good to kiss someone who wasn't Lon. Like a mint after eating something garlicky.'

'I see that,' I say. 'It must be weird for the last person that you kissed to be the worst person who ever lived bar none.'

'And not even a real person either,' she says. 'It does terrible things to my brain. But that is not the truth any more, because I am IRRESISTIBLE. It was only a matter of time before someone took me in a chapel.'

'You said you only did kissing,' I exclaim. 'You'll ruin the poor boy's reputation.'

'I'll *enhance* his reputation.' She grins. She looks more like her old self than I've seen in a while. It's lovely, but I am going to have to tell her terrible things while wheeling an old black bicycle that probably pre-dates Brian, and that's not great.

What would Mamó do? I ask myself. Ruin everything forever, probably.

Fair enough.

'So, Brian says you've been sleepwalking?' I try again.

'Yeah,' she says. 'It's eased off over the past while, but it was pretty bad there for a bit. I'm surprised he told you. I was going to go to Mamó about it, and he convinced me not to.'

'Ugh. Seems like he has to be constantly doing the exact wrong thing at the moment. How did he convince you?' I ask, narrowing my eyes.

'You look like Margaret when you do that,' she scoffs. 'I don't like it.'

'Who is Margaret?' I ask.

'You know her as Mamó.'

'She has an actual name?' I am shocked, and more than a little disconcerted. Mamó is human.

'Yeah, and she is actually as old as balls. Maybe even older. I have evidence. I found her name in the parish records the first time I broke into the sacristy. I've been doing it kind of a lot actually. We should probably move away from the entrance to the church, seeing as I'm talking so loudly about it.'

'You think?' I raise an eyebrow.

'Yeah. I mean, Father Byrne probably won't hear because he's in the sacristy trying to work out who broke into the sacristy, but you can't be too careful these days,' she explains. 'So, the thing with Brian convincing me not to tell Mamó is strange, because we had this big chat about it, but I can't remember the details, they go all foggy when I try to focus on them.'

'I don't like the sound of that,' I say, furrowing my brow. 'Bang of magic off of it.'

'I didn't like experiencing it,' she says, 'and I would like some answers. Or would have liked them anyway, before it all got sorted. What do you think it was?'

I look at her, her hair wild and white around her face, her eyes bright. We've moved further away from the church now I'm holding my bicycle, pushing it where the road meets footpath, and she's on the path itself, looming over me a little. As usual. Catlin's personality is a bullet train.

I think for a minute. 'This is going to sound dramatic,' I tell her.

'Thank GOD,' she says. 'Wouldn't it be dreadful if I was sleepwalking because of something boring like business studies or improperly refrigerated meats?'

'Ugh. MEATS,' I shudder. 'It's probably ghosts. Or a ghost anyway.'

137

'Bridget Hora,' she says.

I nod. 'How did you know?'

'Well –' she shrugs – 'there are dreams that go along with the sleepwalking, and she pops up in them now and again.'

'That sounds horrible,' I tell her. 'Ghosts, and moving around without knowing it, and Brian doing some sort of creepy manipulation charm on you.'

'I wouldn't use the words Brian and charm in the same sentence, to be honest.'

I let out an unexpected cackle, and she joins in. I've missed this. I miss it so much, even while it's going on, the thought of how long it'll be until it's the two of us against the world again makes me so sad.

'It's not that bad actually.' She's looking away from me now, her face tilted up towards the waning moon. 'I mean, it's a break from the dreams of *him*.'

'Lon?' I ask.

She nods.

'Every night, or almost every night. It's like I'm back in it, and I can't get out even though I know how it ends. But Bridget's been helping a bit. I mean, she's a spooky bitch, but when she showed up the dreams started changing, and then she replaced me, with Lon. I know the sleepwalking is probably a sign of some weird terrible ghost thing, but I felt like she was protecting me, and it was nice. To be protected.'

'Yeah,' I say. I wish I could protect her.

'So what's the story? Are you, like, going to exorcise her now?' Catlin asks, her voice a little concerned, like Bridget is a friend who has recently been diagnosed with something.

'We already did a small thing, but not to hurt her, more to set her free. Mamó has some of her remains, and she's trying to work out exactly what Brian's up to, and if there are any more of the missing girls that are being used for cheap domestic labour.'

'That's what he was doing?' Catlin is aghast. 'That's horrible. Ingenious in a way though. I mean, I hate and fear housework as much as the next person, but that doesn't mean I'd harness the dead to do it for me.'

'If you were Brian,' I say, 'that's exactly what it would mean.'

'So . . .' she asks, 'is Brian, like, magic now? I know his dad was into some bad stuff, because he keeps going on about his dad.'

'Such a little rich boy.' I roll my eyes. Catlin grins.

'Oh no, my dad was bad and he left me this castle and these millions and this real heavy chip on my shoulder.'

'It's not my fault I forgot to tell my stepdaughter her boyfriend was a mass murderer.'

'Or that I have a dead girl scrubbing the floors.'

'Or that my wife is packing a go-bag.' I raise an eyebrow.

Catlin does something that's not quite a double take, but very like one. 'Is she really?'

'Apparently we're to have our passports ready and a bag packed. Mam was very clear on that point.' I try to keep the amusement out of my voice, but don't quite manage it.

'Fair play to her. It's nice to see her energised about something.'

'Yeah. She's not looking well, is she, Catlin?' I say. 'I mean, she was in bed when I called over.'

139

'This is going to sound bad, but I haven't noticed. I mean, I know she's not been doing as much, but she's been kind of depressed since everything happened with the two of us. I just assumed she was coping with being powerless and trapped and went about my day. That is bad. Argh. I should try more.'

'We both should,' I say. 'But especially you probably, because you don't work full-time for Margaret.'

'*Margaret.*' She smirks. 'Such a normal name.'

'What would be a good witch name?' I ask.

'Like Luna. Or Silver. Or Ravenstar Nightblossom.' She does wiggly spirit fingers and twirls as though she's wearing too many silk scarves and must let them all fly free.

'Sonata Destiny?' I offer.

She nods. 'Epaulette Moonshadow.'

I like this game. 'Rowan Greentree.' Rowan is actually quite a nice name. And not overly witchy. Just occult enough.

'Cadence Spellcraft,' Catlin says, holding her two hands up to the sky like she's invoking a storm to come down and wash away all other boring names. She pauses. 'But this is Ballyfrann, and so we get Margaret.'

'And possibly Brian,' I add, as if this in any way makes it better, and not much worse.

'It's not fair. Like, if witches had really witchy names it would be so easy to spot them. And avoid them.'

'Hey!'

'I don't mean you.'

We're almost at the castle. I slow my pace. I don't want to go back. I don't want to be launched into the middle of whatever is happening. I'd quite like to order a pizza and

140

just hang out with Catlin for the rest of the day, avoiding the world and talking nonsense.

'What are we going to do?' I ask.

'I honestly have no idea, Maddy.' She sighs. 'It's all too much.'

'If the sleepwalking keeps up, will you come and tell me?' I ask her. 'I won't even say it to Mamó if you ask me not to, but I don't want you going through that alone.'

'Okay.' She nods. 'But will you tell me what you're doing with Bridget? I mean, she's been good to me, in ways, and I'd like to know what happens there. Murdered girl solidarity and all.'

'Of course,' I say. 'It'll probably piss Margaret right off, but that is all the *more* reason.'

'You scamp,' she says, ruffling my hair. She smells a little different, I think. A bit like roses. It's disconcerting somehow. There are all these little changes that I don't get to be a part of now.

The castle looms at the end of the driveway, and before we part ways we hug each other for a long time. Her arms are very strong and tight around me, and even though I can't see a way out, there's a power in being here together.

23

Baby Teeth

(protection: curses, battles)

I made something float today. I was at my altar praying, and I looked at one of the feathers that now litter it, a deep dark carpet of them. The one I focused on was the kind of black that has purple and green filtering through it, and I stared at it and thought about how beautiful it was, and wanted a closer look, but before I went to pick it up it rose and floated to me, like a small gust of wind was fluttering it right where I needed it to go.

I'll obviously need to walk before I can run. But the power, the sense that I could be the dangerous one in the room. That I could have ways to protect myself. If it happened again.

It's heady.

And I can't let it go, or give it up.

It's only just beginning.

The sleepwalking hasn't eased off. Kind of the opposite. But I'm fairly sure that if I told Maddy about it, and that Our Lady of Ballyfrann keeps appearing to me in my dreams (and once weirdly while I was doing the washing-up) and that I now apparently have low-level magic powers, she'd freak out and then I might not get to have low-level magic powers any more and life would inevitably lose some of its flavour. And I suppose I've been avoiding her a bit, in case it accidentally spills out of me or something.

Does that make me a bit like Brian?

Who's to say?

I mean, I'm not hurting anyone, or exploiting anyone. I'm just feeling happier in my own skin. More like myself. More powerful. And yes, the sleepwalking thing is scary, and sometimes I wake up with bloodstains on my hands, clumps of feathers sticking to my skin, but it's not like that's a massive red flag. Farmers kill birds all the time. And cats. Not that I'm even sure that's what I'm doing. If I was waking up in front of a sacrificed goat or something, clearly I'd be worried and tell Maddy and her best pal, Margaret the weird old woman, but I don't think it's necessary. I mean, she healed me. That has to mean something. As well as that, her presence, Bridget's presence – or Our Lady of Ballyfrann's – is making it much easier to sleep. Lon is still in my dreams, but we're further apart now, and I spend my time looking for him, across hills and valleys, in cities and towns. It's almost like a game. When I do see him, he's always near the statue of OLOB (I needed to find a shorter way to say it seeing as she's popping up in my thoughts like every five seconds at the moment), and his back is to me. I get closer and closer and then I wake up somewhere.

And I smile because it's good to be the hunter and not the prey.

Mam was on at me about the go-bag. She drove into Galway yesterday and bought little rucksacks for me and her and Maddy, and travel toiletries, etc. We're to keep them underneath our beds and to 'be ready'. Ha. Good luck finding me if I'm off sleepwalking somewhere, and Maddy is always off on moonlight jaunts with Mamó. It's nice to see Mam with a bit of energy though. Maybe she's getting better. I've been on at her a bit to see the doctor, and she says she's going to. I mean, just because there's magic in the town doesn't mean that all our ailments are magical. And if something happened to her, I don't know what I'd do. We need our mam to look out for us.

Weirdly, no one has noticed that the marks Lon left me with are all but gone. I'm fairly sure they register it on some level, like people meet my eye more, find me easier to look at, but no one has flat out asked me about it. Not even Maddy. And she would have. I don't think she can see it the same way I can. I think that something happens when people look at my face, something that makes the obvious a bit less obvious. And I don't know if I'm doing it without realising it, by instinct, or if OLOB is somehow helping me. I mean, she was the one who healed my face. In some ways it's a pity. Mam would be delighted, if she could see, and I don't think she'd really care who supernaturally healed who and why, as long as I was happy.

Eddie called to check in with me last night, which was

sweet of him. I think that for now I prefer the back and forth of messaging. There's still some residual sensitivity after the way things ended in the church. That feeling when he pulled my ribcage. It's like I know him well enough for me to want to do stuff with him, but I don't know him well enough to schedule regular trauma-unpacking sessions. And I don't have any experience of being the way I am. The way Lon made me.

Eddie seems in good form. Their tractor broke down apparently, but it's easily fixed. I was very excited that he could drive a tractor, and asked him if I could have a go on it when it was working again.

'It's not a roller coaster, Catlin,' he said.

'I know. But I have never been on a tractor and I would like to be able to say that I had, you know, when I get back to school and everyone is boasting about how many tractors they've been on.'

'Will you be back to school in September then?' he asked.

'I think so, yeah. I mean, I'll be a year behind, but I have to go back some time.' I sighed. 'It feels a bit overwhelming when I think about it, but the longer I leave it the bigger it's going to get, if that makes sense.'

'It does.' His voice is really soothing. Not even the voice itself, but the spaces he leaves between speaking. It's like I can hear him listening to me.

'Eddie?' I asked. 'I know this is weird, and please feel free to tell me it's none of my business, but I'd kind of like to know what your deal is with the shape-shifting stuff.'

There was a pause.

'I'm really sorry to ask,' I said, 'but it's just that this is the

145

first time that I've been with someone since . . . and I just need to know that I'm safe, you know?'

'You're safe with me, Catlin,' he said. 'I don't like talking about it. Like, our culture around it is kind of to keep things private, and I have so much figuring out to do about how I feel about it myself that it's hard to put into words.'

'You don't have to . . .' I trailed off, feeling like I'd just changed the tone or something, asked for too much.

'No,' he said, after a beat. 'Look. A lot of what happened to you last year might have been avoidable if people had been honest. And you're honest with me. So I might as well be upfront with you. I've only just started "the change", which makes me sound menopausal but I don't want to call it "the shift" because . . .'

'. . . that would be terrible.'

'It would. Truly terrible. So, there are a few different things that people can turn into. But it's normally mythic. Like, animals that you would find in myths. Hares, swans, cats, things like that. But our family is the most predictable kind of shape-shifter.'

'Wolves?'

'Yeah,' he said. 'It's weird, and it's obviously not ideal. But because we all live together, there's a lot of wisdom shared around it, and we kind of have a handle on how to . . . manage it.'

'It must be hard.'

He paused, and I didn't fill up the space, just listened to him searching for the words.

'It's complicated,' he said eventually. 'But not all bad. I mean, I've only ever been the way I am, and from the family that I am from. And it's not like in films where you lose all control and want to tear everything apart.'

146

Tear everything apart.

Poor choice of words.

I felt my heartbeat begin to quicken. I tried to slow my breath, drumming my fingers along the edge of the table and counting one, two, three, four, five . . .

'So if we were together and you felt the need to . . . change . . . what would happen?' I ran a hand through my hair, and thick white strands snagged on my fingers. It tangles so much more quickly now, I don't know why.

'I'd feel it coming on for a few days beforehand. And I probably wouldn't be by myself. Family members tend to have the same cycle. So the first thing is that you wouldn't be around. And the second thing is that I'd still be me. I mean, you still recognise the smell of familiar people and that kind of stuff.'

'You recognise my smell?' I asked.

'Well, yeah. I mean, smell is a thing when you're attracted to someone, isn't it?'

I got a flash of me burrowing my head into the crook of his neck and felt my skin begin to flush a bit.

'I suppose.'

'So even if I were to be around you, you would be safe. But I might, like, eat a rabbit or piss on a tree or something and that would be a bit embarrassing.'

'Fair enough,' I said.

'Does that help any?' he asked. 'I mean, it's probably not hugely comforting, because wolves aren't the safest animal. Like, it would probably be better if my family turned into golden retrievers or something.'

'Golden retrievers are sound,' I said.

'Wolves can be sound as well,' he told me, and there's a note of something in his voice, defensiveness or worry maybe.

'I think you're very sound, Eddie Collins,' I said to him. 'And thank you for sharing that with me. I get that it probably wasn't easy.'

'Do you still want to . . . ugh . . . I don't know . . .'

'Look, I don't know either. I mean, I do want to see you again, but I can feel really scared really quickly since the thing, and I can't promise that who you are won't be a part of that. I can tell you I like you though. I do like you.'

'I like you too, Catlin Hayes.' I could feel the smile in his voice. But when we said goodbye, I still didn't know.

I closed my eyes and heard his voice say the phrase 'tear everything apart' over and over again.

Bad things can happen very, very quickly.

I need to take my power where I can.

24

Willowherb

(soothing, stopping bleeding)

There's a kind of mushroom called the deceiver mushroom, because it can look a lot of different ways. One of them is a waxy sort of tan, like human skin. They're not the nicest to the touch, but I'm plucking a ton of them under the watchful eye of Mamó, who has come with me today. She has been both criticising the way I harvest things and asking questions about Mam and Catlin, and what they said and did. It's like being interrogated by two bad cops in the one body and I've told her everything, but she keeps making me repeat it over and over again, looking for tiny details, the kind you barely notice at the time, much less in retrospect. I feel like giving her any old answer just to get her off my back, but she would know. Not just because I'm terrible at lying, but because she is an ancient and powerful witch as well as a massive pain in the hole.

'Focus,' she tells me, and asks me things like:

'Did Sheila have dry skin?'

'Was there anything under Catlin's nail beds?'

As if I am the kind of person who spends my whole time looking at the small imperfect details of people's bodies when I'm breaking bad news to them. This might explain a lot about Mamó actually. The glaring. The reluctance to let me have friends. She's always giving me dirty looks when I'm using my phone now, which is unfortunate timing-wise because Oona has been messaging me more and more, and sometimes she calls too. It's nice to hear a voice that's apart from all the nonsense that's going on. Mam hasn't been in touch with Elodie yet, but I passed on her number in case it would help. They could discuss go-bags and men who are not all they seem. Oona says it's more complicated than you would think to leave him.

I'm going to see Oona tonight, which Mamó is not happy about at all, but I need to show up for her, to make sure she's okay. She's going through a lot. But spending time with her makes things more complicated. It's like the ground is shifting under me, and losing my balance is inevitable.

'Mamó?' I ask.

She clears her throat.

'Do you know why it would be complicated for Elodie and Oona to leave Johnny Noone?'

'I have an idea, yes.' Her face is impassive. She's so hard to get a read on sometimes.

'I mean, is it the Collins connection? Is he a shape-shifter too? Could you explain it to me? It might help me to help her.' I grab another mushroom and place it in my bag.

150

'I could,' she says. 'But I won't. It's none of your business unless that little girl decides to tell you herself.'

'She's not a little girl,' I snap. 'And while we're at it, how am I supposed to learn when you only ever give me half-answers?' I'm frustrated. Because she is frustrating.

'A lot of what we do is learning to look and listen to what people are telling you. And not just with their words. You have to notice the details.'

'I do notice the details,' I say. And it's true. I am forever staring at Oona. To the point where it is almost creepy. I like her so much.

'Not the right ones,' Mamó snaps.

'How am I to know what the right ones are?'

'You can't,' she says. 'So you have to notice everything. When you met Catlin outside the church, were her cheeks flushed?'

I think. Hard.

'It's . . . strange,' I tell Mamó. 'When I picture Catlin outside the church, even though I know she has the scars, her skin is back to the way it was before. It's like, there's a filter over the pictures in my head, if that makes sense. I don't, like, trust my brain . . .'

Mamó's eyes narrow, and she leans closer to me. When she speaks, her voice is more intense.

'Did the air smell any sort of way? Was she wearing perfume?'

I try to focus on my sister's face, the church behind us getting further and further away as we walked home. There is something, but it's faint. I'd almost think that I was making

151

it up it's that faint, but something in me niggles so I say it anyway.

'I think so . . . maybe roses?'

Mamó grunts again. I'm not sure if I've done well, or just imagined more reasons for us to worry.

'We're probably grand with the deceivers now,' she tells me. 'Let's go get some purple woundwort. I have to go up to the Noones later on this evening, and you'll come with me.'

My heart stops a little. Oona's house. I've never been inside it, for all that we have been to each other. She's private like that, I don't think the way her dad is makes it easy to have people round. This feels like an intrusion. Like something she won't like. I bite my lip, searching for some reason that I can't go, that is both practical and sensible. I can't find one.

'I have a thing?' I venture. Which is true, I do have a thing. With Oona. as it happens, which will make the visit to her house even more awkward. Like, she won't even be there and I'll be watching Mamó poke around in her life.

'You'll follow me, and you'll take it all in,' Mamó tells me. 'I'll ask about it after.'

Ooh, assessment. Wonderful.

'Yes, Margaret,' I say ruefully, and she turns her head slowly towards me. Her gunmetal grey eyes meet mine.

'Only my friends call me Margaret,' she says slowly.

I look at her steadily. 'But everyone here calls you Mamó.'

'Yes,' she says, and strides on through the forest.

I bet if they could speak, Badb would be allowed to call her Margaret.

I quicken my pace and hear a low rumble from a tree

152

above me. I look up. Button jumps on top of me, growling, and scratches my face. I try to push him off, but his claws have dug right in. He must have been up there, hunting a bird or something. For a cat with one eye, he can see well enough when he wants to, I think, trying to disentangle myself from his small rage.

His ears are twisted into something owl-like and his eye is wild. He used to be so snuggly once. I fling him away and start running towards Mamó. He grasps my legs with his teeth and claws, and I have to stop and pull him off again. Ugh. I'm going to be so humiliated if she notices that I've fallen behind because I'm fighting a cat.

'Button, *stop*!' I squeak, but he's not listening. A grey feather clings to his back. Why can't he just go back to hunting birds? I mean, isn't he hungry? Apart from for revenge? I crouch down to try to shield my face and he's going for my eyes. Of course he is. I manage to hold him off with my two hands, underneath the part that would be armpits if he were a human, and get back up. He's waiting for a chance to attack me again, I can see it. His eye that's sewn shut flashes for a second, as though there were something underneath the surface, a little light, and I want to reach my finger out and trace it, but I also am enjoying not being attacked so I keep my arms where they are and quicken my pace. Angry cats are basically a liquid, so it's not easy to keep a grip on Button. Badb flaps down to a nearby tree branch and begins glaring down with his little pinprick eyes. It's not very supportive, but maybe it does something, because when I release my grip a little Button runs off into the undergrowth with a feral *mrowww*.

He'll be back again, I know it. I sigh. I don't have time for this. There's witchcraft and entanglements and gardens that need tending. I can't see Mamó in front of me any more.

I take the deepest breath and start to run.

25

Whiskers

(safety, speed, perception. also luck)

I'm meeting up with Eddie, Charley, Oona, Fiachra, Cathal and Layla in the shed at the top of the mountains. The youth club we were all in last year has been disbanded, seeing as Lon was a full-on murderer. But sure, that's no reason we can't still all meet up and drink cans, even if most of them still avoid meeting my eye whenever Lon's name comes up. Love Ballyfrann.

I had a dream last night about my dad. I was watching from behind the shoulders of two men. They covered him with petrol and set him alight. His lips were moving but I couldn't hear what he was saying, it was like he was underwater, or I was. I couldn't hear the men's voices but his face was not afraid. It was angry. He was angry they were doing this to him. And I felt the ripple of the flame and then something else, a sort of sucking, and I watched his mouth moving and saw his hands flat upon the earth as the pain flickered across his face, as the fire took him and suddenly I couldn't feel the heat. A gap had widened or a veil had dropped. It was like I was just standing in the forest, on a normal day, watching a recording or a ghost or something.

I caught a flash of blue past the flames, through the trees, and saw the shadow of a cloak, the tilt of a wooden face. She was there with me. Tilting one long wooden finger to her lips and murmuring a *shhh* that I felt travelling right down my neck. Why was she showing me this? I wondered if it was one of her secrets, the three mysteries she'd whispered, and moved to follow her, and even though I wasn't really there the two men startled, pulled their collars up and hurried off. My dad's eyes met mine and I smiled at him. I think he knew who I was, and it sent a shock through me that I was present here, so long ago. How was that even possible?

I tried to send him the message that we're okay. That we grew up safe. To lie, but just a little. But I could see it didn't fully take. He stared at me but I couldn't read his eyes. Was he comforted or was he frightened? Could he even see me through the pain?

I stayed there looking at him till the end, and when I woke my face was wet with tears. I wish I'd seen their faces. Those two men. They have to be the ones who robbed his grave. Them, or others like them. I wish there was a way to talk this out with Madeline, but I don't know when we'll have the chance again, and I don't want to make Mamó, or her, suspicious.

I braid my hair into a messy updo thing, and pull on a nice dress and runners, slick on some make-up. It's a relief not to have to spend hours on it when I want to see people, and even nicer to like what I see in the mirror again. To feel more like myself.

Mam gives me a lift halfway there, because I'm not as obsessed with walking as Madeline, and I'll have to walk home anyway which is irritating enough. I rub the beads on the rosary bracelet around my arm, and remind myself that I am safe. That somebody is looking out for me. I am looking forward to seeing Eddie again, I realise, which is strange.

'Why are you smiling, Catlin Hayes?' asks Mam.

'I'm just happy because it's been a while since I did anything sociable,' I tell her. 'It's nice to feel like I have a bit of a group again.'

'Hmmm,' she says, as though she doesn't quite believe me, and takes a bite from a box of cream crackers she has taken with her on the drive for some reason. Maybe it's to do with the go-bag stuff.

'Are we always bringing snacks in the car now?' I ask. She pulls over into a grassy margin.

'You never know when you'll get peckish,' she says. 'And it's nice to have a problem that's so easily solved. Did you ever hear about this thing called the Dark Web, Catlin? Elodie Noone says you can get new passports and guns and all sorts on it.'

'Yeah, you probably can,' I tell her. 'But should you? I'm not sure this Elodie Noone is a good influence on you. She's probably a dose like her daughter.'

'Oona Noone is a lovely young woman, Catlin. A credit to

her mother. She stayed and chatted with us while we were having tea and everything. She told us all about their life in France. And she was asking after Madeline.'

'I bet she was,' I say grimly. She'd better stay away from my sister. Madeline might not have a soul but she definitely has a heart, and Oona Noone will crush it into nothing if she's not careful.

I say goodbye to Mam, and she says if I need a lift home to give her a call because she probably won't be sleeping. Which is both handy and worrying. I head up the mountain to the little shed we're meeting in. Fiachra and Cathal's mountain bikes are slung against the wall, I notice. Everyone is there before me, and the fire has been lit in the fireplace. They all have bottles full of various things, and some of them have cans as well. Fiachra is sprawled over two beanbags, like a sort of pale giraffe.

'Hey, Catlin!' he says and I instantly know that:

a) He is already drunk,

b) They *alllllll* know that I kissed Eddie.

I love heading into a room where people have been talking about me behind my back. I know that might sound like sarcasm, but it's actually true. It's a reminder that I matter. I take my hip flask out of my bag and take a sip of whiskey. It makes my mouth awake. I find a place to sit, not too near Eddie, and realise I'm sitting beside Oona, who is wearing a navy-and-white Breton top, which is a bit overkill if you ask me. Next it'll be a beret and a big string of garlic around her neck. She's drinking wine. Of course she is. Fair dues.

'Oona,' I say.

'Catlin,' she says back. '*Bienvenue.*'

I narrow my eyes. '*Fáilte.*'

She is beautiful, I will give her that. Like, stunning. Even in her weird Parisian Halloween costume of an outfit.

'*Agus romhat féin.*'

OH FUCK OFF, OONA. I take another sip. 'How are you getting on?'

She shrugs. 'You know.'

I nod. 'Ballyfrann.'

Layla settles herself beside us, crossing her impossibly long legs around each other twice.

'Ballyfrann,' she says, taking a slug from her 7-Up bottle.

'What's in the bottle?' I ask.

'Medicine.' She grins. 'You'd miss Maddy, wouldn't you?'

'Yeah,' I say. 'You would.'

'It's such a pity,' Oona says, 'that she has not the freedom to go where she would like.' Her tone of voice fully makes it my fault and I resist the urge to say something mean about girls who are careless with the feelings of my sister.

'Mamó is scary,' Layla says. 'I wouldn't want to annoy her.'

I swallow. Oh, fuck it.

'Yeah, it's terrible that she's being exploited,' I say. 'No one should do that to another person.'

Oona sighs. 'I agree,' she says, making eye contact with me as though I were an exploiter.

'I'm glad you do,' I say. I wonder if I could levitate her out of the house. I mean, I probably couldn't. And even if I could I probably shouldn't. I take another slug of whiskey and decide to be nice, for Maddy's sake.

159

'Will you get a chance to go back to France for a visit or anything over the summer?'

'I would like to visit my grandparents,' she says. 'But it can be hard to get away.'

'Yup,' I say. 'We went back to Cork for a night there a while back, and it felt so strange to not be here. We were tempted not to come back, to be honest. But Maddy, and my . . . condition make it a bit hard to just go back to normal.' I touch my face, as though the scars were still there.

Layla smiles. 'No such thing as normal.'

'I suppose not,' I say. 'But there is definitely a strange that is less strange than life here is.'

'It does have its benefits though.' Layla smiles at Oona, and I catch a flash of something. An undercurrent What the fuck is that? I wonder. Are they hooking up? Not that it is my business. It isn't. I mean, fair play to them. But Maddy's little heart will break in two and she needs to be strong for giving out to Brian and freeing ghosts and looking at plants and whatever else herself and Mamó do.

We talk about Paris some more, and about how Liam Donoghue thinks it's funny to ask Oona where she's really from, because he doesn't realise people can be both French and brown.

'I wouldn't be too concerned with Liam Donoghue's good opinion,' I tell her. 'Seeing as how he hired a murderer and all.' Lon used to work in Donoghue's.

They look at me. Argh. I brought it up again.

'Sorry,' I say. 'I didn't mean to make it all about me. I just wanted to say that he's not a great person.'

'He's my uncle,' Layla tells me. 'So I can confirm that he is not.'

'I am sorry that you got murdered, Catlin,' says Oona.

'Ah, thanks, Oona,' I tell her. 'I'm sorry that people are racist.'

She makes a very French shape with her mouth, like she has been confronted with a subpar block of cheese.

I clink my glass with hers.

We drink more drinks. I see a small, dry leaf on the ground and try to make it dance. It does, and no one notices but me. I smile.

'Look at you, smiling at a leaf,' says Eddie Collins.

I smile at Eddie Collins. He has a nice face. I like looking at it. Maybe I am a little drunk, I realise. I shake my hip flask. There's still plenty in there.

'It's a good leaf,' I tell him, 'maybe *the best* leaf.'

'I wouldn't go that far.' He runs his fingers through his hair, and I have the strongest urge to reach over and mess it up. 'I mean, it's not even on a tree.'

'It doesn't need a tree,' I say. 'It's a very independent leaf. It's going places.' Though obviously I'm not going to make it go any more places tonight, because that would be really foolish. I don't want anybody catching on that Madeline is not the only witch in the family.

Eddie smiles at me again, and I need to be kissing him so I ask him if he wants to go for a walk, and don't wait for him to answer before heading out the door into the moonlit night.

The small overgrown garden out the back is familiar, and I realise I've seen it in my dream. I followed her here – Bridget, or Our Lady of Ballyfrann – the skyline and the slope of hill

161

the same. If I moved towards the corner, up the hill a little, there would be the cave that wouldn't let her through. I have a flash of thorns instead of teeth, a gaping shout. What does it mean that I have been dreaming of real places here? Crow blood on my feet and feathers in my hair. Could I really travel all this way at night and not remember?

Fear settles heavily in my stomach, and Eddie puts his hand very gently, almost questioningly, on the small of my back. I smile and move closer to him. The air tastes of mystery. I find myself sniffing the air, seeking the scent of roses, but they aren't here, only the low hum of night, the swish of grass and leaf, the rustle of them underneath our feet. I find myself venturing up towards the cave she couldn't enter. I see the entrance.

'Have you been here before?' I ask Eddie.

'Not a big fan of tunnels,' he says.

'Me neither,' I tell him. 'Madeline found something here, I think. A bone or something.' I try to remember if she told me so, but how could I know it if she didn't? She must have done or it doesn't make sense.

'That's horrible,' he says, and I know he knows the kind of bone I mean. The kind of bone that could have been me. I look at my fingers, small and splayed out. He takes my hand. His hands aren't big for a boy, but they are bigger than mine, which is nice. We sit in the cave entrance, and I look at the stones in a circle, with the marks inside. I go to pick up a stone and examine it but Eddie stops me.

'We don't touch those.' His face is serious.

'Why not?' I ask. 'They're only stones.'

'And plants are only plants, but used a certain way they can

162

do a lot of different things. It's there for a reason. Like a sign on a gate about a bull.'

'Mamó,' I say, sighing. Of course it's Mamó. Of course she's up to something. Remembering the dream, and the roar of OLOB, her open maw, I feel my fingers itch to break up the circle, wipe away the shapes and throw the stones into the long grass of the garden. But it wouldn't be a good idea. Not with witnesses.

We need to be careful.

'I'm hungry,' I say. And because Eddie Collins is absolutely lovely, he takes out a Snickers bar from his pocket and hands it to me without a word. I wolf it down, and then he kisses me and he tastes of apples and I taste of chocolate and the two go very well together, but I'm thinking of a wooden face with dents instead of eyes as his hands run over my body, avoiding my ribcage, not demanding anything I can't give. Our skin is touching and my body hums with it, and I find myself pushing against him, asking for more of this, and more. I don't know how much time passes before the door of the shed opens and Charley yells that their lift is here, but I know moving apart feels like a loss. Eddie takes my hand and helps me to my feet. I dust off whatever cave debris is clinging to me, and I reach my hands up and pull a desiccated leaf from his soft hair.

'Go on ahead,' I say, 'I need to call Mam anyway, to check in.'

'Are you sure?'

'I am, of course,' I say. 'She worries. You know how mams are.'

He nods, and kisses me on the cheek before moving away towards the shed. I straighten my dress, run my fingers through my hair, tucking any loose wisps back in place, and dismantle Mamó's circle, stone by stone.

26

Marigold

(vision, expulsion of parasites, finding what's been lost)

I.
Am.
So.
   Late.

The thing at Oona's house took *forever*. Lots of small talk before getting to the point from Johnny Noone; it was like he really wanted to impress Mamó. There were five kinds of biscuits, plus some buttered scones. It would have been kind of nice, if it wasn't so obviously a performance. It was like he was trying to convince us how normal he was, and Elodie was there as well. Her face paler than I remembered, and taut. She looked at him sometimes before she spoke. I remembered that look, from how Catlin was with Lon. My stomach sickens at the thought of Oona living with that kind of tension. Day in, day out. It would have to eat away at you.

Oona's dad spoke in a low, definite voice and paused before responding to Mamó, like she was a guard and he needed to get his story straight. Mamó sat, back arched, eyes fixed on him, and I hope she never looks at me that way. Apparently her usual glare is a casual sort of thing.

'Your cousins are going to keep an eye on you,' she told him icily.

'And do I get any say in this?'

'You don't. Elodie and Oona will stay in this house, and you will go to be with your people until whatever has broken in you has fixed.'

'I'm fine,' he snapped.

Mamó blinked at him.

He swallowed, and lowered his head. His hands were fists in his lap, and I looked at Mamó, thinking, There's no way we should leave him here tonight.

She gave a slight nod and said, 'Pack your bags.'

'And what if I say no?' he asked, with just a little fight left in his voice.

'Then you won't have your things with you when we drop you off,' Mamó said.

He got up, and stomped off like a surly toddler.

Elodie asked me how I was getting on, and was I finding studying hard without school, and things like that, like it was perfectly normal to be an apprentice witch confronted by the hardest parts of a neighbour's marriage. The range was warm, and the kettle sang on top of it. It was a windy night. I answered her questions politely and accepted the offer of a cup of tea, even though part of me wanted to get out of there as quickly as I could, and the other part of me was obsessing about the impact this could have on my relationship with Oona.

I bit into a scone for something to do and saw the teeth-marks I had made in the butter. It made me think of dental records, skulls. Eventually Johnny Noone arrived with a khaki knapsack and we drove up to the cottages in the mountains where the Collinses lived.

'I'm not a bad person,' he said in the car. 'I'm not a monster.'

Nobody said anything.

'I feel really attacked. And it takes more than one to start a fight, you know. Elodie has a temper on her.'

'There's no point laying blame,' Mamó said.

'That's not what I'm trying to do,' he growled.

Again she didn't answer.

They saw us out, and stared after the car as we drove away. I exhaled deeply, and looked at Mamó.

'Do you think it'll be okay?'

'I think they'll be safer now,' she said. 'But he doesn't seem like a man who is overly anxious to better himself.'

'No,' I said. 'He doesn't.'

'Time will tell,' she said. I couldn't read her face, focused as it was on the road. I felt my legs twitch as we passed the turn-off nearest the shed.

'Do you have somewhere else you need to be?' she asked.

'Actually,' I said, 'if you could let me out, I could make my way back home in my own time – Oona . . .'

She stopped the car so suddenly the brakes squealed.

'Out you get, so.'

I gathered up my bag and launched outside. Wondering how to tell Oona where I'd been. Though I have to get used to this, I suppose. Meddling in the lives of those who need it. Working with Mamó has made me part of the fabric of the town now, delivering babies, healing ailments doctors wouldn't have a notion of, sorting things before they become problems, but at the same time we stand a bit apart.

I run up towards the shed. Before I go inside, I know that something's wrong. The lights are on, and I can see movement inside, people. That's unexpected, but there is something else, a warmth in the air, that makes me worry. I don't like that they're here. I don't like the smell of the place. Something is off.

I sigh.

I wish she'd told me that it was a thing with people. I mean, maybe it's my fault that I always assume when Oona wants to meet that she's in crisis. And she could well be, like you can be in crisis at a party. Sometimes being at a party feels like a crisis in itself for me. Ugh. *People*.

I walk in through the front door, feeling a blast of heat from the fire and people's warm bodies. Fiachra is playing a guitar, and Cathal is singing a song while people listen. They stop when I come in, of course they do. Layla and Oona are in the corner, huddled close together, two heads touching.

'Madeline!' Layla exclaims, getting up with a big grin. I love drunk Layla. She is like seven puppies in a trench coat. But I do not have time for even one puppy tonight and I need to make that clear. Okay, apparently we're hugging. We're huggy friends.

167

'You're the BEST.' Layla beams. 'We're so glad you could come. Charley will be sad she missed you, and Eddie.'

'I have to . . .' I start to say.

'Would you like a drink? Madeline Hayes, would you like SEVERAL drinks?'

I feel all welcomed. This is actually really nice. I wish I wasn't super suspicious that something really bad is going on. Maybe it isn't and I should just have several drinks and hang out with lovely Layla, and stare at Oona. The first time we hung out with all the Ballyfrann crowd at night, me and her snuck away for a swim and it's still one of the best things that has ever happened to me. I meet her gaze across the room, remembering. She does a little wave. I wave back.

I need to focus.

Layla pulls me over to where herself and Oona were sitting.

'You missed Catlin as well,' she says. 'She went for a lift. She's been kissing Eddie.'

'I'm aware,' I say. 'She's not big on secrets.' Except for the sleepwalking and the whatever happened with the memory of her skin earlier. Or was that just me? I wonder.

'I need to go outside for a minute,' I say. 'To get some fresh air.'

'I could come with you?' offers Oona.

And I say, 'No, you're grand,' as if I didn't love being around her with every fibre of my being. As if every room she's in weren't the best room in the world bar none.

And it's probably stupid because I do need to talk to her, but the witch in me's awake.

Something isn't right and it's only getting wronger. I weave my way through the overgrown garden, the smell of rust

168

and honeysuckle in the air. I head up towards the tunnel, wishing my phone were charged so I'd at least have a torch or something. My hands reach out for something I can use, a flower I don't recognise. Clustered a little like woundwort, but coloured like a daisy. I remove some mint leaves from my bag and crush them together, rub them on my eyes. Mamó would probably have something better, but I am the one who is here right now. I have to do my best. My vision clears and it's still dark but I can make out shapes with accuracy. I wonder if this is how cats see, little Button with his vengeful heart and creepy little eyes that catch the light and flash. I swallow. Now is not the time to be thinking of possible attacks from furry guys. I need to focus.

I approach the mouth of the tunnel. I notice the stone circle Mamó made has been broken apart, the stones thrown into different corners and the symbols written in the dust erased. I close my eyes and try to picture exactly what it looked like. I let my hands guide me to where the stones are, and begin making a little pile in the centre of where it had been. Some of them are back in the thick overgrowth of the garden, and I retrace my steps and let my instinct find them one by one, until my gut tells me I have enough. The pile completed, I look around to see what else has happened. I can't see any change, apart from that and some footprints, both smallish, but one bigger than the other. Two people were here, and now the circle's broken. I have a sinking feeling as I replace the stones in the circle. I throw the remains of my mint and daisy-looking things into the circle I have made and trace the shapes half remembered from Mamó. She's right, I do need a sharper memory. I rub them out and try again until something clicks inside me to tell me that it's working, maybe not as well as it did before, but as close as I will get tonight.

I close my eyes, place my two hands on the ground and see if I can get the marks to shimmer like Mamó did. It's very pale, almost imperceptible, but there is a small dull ripple of something through them that satisfies me. I close my eyes and inhale the moist air of the tunnel. It smells of old dust, old secrets and there's the scent of roses in the air. Something grabs the back of my head and pulls my hair so tightly that for a second I think I'll lose a chunk of it. I fall on my back, rolling to avoid breaking the circle and turn to face my assailant. Witches don't go down without a fight. Sharp nails carve into my face and I feel the warmth of blood begin to run, I reach my hands out, grab and hold on tight. Try my best to look through the pain, the flow. The figure stares at me, eyes wide and vacant, face pale, but marked with lines that twist around each other, like fingerprints or woodgrain. The flash of something – recognition? fear? – before she turns and walks away. I hear the footsteps fade.

I can't be sure. My eyes. But still . . .

I hear my high, pathetic voice ask:

'Catlin . . . ?'

It sounds so young, like I am just a child. I feel a child. I feel too young for this.

My two hands on my face, and something sharp is stuck inside the wound. More than one of them, as sharp as needles. Splinters. Lots of splinters. Made of wood. I pluck them out one by one and sit beside the circle, to protect it.

I hear Layla's voice calling for me from the garden, and I stay quiet, waiting there.

I wait beside the circle all night long, holding my breath and keeping it intact, my hands tense and my wits about me.

Until the sun begins to rise, and I feel like the threat, for now, has passed.

27

Tangleweed

(connecting, bridging, linking)

I am trying to take the perfect photograph of my breakfast so I can send it to Eddie, who has been messaging me since last night. He wanted to check I got home safe, which was quite sweet, though with those messages I always kind of wonder what the response would be if I hadn't gotten home safe, and was like: No. Help! Come and rescue me immediately!

Breakfast is a boiled egg and toast. I didn't get the top off my egg right, so I'm using Mam's egg for the photograph and she is glaring hungrily at me. Mam is mad for boiled eggs at the moment, she keeps going on about protein. I wonder if that's an essential element of her plan to get away from here. Bulk us all up on protein until we're magnificently swole and then we just like . . . beat on Brian if he tries to stop us leaving? Though she also made him an egg, so that's a big flaw in the plan right there.

Brian does not deserve a boiled egg, surely. But Mam is really good at minding people, and I think she must kind of go into autopilot , sometimes. She's being very nice to Brian, for all that she knows what he did; you'd hardly know she was plotting to leave him at all, like. I don't understand adult relationships, and I worry if she carries on like everything is normal with him, that all of a sudden it just will be, and it will be too late. She will be stuck.

I send the picture, dip my toast into the runny yolk and wish she'd send me a sign, like giving Brian the finger behind his big stupid head or something. Mam sighs and grabs my less neat egg like I've done her a grave injury.

Brian is drinking a smoothie with his egg, which is a disgusting and weird combination of flavours. My stomach is unsettled just looking at him. And possibly from all the drink last night. Brian has gone smoothie-mad recently. He has all these powders and things he puts in them, and even though the flavours are supposed to be 'strawberry' or 'tropical', they all smell, to me, a little bit like mince. Like liquid mince. Maybe *he* is the one planning to get all swole and stop us leaving by sheer force. Though he mightn't need to, seeing as he apparently has no problem using magic to make women do things for him. He'd probably argue that ghosts aren't really people, but seeing as how I almost was one, I have a bit of an issue with that. I take another vicious bite of egg and glare at him. His face is all thoughtful.

'We might need to start a chore wheel,' he declares, stroking his chin, as if that was a perfectly normal thing to say, and then he has another gulp of his smoothie. It's pink today. A little dribble escapes from the corner of his mouth and he dabs at it with a bit of kitchen roll. I continue glaring, but Mam nods.

'That might be a good idea, get everything a bit more organised.'

'What should we put on it, Catlin? Is there anything you would like to be your responsibility?' he asks.

And I know sometimes that the right thing to do is to shut up and smile and go with it.

But.

I'm also me.

So that isn't always an option.

'I don't know, Brian, what did Bridget Hora do?' I ask.

Mam tilts her head to one side, and I decide to stir the pot some more. I know she knows, but I'm not sure Brian does. And I hate the idea of a chore wheel. It's so patronising.

'Mam, Brian might like to explain what I'm talking about. If he's not too busy designing and building his chore wheel. They need to have different colours and a part that spins, so they can be quite time-consuming to make, I imagine.'

Brian's face goes pale, which feels somehow angrier than if it went red. He takes a slow, menacing spoon out of his egg. I crunch the last bit of my toast and take a sip of tea, with a polite smile on my face.

If I wanted to, I could really hurt him.

The thought comes unbidden to my brain, but I know the truth of it instantly. All it would take would be the right prayer, the right moment, and OLOB would help me get rid of him. I mean, if she can help me float things, surely she can help me beat the hell out of someone. Bridget would probably give a hand as well, I can't imagine she's too fond, after what he did to her. It's comforting. I don't have to be afraid any more. I can just be petty.

'It was just a suggestion, Catlin,' he says. 'We all want to live in a nice environment, and we have to take responsibility for that.'

'Now?' I say. 'Because Mamó and Madeline have stopped you from making a ghost do it?'

'Does anyone want another egg?' asks Mam, her eyebrows basically turning into one long straight line across her forehead with how much she wants me to shut up.

'It's not as simple as that,' Brian says. 'Sheila.'

Mam sits down beside him. 'I'm sure it isn't, Brian.' She takes his hand. 'Sure haven't we been through worse?'

'Mam!' I say, even if she's pretending, this is a bit much. 'It could be me. I mean, would you like if I was a ghost doing housework?'

'The part of that that would surprise me the most, love, is the housework, to be honest. I picked up seven cups from your room last week. Seven. One cup of tea basically had algae floating in it, it was that old.'

'I can tidy my own room.'

'I'd believe that. However, you obviously choose not to. I think a chore wheel is a great idea, Brian.'

'Thanks, love, I saw it on one of them American parenting websites.' He smiles modestly, as if the ability to do a Google search is the mark of an exceptional stepdad. I roll my eyes.

And then.

I kind of lose the run of myself, and mutter a little prayer to Our Lady of Ballyfrann to give me the strength to be dealing with this kind of nonsense. Not inner strength, but the kind where I can use my mind to make his coffee tip over into his lap. I visualise it, pooling aggressively on his chinos and then kind of tilt it with my mind, and it just happens. It feels as natural as if I had reached my hand over and spilled it on him myself, but somehow better.

Brian stands up, and coffee drips over the floor.

I whisper a small message of thanks to OLOB for having my back.

'At least it wasn't roasting hot,' he says. 'Would you mind cleaning it up, love? I'll have to change my trousers.'

And Mam gets a cloth and just starts wiping as he leaves the room.

'Why are you cleaning up after him?' I ask. 'Don't you remember that he is terrible?'

'Terrible or not, the coffee can't just stay on the floor, Catlin. I might have lost trust in Brian, but that's not to say he's wrong about everything all of the time. And it suits us all to stay on his good side for now. Besides, the chore wheel, or some way of organising who does what, is a good idea.'

'No, it isn't.'

'You only say that because you get away with doing sweet nothing all day long while myself and Brian take the brunt of it.'

'Let him hire a cleaner, so,' I snap. 'I'm no one's servant.'

'Neither am I, but I do an awful lot of cleaning up after you.'

'That's different,' I point out, because it is. 'You're my mam.'

'And you're seventeen years old, and should be more of a help to me.' She looks me up and down like I'm a disappointing employee and actually fuck that.

'How is *this* what we're arguing about after everything Brian has done?' I ask, very taken aback.

'I won't be around forever, and you'll need to be able to take care of your environment,' she says.

I straighten my back, because I am well able to take care of my environment. I just don't always choose to. Also, I hate it when she plays the I-won't-be-around-forever card.

'You're not going to die, Mam,' I say.

'We all die someday,' she says darkly.

'Yeah, except one of us, *me*, actually did die, so I think it's a bit much for you to bandy it around like a bargaining chip,' I say, my voice rising to a point where it's probably aggressive but I don't care.

'I just want you to keep your room tidy and do the wash-up after dinner. That's not too much to ask,' she says, her lip trembling.

'I do both of those things already,' I say, outraged.

'Not consistently.'

I swear to Our Lady, I almost launch my cup of tea at her head. But I do have some self-control so I just yell, 'I can't believe you!' and stomp out of the room like the ground did something bad and needs to be punished. It's not about the jobs, to be clear. Like, I don't care if I have to do stuff. We did in Cork, and I mean, I don't love housework but it's part of life, like homework and period cramps. Back when I used to get them, that is.

As I march up the stairs I can feel a headache building right behind my eye, and the colours starting to dance around the room. It's as if two long fingers are holding my optic nerve and digging into it until they have a really good grip, and then slowly beginning to twist and squeeze until I either vomit or pass out, or both. I can't think straight, it's like there are all these rainbow fireflies and the buzzing gets louder and I feel the fingers clench behind my eye and I go into my bedroom and light my candles and murmur my prayers until I feel her presence come and soothe me.

It will be okay.
You're not alone.
We'll deal with it together.
Let me heal you, Catlin.
Let me help.

And I feel something strange, almost like a door inside my brain opening and welcoming her to me. It sounds creepy when I put it like that, but it feels somewhere between relief and healing. I'm not alone right now. And I am strong.

28

Clary Sage

(boils, backs, afterbirth)

I can hardly keep my eyes open as I stumble back towards the castle. Whatever was in that cave attacked me, and I hope I'm wrong about who it looked like. I feel sick, and the ground is uneven beneath my feet. The texture of it is all wrong. I can't get purchase. I keep going. I have to get back. Because whatever that was, scratching up my face was not its main plan. There was a reason it was in that cave, and I can't piece together exactly what it was, though I keep trying. Does it want to harness the ghosts of murdered girls, like Brian's father? Is it looking to get revenge? Or power, maybe. Mamó hasn't been clear on what exactly the third kind of magic involves, and I need her to tell me because maybe that's what it is, and I hope to God she hasn't gone too far.

My foot crunches, and when I crouch down it's the body

of another crow, this time with a hole in the centre its breast as though someone had scooped out its little heart. There is something unnatural to this, the same sick sort of thing that clung to the air in the cave. I can feel the danger we're all in building around me, leaking through the pores of my skin. It's oily and pungent and I can't shake it off right now, the dread. When I was scared for Catlin, before, it was sharp. But this is dull. It's bigger and slower and maybe very old. I'm not qualified for this. I need Mamó. I see the castle up ahead. Not too long now. My legs feel like they're going to fall off and the burning in my head is loud as well as painful. The hum of insects and the smell of roses. My vision blurs. I press on. What is it Mamó always says to me?

Do your job.

I have to do my job.

The castle looks grimmer every time I approach it. The walls are stained with lichen, thick with growth. The slate on the turrets is pocked with moss, and the windows look dull and opaque. There isn't any sign of human life. It's far too big for three people to live in. It's too big for five, if Mamó and myself were to count as well. And there are the hollowed-out spaces in the earth around it, leading through the mountains, through the caves. It's a building but it's also a lie. A lot of lies all stacked one on top of the other.

I get to the door of Mamó's flat and try it. It's closed to me, which is unusual. I knock and knock again and ring the bell. I could have gone missing or anything last night, I realise. And no one would have noticed. Badb lands on the edge of the roof and caws at me. I gesture to my bloody face, and eventually

I hear movement nearby. The murmur of voices. She's with someone. My face. I crouch behind a bush until they've said goodbye. It's Charley Collins, I hear the wobble of her voice and see the tilt of her head. Mamó watches her leaving and then turns towards me as though there wasn't a bush there at all.

'Come out now, Madeline.' Her voice is hard to read. I stand. She looks at me. 'Let's get you fixed.'

I go into the bathroom and wash the blood off my face, trying to think how much I should tell her. My head is banging. I go back into the room and she barks at me to sit, so I do. I'd love a bit of sympathy. A crumb.

She looks at the wound closely, tracing it with her fingers as though it were Braille and could be read. I tell her what happened, and why I waited all night, and show her the splinters from my pocket. Touching them makes the hairs on the back of my neck stand up. There's something off, there. She takes them from me with a *hmmm* and puts them carefully in a jar with some rowan berries and a bay leaf.

Last time I didn't speak up in time and Catlin got murdered, so I swallow down my instinct and just say it.

'I think that it was Catlin, Mamó.' My voice is low.

She nods. 'It could well have been. The sleepwalking. And the church-going. She prays.'

'She does. She has an altar in her room.'

Mamó's eyes dart to the splinters of wood. She makes a small sound in the back of her throat and does something that could almost be described as a twitch, if there was a universe where Mamó was the kind of person who would ever consider such a thing.

'I'll be back in a while,' she says. 'And we'll continue. I have to do something to sort these.' She takes the jar and leaves, as though she has excused herself to wash her hands or something. I stare at the jars on the wall, trying to work out what would be good to soothe my face, but the room is very bright all of a sudden and everything clouds together and fades to black.

I wake in the same chair some time later with a crick in my neck. I don't know if it was sleep or if I lost consciousness for a while. I find my charger and plug in my phone and put the kettle on for a cup of tea. Rowan berries and bay leaves were what Mamó put in with the splinters, so maybe they might help the wound a bit. Garlic and dandelion as well. And milk and bread. I lay them out and begin carefully making a poultice. She isn't back, but it's early in the day still. I wish I knew how long she'd be gone. I have so many questions. We have a chunk of spine in the house, for goodness sake – what is so bad about some chips of wood?

The door clicks open. Mamó has returned.

'Right,' she says, dusting off her legs and sitting down. 'We need to talk about your sister and what she's done and what we'll need to do.'

'There was a crow as well,' I say, remembering. 'Its heart was gone.'

'That's not great,' she says. 'How is your wound?'

'I slept for a bit, I think,' I say. 'Or passed out. Probably slept. It hurts. But it's not that deep.'

'It doesn't have to be,' she says, walking over to the counter and nodding at the things I have started. 'These will do. I'll make you something for it. How long has your sister been . . . religious?'

'She's always gone to church and stuff. And liked collecting statues, Mass cards, medals, that kind of thing.'

'Go on.'

'When we got to Ballyfrann, she built an altar to the Virgin Mary in her room. And after everything with Lon, I know she spends a lot of time praying in the church as well. Talking to Father Byrne.'

'And where exactly in the church does she pray?'

I rack my brains. It's hard to think. I never go in there with her, not really. There was a day when we were both in town when I went in though. I was meeting Oona and she was meeting Lon. And the smell of incense was overwhelming. She knelt in front of . . .

'The wooden one,' I say. 'Our Lady of Ballyfrann.'

Mamó nods slowly. 'I thought as much,' she says. 'Do you remember, Madeline, when we spoke of the different kinds of magic?'

I nod. 'Yes.'

'Well, the second one is the sort we encountered with that fox last year.'

My mind flashes to a small bright corpse in middle of a crossroads in the forest. A wild thing ripped apart to make a wish. It felt wrong too, much like the splinters. And Mamó sorted it, or tried to anyway. That was the night it started to feel real to me, and dangerous.

'The Ask, you called it.'

'Yes . . . When Catlin was a child . . . did she always say her prayers before bed?'

I nod. 'She did. She decided to at one point when we were little, and kept going. She was having nightmares, about fire. About Dad. And when she prayed, they stopped.'

'And all along – would you say things came easier to her? Things she desired?' Mamó's voice is hard to read.

'I would have said yes, up until the thing with Lon?'

'That was different.' Mamó keeps grinding plants. 'That was a hard situation. For both of you. But this might be harder.'

'Harder how?'

'There's a point where you can bring a person back. Beyond it, all you can do is put an end to whatever is happening. Our next step is to find out what our course of action is.'

My heart is in my throat. I can't listen to this.

'We don't know for sure though.'

She comes over with a steaming poultice of bread and muck. It smells right. It smells like it will help.

'We don't. But I don't want you to be taken by surprise. This sort of magic, the second kind, people might not even know they're doing it. It just becomes part of the fabric of their lives, of who they are. And then there's more leeway for something to go wrong. Or right, depending on whose point of view you're looking at it from.'

I look at her. She meets my gaze with those bright grey eyes.

'I brought your sister back once, Maddy. And I promise that I will do my best to help her survive this if she can.'

'If she can,' I repeat, my heart filling with something between frustration and despair.

The poultice is making my head muggy, I feel like something is being drawn out of me, not like an infection but like a sort of headache, the kind I used to get when I was healing, with the coloured lights. Like something is pulling them out of my brain. Is switching them off. One by one, click, click.

Mamó guides me to my bedroom and pulls the blanket over me. I feel as if my body and my brain aren't holding hands any more. The sun spills between the curtains but then it fades away and all is darkness I can't see a thing my head is heavy.

I need to think though need to help Catlin I can't let her I can't let them I can't but –

'Go to sleep, child,' she says, not unkindly.

And in spite of everything, I do.

29

Claw Sheaths

(protection, disarmament)

I wake from a dream to a world that is a little bit like one of my dreams. The colours seem intense but also blurry, as though I'm zooming in and out through a slightly smudged lens. I rub my eyes, wondering if it's one of my migraines, but it doesn't hurt. And everything smells like roses. It's her.

Bridget isn't here this time. Her face has been fading piece by piece into the wood, until it's just Our Lady. Watching me. Minding me. When I dream of Lon now, I feel safer, less trapped. Like I could flex my hand and push him away as though he were Brian's coffee. I feel like OLOB has my back.

The daylight filtering through the window is so bright, and I can see all the colours it's made of. The rainbow spectrum of it. I could stare and stare at it all day. But that's not what she wants. I need to . . . something. Something I can't put my finger on.

The church, I think.

If I could see her, touch her, maybe then it would click into place. I quickly dress and put on my darkest sunglasses, the light is so beautiful I can see myself walking into traffic, getting lost . . . It's weird to not know what to focus on.

The church is quite a distance, but the road seems somehow shorter today, or maybe she is guiding me. I go through the dark wooden doors and kneel before her. Everything falls into place as my vision shifts just a little.

There you are.

I smile at her. She's beautiful.

I start to murmur prayers, but they seem to come out in a different language. Something ancient living in my throat. Guttural and beautiful. Worthy of her. I am so absorbed that I don't hear Father Byrne approach. Until he clears his throat and says my name.

'Catlin.'

His wrinkles look really dark today, almost drawn on. Like he's not exactly real. I close my eyes and open them again. That's better. I need to focus. He'll think I'm drunk or something.

'Yes, Father?'

'Praying to Our Lady of Ballyfrann again?'

I smile and shrug.

'Will you come and sit with me a while?' His voice is low.

I look at her, but there's no sense of what the right thing is. Probably less hassle to just go with him, have a chat. Get back to praying after. Work out what she wants, and then do that. I nod, stand up. He sits in one of the pews and crosses one leg over the other, making a sort of triangle in the air.

187

We both stare at the altar, each waiting for the other one to start.

'I've been meaning to have a word with you, Catlin,' he says. 'About Our Lady of Ballyfrann. And your, eh, devotion to her.'

I keep my eyes fixed on the altar. The dark wood. The unlit candles. The embroidered cloths. I have a feeling in the pit of my stomach. Like something's going to happen here, and soon.

He continues.

'The thing is. She's not . . . the Virgin Mary. Not exactly.'

I tilt my head. 'What do you mean by that?'

'Well, you know the story, obviously. Of how she was pulled out of the bog and performed miracles.'

'She healed people,' I say, touching one hand to the side of my face. Where my scars once were.

'Well, there's no real way of knowing who she is or where she came from. The town just assumed. And miracles . . . well . . . they weren't all that happened once she was unearthed, Catlin.'

I shift uncomfortably against the wood.

'What else?' I ask. I don't really care what the answer is. I can see what he is trying to do.

'There were . . . deaths, child,' he says.

'Linked to her?' I asked.

'No. Not strictly, but . . .'

I cut him off. 'There are always deaths in Ballyfrann. It's part of life here. Everywhere, in fact, but more so here. And it's hard, but that's not down to Our Lady, Father. She *heals*. She healed my face.'

I gesture to it, and the reality of her care for me dawns across his face.

'Oh, child,' he says. 'You have been touched by something very old. And old things can be dangerous. Old ways, old Gods. And there is power that we shouldn't have access to, as humans.'

'Magic power?' I ask. It seems strange to speak of everyday magic in a church, where there's a kind of a belief in a different kind of magic, the kind that turns wine into old blood, that assumes that somebody can rise from the dead, turn some food into *loads* of food. That prayer can heal a sickness, staunch a wound. But the magic they talk about from the altar is old, it's not the kind that hums through me, from her. That's new and vibrant. It doesn't want to teach me a lesson, or make me a better person. All it wants is to set me free from the things within me that stop me feeling pleased or good, or whole. And that's worth more than wine and blood to me.

'Yes,' he tells me. 'Some can wield it well, more or less. Mamó, for example, uses her talent to help people. But it wouldn't be for me.'

I look at him. Someone needed to say it. 'You're a priest. That's a kind of power. Having the might of the Church behind you or whatever . . .'

'If I had the might of the Church behind me, Catlin Hayes, I wouldn't be in Ballyfrann,' he says and his voice is . . . not bitter, but tinged with regret.

'Do you hate it here?' I ask.

'I did at first. When I was young, I was full of fire and belief. I thought that the right thing to do and the thing that should

189

be done were one and the same. And it didn't stand to me. I needed to learn humility, they said. But what I learned was more complicated.'

'What did you do?' I ask.

'I was placed in a school where children were in danger from my superior.' He swallowed. 'One child in particular – a girl named Maisy – I thought that if I spoke up, I could help her at least. But what happened instead was that I was shuffled around until I came here. The girl was left where she was, and I heard she died a few years after that. He ended up a bishop.'

'At least you spoke up,' I said. 'That counts for something.'

'Not for Maisy. I stuck my neck out once, Catlin Hayes. Once. It made no difference. And when I saw how much it cost to speak, I wasn't long shutting up.' He was angry at himself, even all these years later.

'I thought the Church would offer me power, protection. A voice that could be heard. But that was only true when I did what I was told. When something offers power, child, it asks for something in return, sometimes too much. I think it's time I took down that old statue, maybe sent it off to get cleaned up a bit. There are other Marys you can pray to.'

His voice is not unkind, but his words are hurting. Can he not see, have I not shown him, that I need her, and she needs me back? We have a bond. The kind that it would hurt my heart to break. My breath quickens in my throat at the thought of losing her, and I can smell the scent of roses rising in the air. She needs help. She needs me to help her. He will hurt her to try to protect me.

'You can't do that,' I say. 'She's mine. I'm hers.'

'I thought you might say that.' His face is stern. 'And that's exactly why she has to go. It isn't safe to put that much of you into a god you do not really know.'

'I know her,' I protest.

'But who is she, Catlin Hayes?'

I smile. 'The Virgin Mary.'

He shakes his head a little sadly. 'Yes and no, child.'

'She speaks to me, Father,' I say, as if that would in any way convince him that everything was fine.

His voice when he responds is low, and deadly serious. 'This is worse than I thought.'

His lips began to move. Which is a game that two can play at. I began to murmur the rosary to her, and ask for her help and strength. For her to stay with me through this, to not abandon me in my hour of need. She answers me.

You need to rescue me.

To take me with you.

I walk towards the statue and grab it from its nook. The candles around her extinguish as I approach, to make my path to her clearer, safer. How can he doubt her kindness when it's so obvious she wants to keep me safe?

I hear his footsteps behind me and feel his hand on my wrist, yanking me back as though I were a dog on a leash and not her servant. How dare he do this to us? I feel my face get warm, my hands balling into fists.

And then a surge.

Her power rushes through me.

Just because his God let him down didn't mean mine would

ever do that to me, I remember thinking, and then I wasn't thinking much at all. Only acting on instinct. I'm not sure whose instinct it was exactly though. I mean, I've never been the kind to just punch someone in the face out of the blue. But I don't like being told what to do or grabbed, which is why she gave me the strength to act, I suppose. Her hands guiding mine. Her voice in the corner of my brain advising me. I hit him and I kept on hitting him, though after the first one he began blocking me with his hands and trying to restrain me. I knew, if I didn't get to take her with me, that she would be put somewhere I couldn't find her. I need to be able to access her. I need to know she's safe.

I'm letting her guide my steps, listening to her direct me. The smell of roses is strong and I can feel a warm breeze against my skin. I have pleased her. She has given me so much over the past while, healed my skin and made me feel like I have some sort of control over my destiny. And, yes, there's the odd bit of sleepwalking, or finding blood and feathers in random places but it's worth it, for the sense of being free from what happened before. And all she wants is for me to love her and be loyal to her. Such a small thing.

I reach the forest, away from any prying eyes, and I feel relief wash over me, and faith. I know we're going home to the castle, and where I have to put her. I wish my feet could move quicker, and all of a sudden I'm lifted off the ground and swept along. It's like the feeling when you're a kid and someone picks you up and swings you around until you're laughing so much you can hardly breathe. That kind of wild, hilarious freedom. This shouldn't be happening, but look, it is! She places me on the ground and I breathe deep and ask for her to lift me up again.

She does.

I'm flying.

30

Orange Peel

(relieves anxiety, draws joy)

When I wake up, it feels like I am in another dream, where Mamó is a burnt-out cop on the edge. She gestures at me to pick up my satchel and follow her into the castle, padding up the stairs as quietly as Button stalking a bird. We don't speak. I suppose there are no explanations necessary really. Not that Mamó ever thinks there are.

When we get to Catlin's room, she kind of launches herself at it and rummages through everything piece by piece. It feels a violation, rooting through my sister's sock drawer looking for . . . I don't even know what. The altar holds Mamó's interest most of all. Mine too. Something about it feels off. Usually I feel the same about it as I would about the bed, or the wardrobe or the piles of clothes that Catlin always has scattered on the floor. But not today. There's something . . .

One of the candles looks like it is smeared with rose petals and blood. Which is disturbing, and also kind of . . . perfect because it is Catlin, and even when she's being a creepy dose she's got a flair for making things look good. Mamó tells me to 'take some pictures on the phone', and I do. We check under the bed and look at the sheets as well, which are stained with mud and dirt. There is a layer of dust building over almost everything. Except the altar, which is obviously well tended to. Somehow it has become the most important thing in the room, I think, and I don't like it.

Mamó takes some of the candles and feathers and places them in brown paper bags in her big bag, and she looks at the edges of the window and on the sill. She checks in every corner, and knocks on the floorboards in case any are hollow. We find nothing, and we don't take that much, but I have a clear sense that Catlin will absolutely know someone was in her room, and she'll be angry. Because as I look at the altar, I feel like we are trespassing. Encroaching on something powerful and private and not for us.

Mam appears at the door, a bit annoyed that we are 'poking around without permission'. Mamó looks ready to throttle her, but in fairness we are fully sneaking around and have taken some stuff. I would be annoyed too. I decide guilt is the way to go, to avoid awkward questions, and give her big wide eyes and ask, 'Is this not my home any more?' And she must feel bad because she offers us tea, which is good, though we don't take it. Apparently there isn't time. When we get back to the flat, Mamó announces, 'It's as I thought,' grimly, then carries on as though that statement needs no further clarification. She rummages around the shelves, yanking jar after jar down and throwing a pinch of this or that into her mortar and grinding it with a pestle as though she has a personal grudge against them.

'What did you think?' I feel sick, worried at what this could mean for Catlin.

'Your sister, or that creature she's praying to, is what scratched your face. We might not be too late though,' she says, as I kind of follow her around, feeling useless.

'What will we have to do?' I ask. 'To help her.'

'That depends on how far gone she is. And if she'll accept the help.'

'We brought her back before,' I say, trying to be hopeful.

'She wasn't given much of a choice in that, Madeline,' Mamó says, and her voice is grim. 'And if she's able to, she might cling to this. Magic, powerful magic, can be addictive.'

'Do you think she's a witch?' I ask.

'I think she's being used by something that is up to something, but there's a power that can come with that.' Great, another super-vague Mamó response, delightful, I feel so confident about what our next steps are.

She looks me up and down. 'Take that face off you. We're heading to the church. Let's go.'

I nod, and follow.

'Oh, and Madeline?'

'Yes?'

'Might as well take the shovel with you, while you're at it.'

Ugh.

31

Blood

(protection, healing, hurting, strength of will)

I need to get something for her. Something he's been using. I'm not sure who *he* is exactly. She won't say. It's probably Father Byrne, or maybe Brian, if it is in the castle. But it doesn't really matter, does it, because she says that when I get it, it will make her stronger, and me stronger too. I'm still giddy from the flying, to be honest. This is moving so quickly, and it's surreal. Of course it's surreal. Like, the Virgin Mary, or whatever she is, doesn't exactly appear and grant magical favours to all the girls. Just me. I have a missed call from Eddie Collins, and I vaguely remember we had plans to go for tea or a walk or something after I left the church. I stop to message him back and I can feel her frustration nudging at me. She needs to go home, I need to take her home, why am I slowing down, do I not love her?

'Of course I love you,' I say. 'Just give me a second.'

I message Eddie to apologise and say we'll catch up soon. She doesn't sigh, but I can feel her impatience. I don't want to displease her, or let her down. But it's important too, to have other people. I like kissing Eddie. It's distracting, and he smells nice, not a bit like dog, which you would kind of expect. Maybe that's insensitive of me. Also, the knowledge that I could probably beat him to a pulp if it came to that will probably actually really help if he does anything that reminds me of Lon again. I mean, not that I would hurt him. Of course I wouldn't. But he can't hurt me. Nobody is ever going to make me feel small and weak and useless ever again. To eat and eat at me until there's nothing left and keep on eating.

Of course they won't, she tells me.

We won't let them.

32

Catnip

(courage and protection during sleep)

Why is life like this? I ask myself. Why do I always end up traipsing after Mamó holding shovels? And why can't there be one member of my family who isn't complicated?

We get into the car and Mamó bombs it into town. We're lucky there's no Garda station in Ballyfrann because the way she drives is one pedestrian away from a murder. She pulls into a loading bay, slams the door and stalks towards the church. I sigh, and follow her.

With the shovel.

Because, of course, the shovel.

If I were still in school. I would surely be bringing the shovel to my debs. I would wear grey, and the shovel would go naked, or maybe wear a jaunty little tiara. We try the church door, but it's locked.

Mamó knocks, pointedly.

Once.

We hear a shuffling and the wide oak door cracks open.

''Tis yourself, Mamó!' exclaims Father Byrne warmly.

'Seán,' Mamó says neutrally.

'I assume you're here about the other one,' he says, gesturing to me. And making me hate him a little. She has a name, Seán. His eye is bruised, and he walks with a stiffness in one leg.

Neither of us says anything, because we don't need to.

He continues. 'She was here earlier.' He gestures to his face, and to the blank space where Our Lady of Ballyfrann used to be.

'That's not ideal,' Mamó says.

'No.' He shakes his head. 'I could probably have stopped her, but I was hesitant to use force. As was she, to a certain extent.'

'Catlin did this to you?' I am shocked. I mean, I kind of wanted to slap him when he made that comment, but a metaphorical slap, not actually beating the pulp out of him. He must be eighty, like.

'She did,' he said. 'But I'm not sure she was in the driver's seat, so to speak.'

'She has her, does she?' Mamó asks, her eyes on the space the statue used to be. The gap it left.

'I'm afraid so.' His face is gaunt, determined. He really is very tall. He looks like a priest who'd throw a teenage girl in the door of a Magdalene laundry in a film. Or, you know, real life. He's old enough. I narrow my eyes. The Catholic Church is not great about lesbians. Or women in general.

Mamó glares at me like she can read my mind, and jerks her head at him. 'Tell him what you know.'

Father Byrne holds up a hand, in the manner of someone used to giving orders. 'First, let's repair to the sacristy. Less of a chance of being overheard.'

I roll my eyes at Mamó, who crooks her mouth a very small amount. We traipse up, over the altar and into the bright room lined with bookshelves and cupboards full of vestments and assorted items of priest-wear.

We sit on uncomfortable chairs, and I catch Father Byrne up about sleepwalking, altars, dead birds, and possible face scratching. He listens to everything I have to say. Every now and then he interjects with a question about Catlin's demeanour, or the exact way the altar was laid out. I answer as best I can, though I don't know everything, and there's something grim about the way the two of them are acting. I don't want them to hurt Catlin, and I don't like the thought of her being . . . whatever this is.

'What does this all mean though, Father?' I ask him.

'I would hazard a guess, Madeline, that young Catlin has been dabbling in prayer magic without realising it. Prayer is a powerful and beautiful thing, but if misdirected it can be a tool to contact other realms. And the things that live within those realms are what we would call preternatural in nature.'

Mamó looks at me. She doesn't have to say it. We both know *we* would not use words like that. It's kind of nice, this slightly ganging up on a priest. I wonder if that's why Catlin beat him up. Father Byrne ignores us and continues.

'I began to suspect Catlin might be in trouble one of the last times she visited the church. She was increasingly focused on Our Lady of Ballyfrann, who may not even be a representation of Our Lady, as I suspect the carving pre-dates Christianity. She found great comfort in prayer, but at some point her praying began to look less like meditation and more like conversation. Her head would move as though she were listening to another person, and the smell of roses in the chapel became more pronounced when she was in there.'

He sighs and leans towards us, his two hands on his knees.

'I should have intervened sooner, but I have developed a fondness for the girl, and I hoped that I was being overly suspicious.'

'Hmmph,' Mamó says, and I know what she's thinking. You can never be overly suspicious. It is one of the tenets of her grumpy, grumpy life.

'I decided to confront her with the possibility of the statue's removal, and as you can see, her response was to beat the tar out of me and take it with her.'

He stands up and goes into the corner of the sacristy, starts feeling the floorboards. A sinking feeling grows in my stomach. What's under there? Is she going to send me back to the door to get the shovel? I mean, not that a shovel matters in the grand scheme of things when someone is basically telling you your sister is in thrall to something very old and very bad. Again.

He pulls on a part of the floorboards and a ton of them rise up at once like the lid of a treasure chest full of old leatherbound books, bottles of liquid, vestments sewn with ancient-looking glyphs, and, more worryingly, weapons – knives, wooden swords like what Brian used on Lon, some ropes, more knives, and an actual fucking crossbow.

'This feels surreal,' I say.

'Reality isn't a fixed state in Ballyfrann.' Father Byrne's voice is low. 'I've had to pick up a few tricks over the years to keep the parishioners safe.'

'And how are weapons going to keep my sister safe?' I ask, gesturing to a quiver of arrows with tips that look like barbed wire. 'These don't look very Christian to me, Father.'

'I'm hoping to use the books first,' he tells me, 'and then decide what else from my arsenal is necessary.'

I turn to Mamó.

'Is this a normal thing? Do you also have an . . . arsenal?'

Mamó snorts. 'I do in my eye. No offence, Seán.'

'None taken.' He plonks a big old book down on the table and begins to flick through it. 'These are some of the notes from the local parish priest before I came here, around the time Our Lady of Ballyfrann was recovered from the bog. There might be something here indicating where her next port of call is, or what sort of impact she might have on your sister, what kind of tributes she enjoys, that kind of thing . . .'

'Tributes?' I ask.

'Yes, these things, the bad ones, usually enjoy a tribute or two. Based on the crows, I'm assuming she enjoys sacrifices, and a typical one might be the taking or the giving of a life in her honour.'

My mouth is open. I can't believe this is really happening. He has to be, like, crazy, doesn't he? Why is Mamó putting up with this?

'Ah yes, here it is!' he exclaims. 'The parish records from when Our Lady of Ballyfrann was found, and the miracles she performed.'

Mamó rises. 'Thank you, Seán,' she says, going over to the book and tearing out about ten pages. 'We'll take it from here.'

'But –' He's irked. Seán was on a roll. Priests hate being interrupted. He swallows. 'I will be needing those pages back.'

'I'm sure you will,' says Mamó. 'And we'll be calling on you if we need –' she gestures to his floor full of weapons – 'any . . . help. Maddy, come. We need to find your sister.'

'Goodbye, Mamó. Godspeed,' he says, but she's already gone. There's work to do. I rise and follow her out of the sacristy, grabbing my shovel as we sweep through the church door, back over the streets to the little red car. She doesn't wear a cloak, Mamó, but she's giving off some extremely cloak energy. She throws the pages in my lap, revs the engine and we begin to floor our way back home.

I start to read.

33

Ink and Paper

(clarity, recall)

The men pulled it out of the bog yesterday. Tim Collins found it, came back 'roaring to us' according to the testimony of them that were there. 'It looked like nothing at first until we [they] cut down deep.' Tim Collins was already blessing himself and falling to his knees before they had her out, Paud Collins says. Apparently Tim's withered hand healed as soon as he put it against the figure. It was at this point that they sought my assistance.

I inspected the figure, but Tim Collins was reluctant to let me take it to the church for further scrutiny. Though I have offered it a home in the chapel, it will remain in his cottage for the moment, as I hesitate to incur the wrath of any member of the Collins family. The figure itself is of a moderate size – perhaps two, two and a half feet tall – almost entirely pale in colour and made of a substance not unlike driftwood. Alternately warm and cold to the touch, it is curved in form, and unmistakably female. Due to this, and the nature of the possible 'miracle', I might assume that it is a religious figure, most likely a representation of Our Lady. Perhaps unsurprisingly, the women of the village seem to have a particular interest in it. Their simple devotion moves me, as it would Our Lady, were she here to see it. And perhaps, I think increasingly, she is.

*

Margaret O'Brien, who seems to make a hobby of thwarting honest people, has been sniffing around the figure. The woman cornered me on my way home from the inspection of the figure with many impertinent questions. Something needs to be done about that creature, and once this business is resolved, I shall make it my highest priority.

*

The figure appeared to me in a dream last night and instructed me to construct a place of prominence within the chapel for her. When I awoke, my room smelled like roses and oil of chrism, and I felt a lightness in my heart and a renewed sense of purpose in my vocation. It is the fondest dream of any servant of Our Lord to be visited in such a way, and I only hope that this humble servant is deserving of such an honour, and up to the task that She herself has set me. Holy Mary conceived without sin, pray for us who have recourse to thee.

*

She is now in place, where she will remain for the foreseeable future. I have made contact with the Bishop, informing him of the incidents that have taken place to date, though I may have to go further still, as he has no great liking for me – the Church has a long memory.

*

She appeared to me in my dreams once more, and asked that candles be lit to her. She told me three secrets but they remain a mystery to my waking self. When I awoke, there were three long grey feathers on my eiderdown, as though from the wings of an angel.

*

The parishioners continue to visit, though several weeks have passed since Our Lady of Ballyfrann took her rightful place in the chapel. It is heartening to see their renewed faith.

*

Joan Delacroix spent three hours praying to Our Lady of Ballyfrann today, and was clearly much moved after the experience. Joan is a quiet sort, she grew up in Ballyfrann, and left, only to return having married the Frenchman, Jean, and him being so often away on business. Her time abroad has given her foreign ways, and they set her apart a little from the other women. But I cannot fault her devotion, or the bread which she so kindly brought as a gift.

*

Our Lady appeared in my dreams again, and took me up the hills behind the O'Brien woman's house and through a tunnel that led into the depths of the mountain. There I saw a cave, a natural and beautiful grotto. Wonders would be wrought there in her name she told me and I believed her, but when I awoke my stomach was very unsettled for several hours and my head plagued with worries I cannot name.

*

Another miracle has occurred. Joan Delacroix is with child. Her husband being away so often, the babe will surely prove a comfort to her. What a blessed occurrence. The village women have become more fond of Joan and have welcomed her more thoroughly into the fold, swayed as they are by this evidence of Our Lady's favour. Yet still, I will confess, my brain seeks to remember the three mysteries which were revealed to me and veiled again . . .

*

I awoke with dirty feet this morning. The taste of flesh on my tongue and the smell of roses on my breath.

What is happening?

I think of the martyrs and all they endured for Mother Church and try my best to be strong and do as she asks of me, though it be difficult to comprehend. God's mysteries are not for man to solve. That woman was in the chapel again today, and I caught her trying to chip off a small portion of Our Lady of Ballyfrann with a class of big flat knife. Of course I sent her packing. Upon examination of the figure, I found berries and various pieces of plant tucked beneath her feet, which can only be the work of that wretch. She is in desperate need of re-education, for if she carries on as she is, her soul will surely be damned. I shall pray on it.

I was so hungry.

*

I have climbed today into the tunnels from my dreams and found them there, exactly as she showed me. My candle flickered, but my faith remained strong and stalwart, and lo, a light appeared to guide my way. Truly this town is a place of miracles.

*

Work on the caverns is being completed by Seamus O'Brien with a team of stout Collins men to help him. Joan Delacroix was in

208

some distress today, as she encountered Margaret O'Brien, who apparently threatened the life of her unborn child in some way. She was much aggrieved. That cursed woman has forced my hand and I must now denounce her from the pulpit, to shield my parishioners from her corrosive influence.

*

Blood in my mouth and one of my teeth missing. In its place a thorn.

*

No word from the Bishop. I shall write again, though part of me has half a mind to shield Our Lady of Ballyfrann from the outside world and its tawdriness and grasping. Here she can be safe. She can be mine, and the people of the town's. Though they do not seem to be heeding my warnings about Margaret O'Brien in the slightest. I observed her yesterday leaving the shop with a basketful of produce I am sure she didn't pay for. Would that people could put their faith in God and only God.

*

Sad tidings today. Joan Delacroix is dead, discovered on the mountainside, surrounded by feathers and rose petals. Her babe seemingly was born, but is now nowhere to be found. I fear the worst and have alerted the authorities. Margaret O'Brien is responsible for this and she should hang.

*

The Guards came to remove the woman, Glory be to God. I spent the day in the caverns in quiet contemplation, praying that Our Lady will bring the babe home safe and sound. I prayed until my throat ached and my heart was full. Until I heard a mewl, like that of a kitten, faint at first, and husky. It led me up and out of the tunnels and into the cottage where that woman used to

209

reside. In there I found a babe, a boy, with a ring of blood around its little mouth.

*

The foundling is in the hands of Lorna Collins and some of the other local wives. Jean Delacroix seems unwilling to acknowledge it as his son. The babe is sickly and prone to screaming until it is fed, and even after.

*

Lorna Collins's little one, Eileen, was found dead today beside the Delacroix babe. They have given the babe to me, to be placed with the nuns. They blame him for the death, and I can see again the paganism of this place. When the surface is scratched, the veneer of civilisation can be very thin. Mrs. Gogan, my housekeeper, is a treasure, and has taken to minding the babe with a woman's natural instinct. It cries constantly, however, and seems to grow more sickly when fed milk, which it regurgitates with great force. I will pray on this.

*

That woman came today, having apparently been released by the Guards, and tried to remove the babe from the parochial house. She arrived when I was saying Mass and Mrs. Gogan was there alone. It is no small credit to Mrs. Gogan that she held firm until I arrived back. The creature asked to speak privately with me, which I refused, and she informed me that the child was not of this world and must be handed over to her immediately, or 'people will die'. I, not surprisingly, took umbrage at her rural superstition and shrewish tone, and she became demonstrably irate, lambasting me with such disrespectful phrases as 'foolish, foolish man'. I drew myself to my full height and reminded her

210

of my station in the community and as a servant of the Church. Unfortunately, this prompted her to draw herself up to her full un-feminine height and stare at me as fixedly as a cat, until I left the room and locked the door behind me.

*

I will not hesitate to alert the authorities again if she targets that poor little boy. Laurent, they called him, after the martyr St. Laurence. I must protect him. Suffer the little children.

*

Laurent is wasting away. He is growing pale and full of vexation. I have been praying to Our Lady to help me understand what he needs to thrive. Though of woman born, I think of him as belonging to Our Lady. Her little son. Christ will come again.

*

I went down into the caverns and I brought her with me. When in place, she turned her head to me, and though she has no eyes I felt her gaze. This place is to be made secret again, to protect the little fellow. I must conceal him here, and do my best to help him thrive and grow.

She told me what it needs.

God Help Us All.

34

Knots

(binding, strength and focus)

They are coming. They will try to stop me. I feel the panic of it in my blood, and try to damp it down. I need to be thinking clearly. To do my best to keep it together. To keep everything hidden for a while. Until I know the best way to proceed. The things she needs from me. I think of Father Byrne's face and feel sick. The further I move away from what happened, the worse it seems. At the time, it was all adrenaline, and it felt necessary.

He has been good to me.

He looked so old.

I can't think about that now.

I run my hands over my hair, it shines. I head inside. The ceiling is high, so high you'd think there would be cobwebs but there aren't. I can't let everything inside today. I need to block it out. I need to pray. I need to open up a door to her. To see what she wants. She has to be my priority, tucked into a nook behind my wardrobe to protect her from their prying eyes. My boots are heavy on the floor and it feels like such a waste of time to walk when flying is so effortless. But we need to be careful. Not forever, just for a little while longer. Just until . . . but I am not sure what comes after that. I know there's something. Wish I could remember. Know exactly.

How I can help and what that help will cost me.

Brian is in the kitchen when I come in, drinking another one of his smoothies. His long fingers wrap around the weird plastic thing with the measuring lines he drinks them from, and for some reason it angers me, the sight of it. I try to swallow it down. To smile.

'Hello, Catlin,' he says. 'How are you getting on?'

'What's in the smoothie, Brian?' I ask, my voice sharp. It's humming at me, the scent, making my lungs itch. Why is it so wrong? Why is my head reeling? I find myself at the cutlery drawer, my hands curling around a sharp steak knife. Not my hands. Hers. I put it down and slam the door again. I can't. I can't.

Brian doesn't seem to notice.

'Protein powder, spirulina, blueberries, banana, Greek yoghurt, apple juice and cranberry juice,' he says proudly. 'Very healthy.'

He is lying, I think.

Why does he always lie?

I need to stop him.

'Sounds it,' I say, trying to slow the blood that's flowing to

213

my head. I feel like I am going to explode. Beside the collarbone there is an artery. I don't know how I know that but I know. My stomach feels sick. What is happening to me? Why are there thoughts in my head that aren't my thoughts? Holy Mother, help me, I think. Guide me.

I think. I close my eyes and feel the sweat beading on my back.

'I can make you one if you'd like?' His voice is high, and there's a sort of rhythm to it, an up-and-downiness. It's disconcerting, like the floor is moving underneath my feet. The thought of one of his smoothies makes bile rise up onto my tongue and I spit yellow acid into the sink.

'No, thank you, Brian,' I say.

'Are you all right, love?' he asks.

My nails dig hard into the palm of my hand and I can't smell roses, only my own breath like curdled milk.

'I think I need to go to bed,' I say, and feel my feet give from underneath me. I hear my stepfather's voice repeating my name, as though calling me would help, as though I'd answer him after all the things I've done. The purple liquid oozing down his throat. A bricked-up wall. My hands.

When I wake, I am in my bedroom, the four posts of the bed casting shadows across the bedspread. Squinting at them, I can see the carvings, the faces, fruits and snakes, wrapping around. I reach a hand to the closest one. It's roasting to the touch. Like fire, like flame. I cough again, and feel more bile coming. I run to the en suite, barely make it to the sink. It's bright yellow again, and shiny-oily. Something else in it when

I look close. I reach my finger inside the viscous goo and ease it out. It pierces at my skin, and blood beads on my fingertip.

A thorn.

Something's definitely going wrong.

I close my eyes and try to search for Bridget Hora's face. It's blurred into woodgrain now, I cannot picture it. I hold the thorn in front of my face and look at it. It's small and stumpy. Thorns stop animals from eating plants. Where were they when I needed them? I wonder. My stomach is unsettled and I can still smell Brian's smoothie – the fruit, and something buried underneath.

I sit on the centre of my bed, and face away from the altar. Bridget Hora, I think, Bridget Hora. Were you angry afterwards, or scared? What made you hang around when others didn't? Was it only the spell, or something else as well? I feel a flicker pulse of something, an almost imperceptible twitch. She's still here somewhere, but she isn't close. I think Our Lady was safer, for me at least, when she was tempered with the ghost of Bridget. Today scared me. I breathe in and out and try to clear my mind of everything. To focus on the details that matter. It's hard. It's like I'm seeing them through layers of mist thick with the scent of roses.

I hear a click, a hiss, and turn around.

The candles in the altar are all blazing, flames handspan-high, wax dripping down in tortured-looking shapes, like burning women.

Would you be powerless again, my child? she asks me, and it feels a little weighted, like a threat. I feel the pucker of my skin, and know she's making my scars bloom bright again.

All she's given she can take away. I've never felt so weak. Not even when he had me on my back. Not even then. That wasn't my choice. And she needs me to choose her. To decide to want this. Her gifts that are not gifts, but something close to bargains, maybe bills.

The three secrets she told me in the dream.

I strain my brain.

I wish I could remember what they were. The candles down to nothing now, the flames still dancing burning. It would be an awful way to go. When I was young, I'd dream of flames licking up walls, of heat on skin that couldn't move away. Of crisping, roasting. Of screams lost in the gasp of black-smoke lungs, the crack of flame. Mam taught me to pray, to counteract that. To press my hands together, say the words. People get surprised that I'm religious. It doesn't seem to fit with who I am. But it does, you see. It fits with who everyone is. We all want things. And when we get them, we find more to want.

And I need more. I need to solve this. To find a way to harness it. I can't give up this power, not now. Not when there's so much for me to learn. An empty grave, the clay shot through with worms, the spade cutting them in two sometimes. If you took your time and looked closely, you might save a few, but not them all. You can't keep everyone happy or safe. At the end of the day, you only have yourself. And other people can't help me with this. I have to choose. But is there a choice, really, in the end? Weakness or strength? Maddy didn't get to choose at all, of course. Her hand was forced by me, and now we're separate. We've cracked in two. I miss her. And maybe there's a way that I could help. If I were strong enough, bold enough.

The first day we went into playschool together, she hid behind me, and I looked back, and I remember thinking, There isn't space for both of us to be shy. One of us has to be brave. So I found the girl with the nicest hairslides and stomped us up to her and said hello. And when lunchtime came, I made sure I demanded pasta with no sauce for her, so she could eat. And I got used to being the brave one, the cool one, the strong one. But it all started there, with fear and love.

Fear and love. Why do they always journey hand in hand?

I go before my altar, flames hovering over candlesticks. And I kneel. They shrink a little, and I hear her voice, not from where she is hidden, but from everywhere, inside and outside me.

Good girl.

Now listen, there are things we have to do.

35

Bay

(prophetic visions, cold griefs)

'"God Help Us All",' I say. 'That's not hugely positive.'

'He wasn't a very positive man,' Mamó tells me, her eyes steel-blue in the rear-view mirror.

'I can't believe he had you arrested.'

'He had no such thing. Sure didn't I deliver half the guards that were there at the time? I had a cup of tea at the station, and then I headed home.' Her voice is almost amused at the cheek of him.

'He would have been furious. If he had known,' I say.

''Tis easy to infuriate a priest,' she tells me. I hold back on pointing out that it's easy for Mamó to infuriate anyone, probably. I can see how priests would be particularly susceptible to her unique brand of annoyance though.

'And probably even easier back then,' I say. 'What do you think of Father Byrne?'

She pauses. I suppose she's wondering how much to say to me. 'He's not the worst and we might need him later.'

'Not now?' I say.

'Faith can be a liability sometimes.' Her voice is low. 'It has been for your sister. She's not exactly in the driver's seat.'

'What do you mean?' I ask, though I suspect I have a fair idea.

'Something's taken hold of her, quite forcefully. She's somewhere between disciple and puppet now. And the less control she has, the harder it becomes for us to remedy.'

'What if we're too late?' I ask.

'Then she will die. And you might have to be the one to kill her.' Mamó's voice is neutral, as though she were telling me how to make a tincture, maybe more so. She can get very het up about tinctures. My heart stops.

'I won't do that,' I say, keeping my tone as even as I can. 'There has to be another way.'

'There's always another way,' Mamó tells me. 'It's a question of how many people will end up paying the price for her choices.'

'The baby was Lon,' I say, though it's a question too, I suppose.

'Yes.'

'And what do you think she wants this time?' I ask, trying to banish thoughts of hurting Catlin from my head. It might not come to that. 'I mean the statue.'

'The statue is a lump of wood,' Mamó tells me. 'Doors are made of wood.'

'But who's behind the door?'

'That's a question for a scholar or a priest. I only know that if it's the same one from before, or even if it isn't, we have to get it shut and keep it that way.'

'You're speaking in circles,' I tell her, frustrated. 'I don't know what we're dealing with at all. And it would help to.'

She opens the door of the car, walks around, and opens the door for me.

'Madeline, these things don't give out business cards. Knowing their names won't help.'

'What are we supposed to do then? What did you do the last time?'

'I tried a few things,' she says. 'None of them worked as well as I would like.'

I think of the leaves and berries by the statue's' feet, of Mamó chipping at it, searching for a way to stave off danger.

Failing.

It's strange to think of her as someone with the potential for failure. She always seems so sure of who she is, of what to do.

'I did what I had to,' she says. 'And it wasn't pleasant. We'll have a better notion of what's needed if we can get it in front of us.'

I sigh. 'How do we do that?'

'Well,' she says, taking a long drag of the air, as though it were a pipe, 'knowing what they want can be a map.'

'What do they want?' I ask.

'The same thing that creature did last year,' she says. 'Your sister.'

'We need to find Catlin,' I say.

Mamó swallows. 'First come into the house,' she tells me. 'We can't be saying everything out here.'

Myself, Mamó and my best friend the shovel clamber into the flat. I begin emptying the jars of stuff we haven't used, and she motions her head for what we'll need to keep and adds several more – some I recognise – hellebore, foxglove, bay – and some I don't. We have it down to a fine art at this stage, the routine: come in, tidy up, then regroup.

'We need to act,' I say. 'We need a plan.' My voice is steady. I sound more sure, much more sure than I'm feeling.

She looks fixedly at me, like Badb the crow regarding a tasty piece of meat. I inhale slowly and stare back, trying to keep a wall behind my eyes, show no emotion. A doctor diagnosing. A detective. Clinical. Detached.

'Well, by all means, Madeline,' she says, 'provide one.'

'Okay,' I say. 'But it won't be flawless. There's some stuff I need to know.'

'Evidently,' she says.

'First, I think we should ring Elodie Noone and get them to take Mam in. She owes you a favour, and Mam will feel like she's helping out or something.' The two of them have been getting on well, and Mam knows a lot of what's going on there. Maybe more than I do.

'That woman owes me nothing,' Mamó tells me. 'But that said, it is not a bad idea. Getting Sheila out of the way.' She says it as though Mam is a puppy who might pee on the rug at an inopportune moment and not a family member who deserves a better hand than she's been dealt.

'I'll phone Catlin and see if she's around. I'll say I got away from you for a bit. She might believe me.'

'Doubtful.'

221

'Yeah,' I say. 'As if I'd be able to get away from you.'

She doesn't react. I'd have been surprised if she had done, in fairness.

'It's worth a try,' I say. Her nod is barely a nod, but she doesn't tell me how foolish I am so I consider it a massive victory. Well done, me! There will surely be a hero's parade for me when this is all over. Or at least an evening off. Ha.

'Okay. So Brian . . .' I say.

'Ah,' she says. 'That's been handled.'

'What did you do?' I ask.

'I handled it,' she says. 'Now, we might need to take some items for insurance. But he won't be able to practise prayer magic for some time.'

I think again of the symbols that she drew in the circle, and the symbols I noticed shimmering on Brian's back in the moonlight the first time I snuck salt under their beds here. It clicks into place a bit. I nod.

'And Bridget?' I ask.

'More insurance,' she says. 'We'll have to take her with us. Parts of her anyway. Just in case.'

'In case of what?' I ask.

'The form something appears in might not be its true face. But it does tell you something. This, presumably, is appearing to your sister as the Mother of God. What does that tell you about what it wants for its child?'

I swallow.

'Resurrection?' My stomach recoils at the possibility of seeing Lon Delacroix again.

'It's a possibility,' she tells me. 'One thing's for sure – it's up to no good. Get out your mobile phone.'

I do, and she gives me a phone number to key in.

'Whose number is it?' I ask.

'Father Byrne's,' she tells me. 'Just in case.' She smooths her hair. 'Time is of the essence. Call your sister. I'll get Elodie Noone on the landline.'

'We have a landline?' I ask, surprised.

'I do,' she says, going underneath the sink and pulling out an old biscuit tin. It says USA biscuits on the side, and is red and gold. I recognise the packaging from Christmases. Catlin would always get the one with the red jelly star on top. I'd settle for the odd pink wafer biscuit. My stomach rumbles. It has been ages since we last ate. Imagine a world where nothing dangerous was going on and Mamó was legitimately just about to surprise me with biscuits.

She pulls out a cream-coloured phone and places it on the countertop. She plugs the cord coming out of it into the socket in the wall and holds the receiver up to her ear to listen for the dial tone.

It mustn't have worked. She bends down, tries again. Then rises.

'Madeline Hayes, what are you doing gawking at me?'

What am I doing? I wonder. It's not like we have all this precious time.

'Go into the other room,' she says, 'and make that phone call.'

My fingers shake as I unlock the screen.

36

Beads

(focus, calling, prayer)

I'm scratching at the walls in Brian's office when Maddy calls me. When I went down the passageway the first time, Lon opened it, and the second time, Brian left it open. I'm not sure exactly how to make it work. And neither is OLOB, apparently. But it's definitely somewhere on the wall. I just need to find a spot that feels a little different.

'Maddy!' I exclaim happily.

'Catlin,' she says, and I can feel the worry in her voice. 'Where are you?'

Ugh, I realise. I won't be able to ask her how to get the door open, because then she'll know that I'm at the door trying to get it open and probably follow me or something. I press my palm to different parts of wall, over and over again.

'Catlin?' she says again. 'Are you . . . drumming?'

I sigh. 'Yes, Madeline, I'm drumming. Myself, Layla and Eddie Collins are a drumming circle now. We go up to the old shed and make beautiful rhythmic sounds on various household implements.'

'It's good to have a hobby,' she says, and I can sense the smile in her voice.

'To answer your question,' I say, 'I'm in town. I went for a long walk and kind of ended up here. I'll wander back slowly. I think I'm going to buy some pick-and-mix in the petrol station.'

'You're taking your life in your hands with those pick-and-mix,' Maddy says. 'They don't have any scoops.'

'It'll build up my immune system,' I say brightly. 'I'll be immune to everything people have in Ballyfrann. Magic, shape-shifting, whatever the fuck else is going on.'

While we talk, one of my hands is still trailing purposefully across the wall, tapping until I hear a click and the entrance opens. And all of it fades away. It's not about my sister any more. It's about me and her in sync, helping each other to make our way through the world. Still I have to keep on talking to her. Pretending that I care. When I just can't right now. The sense of purpose running through me is so strong there isn't really room for other people. But here we are, I suppose. I keep on talking.

'I know what you mean. At least a bit. But hearts are fragile things. You need to mind yours, and I don't say that as someone who doesn't like Oona, because I don't, like, hate her or anything, she just annoys me sometimes. I say it as your sister. You need to find another girl to love.'

'Easy for you to say.' Her voice is thick with something, maybe annoyance. 'C'mere, Catlin, can we talk? I'd love to see you.'

I test the edges of my mind, to see what she thinks, though I know already.

Absolutely not.

'Yeah,' I say. 'I'd really like that. Will I give you a call when I get back from town?'

'Mamó could give me a lift down to you.' Her voice is eager. There's something off about it.

She's hiding something.

'Okay,' I say. 'Sure. I'll be walking back towards the castle, but I'll stick to the road so you can see me.'

'Great,' she says, and I can feel her smiling. 'See you soon.'

Well done.

We don't have much time now. That's bought us a reprieve, but only a small one. I switch my phone off, put it in the pocket of my dress and head on down. To where he killed me once. I swallow.

The air is thick, and smells of something oddly familiar, that catches in my lungs. I cough, but keep on going, through the dark. She guides me and I will not stumble or fall. If I did, she would raise me up. Would carry me. Would see me through. I'm not alone any more. Candle flames appear, and I can't smell the strange smell, only roses. Certainty in me that this is right. This path I'm on will guide me to the light. A better place.

I put my phone back in my pocket, and smooth my hair down. It's not as hard as I thought it would be, to go back into the tunnel, the place where it happened. My feet seem to know the way to go, one in front of the other almost in spite of me. She says I'm safe. I know that I am safe, but it seems like no one's told my body that. I can feel my heart beating faster, my breath sharp in my throat. It's dark but she helps me to see. The walls are lined with jars, some of the things in them are thick with mould. Some of them look like pieces of flesh – hard to tell if animal or human. Could be either really. Could be both.

I swallow. I need to be more brave. I need to take her where she needs to go. My feet scuff on the floor, and the air is dusty, stale. We come to a fork in the path and start to descend. Soon we'll be back there. Where it all happened. I hope I'm strong enough, for what she asks.

You will be, child. Have faith.

And then we're there. It's changed a little since it happened. The bed is gone, the room is dustier, the candles are covered in it, dark wicks almost submerged in powdered grey. She lights them so we can see where we're headed, past the wall with all the girls' names. And my name too. All carved out, like a checklist. We were things to hurt, to throw away. I swallow. Why is she taking me here? It isn't a good place. It isn't right.

Have faith she says again, again, *have faith . . .*

I do.

I do.

I breathe in strength and roses.

Carry on.

227

37

Onion

(protection, spirits, plague sores)

I look down at the oak leaf in my hand. It's shrivelled into nothing. She was lying. Or the thing inside of her was lying. In spite of myself, I feel furious. After all I've done for her, she's in another dangerous situation and I need to go and look for her, and she won't even make it easy on me. Like, not that it was going to be easy. But less hellishly difficult would be something.

Mamó is waiting by the door with her big leather bag, and a look of impatience on her face.

'Where did she say she was?' Mamó asks me.

'In town,' I say.

'And where is she really?' She says it as if there is no doubt in her mind but that Catlin would lie to me. She's right, but it still stings.

'I'd guess somewhere near the caverns,' I say. 'I mean, I can't be sure. It's just a feeling.'

'I have the same one,' she says. 'Elodie Noone should have called your mother by now. I'm just waiting for her car to go.'

'Yeah,' I tell her. 'Mam has seen enough.'

We hear the scrape of gravel on the driveway. Mamó opens the door. We start to move.

'Madeline?' she says, just as we go. But I'm already holding the shovel. It's big and weapony. The last time that I tried to save my sister in this place, a weapon would have been nice to have. For confidence, if nothing else. And, with me not being sure what will happen, if I'll have to fight her, fight for her – it can't hurt.

I think of the cache of weapons Father Byrne has hidden underneath the floorboards, of Brian's bits of girl in his office, of the graveyard where the stone that bears our father's name rests above some earth and an empty coffin. The earth we took. I run back for it, grab the little jar and run back towards Mamó, picking up the shovel on my way. She says nothing, but she waited for me, which generally means I've done something right. Wait, I'm exaggerating. That I've done something slightly less wrong than usual. I hear a mew behind us coming from the overgrown mint.

'Come,' she says, and out pops Button, giving me a baleful glance and hiss. Dirt *and* a cat. We surely are well equipped to take on the Mother of God, I think, and then shake it away. I need to focus, to clear my mind of all this resentment. Of everything that has gone before.

Mamó's tall back ahead of me, and I struggle to catch up, my mind is racing quicker than my legs, but somehow I manage it. I have to. There is no option where I stay in the flat for a little while and have a cup of tea. No option where Catlin's not in danger.

We don't head to the castle, as I thought, but back into the car. Button hops in too, and curls in the gap behind the driver's seat. More dog than cat, I think, until he hisses at me, arching his back, then turns away in a disdainful manner and flops nonchalantly onto the darkly flecked carpet.

'Why is he here?' I ask Mamó.

'He has his reasons, I'm sure,' she says.

'Why aren't we just going through the castle?' My voice feels weak in my throat, as if every time I have a question that's a layer peeled off it .

'Sometimes it's better to use the back door,' she says. 'I have a fair idea where what she's after might be.'

'Catlin?' I ask.

'Whatever's living in her, anyway. Your one.' Her eyes are steady on the road, and she is driving very, very carefully, for a change. It's actually quite unsettling. I look out of the window and see three crumpled crows on the side of the road, small in death, and shining.

'Mamó?' I ask. 'What was that priest, the one who wrote the records, like?'

'Surer of himself than he had a right to be. But he believed it, I think. That he was special, that God was on his side.'

'Do you believe in God, Mamó?' It's a big question but she seems to be in an oddly talky mood, so I might as well. I mean, there is an afterlife, or sort of. Girls turn into ghosts, and linger here. People have souls. My sisters prays to something and it answers. It makes you wonder what is out there really. Beyond us.

'There's more to us than what's here, but I don't think that any of the things that creep into this world have our best interests at heart.' She turns the cold air on and it blasts over me, puckering my skin.

'You've been at this for a long time,' I say.

'Yes,' she says.

'You must be tired,' I say suddenly, without thinking. She doesn't reply. All those years of putting out fires, healing ailments, settling disputes, keeping track of people who are going off the rails, who might harm themselves or others in this town. She's older than she looks, I know that much.

'Did you train other people, before me?' I ask. I think of how she wants me to learn stuff almost by myself, to be independent. How she practically begged me to do this last year, and now acts like my presence is an imposition. I don't know if I'll ever understand Mamó, even if I read every dusty old book on her shelves, the labels on every single glass jar full of who-knows-what.

'Madeline,' she says, 'stop asking questions.'

I fall silent. But there is a long list of questions piling up my head, and we both know it. We pull in to the side of the road and start making our way up to the passageway behind the shed. I'm carrying the shovel, and Button is somewhere, which makes me very conscious of my ankles. And not just my ankles. I mean, he is a cat, and though depth perception might not be his thing, he certainly can jump and climb with ease.

I feel it again. I think of the oak leaf crumbling in my hand, and my skin tingles with something between dread and resolve. I cannot trust my twin to be my sister. I cannot know that she will make it through.

'Mamó,' I ask, 'can you smell roses?'

38

Knife

(piercing, directing)

I would love a big dirty shovel. Like a really big one. Because this is hard going, and she can only help me so much. I'm past the section of cavern where it happened, it wasn't as bad as I thought. I just kept telling myself that he was dead and I was not alone. That she was with me. And she is. I feel her, keeping me warm with gentle breezes, murmuring soft words of guidance, making this place smell of roses underneath the dust. There's something she needs me to find. In the wall. And it's important.

There's a part of the cavern that's bricked up. She has me punching it, but my arms are too weak. If someone built this, and some of the cement looks fairly fresh, maybe they left tools. My knuckles are bloody and I watch her heal them, and then I hurt myself again, and it's still not budging. There's something that she wants behind those bricks. Something precious to her. I have to make sure she gets it, and I will.

I see a big rock that could work and raise it up over my head, She gives me strength in times of need. I throw it against the wall, and it . . . crumbles.

'There's something wrong,' I say. 'Magic or something.'

Pray, she tells me. *Pray*.

And I see what she means. The pain is part of it. It helps. It gives us strength. I beat my fists against the wall again. They leave it stained with effort. Blood.

The circles of blood look just like roses. I smile. I feel her triumph, feel the bricks begin to loosen, crack. I need to keep at it, to keep going. I murmur old words with new fervour. The rosary round my wrist. That word. It means a garden, doesn't it? A garden filled with roses. Beautiful things, but sharp as well. If you want a rose to bloom again, you need to prune it. Cutting makes it stronger. There are things we live through that teach us what we're made of. The last time that I lived through one of those, I emerged a little disappointed. I felt smaller, somehow. Less. But I am so much more now. Drips as red as candle wax down my hands and I keep on hitting. I think of other girls inside this cave. Who were as scared as me, and didn't make it. Shadows clinging to the place their last moments were.

One of the bricks begins to give, and I see that if I had a pointed thing, a chisel or even a trowel, I could scrape along it and prise out the brick. See what's behind there. Why she wants it so much. I kneel and pray for something to come to me, a tool, a help. There's only so far that your pain can take you.

That's not true, she tells me *Suffering is a key. It opens doors.*
Do you suffer? I ask, and she smiles. *No, child. But yours will bring you closer to me.*

I don't mind being called a child compared to her, because technically I am one, and also she is old, older than I will ever be, probably. Though maybe I am immortal now, like Dracula. Maybe if he killed me again, I would rise up by myself and wreak my vengeance. I'd quite like to wreak some vengeance. I think I'd be good at it.

A chisel! I see the glint of it underneath some rubble. Who was down here? Who would want to be? I mean, if you're looking for someone with access and secrets it's probably Brian, right? She murmurs in my head. She's right. I'm getting distracted. And there is not much time. I have a job to do. I chip away at the cement, flake by flake, until the brick dislodges enough that I can start to pull it out from the others. I pull away at it, feeling her watching, approving. I stare inside. It's in darkness, but I can hear rasping there. Something's in there. Something or someone. Ragged breathing, and gurgle-choking sounds, as though someone is trying to say something but they don't have the right things inside their mouth to make it work. There's a smell I recognise from somewhere though. It's on the tip of my tongue . . . I breathe it in, and retch.

The first secret.

I know what is inside.

39

Lemon

(cleansing, banishing, love)

We're through the tunnel and moving towards the caves beneath the castle. The smell of roses is getting stronger the closer that we get, and I keep looking around, expecting to see them gathering around me, sprawling up the wall, thick like brambles, reaching out and grasping at my clothes. It's very quiet. I can hear Mamó breathing and almost sense the sound of Button's little pad-feet as he trots after her, his tail held high.

It's warm, and there's some sort of smell in the air underneath the roses that I recognise. A musky smell, something heavy and lingering. I hear a scuffle, and quicken my pace. Mamó holds up a hand to slow me down, but I don't relent. If Catlin is in danger, the quicker we get there the better. I won't have her taken from me again. She will not die tonight. I chant it fiercely to myself inside my head. No matter what I have to do, my sister will be fine. She will not die.

We turn a corner, and at the end of the passageway it opens out and we can see the shape of her, sitting on the floor, turned to a portion of the wall with one brick missing. Her shoulders are jerking strangely, as though she is a marionette with one broken string and the puppeteer is trying to make her work, get her up again with desperate little yanks.

'Catlin?' I say.

'Madeline?' she says, and her voice is thick with fear. I run towards her.

'Of course you'd have a shovel,' she says. 'I needed one. Or she did. She wants me to . . .' She gestures to the wall. Mamó strides over to it, peeps inside, then firmly replaces the brick in the wall.

'I have to go have a word with someone,' she tells me. 'I won't be long.'

'What?' I ask, outraged.

'You heard me,' Mamó says. 'Keep a good hold of that shovel.' She strides away. I watch her leave, feeling as infuriated as that old-timey priest. The cheek of her.

'The CHEEK of her,' Catlin says.

'I know,' I say. 'It is a bit much, isn't it?'

'I mean, this is not a good situation for you to be in. Or me, really. I mean, I'm beginning to think Our Lady of Ballyfrann might not have my best interests at heart.'

'Oh no?' I say, and snort. 'What part of you thought she did? I mean, there's the sleepwalking, the weird historical murder stuff . . .'

'There's weird historical murder stuff?' Catlin's voice is curious. 'I mean. She didn't tell me about that. Obviously. Who did she murder?'

'Well . . . it was more like people murdering on her behalf . . . I think.'

'You think,' she says. 'Wonderful.' The sarcasm cuts deep. I know she probably wants to downplay how stupid is to get involved with *another* ancient murderous thing, but it's deeply annoying that now I have to cope with it, while she brushes it off like it's no big deal.

'Oh, I'm sorry,' I say, my voice coming out a bit meaner than I mean it to. 'That I don't have all of the facts about the ancient being you've gotten tangled up with.'

'Oh, don't get annoyed, Maddy,' she says. 'I can't take it right now. Look, you know I've always prayed, right?'

'Yeah.'

'And you've not had, like, a problem with it?'

'Not really, but –' It's hard to get a word in though, she's ranting.

'And I think we can all acknowledge that I have been going through some fucking stuff.' She gestures around the cavern where it happened. 'Exhibit A, like.'

'It hasn't been a picnic for me either.' I gesture to Button, who is flopped down beside a stalagmite like a small loaf of treacle bread. 'Do you know how he lost his eye? I did that, trying to find a way to get you back.'

'Jesus, Maddy . . . what do you even want me to say to that? I'm sorry?' she says. 'I'm sorry that I got into an abusive relationship and didn't listen to you and then got murdered,

238

but it's not my fault. None of it is my fault. And I'm sorry that you felt the need to mutilate an animal or whatever, and most days I'm glad I'm not dead, but I didn't make you decide to do any of it.'

'But you did almost instantly start forging a relationship with another ancient thing who means you harm,' I snap. 'I mean, at some point you have to start taking responsibility for your choices, Catlin. They are not good.'

'They are too,' she says.

'You beat up the priest. You lied to me. And you've obviously started digging out whatever's behind that wall, all because Lon's mam told you to. Did I mention that? That the last time she came she only brought fucking Lon into the world?' I'm well aware that I'm on my high horse now, but it's a comfortable horse and I can't imagine getting down from it any time soon.

'OF COURSE,' Catlin says. 'She would be Lon's mam, wouldn't she? I mean, she couldn't just be my cool mystical pal who helps me out. Everyone here has to have, like, a disturbing agenda. Look, Madeline, if you're here to judge me or whatever, toddle off. I can handle myself.'

'Clearly,' I tell her. 'I mean, look how well you're doing, covered in blood and dirt, dismantling walls.'

'Take a look,' she says, her face ashen.

'What?'

'Go, on Maddy. Take a look at what's behind the wall and then yell at me some more if you feel like it. It suits you, being better than everyone else. Just like Mamó.'

I walk towards the wall, tentatively. I wonder if I'm up

to whatever lies ahead. I wonder why my sister is being so frustrating.

'I don't think I'm better than everyone else, Catlin,' I say. 'I just think that today, in this particular set of circumstances, I'm righter than you are.'

'UGH,' she says, and kicks a stalagmite, which looks really sore, but I have no sympathy for her. 'I am so sick of you and your rightness, and you're not even right as often as you think you are. I'm really upset, and you'd rather bicker with me than help me. You love giving out more than you love helping people and you weren't always like this. You used to be the good one.'

'There was never a good one, Catlin,' I tell her. 'And if there was, like, a better twin, it was probably you. I mean, you know that.'

'I don't mean good with people and all that. I mean like *morally* good,' she explains. 'Reliable and things. Trustworthy. But lately you're just bitter, and it's getting old.'

'Oh, shut up,' I say, easing the brick out of its slot in the wall, 'I mean, if we're talking bitter, you're always going on about what happened last year as if you're the only one who is traumatised by it, and that's just not true.'

'I got murdered, you actual bitch.' Her voice is high now, not quite a shout but getting there. I peer through the hole in the wall and sniff the air. What is it? She keeps on going, on a roll apparently. 'And I think I can be forgiven for having trouble getting over it, in the circumstances. I mean, for one thing, the actual murderer who murdered me is behind that wall.'

I drop the shovel.

It's hard to make out shadows in the dark, but I can see a lanky form that seems to be chained to something. And hear . . . sounds that aren't breathing, but aren't exactly words either.

And that's when everything goes black.

40

Eggs

(healing, fertility, secrets)

Okay, so I didn't mean to hit Maddy with a shovel, but in fairness to me, she was being really annoying and I'm fairly sure I did no major damage. I kind of don't remember deciding to do it, really. It felt a bit like the time I woke up on the stairs, mid-sleepwalk. Or when I hit Father Byrne. I was in my body but not fully, and it happened so quickly too . . . all of a sudden it was in my hand and there I was walloping my sister, instead of just shouting at her when she was only trying to help me like a normal person. I felt sick as she slumped to the ground, the shovel is pretty big and brutal and she cut her head on a rock. It bled a bunch, which seemed to wake Lon up a bit. I could hear him behind the wall shuffling more, and all of a sudden my hands were grasping at bricks and trying to dislodge them. It was a bit easier than I thought it would be. She was definitely giving me some strength, and my brain kept saying I don't want to be doing this, it isn't safe for me, or for Maddy, but my body kept right on digging at the wall like I was tunnelling to my own freedom instead of trying to liberate my murderous ex.

It looks like Lon is tied up, as least, but what if he's not? He is a liar, he could be biding his time and waiting to attack. I don't know how long he's been in there, but he's probably starving. My mouth is moving but my voice is not my own.

My Son, My Son, what have they done to you?

THIS FUCKING TOWN.

I've a good few bricks pulled out of the wall now, enough for me to creep in, not that I want to, I drag my feet but she pushes me towards the hole.

'No,' I say, and all of a sudden I'm levitated up to the top of the cave, between the jutting stalactites like teeth. I'm fairly sure she's not the real Virgin Mary. I mean, back in Cork when I prayed to her I never got this level of feedback.

'FINE,' I say, and down I'm set with a plonk. It's not like when I was actually, for far too brief a moment, able to fly. That was liberating. This is like being one of those puppies whose legs gets too tired to walk and so the owner drags it by the leash, or grudgingly picks it up and keeps on stomping. Ugh, why was I so willing to trust someone I couldn't even see or speak to, really? I mean, you would think past experience would have taught me something. Oh great, now I'm untying the ropes around him, at least there are also chains, that's something. Oh, she knows where the key is, that's ideal. Lon, fortunately, does not look well. He's been all cut up, the parts

243

of him I can see are covered in thick, raised scars, and there are . . . there's no delicate way to put this . . . like chunks of him missing. Even if we didn't kill him, it is clear that he has not been having a good time.

I place my hands on him, and light comes forth from them, and the scars start fading. I can feel my own marks pucker and redden again on my face.

Lon's mouth opens, a wide red chasm framed by pearly teeth, and for the first time outside of my nightmares in over a year I hear his voice.

'My Catalina, you've come back to me.'

41

Mugwort

(cramps, sinews, knots, and birth)

I'm on the floor of the cave and everything is fuzzy. Well, not everything. My sister hit me. And with my own shovel. Which Mamó warned me about. She's going to be so smug about this. Not that she'd ever say it explicitly, but we'll both know I was wrong and she was right. Though she probably shouldn't have fecked off to do whatever she is doing, leaving me with Catlin who is obviously possessed by something old and bad, and a cat who probably purred as she knocked me to the ground. I scowl and move my head a little. My vision is a little blurry, but it's clearing some. In the dim of the cave I can't see Catlin, just a gaping hole in the wall where she's removed even more of the bricks. I start and try to get to my feet. Lon's in there and he's probably hungry, I mean it's been a good long stretch.

I can't believe Brian would do this to us. I mean, it has to be Brian doing it, what with him being the one who captured Lon, who claimed to have disposed of his body, and also this being weirdly part of his house. He's using Lon for something. I grab the shovel, and hoist myself up. Okay. I'm standing now. Trying to be quiet, I peer through the shadows to see if I can make her out. I think she might be in there, with him. Lon. On one hand this is extremely worrying, but on the other it means she probably hasn't seen me, which gives me the element of surprise. Or – a bad thing – he might already have her in his clutches. I can smell what I had always thought of as his cologne wafting out through the roses in the air, and now I realise it must just be the strange inhuman scent of him. I very much doubt Brian's been giving him toiletries, though maybe he has. Nothing would surprise me about that man any more.

I hobble towards my satchel and reach my hand in. Mint, rowan berries, a feather, a hagstone and some of Bridget Hora's bright hair. I smear them with my blood and set the hair on fire, count to thirteen, quench it with my hand. It bloody hurts. I take out an antiseptic wipe and clean the wound it has left. I may be a witch, but there is no point in courting infection while fighting demons, or whatever else you'd call them. Right, I think. I've got this. It'll be okay. I straighten up and walk towards the jagged hole in the wall. It looks like when children first learn to draw teeth, all little rectangles jutting out strangely, a dark mouth gaping in the middle. My eyes adjust to the light and I see Catlin unlocking Lon's chains.

I hear my voice ring out, with an authority that surprises me: 'STOP.'

246

She turns and faces me. Her eyes are dark sky blue shot through with golden strands. Not the irises, you understand, but the whole eye itself. They're glowing and there's a sort of shining aura around her too. She stands taller than my sister stands, as though her bones have elongated. I gasp. She's floating two feet off the ground. She looks me up and down and then, with a small decisive movement, goes back to freeing Lon, who is looking healthier than the flash I saw of him before the shovel. There are little craters on his face, as though someone had scooped out chunks, but they seem to be filling up again, plumping unnaturally. I look at her, at him. I have to do something. To make this stop.

I hold the shovel aloft and run towards him, using the metal blade part to shove the floating thing that was or is my sister away from me. She rebounds against the side of the cave with a bump, and I start laying into Lon as though my life depended on it. When actually I'm probably shortening my life with every smash.

'Madeline,' Lon exclaims between wallops, 'be gentle with me.'

'Um . . . No?' I offer, before being dragged away by my furious sister and slammed against the wall. I square my shoulders, hang on tightly to the shovel which, despite being shoved against the wall by an ancient being in the body of my sister I have managed to keep quite a strong hold of. Which is a skill I did not know I had. I lift the shovel again and take another step towards Lon.

Be careful, child. That voice – it seems so wrong oozing out of her throat like the head of a parasite.

'I'm not your child,' I snap, raising the shovel higher for a good swing. 'My mam's name is Sheila Hayes, and she would FULLY support what I'm about to do.' I swing, and Lon crumples to the ground, which is nice. Catlin runs to him and strokes his hair.

'I knew you would come back to me, my Catalina,' he says, and puts a tender hand on the side of her face, with the combined effect of making me physically ill and making it much harder for me to take a swing at him without hurting her.

It looks at me and makes a pantomime of Catlin's smile. I grab the thing within my sister by the shoulders and pull it off Lon, turn to him, shovel still in hand by the way – I am an absolute pro and should probably take up professional shovel wielding when all this is over. The smell of roses and cologne is sickening, and I crush some of the mint in my pocket and bring it to my nose. It helps me focus. I poke Lon with the blade of the shovel, into a corner. When my hair is pulled so tightly my head jerks back and the shovel is ripped from my grasp. I jump back, as far out of the range of it as I can, and glare at the thing that was, and probably still is, Catlin.

Leave us, child. She is ours now.

That voice that's not her voice. It wrecks my head. Catlin has had so much taken from her, her body, her life, her agency and now this thing has taken her voice too, replaced it with something that has no place inside her throat. What would Mamó do in this situation? Apart from hightail it out of here on witch business. If I could get to my phone, and somehow

248

there was coverage in the cavern, I could ring Father Byrne, or even Brian, at this stage. Someone who'd help.

Who are you to stand against us?

But when you are a witch and things go wobbly, it tends to be up to you to set them right. There's no one going to come and fix this for me. I need to work it out. To do my job. I run towards my leather bag, which is conveniently near the mouth of the cave.

Who am I?

Good question.

When I came to this town I didn't know.

But now?

I am a witch.

A friend.

A girl hopelessly in love with a girl who doesn't love her back.

A daughter.

A girl whose legs are strong from climbing mountains and whose eyes and hands can spot the things I need to make the world around me safer, right.

A girl who listens to her gut.

Who loves her mam.

Who hits bad guys with shovels.

A girl who will sacrifice whatever she has left to try to fix this.

The mortal enemy of a very small cat, who is in the right, and Lon, who isn't.

Catlin Hayes's sister and best friend.

I am Madeline Louise Hayes, a girl who knows down to the very marrow of her bones that, try as she might, this ancient bitch ABSOLUTELY cannot have my sister.

Not while I am breathing.

I shove my two hands in my satchel, grab what I can and hope for the best as I feel myself being dragged up into the air.

42

Candles

(intentions, remembrance, hopes)

I'm floating underneath the surface of myself and I can't really see what's happening. It flickers like the fluorescent light through the windows of the swimming pool that night in the hotel. With Maddy.

Maddy . . .

I can't believe Lon's here. That he's alive.

I think the dreams must have been a way he was trying to find me, even before she showed up. To find me and ask for help. As though after what he's done I could still be, in some way, his. Which I suppose, given the way things are going, I am.

And I don't want that. I feel a spark of anger in my gut. My arms hurt. I'm moving them a lot. I think I'm sleepwalking again or something like it. But when I was asleep I wasn't aware of what I was doing. I didn't know. It all came through in dreams. Dreams of holding feathers in my hands and squeezing, squeezing. Dreams of secrets.

She told me three secrets.

The first was Lon being alive. I remember knowing that, and then not knowing that. Maybe she didn't like the way I reacted when she shared it with me. Our Lady gives and then she takes away. My wrists are sore now, and my index fingers and my thumbs, what am I doing now, what am I doing? I try to swim up towards the light, towards whatever's happening. I don't want to see it, but I have to. It feels as though my two eyes are going to pop out of my skull, as though there are weights sewn inside my clothes that drag me down.

Something's wrong. I feel it in my heart. I kick my legs again, again, again. and keep on swimming.

When I break the surface, my hands are wrapped around my sister's throat.

Her skin is purple.

I look down at my hands and try to move them but they will not move. I hear my own voice now, high and desperate. 'Maddy, you need to fight me, you need to move, I'm so sorry I can't stop this, she won't let me, Maddy. Maddy –'

And then I'm pulled back under once again, only this time I can't see anything at all. There's nothing there.

43

Garlic

(visions, fancies, the bitings of a dog)

Being strangled is no craic, I can confirm. Being strangled by your own possessed sister adds a layer of nastiness to it, certainly, but the worst thing about it is the being strangled part. You become just a neck, an aching pair of lungs, a life that's failing. I think I found a way to hurt her though, before she went for me. Which might be why she went for me. To neutralise the threat. I used the fingerbone of Bridget Hora. It was down in the very bottom of my satchel, I don't remember packing it. And I thought to myself, if Bridget Hora was cleaning this place for so long, and growing angrier and angrier, surely some of that anger would be targeted towards the thing that killed her, and the thing that brought it forth? And I thought very hard about her face, and my fingers began to trace little symbols in the air and my lips began to murmur and I added dried ragwort and hellebore and some of the dirt from our father's grave. Some of the after-feather from one of the crows I found. Cupped them close, and thought about her face. Her smile in the pictures. I thought about Catlin's face as well, the two of them together. Maybe there's some way in Bridget has, some plane where she can help my sister out, or make it easier for her to fight this . . . thing. And I knew in my gut, the marrow of my bones, the core of me, there was something to it. When something's there, your body sings with it. I slowly felt my two feet on the ground, heavy and sure. But then she was beside me, snarling, reaching.

I keep on murmuring inside my head, I do not need a mouth to be a witch. I don't need air. Who I am is in the meat of me. I cannot move my hands, my head is exploding. I can see black spots. Is this . . . Is this . . . .

'Maddy, you need to fight me, you need to move, I'm so sorry I can't stop this, she won't let me, Maddy. Maddy –'

Is this . . . kind of working?

I stare at her, watching the darkness swirl across her eyes again like ink and gold in water. She is my sister and she doesn't want this. She is my sister and she doesn't want this. She is my sister and she doesn't want this. Bone and feather, dirt and bloom.

Help her.

Someone.

Help her.

Everything begins to fade away, and I am falling. My eyes. My eyes. But all at once the pressure around my neck eases, just drops away, and two strong arms are holding me. Holding me. Shaking me. Who . . . ? I can't. I can't. Two blue-grey eyes.

Mamó.

My voice. It won't come out. I'm making noises like what Catlin made when he . . . Oh, Lon. Lon is here. I point a finger towards the wall.

'LLLLLuLLL.'

'I know. It's taken care of. Now get up.' Her gentle demeanour is so soothing. But also highly disconcerting. Things must be dire if she's not giving out.

Catlin is slumped on the floor. I point to her. Mamó points to the shovel. Which makes sense.

'ISSHHHH . . .'

'I can't be listening to that voice of yours. Drink this.' She hands me a bottle of something. I take a tentative sip. It tastes *dreadful*, and my throat does not like the liquid, which scrapes it raw. I close my eyes and gulp it.

'What did you think you were doing leaving me alone with her and Lon?' My voice is still quite raspy. I sound like I smoke nineteen packs of unfiltered cigarettes every day, and eat Brillo-pad sandwiches.

'Well, Madeline,' she says, 'I had assumed that after a year of apprenticeship, you would be able to handle yourself in this kind of situation.'

'Evidently not,' I say, with a sigh. 'But I did learn a valuable lesson about not letting go of my shovel.'

'She got you with the shovel as well, did she?' Mamó says. 'Let me take a look at it.'

'Where's Lon?' I ask, feeling panicked by how cavalier she's being about the situation.

'Brian's tying him up,' she says. 'Seán is on the way as well, in case we need backup. It'll get him out of the house, God love him.'

'Should we tie Catlin up too?' I ask, gesturing. 'I mean, she has both knocked me out and tried to murder me, so I think it might be a good idea.'

'Sit for a minute,' Mamó says, taking a length of twine out of her pocket. 'I'll give it a go.'

'Did we not bring better rope than that?' I ask.

'Brian's using it,' she says. 'And besides she's only small.'

I hear Brian yelp through the hole in the wall.

'He was absolutely keeping Lon here, right?' I ask.

She nods. 'It's a complicated one. We'll have to deal with him later.'

Brian's voice floats out from the hole in the wall. 'What was that, Mamó?'

'I said, Brian, that we'll have to deal with you later.' Her voice is incredibly steady, and I imagine anyone in their right mind would give anything they had – savings, promises, kidneys – to not be dealt with by her.

'Oh. Right you are then, fair enough, as the fella says.'

'Is he tied up?' she asks.

'He is.'

She nudges me to get up, go and check. Lon is indeed tied up, and Brian is hunched in an apologetic manner that I'm pretty used to by now. The I-did-unspeakable-things-but-I'm-working-on-myself-did-I-ever-tell-you-about-my-bad-dad hunch.

'Madeline,' he says. 'I don't know how to –'

Lon makes a sound of discomfort, and Brian backhands him across the face. He cringes.

'We need to sort out Catlin, and make sure that this thing can't hurt her again, Brian,' I tell him. 'We can discuss your reasons for lying to us, and keeping my sister's murderer alive, when things are a bit less dangerous. I'm sure Mam, for one, would love to hear them.'

'Sheila . . .' he says, clutching his head with his hands. I don't have time for this.

'Brian, you're an intelligent man. You have to have thought about what would happen if you got found out. The consequences it would have. All you can do now is mitigate them.' My voice is stern. When did I get so stern? I wonder. It's new.

'I'm not sure that I can, Madeline. It might have gone too far.' His face is miserable, and I want to tell him that there's always hope, but I'm not sure he deserves hope.

He hits Lon across the face again, and his expression is strange. I don't know who he's really thinking about hitting. It could be me. Or it could be himself.

Mamó's voice through the wall. 'We need to find the statue. I didn't spot it in her room.'

'And it isn't here – she didn't bring it with her, I don't think,' I say. 'There's a nook behind the wardrobe in her room. She keeps things there sometimes. It might be worth having a second look. Brian, would you mind?'

He nods, and off he goes. My eyes meet Mamó's.

'Before she hit me in the head, I'd started something,' I say. 'And I think that it could work. I think that's why she went to strangle me, and maybe why she couldn't. Catlin's in there, and she can get out. We just have to find a way to make her stronger. And I think the ghost could help – more than one, if we can manage it. The murdered girls.'

Mamó nods. 'I see where you're coming from, Madeline, but it's a risk. Calling things that are and aren't here. Death does things to a person. Changes them, or opens doors inside them.'

'Did you know, when you brought her back, that something like this could happen?' I ask.

She nods.

'And you did it anyway.'

'Would you have had it otherwise, girly? Would you like it if she were in the ground right now?'

'No, but –'

'There are no buts once you've made your bed. You have to lie in it.'

'There wasn't going to be a happy ending, was there?'

She shakes her head. 'There's no such thing. Now, let's try our best to make this right.'

We hear a low moan from the floor. She's stirring. Mamó looks at me, and I run over, grab my satchel, throw it over my shoulder. The shovel too. I mean, it couldn't hurt. I might not want to use it again, but I don't want to be hit with it either. The remnants of the spell staining my hands and in my pockets. I show them to Mamó, and she looks through her own satchel. Tangleweed and marigold and teeth. Baby teeth, but pointed. Some flecks of wood. I remember in the parish records, he said she cut a bit off. Maybe that. She rubs them between her hands and looks at them fixedly. Button trots over and flops on his side, his stomach exposed. He purrs.

'Where's Badb?' I ask.

'Doing something else,' she tells me.

'Great,' I say.

We both inhale as my sister stands up, shakes her bonds off as though they were made of water, and approaches.

Brian runs in, holding the statue under his arm like a rugby ball.

'I found it!' he exclaims. 'And several bottles of my good whiskey. Catlin Hayes, you need to –'

She moves her hand. He crumples to the ground, a sock without a foot. She tilts her head. It's not a human movement, maybe more like an ancient water-beast. Something hungry coming from the depths. It has been waiting.

She moves her hand again and the statue levitates above us and stays in place, suspended in the air. A predator, stock-still, but watching, waiting . . .

'Catlin,' I say.

She doesn't even flicker. Staring steady with those night-sky eyes.

In unison Mamó and I throw the scraps we've gathered on the ground. They burst alight, and a thin trail of fire begins climbing up towards the statue. Catlin tilts her head towards the ceiling and draws the point of a fingernail underneath her eyes. Her skin opens up, and tears of blood run down the left side of her face, and then I feel it, moist against my skin. It's dripping from the stalactites. The smell of blood and roses mixed together sickens me.

Let me do what I came here to do.

I look at her.

Blood drips in my eyes and down my nose. I wipe it off, we

keep on going with the fire. It glows red, and begins to feed off the blood. My father burned to death, and someone took his ashes. There is nothing lying in his grave. But he left us some of his fire. Catlin and me, we both have our strengths. And she is in there somewhere. If we can use Bridget to get her out, then maybe we have a fighting chance. She's floating up into the air, a cloud of blood around her, hair flying and her eyes are wild. She puts her hands up and Mamó freezes, her hands open and she begins to drift into the air. She looks down at me and nods.

Before when she left me, she assumed I had this. Now, in fairness, things have escalated a bit since then. But there is definitely something I can do. A card left to play. Last year, Catlin found a deck of tarot cards, and she read for me. Death. The moon, but upside down. And a hand emerging from the sky, brandishing a big stick. Perhaps they knew how much shovel would be in my future. The thing about the cards, she told me once, is that they tell a story but the story is different for everyone, and every image has many layers. What do I think of when I think of the Virgin Mary? It's not the virginity she's famous for, it's the child she bore. Her only son. And that's where I should strike. I pull Mamó's leg and she comes down a little.

'Do you have your pouch on you?' I ask.

She nods slightly.

I hold out my hand, and she, her face looking as though every movement is a battle, reaches into her pocket and drops it down to me. I smile and run to Lon, who is still tied up but has managed to wriggle towards the hole in the wall so he can get a view of the battles his girlfriend-mommy is fighting for him. I did not think that he could get any creepier, but there he is, eyes shining. He's enjoying this.

'Hello, Lon,' I say. 'Remember me?'

I unroll the pouch, hoping that there's something made of wood in it. Wood was what we used the night Brian brought him to us to be killed. We didn't kill him and I'm not sure what could kill him, but I know that wood can pierce his skin. Can hurt. There is a statue of the Virgin Mary holding the body of her son, face abject. The *Pietà*. I want to get her from the avenging Mary that does battle to Mary with a sad, defeated face. I want her to be that. I want her broken. I pull out a delicate wooden knife carved with intricate symbols. I think this one would be best.

'Hey, Catlin!' I shout. 'Do you think that this time death will take? Where was his heart again?'

She turns to me, and I see Mamó move a little, like someone not straining at her bonds, but testing them. Measuring how tightly bound she is, what she will have to do to ease her way out of them. I slide the knife across Lon's skin and feel a sort of nausea. I hate this, it feels more intimate, more wrong somehow than a giving someone a good honest belt of a shovel. Closer to torture than self-defence. I sigh, tell myself he probably won't die, meet Catlin's midnight eyes and twist the knife. Lon makes a sound that lets her know it hurts. I slice his gag away so she can hear him.

'Mother, please.'

He would call her Mother, wouldn't he? Everything about him is UGH.

I glare at him.

'Madeline, this isn't you. You do not want to hurt me.'

'You're right, Lon, I don't. But if I feel like it's my job, I will.' I glare at him.

He glares back. My glare, however, is better. And also I have a knife, so there is that. I raise it up high and see her float towards me. She moves her hand and I'm not sure what she's doing exactly, but my hands begin to feel as though I've slept on them, and it's a struggle not to drop the knife. I close my eyes and try to feel the ground beneath my feet, the fire we summoned.

And then, Lon's ropes start to come apart.

Which is . . . not great.

44

Ashes

(divination, death)

I'm inside myself, trapped in a weird dream-space. It's shaped like the cavern, but not the way it is. The way it was. Before he took me here, we would visit it in our dreams. The dreams he made me have, I realised afterwards. So like his mother. But at the time I thought it was a sign that I would think about him, and then go to sleep and dream about him. That we were soulmates, meant to be together. He looks at me now with sadness in his eyes and I'm trying my best to hate him, but there are these feelings welling up inside me, and I'm not sure whose they are. They could be his. Or even hers. I don't feel like I'm my own. Not any more.

Lon sits in front of me on a high-backed wooden chair, like the one from Brian's office, and I stand a bit apart. I am wearing a long silk dress that I don't own.

The silence stretches out, but he speaks first.

'Catalina. When I was trapped in there, I thought of you often.'

I nod. I'm sure he did. He probably wanted a snack. My voice is frozen in my throat though, and all I can do is look at him and think how normal he looks, like he's a person and not this creature who is capable of doing . . . I flinch. He is still talking. That much hasn't changed about him at least.

'I dreamed that you would come and rescue me. I tried to reach you, but I was very weak. Brian would come and . . . I will spare you the details,' he says, waving a long, white hand as if I were too much of a lady to hear about whatever he's been up to. I wasn't too much of a lady when he was holding me down and hurting me. A flash of pain. I try to keep it from my face. I'm trying to stay apart from this. I am not safe, not even from myself here. I can feel my skin call to his skin. I know that sounds really dramatic and I can almost see Maddy rolling her eyes at me, but that was what it was like, what it is still like.

I swallow.

'Lon . . .' I start, but he interrupts me, lost in the flow of his own thoughts. In the story of what has happened since he left me. Since we left each other, I suppose. I close my eyes and try to gather myself. What is my brain doing to me? Why do I want to look at him again? To hear him out?

'I would escape from those long lonely days inside my head, to memories of us, and I would try to reach out and to call to you. I wanted to tell you how much I regret how things turned out. How I wished it could have been different. And now . . . my love . . . it can be.' He stands and begins to walk towards me. I take a step back. His bronze eyes bright as coins. I used to read such love inside that brightness, and now I'm not sure it was ever there. His skin. My skin. I flinch. I can't . . . I can't.

'Lon,' I say again.

'I love the sound of my name inside your mouth,' he says, and it is exactly the kind of thing Lon says, so pitch-perfect it could be Maddy doing an impression. I think of Maddy. That helps. Imagine Maddy glaring at him. Possibly while holding a shovel. Oh, she would be so angry if she knew how I was feeling. I mean, I'm angry with myself. His skin. My skin. My heart.

'Oh my Catalina,' he whispers, coming closer but more slowly, taking little steps as though I were a deer that he wanted to feed, not scare away. 'I wish . . . can we just go back to the way things were before? No recriminations. No anger. Just us. Me, and you, and the love that we have for each other. I still feel it. Can't you feel it too?'

'I . . .' My throat is dry and my palms are sweating. My body is humming and it's halfway between lust and stress. I feel a little movement on my back, as though a hand is gently steering me towards him, and I know that it's her. But when we're in the same body it's hard to tell what's her and what is me. I like to think that if I were myself, if I were right, that I could hate him. That I could walk away. But I don't know that I could. I don't know that I can. I know I should. And I know a huge part of me wants to. Is that enough? He's so old, so strong, the son of something like a god. And I am just a girl who makes mistakes. Who keeps annoying people. Who hit her own sister over the head with a shovel because a demon made her do it.

'Don't say that you don't feel it. I know you can.' He moves closer to me again and this time I stand still. I let him come. I don't know what it is. Somewhere between freezing and wanting. Wanting things to be better than they were. Wanting him to be better than he is, and me to be the self I was when he fell in love with me.

'What happened, Lon?' I ask.

'After you tried to kill me, and I don't blame you for that, I probably deserved it after what I put you through –' he says it like it's water under the bridge, and I understand but it isn't, it cannot be, not for me. He put the water under that bridge and I fell in and I am drowning still – 'I was unconscious, I think for a long time. And I woke up in the place you found me in, and every week or so, Brian –' he says the name like it hurts him to say it – 'would come and he would cut off part of my body. A fingertip, a little slice of flesh. And then he would leave. Sometimes he would give me an animal – a bird or a rabbit or something, and I would eat that. But mostly he would cut me and then leave.'

'That must have been hard,' I say, because sympathy is what he seems to expect. And it must have been. I know it must have because it was hard when he ate me, and that only went on for . . . I don't know . . . an hour . . . probably less, although it felt like more. It doesn't take that long, to hurt a girl. I feel something familiar curl in my stomach and I smile. It's nice to have a part of me that's mine. My anger. I need to hold it close. To keep it safe.

'Do you think he did it to punish you, Lon?' I ask. 'For what happened?'

266

He shakes his head. 'No. If it was that, he would have let me die. He wanted to use the bits of me, for power.'

'How would he do that?' I ask.

'So, as you know, my mother is something close to a goddess. I don't know if I've ever seen her true face. But in Ballyfrann people tend to have secrets of that nature. They change shape, they do magic, some of them can fly.'

'Who can fly, Lon?' I ask.

'The triplets will be able to in time, in different forms. And you, my dove, you can fly as well.' His voice is crooning, gentle, like it was before I knew the other side of him. And I can feel the hum of her as well, or maybe it's just me. Telling me that it will be okay. It will be different this time. Our love is inevitable. I cannot fight it. We should be together.

His mouth on mine, his hands entangling themselves in my hair, and I feel the push of my body against his, but it isn't mine. My body isn't mine. He took it from me. And now somehow it has become his again. His hands brush my ribcage so tenderly. Lon is capable of such great tenderness, but it isn't real. This is a dream. I amn't in the world and even in my dream it is a lie. He is a liar.

The liar kisses me.

I wait for him to stop.

And that's when secret number two comes back.

There's nothing I can do.

And she was using me, like he was all along.

A space to fill.

A vessel.

He wants what she wants. To bring another creature like himself into this world.

To use my womb to do that.

I can't let him.

My brain on fire.

My hands just hanging limply at my sides. As if I were the corpse he tried to make me.

45

Bloodwort

(expectorant)

When we were little, we would swap things sometimes. Stickers, dolls, treats. Catlin always ended up with the best thing. Even when I had the choice, I ended up looking at what was in her hand and feeling like I had chosen wrong. That there was a better path, another happiness. As we grew up, it wasn't just with treats and things, it was with people too. The way she drew friends to her was amazing, and I felt a bit like maybe it hadn't been the choices that I made, maybe I myself was the wrong option. She was the better twin, the better path. I don't know if I feel that way now. I mean, we're much of a muchness. I'm more comfortable in my skin, but on the other hand her ex-boyfriend is really hard to tie back up. A wriggly dude. He is, to give him credit, lithe. I don't know if his bones are really bones. It makes me think of rats. They can squeeze through very small spaces because their bones are made of cartilage, the stuff your ears are made of. They bend and alter, when they need to. However, I'm a girl with normal bones, trying my best to keep his bonds tight and wondering how to help Mamó. I can't hear what's going on out there any more, and I'm afraid that it could be bad.

I struggle to pull the ropes tight around Lon, and smear some blood and salt across them and across his face. He winces. He's strong, and he struggles. But something in me is stronger. It's like the certainty I feel when I click into witchcraft is in my muscles.

Lon grumbles at me. 'Maddy, why would you do this to me? You're not cruel. You're kind.'

'I am kind,' I tell him. 'But not equally kind to everyone. And sometimes, the kindest thing to do, in a given situation, is to remove the immediate danger.'

'I didn't mean to hurt her,' he whines. 'It was an accident. I went too far. I can't control myself around her sometimes.'

'These seem like arguments that work better in your head, Lon. You hurt my sister, and when I hesitate to hurt you, it is not because you don't deserve to be hurt. And you know, don't you,' I say, leaning close to him, and meeting his old-blood eyes with a glare that feels more like mine and less like Mamó's every time I glare it, 'that when we killed you, we were both relieved. You needed to be put down. And before this is over, trust that you will be.'

Willowherb and bloodwort, salt and ash from my satchel in a circle around his feet.

'Stay there!' I command, as though he were a dog. That's

kind of unfair to dogs, who if a bit needy are, in general, good boys. Button trots over to me, and I notice he has shed a whisker on the ground. I add it to the circle, and he swishes off, his tail high. I wonder if he's warming to me now. Somehow I doubt it.

Lon slumps and closes his eyes, as though he is asleep. I narrow my eyes, but move away from him to check on Mamó. I'm glad I do. She's still up there, but there are ropes of blue and red light around her, like a network of veins, from Catlin to her, and it looks sinister and like something that shouldn't be happening.

'Catlin!' I bark. 'Catlin! Hey! Catlin!'

She ignores me and goes on being possessed or whatever. I finger the small the hardness of bone inside my pocket and I swallow. Ask for it to give me strength. And then I remember that I am strong. And just because something worked once, doesn't mean it won't work again. In fact, the opposite might be true. I run towards the shovel. It's probably long enough to at least bruise her legs, annoy her a bit. Which might make whatever is curling like ivy around Mamó and pulsing gently stop for a second. When she told me about the second type of magic, way back when, this was absolutely not what I pictured. I thought more about the fox we found slaughtered in the woods. A bright and beautiful flash of orange through the trees, but warped into something wrong. A resource to be used. The wild exploited. No. I think. No.

The grass on the mountains littered with the corpses of crows. Lon's mouth sucking at the hole in their chests. Hungry for whatever heart's available. He won't have her again. I won't allow it.

271

I don't know what's going on, but I think the best thing I can do to stop it is to get my sister back. The earth from Dad's grave inside my pocket. The bones of Bridget Hora. I call on all the loving and the hating dead. I call on ghosts to help. It's perilously close to prayer magic, I realise. The line is thin. I cut myself with one of Mamó's smaller knives and let a thin trickle of blood settle on the earth. Button comes over and licks it with his rough cat's tongue. I stiffen. It's deeply unhygienic, but he looks at me, and I wonder if now we're even, before remembering he is a cat. I will be paying for my crimes my whole life long.

'Bridget?' I ask. 'If you're still here, at all, I wonder if you could help my sister. She's trapped inside herself, and someone else is telling her body what to do. I think it has something to do with Lon. I think . . .'

I glance up at Catlin, hovering and glaring at Mamó with those black eyes. My stomach twists. Her chest. Her chest is wet with blood, and . . . is that milk? Something crystallises in me.

'The last time that she came, she brought Lon into the world and then disappeared for years. I have this feeling she wants to do the same kind of thing again . . . The world doesn't even need the Lon it has. I liked it so much better when he was dead. Dad, I don't know if you're listening as well, like, but it's a lot, and I think that if you have any way of helping Catlin, you should do it. Mamó doesn't seem to be available to help right now, so it's just me, and I can't get inside Catlin's head the way they can.'

I press my hands against the wall of the cave where their names are carved in stone. So many names, so many lives he's taken. I couldn't even stop him once alone, not without Mamó's help.

'Help her,' I beg the girls who came before us to this place. The girls whose lives were stolen.

Helen.

Bridget.

Nora.

And the rest.

'She's trapped inside herself and he is in there. He visits her in dreams. I think. I think that this thing that's taken hold of her wants something from her she won't want to give. And I won't let that happen.'

I feel the pulse of them. I need to find a way to make them listen. I crush the graveyard dirt into a paste, with salt and ash and little flecks of bone. I shove it in my mouth.

It tastes disgusting.

Force myself to chew it, swallow down.

I know what's coming next will not be easy.

I go into the cell. I wake up Lon.

46

Pins

(wishes, curses, making something stick)

So, I've uncovered two of the secrets, out of the three. I'd like to know the third one, and I feel it nagging at the edges of my brain, like a song where you only half remember the chorus and it will not leave your head. I need to know these things. But on the other hand, I do not want to know. I'm still reeling from the first two, and I have the sense the third will burn me up.

Secret One was that Lon is still alive. Which I'm adjusting to. I have to deal with it. Trapped as I am in this prison she has built inside my mind. I do not know what our bodies are doing in the real world and that terrifies me, as I've worked out that Secret Two is what she wants from me. What she has wanted from me all along. Another child for her. A thing like Lon. She wants to have his baby, and the way she wants to have it is by using my womb.

I should have known. I should have guessed from other things. I mean, she took the shape of the Virgin Mary, whose whole thing was getting teen-impregnated by an all-powerful being. I can't believe her. I thought she loved me. I thought that when she gave me power, it was my power she was giving me, not her power flexing through my body, getting ready to fill it up with something worse than Lon. And I know in the pit of me that if this baby happens it will be worse. I cannot let it happen.

I focus on how much I do not want this, on how betrayed I feel. On the rage building inside of the betrayal, right in the pit of my stomach. A hot, humiliated rage that burns my face and sings its way through my veins. I can hear my heart inside my ears. *Thump thump. Thump thump.*

Lon is still pawing at me, but my thoughts are getting clearer, and I reach inside myself. I pray. But not to her. I pray to me. I pray to the girl I used to be before him. The girl who survived the things he did. I don't always feel strong. But I am strong in this. He will not have me. I will not be turned into a thing for him again. My hands snake up to his chest and I begin to push him back, weakly at first, as though my limbs had been asleep, and then with greater force. I feel as though I have more than one set of arms, like I am not alone. Like I have help.

And suddenly their names well up in me and alongside them their faces, feelings, thoughts. A torn blouse, a daisy chain, a promise. A freckled nose, hair escaping from a long thick braid, a baby-blue slip that got sent in a parcel from America, the bright gold of a spud pulled from the earth, earrings shaped like lightning bolts, runes, a Tamogotchi, eyes, so many eyes that shone for him, and shine again but different.

When I died here before, I grew new sisters.

He will fear our names.

'Dearbhla, Sibéal, Amanda, Laoise, Eimear, Laura, Bríd, Sorcha, Bridget, Karen, Gráinne, Julie, Roisín, Gobnait, Violet, Dymphna, Alacoque, Aoife, Fionnuala, Victoria, Elizabeth, Emer, Sinéad. Sally, Ciara, Mary-Ann, Nancy, Susan, Fiona, Delia, Maisy, Laura, Rachel, Caoimhe. Julie, Ava, Sheila, Maria, Antoinette, Cathleen, Martina, Jennifer, Carol, Nora, Lee, Colette, Ellen, Claire, Laurel, Jacinta, Mary-Bridget, Mary, Ann, Marie, Noreena, Savita, Carmel, Sarah, Aoibhe, Scarlett, Dearbhla, Katherine, Cecelia, Lisa, Lillian, Louise, Patricia, Katie, Cliodhna, Shona, Nuala, Shauna, Patricia, Monica, Meabhdh, Jean, Gillian, Elaine, Anna, Sabhdh, Sarah, Adele, Rose, Grace, Joyce, Nicola, Ruth, Frances, Naomi, Elizabeth, Sandra, Dolores, Aisling, Sharon, Lola, Chloe, Helen, Daisy, Megan, Úna, Fawn.'

By the time I finish, he is gone, torn into wisps of nothing. But they're with me, I can hear their voices alongside mine, some husky with the lack of use, others sharp with longing to be heard. And there is one more voice I know as well.

'Maddy?' I say.

She throws her arms around me, and I feel her legs give beneath her. Her face is very pale, drained of blood.

Bridget's voice rises out above the others. It is a little different from my dreams and her face is different too, more vibrant somehow.

'You need to get out of here,' she tells me.

I look at them, my sisters. The shimmer of their skin. And Maddy's too, I realise. She looks like them. She looks just like a ghost.

My heart.

Bridget reaches out her hand.

I take it. And, maybe for the last time, I am flying.

47

Yew

(death, rebirth)

There is a poem they sometimes read out at funerals, about how death is not that big a deal, how the person who has passed has only slipped away into the next room. And that everything you mean to them will stay the same. I don't think that the poet intended it to be used as a guide to breaking into my sister's subconscious with a fuck ton of ghosts, but there are times you have to lean into your intuition.

Lon didn't try to eat me, the way he did with Catlin. He just wrapped his long thin fingers around my neck and squeezed. The pain from earlier flooding back to make it easier for him, I knew right away I didn't have much time. While he was squeezing, he was saying some things, but I wasn't listening. I was chanting the names of the mountain girls, trying to keep the things I had to do fresh in my brain. It wasn't easy. I wanted to fight more, to push him off. To live. Just as I felt darkness closing in I smeared blood, ash and bone across his face. I woke up surrounded by the ghosts of other girls, inside a dream, I think. I can't be sure. I think – I hope – I saved her. I'm watching things from the top of the cavern now. I can see remnants of ghosts, a flash of hair being a stalactite, an elbow poking from the cavern wall, a footstep. And Mamó is on the ground, making her way to the statue, which has fallen from the top of the cavern to the bottom of it. Such a little thing it looks like now. I see Catlin's body on the floor, hair wild around her, skin as pale as death. She looks a little like she did that night.

I hear a noise behind me, and there she is again, another Catlin, this one walking over to the first one. Her hair stark white, her face is marked with red, and I can't read her expression. She's leaning down over the first Catlin and she is calling my name and I'm up here, but then I realise I'm not up here. It's me. I am the body on the ground. I am a ghost who is looking at herself.

And there is bone and ash and blood spattered around the floor, and Lon is nowhere to be seen at all. But I don't feel he's here. Not any more. I think the girls have taken him away. To somewhere where he cannot hurt anyone any more. I would really like some confirmation of that though.

Catlin's voice is deep inside her throat. She's screaming, but it sounds so far away. Everything is getting quieter, paler. I don't know if the next room I go into will be as quick to let me out again. And I don't want to go. Catlin is yelling for Mamó, but Mamó is intent on stopping this thing coming back. She looks so old. Her face is drained of colour and she has big dark shadows under her eyes. Her mouth is set into a grim line. She takes a deep breath, tosses her braid over one shoulder and places her hands over the statue. I hear her murmur words. They sound familiar. They make me afraid. There's something in them, weaving through, that hurts me. That has hurt me, or someone belonging to me. In someone else's voice these words rang out across a forest glade. I almost see them standing over him, and chanting, chanting.

There is a beat, where the statue seems to pulse, as though it were a living, breathing thing in the way we understand life and breath to be. As if it weren't time for it to go. Then there is a shudder through the air of the room, and the next instant it bursts into flames.

And so does Catlin.

48

Shells

(cleansing, containing, going under)

I feel the flames humming through my skin, emerging the way that gooseflesh does. They aren't even warm at first, they curl over me like waves lapping on the shore. I cannot burn up while my sister dies. I close my eyes and I begin to search the quiet place in my mind where prayer once brought me. But instead of focusing on Gods or saints, I focus on my sister. Madeline, the brave, the clever, the kind. She loves so hard that she would give her life up. Even though her life is worth much more. She is worth ten of me, she is worth hundreds. I breathe in deeply, focus on how much I need her to be in the world.

And suddenly I'm back there again, in a forest glade, the leaves whispering their secrets to the air. The place they took his life, where she took me in the dream, back when I trusted her. When I had hope. I can see my old self, and my father. And standing over him is secret number three.

Younger, but still tall and thin and awkward.

My disappointing stepfather.

Of course it is.

Brian was the one to take our father's life. To burn him up. I can feel the fire starting to lick at my skin. It's bearable, but soon it won't be, and I push through the two men as though I were made of smoke and face my dad.

His expression is kinder than it looks in photographs, now I can see the light inside his eyes. And he's so young, so young compared to Mam and Brian now. He barely looks old enough to shave, much less to be a parent. A barista or a bass player, at a push.

Catlin

I hear him think.

How does he know me.

Family

So simple.

Hi, I say to him. Hi, Dad. We miss you.

Tears cut through the flames.

It is the truth.

He starts to speak and I know it's going to be an apology or something sentimental, but I cut him off.

Maddy is in trouble.

And you are too. Come, he says. *Come give your dad a hug. I'll show you how to fix it.*

A burning ghost beside a burning father.

I feel him take my fire inside his.

282

And whisper to me what I need to do.

And fade away.

When I wake up, I smell like ashes, and I look like shit. Father Byrne is staring at me while Mamó smears various ointments over Madeline.

'She . . .' I say, and my voice creaks like a door that hasn't been opened for years

I try again.

'She isn't there. She's somewhere in the cavern though. She's clinging. You need to give her back the soul you took. And more besides. She didn't choose this life, Margaret. You forced it on her and you know you did.'

'I did what I had to do,' she snaps. 'Seán, cover her.'

Father Byrne points a crossbow at me, and I burst out laughing.

'Here to battle the Demon of Teen Pregnancy, Father?' I ask. 'I think I managed to dodge that particular bullet.'

'Time will tell on that one, Catlin Hayes. She's wily,' he says. He sounds a bit like Mamó and I wonder if he's doing it on purpose so she'll think he's cool. If so, it isn't working. She's laser-focused on Madeline, moving her hands over her and whispering old words that sound as though Irish and German had an even more guttural baby. Or like a language that aliens on a show would speak. Warrior aliens.

'If you need a bit of my soul, she can have it,' I offer.

Mamó snorts. 'There's very little of it in you, Catlin. And what was left she probably ate some of to make room inside for herself.'

283

'And Lon and me's demon baby Francis,' I add helpfully.

Neither of them responds. Which, fair enough. I scan the room for Button, and make the weird shushing sounds you make when summoning a cat. He approaches me tentatively. I hold him up, my thumbs cupped under his little furry armpits. He's such a good boy. He doesn't deserve to be in the middle of all of this drama.

'You are the best cat I have ever met,' I tell him. 'And when we're finished here, I am going to give you so many salmon sticks.'

He stares at me, but doesn't wiggle.

And, though it's probably very foolish, I draw on the thread of prayer magic I have, picturing a candle, not on an altar but in Madeline's hand. She is the person that I know the best.

'I love you, Maddy,' I tell her. 'Help me to help you.'

Button hisses, and I somehow know that my sister is listening to me. I see a flicker underneath the skin of his missing eye. And holding on to that candle flame I gently draw a fingertip over the surface of it, murmuring I'm sorries and promising many fine treats to come if only Button will help us out.

There is a moment when he looks at me with his golden and black eyes, and it is like I'm looking at myself. Someone he trusted hurt him too, and he is scarred from it, and he is trying. And he is strong.

And he will help us.

His eyelids part, and underneath is something strange. The size and shape of a marble. But glowing bright, the fiery red of a fox flashing through the snow. The red of a leaf a child picks up to marvel at. The red of my sister's big heart that keeps forgiving me. That keeps on trying.

It plops into my hand, and it is moist.

I kiss Button on his little head and tell him, *Thank you*.

When I turn, Mamó is staring at me. Her expression as always is very hard to read, but Father Byrne has lowered the crossbow, which seems like a good sign.

'Give her this,' I say, and hold a hand over my own throat, clenching and unclenching my fingers until I feel something in the pit of me release, and I begin to cough and splutter. This time, it's less of a magical-animal-companion-doing-you-a-favour type thing, and more like a vomit with rocks in.

Rocks, feathers and thorns.

I sift through, looking for something that I need, and contemplate the many excellent choices I have made over the past few months. Why am I like this? Is there another way for me to be? And, if so, can I be that instead, please? My hand eventually lingers on the smallest stone, with the blue-black shimmer of a raven's wing fluttering weakly inside.

'She's always giving stuff up to save me,' I say. 'The least I could do is return the favour.'

I hand them to Mamó. And sit and wait for whatever comes next. Death, maybe? I mean, it would make sense. But nothing happens, and Mamó grabs me by the shoulder and leads me to Maddy, and she begins to chant. I know the words to this one. I'm not sure how, whether they were sung to me in the cradle, or when I died and they brought me back before, but they are old and deep and they are soothing.

I try to ask Mamó with my eyes if it will be enough. But she won't look at me. And Maddy's face is pale, so very pale.

Father Byrne watches us awkwardly, crossbow dangling from one hand while I feel my heart break inside my chest, as though the fire has torn right through my body, and all that has been left behind is ash.

49

Violet Bramble Rust

(timing, decay)

I'm here. I'm here. I'm here. I'm here.

Keep trying.

50

Graveyard Earth

(calling forth the dead)

'Why isn't it working?' I ask Mamó, hating the plaintive tone I can't keep out of my voice. Of course I know why. I don't have enough soul to give her. I can't make the same sacrifice she made for me. How could I when I only ever think about myself?

'Can I do anything?' asks Father Byrne somewhat awkwardly. He has fully put down the crossbow now and is just leaning against the wall of the cave. I find it hard to look directly at him, with his bruised face. I mean, I suppose you could argue the fact that he was apparently prepared to shoot me with a crossbow makes us even, but I don't really feel it does.

'You could tie up Brian,' I suggest, looking at the crumpled form of our stepfather. 'Unless he's dead, in which case it's probably fine.'

Mamó looks at me sharply.

'He is not a good man, Margaret,' I tell her. 'He exploits ghosts, eats ex-boyfriends and apparently murdered my dad, so I feel like being tied up is the least that he deserves.'

She looks me in the eye, and it feels like she's doing a weird witch polygraph on me to check my story. Whatever she sees there must pass the test because she makes a small sound in the back of her throat and jerks her head at Brian. Father Byrne moves quickly towards a big black doctor bag he apparently brought with him and takes out some vaguely nautical-looking ropes. He bends to Brian and begins binding his arms and legs together. I turn back to Maddy.

'Did you hear that, Maddy?' I ask her. 'Brian killed our dad. Him and his father. I saw it. She took me there and showed me. And he was a witch like you. I could feel the power and the kindness in him. I think he saved my life. At least a bit.'

Mamó rests a hand gently on my shoulder. 'Catlin Hayes. It might be time to call your mother. Tell her to come here.'

And that, more than anything, is what breaks me.

'Can't you do something else?' I plead. 'Is there more that I can give her? I mean, you could take it, everything, from me. Just bring her back. I'll do whatever you say . . .'

'You've done enough. There is more I can do, but I don't know what difference it'll make at this stage.'

Her voice is not unkind. She bends over my sister again, and begins to chant. I get my phone out and walk away from Madeline, leaving her there in the cave, on the brink of death, with no family beside her. If I didn't know what it was like to die, I might say that she probably wouldn't notice. But I remember

Mam being there beside me when Maddy went away to try to help. And it meant something to me. I could feel it even when I was just sensations weakening away.

I have no signal because it's a cavern underneath a big castle, obviously. So I head out of the passageway, looking at my phone to see when I'll be able to get through. I'm almost at Brian's office when notifications start buzzing in.

Eddie.

Layla.

Oona.

Mam.

It's nice to be missed, I suppose. I haven't time to read them though. There's work to be done. Mam picks up on the second ring.

'You need to come here now.'

'Why?' she asks. 'What's happened? Are you all right? Is Madeline all right?'

'Just come home, Mam,' I tell her. 'Drive safely, and I'll be in Brian's office waiting for you.'

I don't want to worry her, or make her get into a car accident or anything. Or maybe I just couldn't say the words. I take a Post-it from Brian's bureau and write down where she needs to go to find us. I'm about to turn and run back to the cave. And then I think. I think of Button. I think of Mamó's age.

I think of the small round stone I vomited out, and how it wasn't enough.

I think of thick black feathers littering the altar where I prayed. Where would an ancient witch put her soul to keep it safe? I wonder. And could I get it out?

I swallow.

I could certainly try.

I run towards the garden.

Just in case.

51

Yarrow

(gonorrhoea, hair loss, battle wounds)

I can feel myself fading into the walls of the cave, joining the other girls. Some of them are here still, I can sense them, like waking up at night and hearing soft breath. I am uneasy, but I can feel that ebbing too from me.

I can feel myself becoming nothing.

Untethered.

And then . . . that voice.

That voice that cuts through everything.

Annoying me.

'Madeline,' she says. 'Madeline. Hear my words. Take whatever form of hand is left to you. And get down here, and hang on for dear life to that shovel.'

A flash of memory.

The tarot card in Catlin's hand that turned.
The hand in the sky.
The stick.
I can remember the feel of it against my skin.
The weight.
I focus and I try.

52

Flesh

(sacrifice and cycles)

I don't know how to call a raven to me. If I were Maddy, this would all be so much easier. She goes on and on about how Mamó never tells her anything, but she's learning plenty. I mean, she summoned one hundred and two ghosts to fight Lon for me. That's not minor witchcraft. That's, like, big. I feel like the things I've done are all from OLOB, or residue from her. I don't know how to witch properly at all. I've always had stabilisers. Big, demony stabilisers that rode the bicycle of me right into the fucking sun. Literally, considering how burned I almost got. Being burned alive was, in fairness, pretty witch of me.

I close my eyes, but all I can think of is her face, and how much I cannot lose her.

I try again.

Where does Mamó's raven hang out?

Mamó's flat.

I go to the door and try it. It isn't locked. Maddy says it is always locked and Mamó decides who to let in. I decide this means I am doing a fantastic job. I mean, Maddy is still dying or dead, so not like super-fantastic, but it is important to keep my motivation up. Lots of dusty books and things in jam jars line the shelves, but apart from that it's a fairly normal flat. They have a sofa, a kettle, an oven. Human things. It's not like cauldrons and broomsticks. I would have a cauldron, I think, if I lived here. It would add something.

Cauldron, I think. Warm fluid. Something to eat. What does Badb the raven like to eat? I close my eyes and picture ravens.

On a battlefield.

Circling.

Cawing.

Soaring.

Tearing at flesh.

Lapping at pools of blood.

Oh dear.

Well, no time to think about it. I grab a saucer from a stack on the countertop and rummage through the drawers for a sharp knife. I run it under the tap for a few seconds, which will do literally nothing if it's dirty but it makes me feel better about what I'm about to do.

I hate the sight of my own blood. You'd think I would be used to it by now, but no.

I slice the soft skin of my inner arm until I've got a steady flow going on, and let it drip into the saucer. I wrap a tea towel around the wound to staunch the blood. It will probably leave a scar. But so does everything.

And suddenly they're there. In the room, as though they were always there. Staring from the shadows. I close my eyes.

'I'm sorry,' I say, thinking of the dark feathers on the altar. Of all the little corpses in the woods.

Badb says nothing, just begins to lap up my blood from the saucer, as delicately as a cat would. Maybe even more delicately. Ravens have an elegance about them. You'd never catch one jumping into boxes on the Internet. I hold my breath and wait until they have finished every last drop of the blood that I had let into the saucer.

They look at me again.

They want some more.

Six more times I fill the saucer for them, and six more times they drink it down in silence. I feel dizzy and weak, and I hold the counter to keep myself upright. This is all taking so much time, I think. Time Maddy doesn't have. She's dying and I'm here in a kitchen, trying to . . . what?

I feel my eyes begin to sting with frustration. Why am I the way I am?

And then Badb spreads their wings, and flies. And lands on my shoulder.

Like. Okay. I'm full. Take me where you need me to be.

And something like a bright hope rises in me. It's very small, and very hard to kill.

Like my sister.

With talons scraping through my clothes, right into my shoulder, I begin to absolutely leg it back to the cavern. There might still be time. There might be time.

53

Hawthorn

(inward torments)

I feel myself begin to want to go. There's a pull at me. Her words are ropes. They tie me here, I want to shrug them off. I can't remember. I am beside a shovel and there's light around me and I want to go into the next place. Maybe it will be warmer there.

A woman comes in and her face is very sad. Who is she? She is running to the one who is speaking and she is screaming, pushing her out of the way. The woman speaking slaps her across the face and I feel a flash of anger. She slaps back. There is no point, I think. I'm going. I am going. I can't . . . I can't . . .

But she, the screaming woman, is putting her hands on my body and it makes me remember that it is mine. My body. And she. I know her. I know her.

I do not want to leave her on her own.

She is grabbing my head and holding it against her chest and rocking and the sounds she makes are echoed by the ghosts inside the walls. The lonely ones. The ones who chose to stay.

And I . . .
I don't know what to do.
I am so weak now. Barely even a breath of a thing. I could flicker, quickly as a candle.

54

Voice

(incantation, prayer)

I plough through the dark of the passageway with the raven on my arm. I can feel its claws digging into me, and the weight of it. When Badb sits on Mamó's shoulder it looks so effortless. I didn't realise that it would hurt. Maybe this carving up my flesh is another part of a price I have to pay. I'll gladly pay it.

When I was inside my head, or wherever it was that she put me, with Lon, my sisters came for me, the ones I grew the night I died and the one who grew beside me in the womb. Who has always been there. All my life. Steadying me. Making me feel braver, better, more. I'll never take her for granted again. I won't even say bad things about Oona, I'll hold my tongue. I'll let her live her life. I will be kinder, gentler, better. I'll do all of the chores on the chore wheel, and more besides, just please. Just let Maddy stay. That's what children do, isn't it? When they don't want something bad to happen. They bargain and they pray. It's not enough. I'm not a kid. I need to focus. Act.

I turn a corner and see Mam clutching Maddy to her chest and the sounds from her are guttural, a keen. Mamó looks at me, as if to say, *What took you?* and the raven spreads its wings and flies to her, alighting on her shoulder.

'Do you know what you're asking of me, girl?' she demands.

'I'm asking you to save my sister's life,' I say. 'And I know you can do it.'

'There will be a cost.'

'I'll pay it. Whatever it is, I'll pay it,' I say. And her eyes are cloudy and hard to read for a bit, and then she says, 'Fair enough.' And holds out her hand. The raven's stomach begins to pulse and ripple and I see a large round ball move up its breast, its gullet to the beak. It looks too big to fit out of it, the size of an eyeball and the grey and green of seaweed clinging to old battered rocks. It rolls smoothly into Mamó's hand.

'Give her this,' she says. 'And hold the fort for me.'

I don't know what that means but I nod as if I do. I have no choice. Mam looks at me, her face is miserable.

'She's . . . .'

'NO,' I say. 'She's not. Or soon she won't be. You need to let me give her this.'

Wide-eyed she moves away, staring at me, as if I were a ghost. And maybe I am part ghost now. Maybe that is what my sister needs to call her back. Mamó follows me and places her hand on my shoulder, it feels as though the raven's claw is on me again. Gripping tight. I bend to Maddy, and pinch her nose to see if she will open her mouth, but she's beyond that so I just kind of work at her jaw until it opens and then shove the marble in and push it down, massaging her throat until it's not a bump any more and has gone somewhere.

We begin to chant again and this time I can feel something different. A hum, a thread, a little spool of life. From me to Maddy and from Mamó to Maddy. My thread is very slender, very fine, but Mamó's is fat as a worm and sturdy as a rope, and they both wind into Maddy until she's all lit up.

I won't survive this.

Another voice inside my head. Mamó's.

I won't be dead. But I will not survive. You'll need to mind me. Turn me. Make sure I'm fed.

I nod. And hear a shovel thud to the ground behind me, as though someone has dropped it.

Ye'll need to watch the town. The girl can do it but she'll need help.

I look at Mamó, across my sister's chest, and nod again.

However long it takes. Ye'll need to wait.

I swallow. *Okay*, I think, and hope that she can hear me. I don't want to reply to her out loud in case it breaks the flow of whatever it is we're doing.

The hardest part I'll ask of you is this: you'll need to leave the door open. A little. Inside your head.

I recoil.

I'll need to be able to keep an eye on ye. And I can use the door in you to do that.

Why didn't you spell this out before?

Time is ticking.

302

I really don't want to be possessed again, but what can you do? I mean, I want Maddy alive. I nod yes to all of it.

Mamó closes her eyes and places her two hands flat on Madeline. The light gets brighter and brighter around the two of them, and then begins to fade around her, till it's almost nothing. Her head slumps down, as though she were gone for a nap, and the raven on her shoulder emits a caw and glares at me with an incredibly familiar expression.

Maddy's eyes flicker open and she begins to gasp and flap like a newly caught fish. Mam runs to her, and I see that she is shining too, around her skin. Something from her hands flows into Maddy, and then the bright is gone and everything is, if not exactly normal, at least the colour it's supposed to be. We hold each other, and I hear their breath moving in and out. And it is the most precious, precious thing.

We're here. We're here.

55

Sleep

(healing, visions, dreams)

Light floods my eyes, and Mam and Catlin are staring down at me. I'm on the floor of the cavern, I can feel the rocks poking into my back. It's very uncomfortable. I sit up a little and Mam pulls me to her chest. I can smell her perfume and feel the soft wool of her jumper and I feel like I'm a child again. Like I am very small and very minded.

Catlin looks at me, and her face is so many things at once I cannot read it. But she wraps her arms around me too, and it's the three of us and we're together. My eyes focus on a point over Mam's shoulder, near the wall.

'Why is the priest staring at us?' I ask.

'Father Byrne was only trying to help,' Catlin says. 'He brought his crossbow. And he tied up Brian!'

'Oh, Jesus, Mary and Joseph,' says Mam, hand flying to her

mouth. 'I hadn't even noticed he was over there in the corner. Brian, I mean, not the priest. Hello, Father.'

'Sheila,' he says, inclining his head.

'I think you can probably head off now, if you'd like,' I say to him. 'I mean, I'm fairly sure that we have enough for what we need to do.'

'I scooped up all the ashes from Our Lady of Ballyfrann into an urn,' he offers helpfully. 'I thought ye might want to keep an eye on them. Or have a use for them. Herself never liked to waste anything.' He looks sadly at Mamó, who is slumped against a rock, eyes staring wide, the light gone from behind them. Her skin is waxy, pale. My heart is in my throat. I gasp and try to get up. Lose my footing.

'Is she . . . ?' My eyes fill up. She certainly looks it. Her body flopped, more awkward than it ever was in life. This can't be happening. I notice Badb, perched nearby, taking it all in.

'Takes more than that to kill a bad thing,' says Catlin, in a voice that's hers and not hers at the same time. 'I'll be right as rain in a few years.'

'Wait, what?' I say, feeling a mixture of confusion and something like relief. That voice. That infuriating, familiar voice. Is it . . . 'Okay. I'm going to need this explained to me in detail.'

Catlin squints at me. 'Of course you will. But first I'll need this body to be put somewhere safe. Get the urn off Seán, Madeline, and Sheila and Catlin, ye can carry me.'

'Catlin, what are you doing?' I ask. 'This isn't funny.'

And then I see her eyes. There is a ring of grey between iris

305

and pupil, stark against the normal hazel hue. She lets out a big sigh, and when she speaks it sounds like her again.

'So . . .' she says. 'You probably have some questions about the deal Margaret and I made to save your life. But the short version is that she's not fully dead, some of her kind of lives in my head, and we need to mind her body so she can go back into it when she's all healed and so on.'

'And how long will that take?' asks Mam, sounding outraged.

'Ah, you can't still be angry with her, Mam, she's saved both our lives now.'

I look at her. My sister.

'Thank you, Catlin,' I say.

'You'd do the same for me,' she says. 'I mean, you basically already did do the same for me. So I suppose we're even?'

I laugh. 'We'll see. Mam, will you help me up?' She puts her arms around me and hauls me to my feet. I'm really thirsty and my brain is reeling from everything that's happened. But someone needs to take control right now. And that's my job.

'Pass me the urn, Father,' I say. 'And that shovel over there will do as a walking stick, while I'm still a bit unsteady. I reckon it'll take the three of you to carry her. We'll leave her in my old room for now, until we know what we're doing.'

'What about Brian?' Mam asks. 'We can't just leave him there.'

'I kind of feel like we can,' says Catlin. 'I mean, he kept my ex-boyfriend alive in a wall so he could do cannibal magic on him, and that is only the tip of the evil iceberg.'

'What did he do?' I ask.

'You don't want to know,' she says.

'When has that ever stopped you telling me anything?' I ask.

'Oh, I'm fully going to tell you.' Catlin smiles. 'But I'm going to give you like half an hour to get used to being alive first. Besides –' she grabs Mamó under the armpits, and gestures to Mam to help her – 'there's a lot to process and I don't want to drop Mamó. God, I'd love to be able to make her levitate again.'

I look at her.

'You wouldn't.'

'Just for handiness.' Her face falls a little. 'You're probably right.'

The two of them kind of drag her with us like a sack of spuds. It's very far from the sort of seamless stride with which she usually moves through the world. My head feels light, and I use the shovel to steady myself.

'I'll follow you,' I tell them, hobbling over to my satchel and picking up some clove, catnip, rowan and yarrow. I close my eyes and reach for anything, but all that I can feel is the lack of energy. There's nothing left in me to do this with. But when you leave the house, you lock the door behind you. Just in case. We don't know what Brian is capable of, and Mamó never made the third kind of magic sound anything less than terrifying. Brian has a history of doing dangerous things when he is desperate. And when he wakes he will be more desperate perhaps than we have ever seen him.

I scatter the herbs over his body and hope that they will work by themselves, at least a little. To keep him sleeping, keep his powers dulled, the threat at bay. As I exit the cavern I hear a whisper, like a breeze or breath. I know it is the girls

I almost joined. The ones who haven't passed on yet. Who stayed. Myself and Catlin will have to do something about them when this is over, be it sending them on their way or setting them safely free. No creature deserves to be tied to the place where they were killed.

I close my eyes, inhale the dusty air of the cavern and set off after Mam, Catlin and Father Byrne, lugging the body of the strongest woman I know, like she was one of us, a broken girl.

56

Ribbon

(setting, binding, sticking)

It's weird, carrying the body of someone you thought was indestructible. I mean, I know old people die, right? And Margaret was fully old. I mean, once you reach a hundred the president writes you a letter or something. Our great-granny got one when we were small, I remember her showing it to us in the nursing home. I wonder did Mamó get a letter? Probably not. She doesn't seem like a birthday card kind of person. Which is a pity, because who doesn't love a birthday card?

'I know she's not dead, Mam,' I say to Mam. 'But you must admit, she fully looks dead.'

'I know.' Mam's face is worried. 'I'm a bit concerned about putting her in Maddy's room. In case she *decomposes*.'

I stare at her.

Father Byrne says nothing. Probably for the best.

I feel a hum of annoyance at the back of my brain. Oh great, she's here. This is going to make a lot of things awkward. Like kissing. I cannot imagine being able to lose myself in someone else's touch if I know there's a magnificent two-hundred-and-seventeen-year-old bitch somewhere in the background, listening in. Like, while I roll my eyes at Margaret a lot, and understand exactly why Madeline finds her frustrating, it has to be said that her power is pretty undeniable. I mean, she can literally stop death.

Not entirely, girl.

I shake myself, as though I were a dog who just hopped out of the ocean. This is going to be so strange. We set her on her back and prop her head up with one pillow. Not two, because apparently she'll get a crick in her corpse's neck or something. Mam tucks her in as though she were one of us.

'How are we going to feed her?' she asks.

'That'll come later,' I say in Mamó's voice. 'First I need to heal a while.'

'SO CREEPY,' Mam says, clutching a hand to her stomach.

'Excuse me?' I say, offended. I mean, it is extremely creepy and awful, but at the same time I don't want to set a worrying precedent where people can just insult me to my face, just because I'm a little bit possessed still. Rude.

'Sorry, love. But, in fairness to me, it is creepy.'

'That doesn't mean you have to spell it out,' I say. 'I wonder if this means Maddy can live with us again. That would be great.'

Mam smiles. 'The thought had occurred to me.'

'I mean, I did promise Margaret that we would both continue her work until she's well again, but who is to say

310

we can't do that from a house that our whole family lives in? Except for Brian, who will need to be dealt with.' I rub my chin. My skin feels coated in a layer of cave-dirt. I'm dying for a shower.

'I should have separated from him after the Lon thing,' Mam says, her face grim. 'I knew I should have, I could feel it welling up inside me, but I wanted to try, you know? I loved him, and we'd moved so far and sacrificed so much. And it wasn't like I could just take the pair of ye back to Cork and slip into our old lives like a cosy dressing gown.'

'How could you have known what he was?' I ask. 'Like, there's no way you could have. We all thought he was nice and that he loved us.'

'What did he do?' she asks. 'What was the thing you didn't say before?'

I rub my eyes with my hands. I am exhausted.

'We should probably wait for Maddy,' I tell her. 'It's not an easy thing to say, and it won't be an easy thing for you to hear. And we'll have to decide what to do with him.'

'What do you mean?' she asks.

I shrug, because I genuinely have no idea. I hope Maddy has some witchy solution to all this, but increasingly I'm learning that it doesn't work that way. It is an aching, bloody sort of thing. Not as simple as an ask, an answer.

'I . . . might go back to the church,' says Father Byrne. 'This seems like a family matter, and I don't want to interfere.' He clears his throat. 'Mind yourselves,' he tells us. 'And if you need anything, ye know where I am.' The tone of his voice implies that where he will be is as far away from our weird family as humanly possible. I suppose it's nice he stuck around this long, not everyone would have.

We tell him, 'Thanks, Father,' and listen to his footsteps going down the stairs. Mam turns and says something about how she'd believe him a bit more if he wasn't halfway out the door when he made the offer, but I leg it after him, and catch him up at the front door.

'Father?' I say.

'Catlin.'

'I'm sorry,' I say. 'For beating you up. Like, I know that I wasn't fully in control, but some of me was, you know, deciding to listen to her. To do the things she wanted. And you've been nothing but nice to me . . .'

'It's forgotten,' he says. 'I've taken worse beatings in my time. I'm just glad that things seem to have resolved themselves. After a fashion.'

'Yeah,' I say, for want of something else.

'Look after yourself, Catlin,' he tells me. 'And you know you're always welcome in the church. If you need a bit of sanctuary from . . . all of this.'

'Thanks, Father.'

'And don't let that one boss you around too much.' He grins. 'Though I'd say ye'll be well able for each other.'

I can feel Mamó itching to say something, but I suppress her a little and just say, 'Thanks, Father,' again, because there really isn't anything else I can say. I mean, I can't take back what I did. I can't change who I am. All I can do is keep trying.

I clamber back up to Maddy's room, and when I get there herself and Mam are staring at Mamó in the bed. It looks wrong.

312

'It's weird to see her sleeping, isn't it?' I say. 'I mean, I know it's not exactly sleeping.'

Mam looks at me. 'What exactly happened to get from where we were the last time I saw you to now?'

I sigh. 'I got possessed by the little wooden statue in the corner of the church and it turned out that the statue was somehow Lon's mam, and that Lon was still alive and they both wanted to get me pregnant, presumably with another murderous demonic sort of creature. And it was a whole thing.'

'Lon was still alive?' Mam is aghast. 'But we saw him die, I thought. I mean, I certainly saw him get very stabbed indeed.'

'Because we stabbed him,' I agree. 'You helped.'

'I'd do it again,' she says, her voice grim. 'He killed you.'

'And Maddy too,' I offer.

'Jesus,' she says, rubbing her hands on her trousers.

'So,' I say, 'about Brian – the first bit of it is that he was keeping Lon alive so he could eat bits of him and gain magical power.'

'Oh,' says Mam. 'So that's what you meant by cannibal magic?' She turns to Maddy. 'Is that a thing?'

She shakes her head. 'It shouldn't be.' She turns to me. 'What's the second part of it?'

I find myself reluctant to tell them. I mean, once they know they'll never not know, and I think who I am most concerned for is Mam. I mean, what would it be like? To love the man who killed your husband? What will that do to her? She's been so fragile this year, so tired-looking. I don't know. I wish there was a way to make this easy.

'Can we be moving down to the kitchen while I'm telling

you this because I absolutely need to eat, and if what Brian was up to didn't put me off my food, nothing will?'

'Of course,' Mam says.

'I'd love a pizza,' says Maddy. 'Like a big cheesy takeaway pizza. With loads of toppings.'

'Good luck finding someone that would deliver to Ballyfrann,' I say.

'I am allowed to have dreams, Catlin,' Maddy snaps. 'I mean, I need something to live for.'

I snort at her, and she narrows her eyes.

'Is that you snorting or Mamó snorting?'

'Me,' I say, 'but I feel like she would agree with my snort.'

Mam clicks the kettle on and takes a fat little loaf out of the bread bin. 'Ye can start with some cheese toasties. You need to build your strength back up.'

She's slicing the bread as though it has personally offended her. I don't relish telling her what happened. I mean, it all worked out, as much as anything that happens in Ballyfrann ever works out, but there's more to come.

'So Brian was kind of helping us, but I knocked him out and he's still unconscious because I'm very strong. Like a bear.' I flex my muscles, Maddy rolls her eyes.

'We'd all have amazing upper-body strength if we were possessed by ancient forces, Catlin.'

'It's like a gym membership. Only with evil schemes instead of whatever people who go to the gym do,' I say.

'Girls, stop.' Mam waves her hands in front of her face. 'I don't think I can handle ye messing while I'm wondering what the story is with my husband.'

314

I take a deep breath. 'You might want to sit down for this,' I say.

Mam sits. I look at her. And Maddy. And I start to talk, catching Mam up on what happened in the cave, and the sacrifice that Maddy made for me. So I could live.

'Anyway, Maddy was a hero and completely saved me, AGAIN. But then when I came back she was dying, and Mamó set the statue of Our Lady of Ballyfrann on fire and then I went on fire, which wasn't great.'

Mam looks at me. 'You don't look burned,' she says.

'I'm getting to that. So I went into this weird dream-space in my head, kind of like where I'd been trapped with Lon, but this time I went back in time or something and saw Dad, and he saved me.'

'Tom,' she says, and there is so much feeling in that syllable.

I swallow. 'Anyway, while I was there, I saw what happened. What they did to him.'

'They?' Maddy asks.

'There were two of them,' I tell her. 'And one of them was definitely Brian. I think the other was his dad.'

Mam's head is in her hands. I keep on going, telling her about the bargain I made with Mamó to save Maddy's life, and what it will mean for the family. I don't go too much into the blood-drinking-raven part of it because we've all had a day.

'Jesus,' Mam says, when I'm finished. 'Is that everything?'

'Probably not,' I say. 'I mean, a *lot* was happening, and all at once. Hard to keep track, but one thing is for sure: we need to do something about Brian. And soon.'

'I wonder was it all a lie,' Mam says. 'Like, did he know when he first met me that I was Tom's widow?'

'That he widowed,' I say, sagely nodding my head. 'I wouldn't be surprised. I mean, he wanted power, right? And me and Maddy, we have it. I mean, he might have wanted to exploit that all along.'

'I thought I knew him,' Mam says. 'I mean, he had me fooled.'

'He had us all fooled,' Maddy says. 'I mean, I thought he loved you too. That he was doing his best for us.'

'Me too,' I say. 'None of this is on you. At all.'

Mam doesn't answer, but reaches out her hands to clasp our hands.

'What are we going to do about him?' Maddy says.

'I have a suggestion,' I say, 'but it's not going to be super popular.'

'Let's hear it,' Maddy says. 'I mean, there are no bad ideas.'

'Um . . .' I say.

'Okay,' she says. 'There are many, many bad ideas. Like, actively terrible ideas. But we definitely need some sort of plan.'

'We do,' I sigh. 'So, I reckon we put him in Lon's room. Like in the wall. There's definitely some cement we can get somewhere, and we can leave a little hole for us to pass him food through . . . and, like, a bucket.'

'Ugh.' Maddy's brow is furrowed as though she's trying to work out a maths problem. 'It seems a bit . . . brutal though.'

'Yeah, *but* so is he. And we both need more energy than we have if we're going to do any sort of successful binding spell, and I get the feeling Mamó is going to have a list of things we have to do to prepare. I have this feeling that's somewhere between a sense that she's annoyed at me and a tension headache.'

'Relatable,' she says.

Mam plonks the cheese toasties in front of us. 'I don't like any of this, girls. I'd like to be able to deal with it myself and spare you both the effort. Or for there to be some sort of gentler way.'

'I don't know that there is one, Mam,' Maddy says, and I nod.

Mam makes a sharp little sound somewhere between concern and resignation. 'Well, eat up, anyway.' She gestures to the plates. 'Whatever happens next, you'll need your strength.'

Maddy makes a sound in the back of her throat. 'I don't like leaving him there. It feels like a loose end.'

'Which we will absolutely tie once we're a bit stronger,' I say. 'Now, who knows where the cement would be?'

'Probably in the tool shed,' Maddy says.

'Eat,' says Mam, again. 'You can wall your stepfather up inside a cavern on full tummies, at least.'

'Delicious,' I say, because it is. 'I don't think food tasted as good when I was possessed by OLOB. It was like there was a tang of iron and roses to everything.'

My phone beeps. It's from Eddie.

'Hey, Maddy,' I say, 'Eddie wants to know if I'm okay. What should I tell him?'

'Who is this Eddie?' Mam says.

Maddy and I meet each other's eyes and burst out laughing. I put my phone away and finish up my dinner. Rinse my plate, and take a breath and get ready to go back there, down to Brian.

57

Dandelion

(purging, procuring rest and sleep)

My head is swimming. I feel like everything around me is watercolour. I mean, I can see it, touch it, but it doesn't seem real. I had this book when I was a kid and there was a bit in it about a little girl trapped inside a painting, and that's kind of how this is. I'm trying to seem as normal as possible, because I don't want either of them to worry.

We're heading towards the cavern, with a thing of cement Catlin made up, a trowel and some spare bricks. Mam is carrying a hamper of food and a small bucket. She insisted on coming too, and I'm kind of glad. I don't want to faint or anything. Catlin doesn't look much better than I feel. Her skin is pale, there are huge dark rings around her eyes, and the marks on her face look livid. I hope he's not awake. I mean, there's only so much fighting evil that one person can do in a short space of time. I might die again if he turns on us. We both might. We're basically like newborn kittens made of tissue paper. And now we have to do some DIY.

The cavern is dark and dim, but we make out Brian easily enough. It looks like the plants did their job, or else he's just really weakened by what happened. His eyes are open, but they look kind of spaced out, blank.

Mam calls his name.

'Brian? Brian?' Like she's on yard duty and he's in big trouble. I can hear sounds in the walls. Like whispers or voices. It's the girls. They recognise me now. They know my name. I'm one of them, except that I survived.

'Sh-Sheila?' Brian says and his voice is so pure normal through the dark that it's jarring. Why did he return to our family?

Mam hoists him up under the armpits, and Catlin grabs one side. I follow them awkwardly. I'm not up for carrying a grown man right now. Though they're not great at it to be honest.

'I could just walk wherever you're taking me,' Brian says. 'I mean, this is obviously straining you.'

'Brian, we *know*,' Mam says and her voice is very quiet and very definite.

'Oh,' Brian says. 'Oh. Right so.' He sighs deeply. 'What are ye going to do with me? Where's Mamó?'

'I'll ask the questions around here,' Catlin says. 'You just keep quiet.'

'What exactly do you want to know, Catlin?' Brian sighs. 'I mean, it must be a lot to take in. I know I've let you all down, but I'd like to help you get closure, if I can.'

'Closure is great,' says Catlin. 'Especially the kind where you brick people up in a wall.'

'Lon wasn't a person, Catlin. You know that,' Brian says, doing himself absolutely no favours. I think Catlin is about to have a go at him for a second, and then her voice kind of deepens and she says:

'We don't have time for this kind of carry-on. Get on with it.' And then sighs and it's like Mamó is giving out to her from inside her own body which is kind of . . . amazing. I mean, even for Mamó, it's a whole new level.

'Brian,' Mam says, 'we would all be better served right now if you shut your mouth.' I wonder if she's going to take the opportunity to tell him that we know about him killing Dad, but she leaves it at that, which is probably for the best. He'd be thinking himself in circles trying to come up with a plausible reason why it was all his dad's fault and he's working on himself and in a better place now, and genuinely loves her and us and all that other stuff he spills out whenever we catch him in a lie. That's probably half of why he hunted Lon down and had us pretend-kill him. So he could be the big man and avoid the awkward conversations that needed to happen.

The names carved into the cave wall warp and blur and I realise we have to get a move on before I collapse or something. Mam and Catlin drag Brian to the hole where Lon was kept, and there are a few moments where we can all feel him almost say something, but he doesn't until Mam explains the picnic basket full of food and water she's leaving, and I hold up the bucket, and then I think it hits him that this is really happening. It's not a great feeling for anyone, to be honest. I never thought

320

I'd be the kind of girl who bricks her stepfather into a small enclosed space while she decides what to do with him.

Catlin scrolls through her phone.

'Are you, like, checking your social?' I ask. 'It's really not the time.'

'No. I haven't even read my messages,' she says, as though this were a sacrifice on a par with her giving up her soul. 'I brought up an article on building a wall from some construction website.'

'Oh,' I say, a bit taken aback. 'Right so.'

Brian is hustled into the cave, and Mam leaves some blunt scissors in there with him. So he can untie himself, but it'll take a while. As Catlin and Mam build the wall, we argue over the wisdom of leaving one brick loose, and decide we kind of have to do that, in case he chokes or gets really sick or something.

'That means one of us is going to have to sleep here,' Catlin says. 'To keep an eye on him. It should probably be me tonight because you're in no shape, and I have Mamó in my head to keep me company.'

'I could do it,' Mam says, but her face is so, so worn out and sad. She's obviously hurting. My eyes flicker to Catlin's, there's just no way. It would take too much out of her.

Catlin sighs. 'You should be taking care of Maddy, Mam. She's not well. I mean, look at her. She needs you.'

Mam looks at me, and nods. What do I look like? I squirm a bit.

'She looks terrible,' Mam says. 'But you're not much better.'

'I'm strong enough to do what needs to be done if it comes

321

to it,' Catlin says, and I can feel the effort of her pushing the doubt out of her voice, in case Mam or Brian get a sniff of it.

'I'll bring you a sleeping bag,' Mam tells her. 'Maybe a few blankets too.'

'And a hot water bottle,' Catlin adds, because she is Catlin. 'Oh, and like a little flask of tea, not normal tea but something that'll stay warmer for longer, like peppermint or lemon and ginger.'

'Grand,' says Mam.

We hear some muffled swearing through the small hole we've left in the wall.

'I think he cut himself with the blunt scissors,' Catlin says. 'I hope you don't get tetanus, Brian. Because we're calling no doctor.'

'Was that her or Mamó?' Mam whispers to me.

'I think her?' I shrug. 'Hard to say though.'

'Right,' Catlin says. 'You put Maddy to bed, Mam, and then bring me sleeping things. I'll watch the wall and make sure it dries and stuff. Maybe when you come back I can have a pee break. Taking over from Mamó is going to be the most fun ever!'

'You're not taking over from Mamó,' I say. 'If anyone is, I am.'

'I'll put Maddy in your bed,' Mam says. 'Because that woman is in her one.'

She wraps her arm around me and I lean into her. It's really comforting. I close my eyes and hear the sounds of the cave. The drip of water, the shuffles of Brian, Catlin's breath, and something else. The non-sound of the murdered girls still waiting.

322

Helping them is on the to-do list.

After get well/don't die (again).

Deal with the Brian thing.

Work out what our lives will look like without Mamó bossing me around (as much).

Keep Mamó alive.

Sort out where Mam is going to live if her and Brian split up.

And where we'll live too – should we, like, renovate the kissing shed? Would that be an idea? Or could we stay in Mamó's flat, to keep an eye on Brian, for all the good it'll do.

'Oh!' says Catlin, obviously doing the same thing in her head. 'We need to give Button some salmon sticks.'

'I will give him all of the salmon in the house, if there is any,' says Mam, 'if the two of ye stop talking and let me put Madeline to bed.'

'Fine,' says Catlin, waving her hand in the air. 'See ye.'

We stumble off, and leave her to the dark.

58

Woodchips

(age, energy, protection, other things depending on the wood)

It's not bad, living in the cave where I was murdered, considering. I mean, at least the guy who murdered me isn't still in the cave. As murderers go, I'd much rather be watching over Brian than Lon. Even though he did try to convince me to break down the wall and empty his bucket yesterday. I refused, of course. It's been like four days, he cannot have peed five litres.

I hear him rustling around. I hope he doesn't talk to me, because I find it really hard to not answer back. I can't even use my phone here, like. Not to contact anyone. Being Brian's jailer is so *boring*. I mean, I thought it would be all tension and intrigue, but it's basically babysitting a brick wall in a damp cave with no Internet. And I'm over it.

I hope Madeline gets better soon so we can do the binding spell or whatever.

Not 'or whatever'. There are very specific things you need to do.

I sigh. She's up. GREAT.

'Hey, Margaret. How you keeping?'

I'd be better if I had more faith in your ability to do your job.

'I'm well, thanks. Watching Brian. He's behind that wall there. Just hanging out being a murderer. Him and his pee bucket and a picnic basket of food and water.'

With Margaret, I try to keep it positive. If she says something that makes me feel bad, I just kind of ignore it and carry on. I'm not sure how effective it is as a strategy, but it really annoys her and that's something.

I wonder should I contact Eddie the next time Mam comes to give me a break. He is very concerned about me, which is nice. I suppose there is no reason he, or Layla, or Charley, or even Oona couldn't come here and hang out. I mean, Brian is hardly going to burst out of the wall with a knife and fork in his hands and eat them. As far as they know, it's just a wall. And possibly a muffled voice and clanking.

Don't.

I fully should. It would make the time pass so much quicker. Mam tries, like, but she's busy tending to Maddy and giving Margaret sponge baths or whatever else she needs.

She doesn't –

'Oh, she fully will have to at some stage though. I mean, unless there's a spell for cleaning comatose witches.'

I feel Mamó bristle at the thought of how helpless her body is without her in it and feel a bit bad.

325

There is a shuffle through the wall, a muffled throat-clearing.

'Brian,' I ask, 'did you, like, know who Mam was when you met her?'

Silence.

'Did you roofie her with magic to make her fall in love with you?'

A noise I think sounds more like no than yes. It's hard to tell when there is an expertly built brick wall in the way. I'm actually really proud of how it turned out. And not a complicated kind of proud, like with the witchcraft stuff. When you're good at building walls, there aren't any *terrible* consequences. Which is nice. Consequences are the worst. I scan my brain, but Margaret has apparently fecked off.

I go into the part of the tunnel where my phone half works and tell Eddie to call over at four if he can, that I'll meet him at the back door and sneak him into the murder cave. I might even see if I can steal some drink. I have been very responsible recently, and that's admirable. But I deserve a break, and also kissing. And who would blame me for not wanting to be alone in the cave? I mean, it's *self-care*.

Plus, I don't want to go to sleep again.

I'm worried what my brain will do to me.

59

Ash

(stitches, venomous beasts)

I don't like being bed-bound. At least I have a bit more energy than I did the last time I almost died, but I suppose then I had lost a lot of my soul, whereas now I have almost too much soul – mine, Catlin's, Mamó's. I mean, that's legitimately a lot. More than most people have. An embarrassment of soul. Oona says she doesn't have one at all. I didn't know that about her. She came to visit with her mother, who has been helping Mam thorough the aftermath of what happened. Though it's not going to be aftermath until we deal with Brian, really. It's more the middlemath, if that's a thing.

It is strange having the girl you've spent over a year being in love with sitting at the foot of your bed. Part of me is very happy about it and the other part wants to have a bit more notice, and the energy to brush my hair and put on some concealer.

Apparently coming back from the dead makes me break out, and I can feel a crop of sore spots erupting on my chin, which is frustrating. It's not even technically my bed, it's Catlin's. I'm just occupying it until Mamó gets her own room, which Mam claims to be 'working on'. It doesn't really look like Catlin's room though, because all of the religious paraphernalia has been removed and packed up into old suitcases, which Mam has lashed in the attic. She was going to put it in bin bags but I stopped her, because not every statue of a religious figure is possessed. I also remembered how it felt to me when she used to clean the salt, bark, leaves and berries from my room. How it felt like she was wiping some of me away.

I've been having nightmares where I can't breathe. I'm wearing a necklace and it's pulled too tight, I'm trying to climb out of a window and it slams down on my neck, I'm underwater. And it gets darker and darker and I can't see and then there is the light again and that sense of floating. It's like the part of me that dreams – my subconscious or whatever – is trying to make what was supposed to happen happen. To put me back where I belong, in death. It would probably have been better for Mamó to be here right now and for me to be wherever I would have gone. Not for me, I mean, I like that I'm still alive. But for the town. It's going to need her so much, and there's so many years of experience and knowledge that I don't have. I've barely scratched the surface. And what is it going to be like being a witch with Catlin? I mean, she's not the most responsible. She might want to start charging money for the work we do. When it doesn't really work that way.

* * *

Oona is looking at me as though I am an interesting painting. Her head is tilted slightly to the side. Her hair has gotten longer, I realise. It brushes her collarbones now.

'Are you all right?' she asks, and I nod.

'Yes. I'm just feeling weak, I suppose. And wondering about what to do next. It's hard to know what the right thing is to do. I mean, with Brian. Mamó didn't even know what he was up to . . . I mean, the Lon thing.'

I've told Oona about Brian because I had to talk to someone about it; even just to say it out loud kind of helps. I haven't exactly told her what we've done with him while I'm waiting to heal because I don't want to take the chance she'll tell someone. A lot of people in Ballyfrann have a huge amount of respect for Brian, and an angry mob looking to free him is the last thing we need.

'There might not be any one right course of action. There wasn't with my father,' Oona says. 'I mean, my mother tried a lot of things before she asked for help. And none of them were right.'

'I felt bad that I didn't tell you before, about calling to the house with Mamó. It felt so wrong to be there without you knowing. To be meddling like that.' I chew on my bottom lip awkwardly, waiting for her to give out to me or something. Her face is calm though, kind.

'Madeline, it is your job. It helped.'

'Are you in touch with him?' I ask.

'A little.' Her hands are in her lap and she is twisting at the rings around her fingers as though they were a puzzle she

329

could solve. 'It was nice having your mother in the house, she made us try our best to be positive. I mean, it's difficult. I am tired of being worried and angry all the time.'

'I know what you mean,' I say. 'I spent so much of this year resenting where I was and how I ended up there, and now I'm looking back on it like it was a holiday or something because what's coming seems like it's going to be so hard.'

'It will be,' she says. 'But you will manage it. I know you.' Her eyes are so beautiful, I think – not with the usual pang in my heart when I look at her, but just with a sense of how nice it is that Oona's beautiful eyes get to be in the world, and how lucky I am that sometimes she looks at me with such compassion.

'I'll try my best.' I smile. 'So, is there any of the good kind of interesting thing going on?' I ask. 'Any girls?'

'In Ballyfrann?' She snorts. 'Not really. Not since you. There was a girl, and I thought that maybe . . . but it turned out she liked somebody else. And that was hard.'

'I can imagine,' I say, thinking of how I never felt like I was good enough for Oona, and compared myself to her ex in France, Claudine.

Oona sighs. 'It happens. I mean, at least I am not the only lesbian in Ballyfrann. It's good to be able to talk about it with someone who gets it. When I talk to my mother, she's very enthusiastic. Like, more than she would be if I were into guys, I think. She means to demonstrate that she is supportive, but I find it a little creepy. In a nice way.'

'I get that,' I say. 'I mean, when Catlin was with Lon she said some horrible things to me, and sometimes when I talk about who I like or something, she's like bending over herself to show that she's sorry and that she's not a bigot or anything and it makes it feel like she's adjusted the dial so it's no longer about me at all.'

'Straight people need to stop,' says Oona.

'Hey!' I say. 'My sister is straight.'

'And you almost died trying to stop her.' She smiles her wide, beautiful smile, and I grin back. She sits closer to me and reaches out a hand to touch my face. A year ago, six months ago, it would have made every part of me wake up, but now I feel the kindness of her and it's enough, it's more than enough and I am grateful for it.

'I am glad you are alive, Madeline,' she says. 'I will let you rest.' And she kisses me softly on the mouth. It's very sweet, and very tender, and I remind myself it's not the beginning of anything. There are lots of different kinds of love, I suppose, and almost love is one of them. I glow with that until I fall asleep.

60

Sugar

(enticement)

I should have possibly thought it through before I invited a boy I'm kissing to come to the place where I got murdered by the boy I kissed before him. I was thinking about warmth and companionship and being distracted from the crushing boredom of staring at a brick wall, and not so much about my trauma. Which is nice, it's good that there are times when I don't have to think about it. I mean, I used to be quite positive as a person. I like to think I still am in ways. But getting hurt, physically and emotionally, it changes you. And I will never not be the girl who got murdered in a cave. I suppose I can add the girl who got possessed and almost impregnated to that list now.

It starts off being really nice to see Eddie. Mam is off doing the shopping, so we made sandwiches in the kitchen and filled thermos flasks full of tea, before heading to Brian's office and the cave. He is impressed.

'I didn't realise there were secret passageways,' he says. 'I mean, I knew there'd have to be some way to get to the cave from the castle, but I didn't think it would involve secret doors in walls.'

'I don't even think of it as weird any more,' I tell him. 'It's just another part of the house. The part where terrible, soul-destroying things happen and the family is changed forever.'

'We call that the kitchen in our house,' says Eddie, and I snort, and then feel bad for snorting because for all I know there could be bad stuff going on, so I ask him, 'Is everything okay at home though?'

He smiles. 'Yeah, was just trying to be funny. I mean, this is a bit intense. As well as a cool adventure and an excuse to spend time with you.'

'Good,' I say.

'My family is kind of weirdly normal,' he says. 'Apart from the whole shape-shifter thing. But that's what normal is for our family.'

'When Maddy started being a witch,' I tell him, 'part of me was taken aback, but more of me was kind of . . . not relieved, but it made sense. It was like there was now words, or an explanation, to put on the part of her that was always there, whether we acknowledged it or not. And that's a good thing. Like, people are going to be who they are, there's kind of nothing you can do to stop them.'

'I suppose.' Eddie's voice is low, thoughtful. We're almost

at the cave and he's tried to hold my hand a few times, but I have a torch and a basket of food, so it's not happening, and I prefer it that way. I want to be strong here, in this place.

'Of course,' I say, 'I didn't think that I could be a witch then. And the prayer stuff – I mean, aside from the possession. It makes me wonder. I've always prayed, and life has always been a bit easier for me than it has been for Maddy and I kind of thought it was because of my personality, but what if it was just prayer magic without me realising it, and I've been, like, tricking people, a bit like the way Lon tricked me?'

'It's a possibility,' says Eddie. 'But I mean, you were still praying and going to Mass and things when you got together with Lon. Like, bad things still happened.'

'Only after we moved here,' I say. 'I mean, apart from Dad dying.'

'Do you regret it?' he asks.

I shrug. 'Yes and no. I mean, I'd rather the bad things that have happened to our family hadn't happened, but we kind of are where we are now and have to deal with that. Regrets are kind of pointless. All we can do is decide what to do next to try to keep each other as safe as we can.' My voice is really low and serious, and normally I'd try to lighten the mood a bit but we're in the cave now and the weight of everything that's come before is on us.

'I'm glad you're here anyway,' Eddie tells me, and it is nice to hear him say that. I mean, I'm glad someone is.

'It's cold,' I say, and he opens his arms and gives me a big hug. It feels really nice, but then Brian shuffles behind the wall, and kind of ruins the moment. I can't have nice things even for a second.

334

'Who is behind the wall?' asks Eddie.

'Well,' I say, 'initially it was Lon, and now it's Brian, who it turns out was eating bits of Lon for the craic.'

Eddie swallows. 'That's dark. What are you going to do with him?'

I lower my voice. 'We're going to do a binding spell once Madeline is stronger, and see how that takes.' I raise my voice again. I actually want him to hear this bit. 'And I suppose work out where we're going to live. Like, Mam is definitely going to leave him. It was touch and go after the last time, and this time it's way more his fault.'

'How so?' Eddie asks.

'Well, the keeping Lon alive to eat bits of him for one thing.'

'Yeah, but that was a magic power thing, not a serial-killer thing . . . I mean, it's Brian. Brian,' Eddie says.

'He lied to us,' I tell him. 'And there's more to it than that as well, but I'm not ready to talk about it yet.' I think of Dad's face in the woods. And how, even on the brink of death, he helped me. It isn't fair that we don't get to have him in our lives because of something Brian did.

'Eddie? Eddie Collins?' Brian's voice is coming through the wall more clearly than usual. 'Any chance you could tell your father where I am?'

'He'd be delighted to,' I tell Brian. 'He can also tell him exactly what you did to get there. All of it.'

'It's more complicated than it seems, Eddie. Sometimes people have to make choices to protect the people they love.'

'Ha,' I say. 'Some job you did protecting us.'

'Catlin, do you not think it's a bit . . . much . . . keeping him bricked up?' Eddie says. 'I mean, it's probably not even necessary.'

'Mamó thinks that it is necessary,' I say. 'We're in contact with her.'

'Oh,' he says. 'Okay then.'

'But,' I tell him, 'I'm not sure I appreciate you calling me out on the hard decisions that I am having to make to keep my family and this town safe.'

'Catlin,' he says, 'I'd rather say it if I have a worry. Like, to your face, and not behind your back. That way we can talk about it, I can feel better and Brian can stay in the wall.' His shoulders are slumped and his hands are in his lap. It is a lot to take in, in fairness. I'd told him most of it already, but it's probably different seeing it.

'Well, I would rather you just trust me,' I say. 'I mean, I know I got possessed and I punched Father Byrne in the face and did all kinds of horrible stuff, but I'm better now and I'm trying to make things right.'

'Wait, you punched Father Byrne in the face?' Eddie says. 'He has a crossbow, Catlin, you could have really gotten hurt.'

'I do feel bad about it,' I say. 'And I apologised to him.'

'I mean, you were possessed,' Eddie says. 'It wasn't exactly you.'

'It was me when I was kissing you in the sacristy,' I tell him, leaning closer. And then we start kissing again, but my body starts to remember how dangerous it is to kiss boys in caves and I freeze up, and I think that he will notice, because he really seemed to the last time, but he keeps kissing me, even

336

though I'm not kissing back any more, and his hands are on me, tangling through my hair and stroking my back. I can't move. I stay stock-still for ages, and when he breaks away my face is wet with tears. What's wrong with me?

'What happened? What did I do?' he asks, and his face is panicked. I try to catch my breath enough and gather my thoughts together enough to find the words to make it okay, but it isn't and it won't be.

'It's nothing you did,' I say. 'I wanted to kiss you. But . . . I don't know if I should be kissing anyone for a while. And definitely not here in this place, with my evil stepdad on the other side of the wall, like.' I smile, like the panic has passed, like it's all a big joke, but all I can think is that I want him out of here. That I don't feel safe. I wanted to feel safe. Why can't I?

'Can I give you a hug?' he asks, and even though I don't want him to, I say yes and he gives me a hug and I put my two arms around him and squeeze, and think of how nice he is and how good it feels to be around him sometimes and how it will never, ever work now because something in me that I thought was healing maybe is now more broken than it ever was.

And when he's gone, and the cave is dark and silent all around me, apart from the odd noises from the other side of the wall that are definitely Brian and not rats, because I cannot handle rats on top of everything else right now, Mamó slips into my brain to tell me that Maddy is almost strong enough, and to start gathering the things that we'll need for what we'll have to do.

61

Jars

(containing, concentrating)

I'm shaken awake. The moon is fat tonight, the light filtering through the window of Catlin's room. I jolt upright, and see Catlin's face glinting at me in the moonlight. 'You never close the curtains,' she says, and I nod, because I don't. I like the sky, and it doesn't seem to bother me, waking to the changes in it.

'No,' I say. 'I don't.'

'We have to do some witch stuff now, to Brian. It's a whole lot, but we can't wait any longer and Mamó thinks you're strong enough,' she says. 'I mean, we'll both have to rest up for a good while afterwards, but if we get it done, and sorted, then Mam and Brian can sort out the complicated bits like where we're going to live and all the stuff they need to do before they can get divorced.'

'Poor Mam,' I say. 'She deserves to be happy. I wish she could be.'

'She doesn't need a husband to be happy, Madeline. She has us, her two beautiful undead daughters. Surely every day is a lottery win when you're our mam.'

'Surely.' I smile. 'She must particularly enjoy the helping-me-to-the-bathroom part of this whole endeavour. My legs kind of went on strike once I was able to lie down.'

'Are they working again now?' Catlin asks, her face concerned. 'Because there is no way I'm lifting you into the cave like a baby.'

'You're so lazy,' I say.

'I really am. Which is why it was a massive sacrifice to give you my bed so I could babysit a wall, with only the pensioner in my head to talk to . . . *Less of that now and get on with your work* . . . .fine.'

It's strange how easy it is to tell when Mamó is speaking through her mouth. 'Are you and Mamó having full-blown out-loud conversations now?' I ask. 'That's going to make school difficult.'

'That and about a million other things.' She smiles. 'You could probably come back too, if you wanted, now that she's gone. Like, no one would stop you.'

'One of us will have to see the clients,' I say.

'Yeah, but who is to say it has to be you the whole time? There could be an upside to this whole Mamó-being-in-a-weird-coma thing. *I said get on with it. You need a cursing stone* . . . What's a cursing stone, Madeline? It sounds mean.'

'It is mean,' I tell her. It's basically a stone with a dip in the middle you can collect water in and it's for cursing. Is that what we're going to do to Brian?'

Catlin looks at me, but the expression in her eyes is all Mamó.

'*We're going to extract a promise from him, girl. And we're going to make sure it's worth his while keeping it.*'

'By cursing him?'

'*Well, trusting him to behave himself didn't exactly work, even with a layer of magic to it. Now, we'll need an onion, a lemon, salt, rainwater, earth from a grave, hawthorn and rowan berries, yew needles, claw sheaths, some of your hair and a knife. Other things as well, you'll know by instinct.*'

'And the shovel?' I ask.

'*No shovels this time, girl.*' Her voice is gruff, but slightly amused. A kindness to it.

'What are Bridget's remains for?'

'*You'll have to ask her,*' Mamó-Catlin says. '*You'll need a candle, a circle of salt, sand and ash and some rosemary and bay for that. And bone.*'

All of a sudden Catlin is herself again.

'Did you hear all that?' I ask her.

'Yeah, I can always hear what she says.' She quirks her mouth. 'I can't always answer back though, which is annoying because she loves giving out and it's really . . . ow!' Her hand flies to her mouth.

'What happened?' I ask. 'Are you okay?'

'I bit my tongue,' she grumbles, 'and I'm not sure if it's her or not, but it's pretty sore. *I have better things to be doing with my time, Catlin Hayes, than making you bite your tongue.* Oh my God, shut up, Margaret.'

340

I stare at her. My mouth is open.

'This situation,' she says, 'is not ideal. For me or for Mamó. But here we are.'

'Here we are.' I sigh. 'Let's get all of the stuff she asked for together. She keeps her cursing stones in the glasshouse, buried in the herb garden and under the sink. We'll need a small one for this. I feel it.'

'You and your magical feelings.' Catlin grins at me. 'I know this is a bad situation, but part of me loves that we get to do this together now. It's a rush.'

'Yeah.' I smile back at her. 'It really can be.'

I pull on my clothes and a sturdy pair of boots. We pad downstairs, trying not to wake Mam, who is sleeping in a different room to normal at the moment so she can check on Mamó and me in the night. I've already woken to her face staring down at me ominously once, around half past one in the morning, so I think we should be safe. Catlin is enjoying this, her face is all flushed and enthusiastic.

I turn the light on when we get to the kitchen, even though the moon is full, and search for the lemon and onion. I don't have my satchel with me, so I put them into a canvas tote bag Mam got in Lidl when she did the big shop. It feels a lot less witchy, but it's not about the look of things, it's about how they work. And it'll do the job.

'I'm excited to see the cursing stones!' says Catlin, as though they were a ride at Disneyland.

'They're not that great,' I say. 'They make the bones in your hands feel weird – you'll see.' I feel a bit like I'm her nana, telling her witchcraft isn't all exciting midnight spells and

341

collecting mysterious objects. I should lean into the fun of it. Because it is fun as well. I can feel the excitement of what we're about to do, the bigness of it coursing through me. The good stuff, Mamó calls it. And she's right.

'I wonder, Catlin,' I say, 'if he knows where Dad's body is.'

'He probably used it up,' she says, with a wince. 'Ate it or something.'

'Don't say that.'

'Why?' she asks. 'It's clearly what he does. But yeah, if there's any left we should try to get some. It feels wrong that his grave is empty.'

'Like a question mark.'

'Yeah.' I look at my hands. I think Mam must have scrubbed them clean; the skin is pinker than I'm used to and there's no dirt underneath the fingernails at all. My nails have grown a bit, and I resist the urge to bite them down. I need to stay calm. I'm the expert here, I suppose, for all that Catlin has Mamó living in her brain.

'We have what we need from here. Let's get the stones and then the stuff from Mamó's and we can maybe start a bit of it there, before we go down to Brian,' I say.

'That sounds like a good plan.' Catlin's face is flushed. 'I really don't want to mess this up, Maddy. I mean, before, there wasn't time to worry, but the past few days, all there's been is time. And the worry creeps in.'

'You never used to worry,' I tell her. 'You used to find it way easier than me to shake things off.'

'I think it's crept in after Lon,' Catlin says, her voice low, as we move outside and through the dark of the gardens. 'It's

342

like a huge part of who I am has changed. And when I try to get back to who I was, like with Eddie . . .'

Her voice is soft when she speaks of him, a softness I haven't heard before.

'Are you two together now?' I ask.

She shakes her head. 'The physical stuff is kind of . . . difficult right now,' she says. 'It's lovely for a bit and then all of a sudden I remember things and it's not . . . right. Anyway, enough about that. I don't have the time to be unpacking my big bag of trauma when we've witchcraft to do. Where do we begin?'

I can tell she doesn't want to talk about it any more, so I just say that I think there are a couple of small cursing stones near the rosemary bush. And then there is nothing but the quiet shuffle of our hands against the earth, inside it, in the moonlight. There's something peaceful in the two of us working side by side towards a common goal. A sort of rightness.

'I think I have one!' Catlin exclaims. 'I'm going to curse everyone so hard, it'll be class.'

'It doesn't work that way,' I say. 'Besides, we kind of only want to curse one person.'

'Do you think he could be possessed, Madeline?' Catlin asks. 'Like by the ghost of his dead mean dad or something? Like, it would explain why he was sometimes nice and kind but also doing terrible things behind our backs.'

'I think he got used to getting what he wanted,' I say. 'And I think he was kind to Mam and us because we had something he wanted. I don't think there's a way out of this where he's a good person.'

'But he's not all bad either,' Catlin points out.

'No one is,' I tell her. 'But if you do enough bad, for long enough, eventually someone has to stop you. And that's our job right now. It's getting cold. Let's have a cup of tea and get to work.'

We traipse towards Mamó's flat. Before we enter, I set the cursing stone out on a windowsill, positioned to catch some rainwater, if there is any. I see Badb's silhouette, perched in the trees. Though the moon is bright, it's like they're occupying negative space and I can't even make out the glint of their eyes. I shudder, in spite of myself, and am glad to enter the familiar place, which oddly feels a little bit like home now.

62

Saucers

(queries or requests)

The saucer stained with my blood is still on the worktop, so I take it to the sink and wash it while Maddy gathers the bits and pieces. There's another thing we need to do here as well that I haven't told her about, and it won't be easy. I put the kettle on. I want to make sure that she's taking breaks, sitting down a bit. This next step is something *I* need to do. Mamó said it was more suited to my talents.

We have to talk to Bridget. Have to ask her a favour. She's done so much for us already. She might say no, Mamó says. And that's okay if she does. There are other ways around it. It's just this is the cleanest one, the best. I gather salt and sand and ash. I've brought the earth from our father's grave with me as well, in the pocket of my dress. It feels like he should be here to see this, even in some small way.

'Is that a blood saucer?' Madeline is aghast. 'Don't just leave it on the draining board.'

'I used hot water and washing-up liquid,' I say. 'Besides, it's my blood. It's probably really clean.'

'It's disgusting,' she says. 'And what's your blood doing in a saucer anyway?'

'I fed it to Badb to get them to show me a way to save you.'

She sighs. 'Nothing is ever direct with Mamó, is it?'

'No,' I say. 'And it wasn't like we had all of this spare time. I mean, you were legit dying. And there I was, giving free refills of vein-juice to a . . . whatever Badb is.'

'A raven.'

'I think we both know they're more than a raven, Maddy.' I tilt my shoulders back, so they click, and turn to face her. 'Okay. So while we're here we're just going to do a quick little séance-type of thing, no big deal. Mamó's plan is that I call Bridget, just to see if she'd be open to being part of the spell we're working on Brian. A sort of alarm-slash-punishment system. Mamó thinks because he forced her to be a servant for so long, and also was complicit in Lon being allowed to do Lon things, that she might actually prefer keeping an eye on him to whatever afterlife awaits her. Some ghosts want to go into the light, but others prefer to settle scores. And we need to find out what kind of ghost Bridget is.'

'Fair enough.' Maddy looks surprisingly unruffled. 'I was wondering what we'd need to combine with the cursing stone to make it stick. And apparently it's the spirit of a murdered girl.'

'Right,' I say. 'I've some bits gathered, but we'll also need a black candle and a white candle. And something of hers. We need a bowl of pure water. We need salt and a mirror. Two coins, half a lemon, ash. A handful of yew berries.' I screw up my eyes, trying to tap into my intuition, before sighing when it bites me in the neck. 'Ugh. And we're probably going to need some of my blood again.'

I take the saucer off the draining board. Madeline begins to move the coffee table, but I stop her.

'You sit,' I say. 'Tonight is going to be a lot, and you need to conserve your strength.' I pass her a cup of tea. 'There's no milk though. Because it's gone off.'

'It would have,' she says. 'I think we need an oak leaf too. One each. I'll go and get them.'

'What are they for?' I ask.

'We need to know if it's really her.' Her mouth is set tight. 'This helps with spotting lies.'

'You've used it on me before,' I realise.

'I have,' she says, 'and you were lying.' She takes a long sip of her tea and we meet each other's eyes.

'What we're about to do, Catlin, is serious,' she says. 'It's powerful stuff. Are you sure you want this?'

'I don't know what I want, Maddy,' I tell her. 'But I wanted you to be alive and here. And I'm willing to hold up my end of the bargain that I made. This isn't like a hobby, or a thing to try out. It's our job now. And it's very weird, but there it is.'

'You sound so sure.'

'I've a ghost in my head,' I tell her. 'If I didn't know who I was, I'd really be in trouble.' I move the coffee table from beside the armchair and assemble the things that we will need to start the night's work.

When everything is ready, I turn the lights out and light the candles. Maddy sits in the armchair, keeping an eye on me, the oak leaf in her hands.

And, for the first time in what feels like forever, I start to pray.

63

Water

(life)

Here you are. Look at you. Look at what they did. You were a girl. You are a girl still, but older, and not older. If it hadn't happened you would still be quick. You would be grown. There are so many lives you could have led.

He started off chatting to you on the walk home from school. The part of the road where you would branch off. He would be there, and you would pass each other by. You got used to it. He was handsome. You liked it when he smiled at you. You wanted to get out of this place, and you knew you probably never would. Or only for a few years. People kept on coming back, and staying. They like to be with their own kind, but you wanted something other for yourself. To know all different kinds of people.

Before him, the only person you had ever kissed was Carol Collins. And it was just a few times. You felt her move away from you. Decide that you were not something she wanted. It stung you, and you didn't like the feeling. You wanted to show her how much you didn't care so you started taking more care with your clothes, your hair, your make-up. Getting the bus into Galway to buy the things you needed. Like they were armour. Mammy gave you some of the egg money. She must have known there was something eating you. You didn't tell her though. You couldn't put it into words. You didn't want it to be true that Carol had had a taste of you and sent you back. You didn't want to make a big thing of it. It was the biggest thing you'd ever felt though. You couldn't help it.

And there was him. He was handsome, and he was dangerous. You'd seen him out with different girls. No one from here. Not since you could remember. And he was older, but that made it more interesting in ways. He had his own money. Had a car. He could buy you things. Could sell you things. He sold you on himself. On the both of you together.

Mammy called him flashy and she was right, but you needed something flashy, something glittering, to take your mind off all the things you still could not help feeling. When he kissed you, though, his lips were cold, and you had to think about what to do with your hands. You didn't want to draw him, drag him, into you.

When he showed up in your dreams you were surprised. He called you mysterious. Inscrutable. Distant. Icy. He described you as though you were a lady in a book and not a real, warm girl. He knew that you were real and you were warm though. You could feel the craving in his hands.

350

He told you that he loved you and you decided that you loved him back. You put mousse into your hair and spent ages getting your fringe just right, doing things with eyeshadow. He always noticed every little detail. And you decided that you loved him back.

And you decided that you loved him back.

When he hurt you, were not surprised though. You could always sense the something in him that knew you weren't there. Not all of you, not really. The little distance that had drawn him in because of something you held. A certain power that he didn't like. And you had decided that you loved him, and so it was impossible for you to walk away. Because you loved him. So you coped with it. And he would talk about when you were married. About what that would be like. About the children you would have together. And you would feel a shudder in your womb at the thought of hosting something like him. You could feel the wrongness of it for a child of yours, but somehow you deserved that very wrongness. It made no sense. It made no sense. But there you were. You didn't see your friends as much. That had started before him anyway. You didn't want to see her. He'd go into the shop for you, where she worked part-time, to buy your cigarettes. He always bought you the brand that he liked, and there was no point arguing. They made your mouth taste like it was his mouth.

When he killed you, it wasn't a surprise. It hurt. It hurt so much. But you had been dying for a while before. There was less of who you were left in you. Very little left to take away. But what there was. That piece of you. That piece he couldn't touch. It scratched. It fought him. You bit, you kicked, you screamed.

351

And no one came.

Until afterward, when there was a use for you. Like boiling bones for stock, they gathered the remains of your poor body and they took them for their own. They didn't even let you keep your soul. Put you to work, making life more comfortable for them. There was a little bit of magic in you. Of course there was, look at where you're from. It hadn't been enough to keep you safe. You kept on going and you did what you were told and fell into a rhythm of it really. But sometimes things would happen. You'd see or touch something –

A braid of brown hair coming softly loose.

A snowdrop bursting through soil.

A wide bright smile.

An egg.

A bowl of porridge –

– and it would give you a memory of life. It wasn't your death that made you angry, hungry. It was your life. The life you wouldn't get. All of the tastes, the moments. When they freed you, anger filled you up and you went into her dreams and found they were another kind of trap. You went into the walls and found your sisters. And after you had torn the thing apart, you waited there. You could have gone. There are so many places where the dead can go. Nothing tethers you but your own self.

And yet, here you are.

A cold, stale place a little like his mouth.

You find you do not move.

You do not remember how to move.

And when she calls – the girl – the noisy, messy one. The one

whose dreams did not belong to her. She makes an offer. And you
remember how it felt to want.

    Yes, you could want this.

    A purpose, and a little taste of breath.

64

Stone

(blessing, cursing, holding, protecting)

Catlin is sitting in front of the flame, and her lips are moving quickly and deliberately. One hand is placed in a bowl of blood and lemon-water, the other in a bowl of salt, sand, earth and yew berries.

The candles flicker and her breath comes quick and shallow. I have a sense that if I reached my fingers out to grab her, they would pass right through as though one of us were made of smoke. He head tilts to the side, as though she is responding to someone, but it stays that way for an unnaturally long period of time. If I wanted to, I could blow out the candles, move her hand. I can end this, but she doesn't seem to be in danger. I don't feel a sickness in my gut. Or an unnatural warmth.

It's easier to be the one doing it, I think. Or I prefer it

anyway. I'm worried about her, and I don't know what's going on, beyond some sort of bargain with Bridget Hora's ghost. I have tucked the oak leaf into her bra strap against her skin, and I am holding mine in my hand. So far they're whole. The room is dim, I hear the tap of rain against the window. A knock at the door.

Thud.

Thud.

Thud.

I rise from the chair, and begin to walk towards it. To see who it could be. And Button emerges from behind the coal scuttle, where he's been curled up, and runs to the door, and stares at it and hisses.

Okay, I think. Okay.

I sit back down.

Catlin's eyes are wide open now and moving around, pupils shrinking and dilating though the light isn't changing. Her shoulders rise and fall.

Thud.

Thud.

Thud.

I stay where I am. I don't acknowledge it. I clutch the oak leaf and focus my gaze on the salt and dried matter under Catlin's hand. Thinking of the ways that I have used it in the past. Under beds and tucked in pockets, school bags. I think of pouring circles of it out around the two of us, like a border or a boundary that can't be crossed. I think of the two of us together. And how much we have given to keep each other safe.

I think.

If I do nothing, she'll be in no danger.

The leaf remains intact.

I think.

What's behind the door?

My palms begin to itch.

Button climbs over to me and sits in the centre of my lap, settling like a loaf of soda bread. It feels as though his legs have retracted into his body. It feels as though he weighs more than a cat. A low rumble emerges from him.

Thud.

Thud.

Thud.

It's not a purr. It's a warning. Catlin opened a door to let Bridget in, I think. And something knows that there's an open door. They want to find it. I stare at the salt, and feel the warmth and rumble of the cat holding me down. Grounding me. I can't believe he had my soul inside him all along. Behind that eye of his, the one I ruined. I can't believe he gave it up for me. I look at the salt, and I think of the clumsy kitten that he was, and how I was probably the first thing to have hurt him in his little life. There is a tiny dent between his shoulder blades. Cats can separate them, can't they? To sneak out windows, go about their business. Button was hurt, I think. But he survived.

Catlin's body ripples up from the floor, as though something has passed through her, and her head flops forward. I can't hear the rain against the windows and I wonder if it was really rain at all or something else. The candles quench themselves, and I gently remove her hands from the bowls – water first, then salt – and place her head on her hands. I turn the lights back on and pour her a glass of water. I can hear her breathing as though she were asleep. It goes on for about another minute, and then she pushes herself up, looks at me and starts to cry and cry. Proper sobs as though she were a little child. I hold her in my arms and tell her it will be all right, all right.

'I know,' she says. 'It's just . . . It's just so sad. She was only just beginning everything. He took it all. She never had a chance. She never had a chance. And it's so *cold*.'

'It's okay,' I tell her. 'Take some time. Have a drink of water. Sit.'

She rises, and plonks herself into an armchair.

'I'll be okay, Maddy,' she says. 'It's actually fine. I just need a second. It was a lot. But I saw her, and we talked . . . well, more communicated really. It was . . . weird. Like being in another person's body, but she could hear my thoughts. A bit like me and Mamó are now, maybe.'

'But she'll do it.'

'She will. Oh, Maddy, she's so cold. She just wants to be warm. It's not a lot.'

'No,' I say. 'It's not a lot to ask.'

'So now we make the amulet,' she tells me. 'That part is more you than me, I've no idea what to do, beyond what Mamó tells me. And when we're done, then we go see Brian.'

'Okay,' I say, and get up from my seat again. 'We have the bits we need for this. Let's get on with it.'

Catlin stands up and puts the coffee table back. I go over to the window again. The moon must have gone behind a cloud. Outside is pitch-black nothing.

Darkness.

Silence.

65

Butter

(changing, smoothing, easing)

Watching Maddy work is kind of amazing. When she studies, there could be an explosion in the room and she wouldn't even notice. Though when it was homework, as opposed to witchy stuff, I suppose I didn't get how much of a skill it was to be able to shut the world out, laser-focus. It was harder for me. I suppose that's why I needed prayer so much, to find a quiet space within myself.

She has jars of things and handfuls of things and she's lashing them into each other, boiling something on the stove and then straining it through a piece of cloth. She pours some of the strained liquid into the cursing stone, and it drinks it up. The water disappears, and she pours again, again, until it seems to be sated. I'm braiding Bridget's hair, and some of ours, through a ribbon we're going to use to fasten it to Brian. There isn't a hole through the stone, but apparently that doesn't matter. I tie seven knots into the hair and ribbon, and with every one I can feel the tug of Bridget at the corners of my brain. She's hungry for a warm place to live. I cannot blame her, it has been so long. More than twice the time I've been alive. I bind her to the ribbon, to the spell.

I think of Carol Collins and her big brown eyes that always look both hopeful and sad. A Labrador, I called her in the car on the way back from Cork. I hope that Bridget can see her again. I mean, so much time has passed. But I think she would want to. A hum of agreement turns my skin to gooseflesh. Maddy works on.

After a time, she looks at me and I know that we have to do this next bit together. We place our hands on the cursing stone and I think of Bridget, and how the parts of her were shaved away one by one like curls of wood. And how, in spite of everything, she's here. Even after death she has persisted, and she wants to help. I don't know if I'll ever be like that. That kind of strong. I meet my sister's eyes and call her through the ribbon. The hole in the stone opens like a maw and gulps the ribbon knot by horrid knot.

The lights go out in the room, just for a second, before they start up again. I hear my own nervous laughter.

'Did it work?' I ask.

'It felt like it did,' Maddy says, her face all serious. 'But the only way we'll know for sure is to keep going. Try it out on Brian.'

'Back to the wall, so,' I say, trying to make it sound like it is nothing. But the bigness of it lodges in my chest. This kind of power. It's exciting, but it's skating very close to something else. Something sinister. I can see why Mamó wanted Maddy to stay away from other kinds of magic, from prayer and flesh. What hums through her is more, far more than whatever little bit of it I have. If something got its teeth into my sister . . . oh, it would love it. It would have a feast.

She needs us, girl. To keep her tethered here.

My skin crawls, thinking, till Maddy grabs my shoulder and tells me to get up, we have to go.

66

Flame

(transfer of energy)

'Can we do something first before we go?' Catlin asks, and I roll my eyes.

'What could be more important than taking care of Brian?'

She swallows. 'See, that's the thing. Bridget, she was – she is – so cold. And the other girls. I mean. They saved my life. And they're still in the walls.'

'Can that not wait though?' I ask. As soon as it's out of my mouth I realise it can. But it shouldn't have to.

'See, it's all about stopping people, what we've been doing, Maddy. And I mean, I always thought that with Mamó, your whole deal was helping people. And it could be you or me in there – in the cold, in the dark. And I would want someone to put us first . . .'

'You always want someone to put you first,' I say.

'Fair, but we're going to have to be cruel to Brian, Maddy. And I can live with that. But let's choose to be kind before that. They shouldn't have to spend eternity there, as a resource for somebody to use. I hope that someone would do the same for Dad. If that is what they did to him, you know?'

'Yeah,' I say. 'When did you get so thoughtful?'

She grins at me. 'It won't last. And we can do what we need to do for them from here. You and me, we are connected to them. That'll be channel enough. I don't want to give Brian a chance to see what we're at. To strategise. Mamó knows the words we have to say. What herbs to use.'

I close my eyes. 'Chamomile, hawthorn, lavender, oats, a bit of yew and . . . we could use roses, but I think maybe we'll substitute yarrow.'

Catlin nods. 'Not a big fan of roses any more.'

I pull the things I need from off the shelf, and arrange them inside a circle of tea lights Catlin builds. We stand in the centre and join hands.

'Mamó is going to give me the right words now,' she says, and her face is very solemn.

I close my eyes and listen to that voice, somewhere between my sister and my mentor chanting. It sounds a bit like the words that Mamó used the night she made the circle in the cave. I sense the lights go out, the candles flare.

After a while, I start to join in for the bits I recognise. There are some parts that repeat again, again. It's gentle this time, much more so than with Bridget. It's not forcing anything open. More lighting up a choice. A route to take.

I feel a presence in the circle with us. Another, and another.

363

One by one. Girls cupped in the centre of us. Our saviours and our sisters. This feels right.

By the end of it, Catlin's voice is breathless.

When I open my eyes, the tea lights are floating somewhere near our shoulders. We look at each other, tears streaming down our faces, as they slowly lower down and fizzle out.

'I think we can go now,' Catlin tells me. 'Madeline . . . will you hold my hand?'

I do. We venture out into the night.

67

Oats

(itches, stitches, ease)

My eyes adjust a bit faster than they used to, but Madeline seems to move as easily as a cat through the dark. When I turn towards her, I half expect to see the weird reflective glow that Button has. It doesn't take long to get to the cave, and when we do, Madeline looks at me.

'What?' I say, though I know it's the wrappers and cans and other bits of me I've left strewn all over the place. I hate looking at places through tidy people's eyes. It's so annoying.

'I'm saying nothing,' she tells me, as if she were making a huge sacrifice.

'It's a MURDER CAVE, Madeline,' I point out. 'Not like a fancy show house. No one cares if you leave a chocolate-bar wrapper on the floor of a MURDER CAVE.'

She sighs. 'Let's not get into it. It's not my job to give out to you about tidying. BUT we need a clean space to work on, so can you at least collect all your bits and, like, put them in a trash pile and then maybe after all this is done you can go live in the trash pile like the trash demon you are.'

'Too soon,' I say. 'I basically was a demon like five seconds ago and I'm still recovering. I may be messy, but you are insensitive. And who's to say what's worse?'

'Um . . . you are also insensitive?' Maddy says. 'At least I put stuff in the bin.'

'I'm not insensitive to me,' I say. 'I take really good care of myself. It is a skill. Now, let's pull some bricks out of a wall. Do you want a chisel?'

'No,' says Maddy. 'I'm going to use my shovel.' She picks up a shovel lying at the edge of the cave, behind a pile of rocks and gives it a little squeeze like, *Hello, Old Friend*.

'You're really into that shovel,' I say.

'We've been through a lot together.' She smiles at it fondly.

'Yeah, like the time I hit you in the head with that exact shovel,' I say. 'Memories.'

'Let me have my little bit of shovel nostalgia, Catlin.' Her eyes are bright. 'It was pretty handy last time that we did some very dangerous stuff.'

I look at her, all business, and begin picking up my wrappers one by one and leaving them beside the pile of rocks where the shovel was.

'You take the shovel,' I say. 'I will use this chisel, which has never yet helped me out in a crisis, but looks like it could fully murder almost anyone, so could probably be handy at close range.'

366

'At close range,' Maddy snorts. 'That's some Father Byrne-type weaponry nonsense.'

'It's hard to talk about weapons without sounding like a bit of a prick, to be fair,' I say.

'They're not weapons, Catlin,' she says. 'At least they're not supposed to be. They're tools. We're not going to, like, murder Brian.'

'Glad to hear it,' says a muffled voice from behind the wall.

'SHUT UP, BRIAN!' we both say.

'Fair enough,' he says, which doesn't count as shutting up and is Brian all over. Very nice, very polite, not doing anything he's supposed to unless he feels like it.

When I've cleared a space, Maddy lays out all the bits Mamó had us collect, and some extra bits as well – leaves I don't recognise, some coloured powders, a bunch of twigs.

'What are those?' I ask.

'Those are just in case,' she says. 'I don't know if we'll need them, but if you feel you might need something and you're about to do something witchy, it's always best to bring too much rather than too little . . .'

'I'll get started on the wall,' I say. 'There are some loose bricks, and I'm sure once we knock a few in, he'll be able to climb his way out, he's quite skinny.'

'No problem, Catlin, as the fella says,' Brian says, ingratiatingly, and I roll my eyes. Why does he have to continue to be such a stepdad when we're trying to neutralise him?

'How's Sheila getting, on girls?' the wall asks.

'She's doing great,' I tell him. 'Apart from being married to you. But that's easily fixed.'

Maddy twists her hands together nervously, scanning all the bits she has laid out.

'That should just about do it,' she says. She moves past me with the shovel, her face intent. I have to duck to avoid getting brained by it.

It takes a while to dismantle a wall. Particularly when you're both absolutely wrecked from all the horrors that have been visited on your bodies recently. I mean, both of us could have died *several* ways, never mind all of the psychological trauma we're after going through. We don't speak that much as our bodies settle into the rhythm of the work. Every now and then one of us lets out a grunt or something, and I feel every breath of air entering my lungs as though it takes an effort to breathe it in.

Once we've prised a few bricks out, Brian starts to help. He looks a bit dishevelled, but not that much worse for wear.

'We'd be faster if I had a chisel or something,' he tells us.

'We're not giving you a weapon, Brian.' Madeline rolls her eyes. 'You murdered our dad.'

'My father murdered your father. I was an accessory at most,' he says.

I stare at him.

'Brian, I was there. I saw your face.'

He moves his gaze away from ours, towards the ground. 'I don't know what you think you saw, Catlin, but I will say I'm not proud of the kind of man I used to be,' he says. 'And there are, obviously, still times when it's a struggle for me to do my best. But I am trying, girls. I really am. And I want you to believe that.'

Madeline lets out a long, irritated sigh. 'Brian. You obviously haven't been trying hard enough. Now, are you going to make this harder than it needs to be?' She rolls up her sleeves, and her neutral, slightly exasperated expression is pretty intimidating, I have to say. I mean, it would almost work on me. And I've seen her cry because it was Wednesday and there were no more biscuits in the press. (I ate them all, but did feel bad, in fairness.)

'Rest assured, girls, I'll give in without a fight. It's the least I can do.'

'You're very clean,' I say. 'Considering.'

'I do what I can to feel human.'

'Yeah, abusing ghosts, cannibal magic, murdering people and then marrying their widow. Normal human things for normal human men,' I say.

Maddy furrows her eyebrows at me, but I can't help it. Sometimes I just have to say a thing.

'Well . . .' His voice is a bit sheepish, like he's been caught eating the last yoghurt.

'Well nothing, Brian. Some people go travelling or do a charity bungee jump or something when they feel the need for a bit of adventure. There are a lot of ways of being in the world that aren't actively evil. It feels like, if you wanted to change, you would have changed, you know?'

Even as I hear my own voice say it, I know it's not that easy. I look at Maddy and get a flash of my hands around her throat, squeezing, squeezing, squeezing.

There are things I did I can't take back.

369

68

Lavender

(the tremblings of the heart)

Catlin can't help herself. She keeps on chatting to Brian. I could throttle her, if I hadn't been throttled so often recently, and didn't know what it felt like. I wouldn't do it to someone now. At least until the memory fades. I rub my neck. There are still marks on it. On Catlin's too. Bruises take a good long while to fade when they're that deep. It's blood beneath the skin. Bleeding, but less showy.

'There should be enough bricks now that you can crawl out,' I say to Brian. 'Move.'

I feel that it's important to limit chat with him, because he's so fucking plausible all the time. He'll have us convinced it was all a bad mistake and that we should all move back into the castle, try again and he'll give us trust funds or some such rich man's nonsense.

Meanwhile, Catlin is interviewing him, like he's a guest on a podcast designed to annoy me.

'So, are you human, Brian? Or is there more you haven't told us yet?' Her voice is deceptively calm, almost professional.

'I am human, Catlin. Girls –' he says. 'But you know, even without innate magical talent, a person who applies themselves and learns can access certain powers. It's just a case of knowing how to go about it.'

'Like sacrifice.'

'Like sacrifice.'

'And murder? Was Lon, like, in your smoothies, Brian?' Catlin asks, and I have to bite my lip to stop myself from yelling at her. I want us to present a united front.

'You're very observant, Catlin,' he says. 'He was. I found it easier to do what needed to be done if it looked a little less like what it was, if that makes sense.'

'It does,' she says. 'Did you, like, grind him up?'

'I got a contraption off the Internet that dehydrates things,' Brian says. 'Once something is all dried up, it's easy enough to crush it to a powder. And he was quite old, as the fella says, so there might not have been as much juice in him as the next man.'

The tone is almost jovial, but when I look at Catlin there's a hint of something in her eyes that is deadly serious. She's up to something too, I realise. Maybe trying to lull him, maybe trying to glean more information . . . I nod at her.

'Fascinating,' she says. 'Did your dad teach you about that kind of magic?'

'He did,' Brian says. 'He was something of a seeker of arcane

371

knowledge. And as he acquired more and more of it, he became hungry to know more, and to do more. He thought it was unfair that some people have innate ability, while others have to struggle for every little bit of what they get.'

'The mountain girls,' Catlin says. 'It wasn't just Lon who killed them, was it?'

'No,' Brian says. 'Initially my father turned a blind eye – Lon stayed away from locals, mostly – but then one of the girls turned out to have some sort of magical ability, untapped of course, and he realised the potential in that. I mean, given Lon's proclivities, that sort of thing was going to happen anyway. What harm in guiding him a bit? And once they were dead, I mean, they weren't using their bodies any more, so . . .'

'You scavenged the leftovers.' Catlin says grimly.

'We never called them that.' His voice is shriller now, defensive.

'But you used them like that,' Catlin says, meeting his eyes directly. 'If I had died, if Maddy hadn't been able to save me, Brian . . . would you have used my body that way too?'

There is a universe, I think, in which Catlin would be an excellent barrister. She's making Brian visibly uncomfortable in his skin. He's twitching. Is he frightened?

'No. Of course not,' he protests, his Adam's apple bobbing in his throat. 'You're my daughter.'

Catlin runs her fingers through her hair, absently removing a desiccated beech leaf, which she crumbles and discards.

'I'm not your daughter, Brian. I'm the daughter of the man you killed. One of them anyway. Now, 'tis time for you to get over there. Maddy has it all set up.'

Brian looks at me. I nod. I think Catlin is being Mamó now. A bit. Her voice is different and she used the word *'tis*.

Catlin turns and glares at me. Her eyes are weird. It's definitely her. I smile. I've missed the old bag.

'This will do,' she says, taking in the things that I've laid out. 'Brian, you'll need to lie down on the ground.'

I breathe in deeply. 'We're going to need you to open your shirt.'

'My goodness, girls,' he says. 'This is all very serious.'

'I didn't realise,' I say to him, 'that you were under the impression that it should be funny.'

Catlin meets my gaze, and I can tell she thinks he's planning something. I think so too. He's talking too much, trying to distract us.

'I hadn't used prayer magic, or blood magic, you know, for years, before ye came along,' he says, 'but when I met Sheila, and we moved here and became a real family, I got so scared I'd lose you. Mess it up. Which I suppose I have . . .'

He trails off, as though he was expecting one of us to contradict him. We don't oblige.

'And I wanted to keep you here. I wanted things to work out. And so I slipped. Just a little bit.'

'The fox we found at the crossroads . . .' Catlin says.

'A sacrifice.' He nods. 'I wanted you to stay here. With me. I didn't realise that it would happen the way it did. I didn't mean –'

'Get on the floor, Brian,' I say.

He doesn't move.

'And then with Lon. He'd hurt you. And I hadn't been able to protect you. And I felt so frustrated, so powerless . . . I wanted to be able to set it right. To be a good father. To keep you safe. And to do that, I needed to be stronger than I was. Mamó had been policing me for years, keeping an eye. Binding me. I let her, because I didn't want to be like my father. But I needed to be able to do something. And not just sit there if something happened again. And he deserved everything he got.'

'Get on the floor, Brian,' I say again, but he keeps on going.

Catlin meets my gaze, like is he legit making a villain speech? I nod, because apparently so. But I have a sense there's more to it than that.

'It felt good, to have magic flowing through me again. To be capable of things. I had to be careful about it, because Mamó was always watching me.'

'She was right to,' Catlin says, and her voice is low. 'You needed watching.'

'I'm not a child to be chastened,' Brian snaps. 'I make my own decisions, and I thought it through. Of course it's more difficult now. With what you did to Lon. But not impossible.'

'Brian,' I say, 'why aren't you on the floor?'

'Oh, Maddy,' he says. 'You were always my favourite. I'm sorry to have to do this.' And he raises his hand.

Catlin lets out a belly, bone-deep sigh.

'Oh for the love of God, young fella, would you ever just do what she tells you?'

'Mamó?' Brian squints. 'I had a feeling you'd be showing up at some point.'

Someone else's smile on Catlin's face.

'Are you going to be a good lad?'

Brian looks at her, and slowly shakes his head.

'Well, isn't this a turn-up for the books? I'm afraid not, Mamó. I tried and it got me precisely nowhere.' The ground begins to shake as Brian's outstretched palm moves up and down. I plonk my two feet solidly on the floor and refuse to let it unbalance me. My feet are plugged into the ground. They know it well. It is their home, and will not fail me now.

Catlin's lips are moving, and I'm picking up some salt and yew berries from the ground. Some lavender, grown in the earth from our father's grave, as well, and some of Button's claw sheaths. The onion, rowan berries and an egg. The spell is nearly done. Once we get him lying down, it won't take long and it will stick. My head is clearer than it's been in ages, laser-focused.

My sister raises her hand, fingers splayed out, and one by one she begins to close them, starting with the little finger, which is unnatural somehow. I can't close mine all by itself. The expression on her face is both benign and intent. I'm not sure how much is her and how much is Mamó, but the two of them are definitely up to something.

God help us all.

69

Roses

(binding, cooling, purging)

Brian is such a *pain* in the *hole*. This is worse than the chore wheel. The ground shaking is giving me motion sickness and, like, he has to know we're going to wear him down eventually. His face is all screwed up and the tendons in his hand are standing out.

Mamó is in the back of my head, but she's weak. I look over at Maddy, who is standing with her arms folded, looking at Brian like he's just spilled red wine on a tablecloth in her restaurant. Real this-is-my-place-of-business-and-you-have-inconvenienced-me-with-your-bad-manners vibes. It's halfway between Mamó and Mam and thoroughly intimidating. I find myself wanting to tuck in my shirt and straighten up my spine.

Small rocks tumble from the ceiling of the cave. Some of

them get in my hair. They're going to be so annoying to get out. My hair tangles more easily now it's white. The texture is a little different and it snags much worse on hairbrushes. I do not need to be adding cave-dust to the mix.

Would you stop thinking about your hair and do your job?

Ugh, Mamó. I can see why Maddy got annoyed with her. She's obsessed with work. I close my eyes for a minute and murmur a prayer to Dad, to the ghosts. I feel a tunnel opening up in my brain, a kind of peaceful hum. It's me and the rhythm of my voice, of my thoughts. I can still see Brian, and his hand and his defiant face. He looks like a small child, not a man. Something in his stance.

'You don't have to do this, Brian,' I say. 'You're choosing to. Because you are a pain in the hole.'

'Language, Catlin,' he says with a grin.

I sigh. 'Look, you might think because you killed my dad and ate my ex that I should be intimidated by you or whatever. Maybe you think that you need to act up because your dad was this big monster guy you have to live up to or something –'

'Don't psychoanalyse me, Catlin Hayes. This has nothing to do with my father.' His mouth tightening, becoming more irate.

'You're the one who is always going on about him, Brian. I don't care why you're doing what you're doing. I do, however, care about being in a cave that seems to be collapsing. It's annoying. Look.'

I raise the other hand, and replicate the movement from before, folding my little finger first and then the rest of them. If Madeline was doing this too, we would totally look like we were about to break into some weird dance routine. I pull on

377

the calm and the certainty that prayer gives me, and I feel Mamó nudging at me. It's very strange when something inside your brain starts nudging you. Half physical, and half like an intrusive thought.

'You could just let me go,' Brian says, either deluded or bluffing. 'I can make this stop.'

'Oh, I can make it stop right now,' I say, splaying out my fingers and realising that it's actually true. The shaking subsides. I lower my shoulders a little. I hadn't known I'd been bracing myself. 'I'm going to ask you one last time, will you please get on the floor and let us bind you so you can maybe stop having so many creepy and disturbing secrets and, like, start divorcing Mam.'

'You can't tell me what to do any more,' Brian says. 'I'm not some pup to be neutered.'

'No one wants to neuter you, Brian.' Maddy's voice cuts through the air. I can feel her getting ready to do something. She has a rake of leaves and bits of dirt. I'll probably have to learn all the leaf and dirt names over the next while. It's going to take ages. I can feel my thoughts annoying Mamó, which is quite satisfying. I wonder should I leave Maddy to it. I mean, she's far more witch than me.

She won't have enough in her for two fights.

I can sense the truth of that. The binding won't be easy for her. Even with my help. I unclench my hands and lower them, walk towards Brian.

'Brian,' I say, 'did I ever tell you what happened to Our Lady of Ballyfrann?'

'I don't . . .' he starts, but he's looking at me.

'Well, she tried to take me with her when Mamó burned her. But she couldn't. And now she's ash. But she was never just a thing that was carved in wood. She crept into my brain. And there are times when I'm not sure that she's entirely gone. I have these dreams still . . .'

Brian is looking at me, and his expression is hard to read. I hope he doesn't want to put me in a smoothie or anything. I would hate that.

'. . . these fever dreams. And when I wake I'm not where I expected to be. In the cave sometimes I would wake up clawing the wall. Because she wants to get to you. When you hurt someone's child, an old, wild, fierce thing's child, it doesn't forget. And whatever shadow, whatever little stain of her, is left behind in me, it remembers what you did to Lon. Bone-deep. And if I let that rise within me now . . .'

I arch my back, deepen my voice, let my eyes darken and allow Mamó to lift me off the ground, just a little.

'. . . well, it would be the worse for you.'

I raise my hand, and swish it to the side.

'GET ON THE FLOOR.'

He stumbles and he does. Lies worked! I am a genius!

When I turn to Maddy though, her face is pale. She looks afraid of me. I cannot reassure her without alerting Brian, so I just shrug and tell her, 'Let's get on with it.'

70

Oak

(spitting of the blood, allaying heat, truth seeking)

I put down the bits I'd gathered and shake a circle of salt around Brian. I add rowan berries, yew needles and the claw sheaths from Button around it. To protect us, and make it harder for him to access whatever power he has left. I can't feel much of it on him, but my heart is racing from what Catlin said. The words are words, but the eyes and levitation. She couldn't do that by herself, not without help, and Mamó isn't into that kind of showmanship. Something I'll have to deal with after this, I muse. Carefully and quickly.

'Open his shirt,' I tell her, not meeting her eye. I'm worried she'll find something in my gaze that she won't like.

'Ugh,' she says. I give her a sharp glance and her expression shifts and she says, 'Excuse me, Brian,' and carefully unbuttons it, one by one.

Brian is silent, but his eyes are furious and I can tell he wants a way out of this. It feels strange, having someone helpless and unwilling on the floor. I'm not comfortable with it. But at the same time, what can we do?

I take the cursing stone out and hold it up.

'This will make it difficult for you to access your magic, Brian,' I tell him. 'And if you try, we will know. And there will be consequences.'

I hold it over his chest and focus. Catlin holds him by the shoulders, not unkindly. I close my eyes and focus on what needs to be done. Push my worries away, and concentrate on the part where his ribcage ends and the flesh is soft and giving. His chest hair is sparse and patchy. I close my eyes and think about that small space of flesh and feel the weight of the stone in my hand. It feels unwelcome, making my skin hum with revulsion. I think of Bridget Hora, and try to send some good wishes and thanks through the warmth of my skin. I hope she'll find something to comfort her here, not just the revenge. It's not enough.

I hear a low sound and realise it's coming from my throat. Catlin's voice joins mine and our hands reach to the point on his chest. A little hole the size of a full stop begins to open, yawning like a mouth until it's wide enough to accommodate the cursing stone. I drop it in and almost expect to hear the splash of water, but the sound is more a meaty sort of suck. The hole closes slowly over, and Catlin takes her finger, dipped in a mixture of water, ash, earth and blood, and begins to trace symbols over his skin, presumably guided by Mamó. I feel the tension of the spell still pulling at me and keep my hands where

381

they are. Brian's chest rises and falls. His breathing is regular, and so is his pulse. We haven't hurt him. He will be okay.

Eventually Catlin finishes, and her eyes look at me, the steel grey-blue of Mamó's, with an expression of something close to satisfaction.

We both exhale deeply, and it's like the bubble we were in pops and the air begins to smell like air again. I can feel the grainy rock beneath my knees, and smell my own sweat. Brian looks like he's asleep.

Catlin buttons up his shirt and smooths it.

'It worked,' she says, her voice a bit triumphant. 'You were amazing.'

'So were you,' I say. 'Did . . .' I want to ask more, but she holds a finger to her mouth and gestures down at Brian.

'We'll talk about it later,' she says. 'Let's get him to a bed. He absolutely reeks, but I can't face helping him shower or anything.'

'STOP,' I say. 'I don't need that image burned on my brain.'

We gather all our things, except for Catlin's little pile of rubbish, which is still there annoying me. Though not as much as the nagging sense that there might be more going on with her than I realised. Again. We pick Brian up, move the rubble that fell from the ceiling away from the passageway to his office, and begin to drag him home. He's very heavy, and Catlin tries to take the bulk of him, but I tell her I'm okay, and able for it. It's true. There's a sense of something like euphoria that's keeping me energised. I mean, I'm fully sure I'll crash later, but for now I feel like I could eat the moon.

'Maddy?' Catlin's voice is low, serious.

'What?' I ask.

'I hope we never have to come back here again.'

'Me too,' I say. The last thing that I see before I turn into the darkness of the passage is the list of names carved deep into the wall. The ones who didn't get to leave here living. I murmur gratitude into the dim.

71

Braid

(uniting, linking, tangling)

Part of me wants to raise my hand again and knock the whole cave to the ground. It would probably do something to the foundations of the castle, and I'd need Mamó's help, so it isn't as though I'll actually get to do it, but the thought is really satisfying. Maddy keeps giving me suspicious sidelong glances that I'm sure she thinks are subtler than they are. We'll be having a perfectly normal conversation about how weird our stepfather's chest hair was and all of a sudden her face will alter, just a very little, and I know she's worried I'll go full Our Lady and start flying around the place, causing havoc and trying to knock myself up again.

Which I won't.

I mean, there's obviously some stuff that lingers after something like that leaves you. But it's definitely trauma and not demons. And Mamó did help with the levitating and the eyes. Once she got what I was up to. The woman knows the value of a good threat, well applied. It takes ages to move Brian back through the tunnels. I hope he's the last unconscious human I'll have to drag out. It kills the upper arms. We plonk him in his office chair when we get in, the morning light is filtering through the windowpanes, and we knock on Mam's bedroom door, until her very sleepy, quite annoyed voice tells us to come in.

She's in her fleeciest pyjamas and there's a pint glass of water and a packet of crackers by the bedside lamp, which I flick on.

'Have you been night-snacking, Mam?' I say, as she blinks her way fully awake.

She nods. 'It's just to settle my stomach, you see . . . Wait, girls, what's happened to ye? There's all rocks in your hair.'

I put my hand up to the crown of my scalp and rub. It feels like I'm exfoliating.

'Oh, that,' I say. 'Well . . . we kind of dealt with Brian.'

'I wish you'd tell me whenever you're off doing this sort of thing,' she says, sitting up in bed, her hair falling around her face.

'We didn't want to worry you,' Maddy says, sitting on the edge of the bed.

'I understand that, but finding out after the fact is also very worrying. And if ye don't tell me when you're off doing dangerous stuff, I kind of always wonder if ye are. And it's stressful.' She fiddles with the buttons on her pyjamas.

'We'll tell you from now on,' I say. 'I mean, if we know in advance. Sometimes things just happen.'

'Don't I know it?' she says. 'Okay. Let's get on with it. What happened with Brian?'

'We put a sort of blocker on his magic,' Maddy says. 'To stop him from using it in future.'

'And if he tries to, we'll know about it,' I add.

'That's something, I suppose,' Mam says. 'How did he take it?'

'Not too well.' Maddy smooths the covers on the bed. 'We had to persuade him to go for it, in the end.'

'But he did go for it?' Mam says. 'That's good.'

'Um . . .' I say. 'Not so much go for it, as have no option. I had to . . . threaten him a bit.'

'Catlin Hayes!' Mam's voice is sharp, as though I'd crawled home at three in the morning without messaging to let her know what was wrong.

'What?' I ask. 'I mean, there weren't many options if he wasn't going to cooperate. Plus, he started it. With Dad.'

Mam's face is impossibly sad. 'I suppose he did, love. I wish that things were different though. I don't like the idea of ye going around threatening people. I used to be able to protect ye . . . I feel so lost.'

'You're not lost, Mam,' Maddy says, holding her hand. 'We have you. And we're not going anywhere.'

Mam doesn't look too comforted by that, and her eyes flicker to the door. 'Where is he now?'

'We left him in the chair in his office, sleeping it off,' I say. 'We'll put him to bed eventually, I suppose. But we weren't sure where . . .'

'Not in with me, that's for sure and certain.' Mam's face is grim. 'He's lost himself that privilege . . . I wish it was the kind of thing where we could just call the guards and go through the proper channels, instead of all this . . . stuff. It's too much to be putting on your shoulders, girls. It isn't right.'

'We can handle it, Mam,' I assure her. 'We're witches, and also kind of Draculas now.'

'Speak for yourself,' Maddy tells me. 'I'm a Carmilla, if anything.'

'Is that a lesbian Dracula?' Mam asks. 'I'm not up on all the lingo.'

Her face is a weird mixture of confused and loving, and we both give her the biggest, biggest hug. She smells like home and safety, and I feel tears of relief welling up behind my eyes that the three of us are here, and we're okay. I try to push them down. I feel like if I start I'll never stop, but then I see that Maddy's eyes are wet, and that's me gone, everything that's happened in the past few months streaming out my eyes and down my face. My arms are shaking and the two of them are rubbing my shoulders and my hair and telling me that it will be all right, all right, it's over and we're safe now.

'I think that's why I'm crying,' I say between the snorts. 'Because I have that bit of space to let it in.'

'I get it,' Maddy says.

'The stuff I said to Brian,' I tell my sister, 'it wasn't true. Mamó helped with it. I just didn't want to fight him, you know? Or for anything else to happen to you.'

'I know,' she says. 'I mean, at first I wasn't sure. You're a very convincing liar.'

'I know,' I say. 'And I absolutely had him. It was class.'

387

'It was a bit,' she says. 'And that thing with your hand – how did you do that?'

'No idea,' I say. 'I think it was mainly Mamó.'

'I'll miss her,' Maddy says. 'Even though she wrecked my head so much. Is that weird?'

'No, a-girl.' I pat her shoulder awkwardly. 'It isn't weird at all. You both did well.'

'Was that . . . herself?' Mam asks.

I nod, and she recoils a bit and looks at me warily.

I decide to go downstairs, make the tea and give Maddy and Mam a bit of time together. And myself a break from suspicious sidelong glances I could do without.

72

Wood Sorrel

(mouth sores, cleansing blood)

We're making up a bed for Brian in the blue bedroom. Mam looks tired, and I need to gather my thoughts a bit. We were going to leave him in his office, but it felt weirdly rude. I mean, it is his house. I think Mam just wanted to do something with her hands, to be honest. She cleans when she gets anxious. I can't blame her, this is all a lot to process. I wish, in some ways, that Mamó was living in my brain. It would be nice to be able to dissect this with her, without Catlin being there as well. It's not that I don't trust her. I'm just a little wary. She can be so flighty at the best of times, and this is not the best of times. Also, when she was possessed she lied to me a lot, which kind of showed me that she could. She has the skills.

I have to pull a dustsheet off the bed, and when I shake it, it makes me sneeze. The blue bedroom is rarely used; I don't think we've been in it since the early days of living in a castle when we used to ramble around looking at things like it was a museum as well as our house. The bed itself is pretty normal, not a four-poster, just a dark wooden headboard. We should probably clear a room for Mamó as well at some point. I imagine Catlin will want her room back, she has not traditionally been that big on sharing.

Mam is furiously polishing the bedside locker, which is pretty unnecessary. I mean, it's not like he deserves her efforts, but I don't want to disturb her when she's in the zone so I sneak out and pop in to check on Mamó. It's weird to see her waxy and still. She's always moving, doing something. Even when she's standing still, there's an odd twitch, the sense of a trap about to spring at any moment. *It isn't her*, I tell myself. *Not really. More of a shell.* I touch her hand, and her skin doesn't feel like skin. It's thick and cold. I hope there's a way to keep her body alive enough to welcome her spirit back when she's ready for it. Magic is a stopgap, but we can't sustain a drain on both our energies. Particularly if something happens again, like with Catlin. I know she thinks that she was lying, back there with Brian, but it had a little ring of truth, like all the best ones do. There was a sort of flourish to it, that wasn't very Mamó, and I don't know how I feel about it. I'll need to watch her very closely over the next while, just to be sure.

I go into the bathroom and splash water on my face. What I want to do is to go back to bed for like three weeks, but there's so much to be sorted out, and I know that every plan I have will involve back and forth with Mam and Catlin. It was easier, in a way, when Mamó could just sweep in and dictate the terms. Though she still might yet, if we do something that displeases her. Like breathe or exist.

I wish I could just be a normal girl for like a second. Working to get over Oona, studying for exams. Like, what if this castle was just a very big house and no one got murdered and everything was fine?

How did my sister being able to levitate become more realistic than me being able to go to college? Or even have a debs. I'm not a big fancy-event type person, but I would love to dance with Oona, maybe sneak away for moonlight adventures in formalwear. I want my heart to stop because she looked at me, not because I got strangled to death by stupid Lon.

I shove my face into a towel to dry it and let out a little scream. Just one muffled scream. And then I head back down to the office to help Mam lug Brian to bed. We'll make it work. We will. It will be fine.

73

Milk

(nurture, bargains)

The tea is cold in the pot, by the time Maddy and Mam finally come back down from whatever the hell took them so long with Brian. They could have brushed his teeth, tucked him in and read him a fairly hefty bedtime story at this stage.

'We had to move him, Catlin,' she says when she sees my expression. 'And it's not like he's a small man.'

'But – tea!' I say, gesturing to the teapot, the mugs. The little plate of assorted biscuits. I did guest-level effort for nothing. Mam, bless her, makes appreciative sounds as she enters the room. She loves eating plated biscuits. I don't know why – a packet is more than grand, like.

'Was it awkward?' I ask. 'I would have helped. Maybe Mamó would have helped me levitate him!'

A contemptuous snort emerges from my mouth.

Maddy smiles. 'I've almost missed that snort.'

'Ugh,' I say.

Mam gets up to put the kettle on, and Maddy makes eyebrows at me like I should hop right up and do it for her, but she has legs and I already made tea which no one drank, so I settle in my chair and make eyebrows back.

Maddy does a snort of her own, gets up and starts pointedly helping Mam. I'm so glad she's back. What a ray of sunshine in my life.

'Now, don't bicker,' Mam says. 'I've had enough nonsense without the two of ye starting.'

'We're not starting anything, Mam,' Maddy says. 'We're just tired.'

Mam sighs. 'Me too,' she says. 'There's something about putting your unconscious husband into the spare room after he's been defeated by your daughters that takes it out of you. I might take this up to bed with me.' She takes a sip and rises, turning to go before coming back for the plate of biscuits. 'Also these.'

Maddy and I look at each other agape. Mam is a huge advocate of not eating in bed in case you rot your teeth. This is very out of character. Also, the last chocolate Hobnob was on that plate and I was eyeing it, and genuinely deserved it more seeing as how I had to levitate earlier, which takes it out of me now that I don't have Our Lady of Ballyfrann flooding my body with those good being-possessed endorphins or whatever.

Maddy and I sit at the table. All bets are off, we realise. I pour myself a big mug of tea and go to the cupboard in search of chocolate digestives.

'No plate this time?'

I hold the packet out to her and she takes one, with the air of a condemned prisoner smoking their last cigarette.

'How was Mam with seeing Brian? I mean . . . what we did to him was a lot. He was pretty banged up.'

'She was oddly stoic,' Maddy tells me. 'Did a lot of polishing and dusting and sweeping and swearing at the spiders in the cornicing before we moved him in there though.'

'Like he's going to notice,' I say.

'And even if he did. I mean . . .' She trails off.

'Anywhere is going to be a fancy hotel compared to his little walled-up cell with the pee bucket.'

'Doubt he'll be too happy though,' she says, grimly taking a slug of tea. 'We'll have to keep an eye on him once he wakes.'

'How long do you reckon it'll be?'

'Hard to say. A few days, maybe? Hopefully. I'd like a bit of time to gather my thoughts. It's hard to know what to do next. Sleep for a week, ideally.'

'I know,' I say. 'Should we, like, be moving out?'

'We could all move into Mamó's apartment for the time being, I suppose,' Maddy says. 'If it came to that.'

'It would be pretty small for three people plus one vacant body though, surely?'

'Not necessarily,' Maddy says. 'I mean, it's smaller than a castle, but not teeny tiny. And it would be a way to not be too near Brian while we plotted out our next steps.'

'Mam could always go stay with Aunty Laura in Cork for a bit,' I say. 'A break from Ballyfrann would do her good.'

'Yeah. She probably wouldn't though. I mean, would you

leave your kids with the man who murdered their father?'
Maddy's face is grim.

'Fair.' I crunch savagely down on another biscuit. 'You know what? I feel like this is a tomorrow problem. I'm going to bed as well.'

'In with me?' Maddy asks.

'Well, it is my room. Plus I'm hardly going to spoon Mamó. For one thing she'd have to be the little spoon and it wouldn't suit her.'

Maddy snorts again, and puts her mug in the sink.

We head upstairs.

74

Nightshade

(sore throat and stinging eyes)

Pale light filters through the slats in the shutters, and I stretch my legs out long. Catlin is still asleep. It's strange being in the same bed as her again. We used to sleep beside each other all the time, especially the first few weeks here when we were getting used to how things were. I can hear the regularity of her breath and smell the familiar scent of her room, of candle wax and incense. The faintest trace of roses lingers on, I suppose it will take time before it's gone entirely. You can't just wipe away something so big.

Catlin's altar is still there, but covered with a cloth now. The bulk of it feels a bit like a threat.

'We could maybe take that down?' I say, and she makes a half-awake sound that I think is affirmative. But not affirmative enough, so I keep going. 'You know, so you don't get possessed again.'

She opens one eye, balefully, like a cat. 'Great job waking me up, Maddy. Being witches together is surely going to be a grand adventure.'

'It has to be said, Catlin.' My voice is serious.

'But does it have to be said before 9 a.m.?' she asks. 'We had kind of a big night.'

'True,' I say. 'But I don't want any more big nights. And, like, you didn't know you were getting possessed the first time – how can you be sure now?' I bite my lip.

'I did a bit, like. Not that I knew I was getting *possessed* possessed.'

'Instead of regular old possessed?' My voice is more suspicious than I intend, and I see hurt flicker briefly across her face. I should probably feel bad about it, but I don't. This needs straightening out, one way or another, and I don't have time to be pussyfooting around her feelings. I'm thinking like Mamó, and it's jarring.

'Well, I did wonder a bit about the sleepwalking and the feathers and blood, of course I did. But I thought she was helping me, not using me . . . you know?'

'I really don't,' I say, turning my head to face hers on the pillow. 'That's why you need to explain it to me.'

'I shouldn't have to explain myself at all. You should just trust me,' she says.

'I do. But you were very convincing last night, and I think we need to talk about it.'

'Ugh, look, for one thing there's no space. Can you imagine Mamó sharing whatever bit of my brain she's occupying with a demon? She'd bate them.'

'It's true,' I say. 'She would.'

'I mean, it's not like I meant to get possessed, but having been possessed, let me assure you that I definitely mean for it never to happen again.'

'It did not look great.'

'There were bits of it that were, like the scars fading, and the being really strong and able to fly. But the being lied to and exploited parts were no craic.'

I hear the effort it takes to keep her voice light.

'I'm sorry,' I say. 'I just –'

'No. Maddy, we have to be able to talk about this stuff. If we're going to work together we need to trust each other, and that doesn't mean no secrets, but it kind of means no secrets that could get people killed.'

'That is a fair and sensible rule,' I tell her.

'I know. Who am I – you?'

I laugh. 'I don't feel sensible. So much of this year was just me feeling on edge and resentful of Mamó and like I would never know enough, or be enough.' My voice is cracking a little, it's been so long since both of us were beside each other like this, sharing parts of who we are.

'You already are enough, Maddy,' she says. 'This witch thing, it's part of you. And it's amazing. But it's not your value. Like, if you lost your powers tomorrow, you would still be my best friend.'

'I'm just worn out,' I say. 'It takes it out of you, this kind of stuff.'

'Yeah,' she says. 'I wish I could just go back to sleep, you know? And stay that way. There's so much to do. Like, we've dealt with most of the supernatural stuff now, hopefully, but there's still all this life stuff.'

I nod. 'Welcome to witchcraft. I might get up, make us some coffee.'

'Witches brew.' She smiles. 'Let me do it. I'm no herbalist, but I can get you nice and caffeinated. And I'm sure if I go wrong, Mamó will help me.'

'Help is a kind word for it.' I smile too.

'That is one thing,' she says. 'A silver lining on the big cloud of all the stuff that's happened.'

'What?'

'You won't be going through this alone any more. I'll be there with you. And we can help each other when it's hard.'

'Always,' she says. 'Well, always from now on. I wasn't much help when I hit you with the shovel.'

'That wasn't you,' I say. 'I know that.'

She squeezes my shoulder, and I curl my face back into the pillow. I can hear the soft pad of her feet as she gets up, the creak of the door. Some of the tension has left my body. It will be nice to have her there with me. To share the burden of it, and the promise. I close my eyes, and feel my brain begin to drift back in the general direction of sleep.

And then the screech of Catlin's voice pierces the air.

'Maddy!! You need to come quick. It's Brian! He's gone.'

Borage

(persistence, drooping spirits)

Dear Sheila,
I don't know what to say to you. And I can't bring myself
to face you, after what I've done. Know that my love for
you was real, and I would have done anything for you
and the girls. That's partly why I slipped. I wanted to
be the husband you deserved. A protector in every way.
And I know it's old-fashioned, but I wanted to take care
of you, you've had to be so strong and for so long, and
much of that was my fault. I wish that I had been a
better man. I hoped, for a time, that I had learned how to
be. But it seems life had a few surprises in store, and the
thought that you would leave, or that harm would come
to you or the girls . . .

There's no excuse, but that was my excuse, if one
was needed.

When I met you, I knew who you were. I knew what he had been, as well. His magic was the reason that we did what we did. I've spoken to you at length about the scars that being my father's son left on me, and over the years I have checked in on your family from afar. I wanted to see that you were all right, thriving. I should never have allowed our paths to cross in person. But they did. And once I'd met you, I couldn't help myself. I fell hard, and perhaps all the harder because I had a sense of how fragile our love was. Built on, if not a lie, then a deception. The omission of a truth that I regret so deeply to this day.

There have been things I've done with an agenda. Loving you was never one of them. I hope you can believe that much, at least.

As for what happened when I was a young man, I hope that you realise that who I was then and who I am now are very different people. No apology will ever be enough, but I am so deeply sorry, my love. I was raised to prioritise pursuit of power over basic humanity, and it took me well into adulthood before I became strong enough to question why. When I feel threatened, or afraid, my default is still to try to find a way to make myself stronger, more able to cope, more able to protect the people I care about. The ways I have learned to do that aren't right. But, in the dark, they feel like all I have, if that makes sense. I don't want to excuse myself, Sheila. But I do want to explain, at least a little. In the hopes that you will understand at least how very precious you are, and how much our time together has meant.

I will need some time to recover from what the girls did to me. I understand they felt they needed to, and I think they understand as well that I would have preferred that they did not. And I think that we need space from each other for a while. Please remain in the castle and use my money, if it will make life more comfortable. Madeline will have to stay in Ballyfrann, and I don't think that you could ever bear to leave, knowing that one of your daughters remained behind.

I know that there is no happy ending to our love story. But I did and do love you, Sheila. Very deeply. More than I thought a heart like mine could love. And if we remain apart, it affords me a certain measure of hope. Hope for a world where things could have been different.

There isn't time to write more, as I have to 'hit the road', as the fella says. I really think this is the easiest way for all of us. I'm trying to do the right thing here, I promise. There's no need to be worried. Know that wherever I am, you will be in my thoughts and in my heart,

Your,

Brian.

P.S. I'm attaching the contact details for my solicitor. If you have any queries about the estate, she should be helpful.

* * *

'He didn't mention me at all,' I say, a little put out. After I defeated him and everything.

Mam is crying quietly, and I wrap my arms around her. 'It'll be okay,' I say.

'How did he get away?' Mam asked. 'I thought you fixed him.'

I sigh. 'The spell we did was to prevent him using his magic. It can't prevent him using his legs, or his car. It's weird though, I really thought he'd be out like a light for way longer.'

'Me too.' Maddy's face is grim. 'We should have double-checked – poked him with a stick or a pin or something.'

'We tried our best,' I say.

'We should have done more.' Her voice is low, she's angry at herself. She shouldn't be. She's tried so hard.

'Look, it's not the worst,' I tell them, brushing cave dust off the fabric of my clothes. 'It was a sad "I have to go, my love" kind of letter, not an "I will be back to wreak vengeance on ye all". Which is positive. Plus, we know that we can find him if we need to –'

'*If* we need to?' Maddy says. 'I think we probably will need to. I mean, do you trust him to just, I don't know, *Eat, Pray, Love* his way around the globe?'

'Um . . . Are you forgetting Bridget?' I tell her. 'Bridget will totally have our backs. She'll let us know if he gets up to anything.'

'Can we even contact her long distance?' Maddy's brow is furrowed. 'How would that work?'

'Um, she's a ghost, Maddy. Every time we contact her it's

403

been long distance. It should be fine. We won't need like a loudspeaker or bigger candles or anything.'

Mam looks at us, her eyes narrowed. 'Who is this Bridget?'

'Bridget Hora.'

'Oh.' Her face relaxes. 'Okay. Should probably have gotten that from the part where you said she was a ghost.'

'You have a lot on your mind,' I say. 'Now, how about some breakfast?'

'You cannot be hungry now, Catlin Hayes.' She smiles.

'I actually am though, I'm starving. Apparently disappearing stepdads make me hungry.'

'Did he take the car?' Maddy says, peering out the window. 'It isn't there . . . How are we going to get around?'

I shrug. 'Mamó's car, probably. Oh, and we should definitely learn how to drive, if we're going to be the town witches.'

Maddy nods. We make our way down to the kitchen, and I start plonking food on plates.

'There are times,' says Mam, 'where all you can do is eat. We'll need to be living apart for a few years anyway, before I can divorce him, so this makes that part simpler, I suppose.' Her mouth is smiling but her eyes are sad.

'You'll miss him,' I say.

'God, no.' She laughs. 'I'll miss who I thought he was. But I've been missing that person for a long time now. And there's a lot to look forward to as well. For one thing, it will be nice to have the both of you back here with me. We might start closing rooms though. Make the place smaller, a bit more like a home.'

'We'll still have to do the work Mamó left behind,' Maddy says. 'It won't be like it was.'

'I know that, love,' Mam says. 'But I'll take what I can get.'

She picks up a little basil plant that has been withering on the windowsill and runs her fingers over it, puts it back and strokes her stomach. Smiles.

'Tom used to get me to do this when I was pregnant with the two of ye,' she says. 'Rub my hands over sickly plants, to see what happened. I haven't thought of that in the longest time.' Her face is serene. 'We need to treasure all the good memories we have too, girls. And there are so many.'

Maddy takes a bite of a rasher sandwich, ketchup and melted butter oozing out.

'Do you think that maybe you're starting to remember the parts you couldn't before, now that we know what happened to Dad?' she asks. 'Because that would be wonderful. I mean, to have some answers. To know.'

'I don't know,' Mam says. 'It's early days yet. Maybe. I do feel something different in me.'

'Mam,' I say, holding the little pot of basil, watching new green shoots unfurl, 'did you just do a magical pregnancy test?'

She smiles and rubs her stomach. 'I don't know if I'd call it magical, exactly. But there's definitely a baby in here. That's part of why I've been so tired recently. It always hits me hard, the first trimester. And now that Brian's gone, I don't have to be so secretive about it.'

Maddy's mouth is open. 'It is Brian's then?'

'Maddy!!' I say. 'It's none of our business . . . but is it though, Mam? Is it Brian's?'

Weirdly I want the answer to be yes. I mean, better that

405

than anything more supernatural. I can tell Maddy is thinking the same thing. We meet each other's eyes.

'Brian doesn't get to be part of this family any more,' Mam says. 'No matter what. This baby's ours. And that's all that matters.' It's not a definite answer, but it's close enough and now is probably not the time to go into the wheres and whens of how the baby was conceived. Though there's probably never going to be an ideal time to have that conversation with our mam, who is looking at us as though we were little kids again.

'Girls.' Her face is bright. 'This is a lovely thing.'

I feel a smile broadening across my face, and looking over I see the mirror of it on my sister's.

'It is,' she says. 'It really is. Come here.'

We hold each other. And I look at the small plant on the windowsill, a small bright flash curling from dark earth.

'Maddy?' I ask. 'What does basil do? I mean, in witchcraft?'

'Lots of good things, Catlin,' she says. 'Lots of new good things.'

Juniper

(safety and speed, countering poison)

My sister is an actual terror. She has invited everyone: Layla, Oona, Charley, Eddie, Cathal and Fiachra to come to the castle, and raided Brian's wine cellar. Mam is out in Galway with Elodie Noone, at a restaurant. The marks on my throat are nearly gone, and I can eat and drink without remembering Lon's hands. Which is something.

At least with them all here, she won't be able to continue her troubling pregnancy calculation obsession. She's convinced she's worked out the last date that Brian and Mam had sex, and keeps talking about it because she likes the way my face looks when I'm traumatised.

I don't know how I feel about the baby. Like, part of me is excited and hopeful – a small sibling! And the other part is worried about what it means, and the kind of world they'll be coming into. And the timing isn't what you'd call ideal. At least Mam seems happy. She's taking naps, cooking a lot, and staying off the Dark Web. As far as we know. I feel like we're inching our way closer to normal. Or a strange that's easier to bear. Catlin helped me make some salve last night. It will be really good for Wendy Collins's joints. She broke her shoulder last winter, and since then it's ached a little, and what we give her helps. People aren't visiting us as regularly as they did with Mamó, but they are coming, one by one, with troubles and concerns. And we do what we can. Bit by bit, and day by day. Catlin is actually very good with them, of course she is. She's Catlin. Some parts of this – the plant stuff especially – don't come as naturally to her as they do to me, but she has strengths as well, and she wants to learn. Sometimes when everything is done and I want to go home she'll be reading over labels or notes Mamó left. I left her in the flat last night, Button purring on her lap. He's become sort of friendly again. He won't sit on me, but he's stopped hissing, and that feels as close to forgiveness as I'm going to get. It's probably more than I deserve. We don't know where Badb is, but we reckon they won't be back until Mamó is too. We're not doing too badly at keeping her alive so far. There's a mixture of the medical and the magical involved, but she tells us what to do, and gives out to us when we get it wrong. Which is both irritating and helpful, a bit like the woman herself.

We're watching movies on Brian's big fancy TV, and eating popcorn. It's very wholesome. It's kind of nice to just feel like a girl. To watch a movie. Oona snuggles beside me on the couch, her legs twisted up underneath her like a mermaid's tail. She places her head on my shoulder. My heart leaps a little, in spite of itself. I lean my head towards hers, until we're so close that we're two people making one shape. Catlin sits between Layla, Charley and Fiachra, but I see her eyes skimming over Eddie when she doesn't think he's looking. I see him look at her, and I know that if she were feeling up to it, she could have him back in a flash. But what can you do? What we've been through has shaped us in different ways, and she needs to be by herself for a while. Or as by yourself as you can be with a two-hundred-and-something-year-old witch living in your head.

Oona's hand strokes my leg through my jeans, absently, as though I were a cat, and I feel my body wake up. I keep my eyes on the screen, but my heart is racing, and I'm not sure what it is she's doing. I mean, to snuggle with me like this out in the open feels like a bit of a statement. But of what? Is it that I'm a friend she's close enough to to express affection that way, or something more? She doesn't rub her other friends. I'd have noticed. Layla meets my eyes and looks away, her expression hard to read. Fiachra and Cathal are drinking cans and talking about mountain bikes. I have this sense of how much is going on around us. While we were fighting with each other, getting hurt, everyone else was fighting their own battles too. And we might never know what they are exactly, just like we've only told a little of what happened. There are things we do not talk about here, in Ballyfrann. And it used to frustrate me so much, this lack of straight answers, but more and more I get it. Because it's nice to just be in the world, and not to count all the things that could go wrong, the worries that could arise. I mean, you'd never be done counting, really.

I remember when Mamó said that her friends called her Margaret, and the thought of having no one left who calls you what your friends call you, it's lonely. I suppose she'd consider it strength. But there's strength here too. In the big hug Layla gave me when she saw me that said, *I'm glad you're here*. In Eddie being pure sound and normal, even though he can't be with the person he cares about. In Catlin, aggressively trying to determine details about our mother's sex life in front of all our friends, to the point where Cathal asked her to 'please stop'. In Oona, warm and real and here and maybe not in my arms exactly, but oh so close to them that my heart swells with it. I am so full of where we are right now. The sky is dark outside, but the moon is a shining sliver. My body and my heart are healing slowly. And it takes time. It does. But here is hope.

I look at Catlin. We are both alive. We're here. We're here. And I can tell she feels that deeply too. Her face is shining, reminding me of who she was before. And who she is now too. Still capable of joy, of mischief. Of anything she sets her mind to really. I'm glad she's on my team. I'm glad we're here.

'Are you going to kiss her, Oona?' she asks. And I swiftly revise my opinion. She is the worst. I should fully have left her with the ghosts.

'Catlin!' I say. 'You can't just go around asking people if they're going to kiss each other.'

'Why not?' she asks. 'It makes the world more interesting.'

'Does anyone want another drink?' I ask, deciding to take a little breath of fresh air to avoid strangling her. We've been working our way through fizzy drinks, tea, coffee and two dusty bottles of red wine from Brian's cellar that Catlin claims no one will miss, because Brian is gone and 'it's not like Mam will be drinking any time soon'.

'I'll help you,' Oona says, getting up.

Catlin waggles her eyebrows at me, and I furrow mine back.

'Could you get another bottle from downstairs, please?' she asks, in the voice she uses when she's pretending to be Mamó, which worked for about five minutes before we realised that Mamó wouldn't want us to loan Catlin fifty euro so she could buy a bag shaped like a frog.

'That doesn't work on me, Catlin,' I say. 'Not any more. And you're fully paying me that money back.'

'Let it go, Maddy,' she says. 'It'll make you feel much better, I promise you.' I narrow my eyes at her, but I'm not really all that mad. Oh no, going downstairs to a dark room with a beautiful friend. What an unfortunate turn of events. However will I cope?

We move through the door, towards the kitchen. Oona takes my hand. Our fingers interlace. I put the kettle on, and get out cups and glasses one-handed. I can feel her skin against my skin, starting in my toes and pulsing through me. There are different kinds of magic in the world. People can be a kind of magic too, if they're the right ones. She looks at me with her brown eyes. Her hair glistens with that watery sheen.

'I missed you,' she says.

'I haven't gone anywhere,' I tell her.

'This year, you kind of have,' she says. 'The arrangement that you had, it made things hard. And even when you were beside me, I didn't know when I would see you again.'

'That wasn't my fault,' I say, feeling kind of defensive, to be

411

honest. 'I mean, I didn't like it either. I missed people. I missed my family. And of course I missed you. I mean, you know I did.'

'I don't think you are as easy to read as you think you are, Madeline,' Oona says. 'You hold a lot inside.'

'I have to,' I say. 'I mean, particularly this year, there was no one really there to talk to.'

'We have phones. You could reach out. I did, when I needed you.' Her face is serious. 'And then with what happened, I mean, you didn't ask for help.'

'It happened very quickly,' I say.

'You could have died.' She looks even more serious when she says that. 'When I visited before, you looked so weak. And I would hate to lose you.'

'You won't lose me,' I tell her, but I feel so confused. What does she mean? She's standing closer to me than she normally does, and I can feel the warmth of her body, but I don't want to misinterpret. I make the tea. I pour the drinks. I feel her eyes on me all the while. And every fibre of my being wants to turn around and reach out to her, but I've only just begun to feel like there's a universe in which I can be normal around her, and that's hard won.

She moves towards my back, and I feel her hands on my ribcage. I lean in to her and can smell the lavender-freshwater scent of her. Feel the warmth of her skin through the fabric of her top. She burrows her face into the crook of my neck and inhales.

'I love the way you smell,' she says. 'I always have.'

I turn around and look at her.

I'm speechless. She reaches her hand to the side of my face and kisses me very slowly and very deliberately on the mouth.

'Oona?' I say.

She looks at me steadily and for a long time.

'Yes.'

'What's changed?' I ask. 'I mean, I like you so much. Like, SO much. But I thought it didn't go both ways. But now.'

'Now,' she says. And looks at me. 'Now things are different. When the stuff happened with my dad this year, I only wanted to talk to you about it, and you were there for me, even when it was hard for you to get away. And when nice things happened too, you were the person that I wanted to tell. I thought about you, Madeline. So often, all the time. I even put a bay leaf with your name on it under my pillow so I would dream of you.'

'And did you?' I ask. My chest hurts. It's like my heart is waiting for permission to beat.

'Yes.' Her voice is soft but very certain. 'I did. This year has been horrible, Madeline. Horrible. And it's made me think about what I want. Who I want. And I want you.'

I swallow. We're standing far too far apart.

She looks at me. With those big eyes.

'I mean, if you still feel that way about me.'

'Oona.' Her name comes out a sigh.

'Madeline,' she says.

I say, 'Come here.'

Basil

(birth, love, courage, luck)

Oona was the last person to go home. Mam dropped her and her mother back, and now we're tidying up the sitting room. Which is good, because I am dying to know what went on with the mixed signals and then the extremely clear signals and then the pair of them basically disappearing to the wine cellar for almost the entire duration of the second film. I mean, I thought I was the one of us who hooked up with people in caves and cave-like locations, but nope. I just ate jelly beans and drank a glass and a half of red wine that tasted like dirt and left a weird coating on my tongue.

I raise my eyebrows.

Madeline looks away. But I can see an enormous grin spreading all over her face, like it was Christmas morning.

'Don't ignore the eyebrows,' I say. 'You're going to tell me what happened anyway. It's not like you can avoid me. We live in the same house. And work together. And I will follow you around demanding information until you crack.'

'I mightn't crack,' she says. 'I'm very strong.'

'You can be,' I say, 'but not really around Oona. You go all squishy.'

'I do a bit.' She smiles again, cracking instantly. 'She likes me back. She says it just took time for her to get over her ex and realise how much I meant to her and things.'

'That's lovely, Madeline,' I say. 'I'm really happy for you.'

'You're not going to say anything mean about her?' She looks perturbed. 'Because I'm kind of sick of calling you on that, like, you don't have to be her best friend, in fact it would be weird if you were, but, like, you need to accept that she's a person who matters a lot to me and deserves your respect.'

'Jesus, Maddy,' I say. 'That's a lot to ask. You know full well I barely respect anyone.'

'True.' She smiles. 'But you need to be nice to her and about her or I'll turn you into a frog.'

'You can't do that,' I say.

'How do you know?' She waggles her fingers. 'Like, you've only been my co-witch for five minutes.'

'So are you two *together* together now?' I say.

'I think so.' She smiles. 'I mean, we didn't label it or anything. But we're going to meet up again tomorrow and she gave me a kiss when she left, which must have blown the head off Mam, because she gave me a big hug and was being far too smiley before she went to bed.'

415

She's wiping off the coffee tables, and I've all the cups and glasses collected now.

'We put an awful lot of tea and wine and cans of things away for a small group of people,' I observe.

'It was nice,' Maddy says. 'Like even apart from what happened with Oona. I felt like a real person again, and not whatever this town turned me into.'

'I kind of love who this town has turned you into,' I say to her. 'You're fearless. But I know what you mean. It was nice. I think we should try to make sure we fit some normal teenage stuff in.'

'Yeah,' she says. 'Mamó wasn't big on normal teenage stuff.'

'There was no such thing as a teenager when she was growing up. They were probably all running farms at seven and having a family of five by the age of twelve.' I roll my eyes. 'We're from a different time, Maddy. And that's okay. Like, we're sacrificing lots by doing this. But giving up everything? I think it would have to drain you dry, like. I don't know how you managed it . . .'

Her face is very serious. 'I didn't. Catlin, I was so, so lonely this year. You have no idea.'

'I was lonely too,' I say. 'I'm so used to having you here, I mean, you've always been there. Literally since birth. And I missed having someone to talk to who understands me properly, you know?'

'I do,' she says, and smiles. 'Catlin?'

'Yeah?'

'You wouldn't fancy going for a walk after this? The moon is out, and I just have this feeling like I need to be under it.'

'If you'll let me take this along in a flask.' I brandish half a bottle of wine. The label says it's twenty-five years old. I hope Brian was saving it for something special.

'You and your wine,' she says. 'You don't need drink to have a good time, you know.'

'I do know,' I say. 'But by bringing drink, it's like I'm deciding to have a good time. Like, invoking the fun gods.'

'No more invoking any gods for you, Catlin Hayes,' she says. 'You're barred from gods for a bit.'

'Fair enough,' I say. 'Let's get this finished, and wrap up warm.'

'Good stuff.' She follows me into the kitchen to wash the cups.

'Warm like the embrace of your fancy new girlfriend,' I say, raising an eyebrow in a suggestive manner.

'Shut up, Catlin,' she says, but it's with such a big grin. It's lovely to see her shining with whatever happened between them, I don't think I've ever seen this side of her before. Not exactly.

'Never,' I declare. 'I don't know how, and I refuse to learn.'

And it's the truth. There's too much shutting up in the world, and not enough looking at things head on. I don't want to learn to be quieter. I want the people around me to be louder. To ask for what they want and name what they feel. I want that for me too, because it's gotten harder over the past while. Too much to bottle up, I suppose. But I'm on the road back to something like the girl I used to be, or maybe a mix of her and what I've learned. And it's kind of part of this whole witch thing, isn't it? To speak your mind.

And to know when to shut your mouth as well.

I roll my eyes. Maddy looks at me. Sometimes people ask us if we have a weird psychic bond because we're twins. And obviously we don't, but sometimes she comes pretty close to reading my thoughts like a book. It's kind of creepy and kind of lovely also.

'What?'

'Nothing,' I say. 'Just Margaret giving out.'

She smiles, wiping a cup. 'It still feels weird to call her Margaret.'

'We're pretty good at embracing the weird though.'

'That we are,' she says. 'That. We. Are.'

Outside the sliver-moon shines wicked bright.

Acknowledgements

It has been a joy to return to Ballyfrann with the team at Hot Key Books, in particular the amazing Georgia Murray her insight and understanding, Talya Baker for her keen eye and warm heart and Jane Harris for her belief in my writing (and being there to celebrate some of the lovelier parts of having a book in the world).

My agent, Clare Wallace has been such a gift to *Precious Catastrophe* and all my work. This book was written during an intense period of change in my life, and I'm hugely grateful for her support, and her belief in me and my voice. Sheila David has been incredible to work with also, and I deeply appreciate her wisdom, skill and kindness.

To Claire Hennessy, Dave Rudden, Sarah Davis Goff, Sarah Griffin, Louise O'Neill, Juno Dawson, Celine Kiernan, Melinda Salisbury, Moïra Fowley-Doyle and every other writer, reader, blogger, reviewer and sound witch who took the time to share their love for *Perfectly Preventable Deaths*. Your generosity of spirit meant so much, and made the hard bits of writing this book easier to weather.

To my extended family, the Sullivans and Kings. I keep

writing stories, and time and again you show up to support them. It's no small thing, to be part of such a tribe.

To Mam, Dad, Tadhg and Cam. With love and hope that we'll all be in the same place at some point soon.

And to Diarmuid, Bonnie and Arthur. My home. My heart. My cat.

Deirdre Sullivan

Deirdre Sullivan is a writer from Galway, Ireland. Her first book for Hot Key Books, *Perfectly Preventable Deaths*, was shortlisted for the Irish Book Awards in 2019. *Savage Her Reply*, a companion to Deirdre's award-winning collection of fairy-tale retellings, *Tangleweed and Brine*, won the KPMG Children's Books Ireland Award 2021 and the Young Adult Book of the Year Award at the An Post Book Awards.

HOT
KEY
BOOKS

Thank you for choosing a Hot Key book.

If you want to know more about our authors and what we publish, you can find us online.

You can start at our website

www.hotkeybooks.com

And you can also find us on:

We hope to see you soon!